"You're going to think Meg Gardiner is a gift from heaven for thriller/mystery readers."—Stephen King

China Lake

"Do me a favor, okay? Lay your hands on . . . *China Lake*. [It] had me at page one. Miss Gardiner makes it all work. . . . Amazingly entertaining." —Stephen King

"[An] exciting mix. Great stuff."

—*Independent on Sunday*

"With a colorful cast of richly delineated characters, a protagonist with whom the readers will easily identify—all big hearted, quick tongued, and hair-trigger tempered . . . a fast-paced ride through some of the more dubious nooks and crannies of the American dream."

—*The Guardian* (UK)

"Fast and hard-edged. Buy it, read it."

—*Hull Daily Mail*

"A cracker, with memorable characters, memorable lines, and a plot that races along to an explosive ending. A great summer read." —*Huddersfield Daily Examiner*

"Very well written, racy, and witty."   —Tangled Web

"From beginning to end, *China Lake* is a book no reader of thrillers will be able to put down. Great characters, dynamic plot, nail-biting action—Meg Gardiner gives us everything."   —Elizabeth George

Kill Chain

"Evan Delaney is a paragon for our times: tough, funny, clever, brave, tireless, and compassionate. The pace and inventiveness never flag, and the climax . . . is both nail-biting and moving. But the brilliant writing is what puts this thriller way ahead of the competition. Intelligent escapism at its best."   —*The Guardian* (UK)

"I loved every minute of it. A breathtaking thriller, gripping and relentless."

—Caroline Carver, CWA Dagger–winning author of *Blood Junction*

continued . . .

Also by Meg Gardiner

China Lake
Mission Canyon
Crosscut
Kill Chain

The Dirty Secrets Club

JERICHO POINT

AN EVAN DELANEY NOVEL

Meg Gardiner

AN OBSIDIAN MYSTERY

For my children, Kate, Mark, and Nate

ACKNOWLEDGMENTS

A number of people have helped with the creation of this novel. For their support and advice I would like to thank: Paul Shreve—husband, guitar player, and my everything, day and night; the writers' group—Mary Albanese, Suzanne Davidovac, Adrienne Dines, Nancy Fraser, and Tammye Huf—for never letting me get away with less than my best; Caroline Carver; Marilyn Moreno and Hector Moreno, attorneys at law; my editor, Sue Fletcher, for her clear eye and inerrant sense of direction; Swati Gamble; and for his wisdom and belief in me, deepest gratitude to the late Giles Gordon.

1

It's only rock 'n' roll, I hear. What a lie.

We know—any of us who has held a lover skin against skin while a song aches from the car radio. Anyone who has shed rage or sorrow to a thundering backbeat. Anyone who holds a guitar and strikes a chord and hears the shout rise from the crowd. We know. It's glory, it's riches, it's a craving. It's immortality. And as I drove through a winter storm, with rain drumming on the windshield and dark rhythms pounding in my ears, I was about to discover another truth. That night, it was also death.

I pulled into the driveway just as the sofa tumbled off the balcony in front of me. It was on fire, an orange shriek in the night. I braked. It hit the driveway and a burning cushion bounced onto the concrete. Though the rain was a cold lash, the fire burned bright. People stood in the street, cheering. Sorority girls danced under the flame's light. From the house came hoots and braying, and a keg flew off the balcony. It crashed in front of the couch and flailed beer in an arc. The girls dashed away shrieking.

Welcome to Friday night in Isla Vista.

My stomach was roiling. Eleven p.m. on a February night, and the phone had stabbed me awake. *Can you come? We don't know what else to do. He had your phone number with him.*

Midterms were over; that's why IV was romping

tonight. Take fifteen thousand college students, add testosterone and ethyl alcohol, and you get *The Lord of the Flies* with a Top 40 soundtrack. I rolled down my window to double-check the address. Del Playa Drive—when I went to the university, I had neither the cash nor the cool to live here. The wind kicked up, blowing rain onto my face. I wiped my eyes, backed the Explorer onto the street, and parked. This was the place.

The house sat on the beach side of the street, the choicest real estate in Isla Vista, on the cliff overlooking the Pacific. The paint was peeling off the walls. I headed for the door, hunching against the rain, smelling salt air and acrid smoke. A young man strolled around the side of the house, ribboned yellow by firelight. Ten feet from me he pulled a full frontal, unzipping his combat trousers and pissing against the side of a car.

"Hey." I turned my face away. "This isn't *America's Rudest Home Videos*. Keep it to yourself."

Rain and beer spray were dousing the sofa. I walked to the door, hearing music pound, feeling my throat go dry, wondering how it had come to this.

I knocked.

It made no sense. Even given a family taste for liquor and too much time staring face-to-face with tragedy. This was wrong. Someone had made a mistake. A voice in my head said, *Denial is a river in Egypt.*

The door opened. Music jackhammered from the stereo. The man holding the knob was older than I expected—early thirties, my age.

"Evan?" He had the desiccated look of an old surfer. "I'm Toby. Thanks for coming." He let me in. "Nobody at the party seems to know him, and I didn't know what else to do."

The living room throbbed with dancing college students. It smelled like Doritos and tequila. We cut a path into the house.

"Where is he?" I said.

"Locked in the bathroom. Look, obviously he has issues, but people at the party want to pee."

"I hate to tell you, but they aren't waiting for the john."

He frowned, walking down a hall toward the back of the house. "Who is he, anyway?"

A strong spirit going out like the tide. A ghost. My life.

"My boyfriend."

He stopped at a door and knocked. Inside the bathroom, a man said, "Fuck off." I felt heat behind my eyes.

"Evan's here," Toby said. "Why don't you unlock the door?"

"Go away."

Toby looked at me and held up a bobby pin. "This will pop the lock. I just didn't want to have to haul him out, maybe start a fight. Want me to open it?"

I couldn't find my voice, so I nodded.

He leaned against the door. "Blackburn, she's coming in." He stuck the bobby pin into the lock and turned. Gave me a sad look. "Good luck."

He pushed the door open.

The bathroom smelled like ripe socks and mildew. My head throbbed and my eyes stung. He was sitting in the bathtub, head in his hands, dark hair falling over his face.

He turned his face to the wall. "Close the door. Don't let them see."

I shut the door behind me. And shut my eyes, fighting the sting. But still I saw him—his rangy frame, his handsome features, his blue eyes. Relief coursed through me. God. I sank against the door frame.

It wasn't him. Of course it wasn't. How the hell could I have believed it? I felt ashamed for buying any bit of it.

"Come on, I'll take you home," I said.

He put up a hand, as if fending me off. "I can't go
out there."

"Why not?" I crouched next to the tub. "What's
wrong?"

"You have to promise me."

"Are you in trouble?"

"Don't tell him."

"Who?" I said, though I knew.

"My brother. He'll go ballistic. Promise you won't
tell Jesse."

I put my hand on his arm. "P.J.?"

His eyes met mine for an instant before he looked
away again. Relief drained from me as fast as if someone had pulled a plug. I had seen that look in his eyes
before. Years ago, on that awful day. He slumped
back in the tub.

"Something's wrong. Tell me," I said.

"Oh, fuck." He started banging his head against the
tiles. "She went off the balcony."

Bang, *bang*, again and again.

"Over the edge. All the way down into the waves."

I grabbed him. "Did you call nine-one-one?"

He scrabbled for the faucets, but I tipped him over
the edge of the tub and hauled him up. I yanked open
the door and shoved him out into the hall, pulling out
my cell phone.

"Did you tell anybody?"

He shook his head.

I urged him into the living room, jostling through the
throng, and into the kitchen. Half a dozen girls stood
gabbing, making a batch of margaritas in the blender.
P.J. kept his head down, as though he were a dog being
punished. I opened the sliding-glass door to the balcony
and pushed him outside. The wind drove nails of rain
against my face. I dialed 911.

The balcony ran the width of the house. Beyond
the railing, forty feet below, the surf pounded the cliff.

It was a huge, roaring tide. The light from the kitchen petered out, but I could see that farther along the balcony a bedroom door was open, the drapes billowing out.

The dispatcher came on the line. "Nine-one-one Emergency."

"I need a rescue. There's been an accident at a house on Del Playa."

P.J. blinked. "No. You promised you wouldn't tell."

Before I knew what was happening, he grabbed the phone from my ear and stumbled back toward the kitchen door, mashing buttons.

"You promised," he said.

"Dammit." I grabbed his hand and pried at his fingers, but he clenched the phone to his ribs. "We have to get search and rescue out here. Now."

His chest heaved. "No, we don't."

"Yes. Now."

The rain was flattening his hair against his head in stringy tails. "We don't need search and rescue. I think . . . I mean, I think I'm wrong. It didn't really happen."

Shit. "Don't give me that."

He stared into the storm. "I think I just freaked out."

"Truth. Right now. Did a girl fall off this balcony or not?"

"I don't know."

Planting both hands against his chest, I pushed him back inside the kitchen, where I could get a good look at his eyes in the light. He didn't resist, just shivered and stared out the door at the ocean. I backed him against the counter.

The margarita girls said, "Hey, what?"

I wiped rain from my face. "Look at me."

His gaze tagged me and jumped away again. His pupils were the size of fleas.

"What did you take?"

A shrug.

"Coke? Speed?"

The girls grabbed the blender pitcher and left the kitchen. P.J. didn't respond. I put my hands on his cheeks and held his face.

"How much, P.J.?"

His skin felt hot, the rainwater warm against my palms. He wasn't as tall as Jesse, didn't have his shoulders, but otherwise the resemblance gave me a punch at the thought of everything that separated the two of them.

I shook his face between my hands.

"Some E," he said. "And maybe a few lines."

Exhaling, I let my hands drop. "What happened here? Tell me."

He stared out the door again. "I don't know. Me and some guys were here in the kitchen. People were everywhere. I couldn't get a clear look."

"What did you see?"

"Something out on the balcony, like voices. But it was so loud, the music—and that sliding-glass door was shut, and the lights here were reflecting. The rain—on the glass it looked so bright." His knee began jittering. "I don't know. It just scared me."

He was wired to the ends of his hair, bouncing toward hysteria, and I still didn't know if he'd hallucinated it or not.

He began shaking. "It was freaky. So freaky."

I looked around the kitchen. The phone had been torn out of the wall, leaving a gaping hole. Written in marker beneath it was, *No more coffee for Alex.*

"Give me my cell phone, P.J."

He clutched it like a precious toy. "You won't call?"

"No."

Slowly he extended it to me. I closed my fingers around it, waiting. It rang.

I answered. "Here. A woman fell off the balcony."

It was the emergency dispatcher calling back. I gave

her the address. The last I saw, P.J. was running through the crowd toward the front door.

Keep it to yourself. Prude. Priss. Got a look at it, and that's all she could say? Frigid bitch.

Just like he'd hoped.

He walked away from the house with the hood of his sweatshirt pulled low over his face. Keeping his head down, when he really wanted to laugh and pull off his clothes and sing. The rain felt great, coming down hard now, like it *knew*, and was showering him with applause. It had been perfect.

Except for running into that woman. Ice queen. Lady *Rudest Home Videos* thought she was a comedian.

But the joke was on her. She saw what he wanted her to see. And she got a good, long, beautiful look, too. Whip it out and they never noticed your face. Wang dangling just blew their minds.

He balled his hands. They weren't exactly slick, more sticky. He held them out and spread his fingers and let the rain lick it off. He wondered if it got on his dick when he whizzed on that car. An ache began in his crotch. But he couldn't pull down his pants and let the sky kiss it all away. Not on the street. But that was okay; it was only blood.

He walked, feeling his hands turning clean. Perfect, yeah, it had been fucking perfect. And gone in a flash.

He should have gotten it on film.

2

The searchlight arced white across the black ocean. A firefighter stood against the balcony railing, swinging the light over the heaving water. Two Water Rescue Jet Skis cruised the surf, looking for the fallen girl. Their engines had cut back, close to idling now.

The fire captain came in from the balcony, his hat and yellow turnout coat shining with rainwater. He moved like a boulder. In his hand a radio squelched.

"Ma'am?"

I looked up from my seat at the kitchen table. "Any sign of her?"

Music was still trickling from the stereo, but the house had emptied out. Nothing kills a party like firefighters showing up. With sheriff's deputies.

The captain wiped the back of his hand across his forehead. "Run it past me again. Exactly what convinced you to call us?"

"A friend told me that a woman had fallen off the balcony into the water," I said.

"But you didn't see it happen."

"No. But—"

A deputy came in with raindrops clinging to his crew cut like dew. "Excuse me, but who are you?"

"Evan Delaney."

He wrote it down. "And the woman who fell, what's her name?"

"I don't know," I said.

"What did she look like?"

"I didn't see her. It happened before I got here."

The fire captain set his radio on the table. "So you don't actually know that anybody fell over the edge."

"No."

"The thing is," the deputy said, "nobody's missing."

Into the kitchen walked Toby, the man who'd let me into the house. The deputy turned to him.

"Isn't that so, sir?"

Toby scratched his nose. He was nothing but dark tan and stringy muscle, a walking stick of beef jerky.

"Nobody said anything to me. If somebody went over, I'd have known. They'd have screamed; I would have heard it."

Spoken like a landlord concerned about liability. The deputy was nodding.

"No, you wouldn't," I said, "not with the storm, the music, the blender, the couch being torched—and besides, somebody *did* know. My friend told me. If I'm wrong, I'm sorry. But a woman might be out there in the water, and I couldn't ignore it."

The fire captain picked up his radio. "I'll send the Jet Skis down the shoreline, but with this surf I can't keep them out there for long."

The deputy ran his hand across his head. "This friend of yours. Was he . . ."

"Wasted," Toby said. "Out of his head. Not that he got that way here at the party. I mean, he showed up that way. I didn't know him."

"Where is he? Can we talk to him?"

"Gone," Toby said. "Out the door like a shot."

"What's his name?"

"Blackburn." Toby took a folded sheet of typing paper from his shirt pocket. Unfolded it, peered at the text. "Jesse Blackburn."

I rubbed my eyes. "No, it isn't."

"Yeah, it says right here." Toby handed me the paper.

It was an e-mail from me to Jesse, giving him my new cell phone number. "Where'd you get this?"

"He brought a guitar. Found it in the case."

Why had I thought I could keep Jesse out of this? I felt as though a landslide were starting under my feet. And it was going to take me down.

"The man who was here wasn't Jesse; it was his brother, P.J.," I said.

"P.J.," the deputy said. "What's that stand for?"

"Patrick John."

Thinking, *Rhymes with here and gone.*

Toby watched me drive away. He stood with the engine crew on the driveway, by the smoldering sofa. The headlights flicked across his eyes when I turned the wheel. His look seemed to say, *Thanks for the trouble. Thanks for nothing.*

I drove to the end of the street, got out, and found a path between houses to the cliff. The wind buffeted me. I could see nothing, hear nothing but the cold roar of the water. It sounded inexorable.

P.J., what happened here tonight? Were you telling me the truth?

He knew how to tell the truth, to break the worst news. He'd broken it to me. But tonight I didn't know whether his tangled story came from fact, imagination, or cocaine.

Getting back in the car, I drove to his apartment building a few blocks away. The Don Quixote Arms, student squalor at its finest. It took three minutes for P.J.'s roommate to answer my pounding. His eyes were gluey with sleep, and he hadn't bothered to remove the stud from his lower lip before bedtime. His T-shirt said, *If I gave a shit, you're the person I'd give it to.* When I asked for P.J., he scratched under his armpit.

"He doesn't live here anymore," he said.

"Yes, he does. That's his acoustic guitar by the sofa."

"Does he owe you money?"

Next door the curtains fluttered. I walked over and knocked.

A woman called from behind the peephole, "Who is it?"

"I'm looking for your neighbor. P. J. Blackburn."

A hand drew back the curtains. I saw cautious eyes and a receding chin. "He went to a party. Over on Del Playa."

"I know. Did he come home?"

"No." She peered, waiting for me to go away. I didn't. "I would have heard him. He hasn't."

Back in the car I slumped against the headrest, listening to the rain. Procrastination wouldn't make this go away. I took out my phone and called Jesse.

Outside Chaco's on State Street, wet asphalt shone gold under the streetlights. Palm trees thrashed in the wind. I pushed through the door. Inside, a lively crowd was listening to indie rock, a local band on the little stage, the wispy girl singer tilting her head toward the microphone, eyes shut, deep into it. I scanned the room. Jesse wasn't here yet. I worked my way to the bar.

The music swelled, drums crashing. But I heard the ocean booming against the cliff. I couldn't stop picturing her—feeling solid wood slip away from her and seeing the balcony recede. Plunging into bitter waves. Struggling up to reach air. Breaking the surface, only to find herself alone.

The song finished on a minor chord, the airy singer smiling, hands at her side, the crowd applauding. The room felt as if it were rolling.

I rubbed my temples. This wasn't news you gave over the phone. Besides, when I called him Jesse had sounded up, saying, "Let's catch a late set." Hearing enthusiasm in his voice had touched me. Joy, any spark at all, had been missing for a long time. And if it was finally rekindling, I was going to douse it once I told him about the mess in Isla Vista.

Patrick John. Make that going, going, almost gone. He was enrolled at the university, but at twenty-three was nowhere close to graduating. His curriculum emphasized recreational chemistry. He spent most of his time playing guitar, working odd jobs, and nosing around the edges of the music industry.

I glanced toward the door, watching for Jesse. It cut at his heart that his brother vanished when push came to shove. But as angry as I felt, I could never resent P.J., because he had been here for me when it counted.

That day—a gleaming Saturday morning, when the hibiscus in the garden flared red and the scent of jasmine saturated the air, he rang my bell. I saw him through the French doors, a big kid in a baseball cap, wiping a runny nose, his foot jittering up and down. I knew right away he could only be Jesse's brother, and my bad mood deepened.

I opened the door and stood there with my bare feet and messy hair and burr-under-the-saddle grouchiness, saying, "Make this a good story."

His blue gaze jumped around. "Jesse asked me to come over."

I crossed my arms. "To tell me why he stood me up last night?"

My new boyfriend, apparently, was a chickenshit. Wouldn't you know—star athlete, absurdly sexy, with a blinding grin and switchblade wit. And he had sent his brother to deliver the basket of excuses.

So I thought. I didn't know that I was standing at the edge of a divide, and P.J. had come to take me across.

He wiped his nose again and met my eyes. "Jesse's been in an accident."

Now the band started a new number, up-tempo. The singer yanked at the mike and growled and sang. Next to me, a man took a seat on a stool and reached for the peanuts on the bar. He wore an aloha shirt and sweet cologne. The bartender asked what I wanted. I ordered a beer.

I could still see P.J. standing on my porch. Those few last seconds of sunshine and blue jays crying in the trees, the smell of freshly cut grass, my sleepy-headed annoyance, before I grasped it. Accident. P.J. was almost falling over from fear and grief. It was beyond bad. The white noise started in my head.

The man on the stool picked through the peanuts. "Yeah, this band's halfway decent. But they could mike the vocalist better. The monitors are wrong, and the mike's too hot."

Evidently he was talking to me. Taking off his glasses, he smoothed his Pancho Villa mustache and hunched against the bar, squinting at me as he chewed. His front teeth protruded—usefully, because several others were missing.

"They play here regular. Like a house band."

He worked his rounded shoulders back and forth, as if his aloha shirt was itchy. His hair dragged over his collar, the color of compost. He had seemingly fallen through a time portal, direct from the set of *Hawaii Five-0*. He would have played a police infor-mant, a nervous loser known as Gopher.

"But if you're into chick singers, she ain't shabby. I see why you like her."

Was I really that distracted, or was this guy having an entirely different conversation, one in which I was answering him? My beer came. I put a twenty on the bar and waited for my change.

He grabbed a cube of sugar from a bowl on the bar and leaned toward me. "You dig all this he-done-me-wrong stuff. I can tell. You got the aura." He squir-reled the sugar cube into his mouth. "But sure, why not, I'll dance with you."

The band hammered away, but nobody was dancing. "I'm waiting for somebody."

"Gotcha, when he gets here it's adios." He chose another sugar cube, sniffed it, and nibbled.

"Wrong. It's adios right now." I turned, planning to find a table, and saw Jesse coming through the door.

He smiled, making his way to the bar. I knew I was about to blow that smile away, but as always I just watched him. He was tall and long-legged, with mahogany hair and looks that made me plain crazy. Even when he was smiling, his gaze told people they'd be foolish to cross him. He could be all edge, all fight, and still take me with effortless, athletic fluidity. He had almost taken me to the altar a few months earlier.

"Okay, we can get out of here, but where you wanta go?" Gopher said.

I felt his fingers on my arm. They were moist, and were leaving a tacky handprint of sugar on my skin.

"No." I lifted his hand off. "That's him."

He followed my gaze. "The guy on the crutches?"

Jesse picked his way between tables. His gait was slow and careful. The bartender was at the cash register, getting my change. Gopher stared at Jesse.

"What happened to him?"

Jesse walked up. He took in Gopher and my pinched face. He gave me a deadpan look.

"You disobeyed orders, Rowan. You left them alive," he said.

God, he had perfect timing. It was dialogue from my new novel. Nice to know he was actually reading it.

"Screw orders. Firing into a church is just bad manners," I replied.

Gopher was gaping. I suppressed the urge to smile.

"Now, let me finish my drink, or I might top you," I said.

"Killing over a beer is pretty damn rude, too." Jesse looked at Gopher. "But people who stare—offing them is a public service."

Peanuts dribbled from the man's hand onto the bar. Inching off the stool, he slunk into the crowd.

I stretched and gave Jesse a fat kiss. "Score one for sci-fi." Waving to the bartender, I raised my beer bottle. *"Uno más."*

Jesse shook his head. "Make it coffee."

I looked him over and saw tension along his jaw and tightness in his shoulders. Avoiding alcohol meant that he was maxed on pain medication. He had to be feeling like hell.

A day in the life, when your back's been shattered by a BMW that was going flat out when it hit your bike. When a training ride up a mountain road killed your best friend and blew your future sideways faster than you could blink.

"I have breaking news," he said.

I took the coffee mug from the bartender. "So do I."

"Me first." He walked to a table, balanced with the crutches, and sat down. "I had dinner with Lavonne tonight."

I gave him an exaggerated head-to-toe. His khakis were ripped at the knee. His T-shirt advertised Santa Barbara's favorite surfboard product, Mr. Zog's Sex Wax.

"You missed the class on sucking up to the boss, didn't you?" I said.

Lavonne Marks was the managing partner at Sanchez Marks, the law firm where Jesse practiced. She was half Hellfire missile, half Jewish mother, forgiving of his shaggy hair and pirate earring, as long as he tore opponents apart on cross and ate a nutritious lunch. I sat down.

"She's going to offer you a job," he said.

The band launched into a new number, the guitarist taking off like a dragster, the drummer hammering on the crash and ride. I stared at Jesse.

"Full-time?" I said.

"You're already putting in twenty hours a week for the firm."

"Maybe five at the office, though."

The rest involved writing briefs, making court appearances, occasionally serving papers. Full-time meant my own office, with a view over red tile roofs. Health insurance, a retirement plan. Business cards.

"Partnership?" I said.

"Figure three years down the line."

And a chance to work down the hall from the man I loved. Fifty hours a week of togetherness.

I looked at him in the amber light. "Lavonne asked you first, to see if you'd object."

"I don't."

Full-time. Dark suits. Panty hose. Good-bye to freelancing. No more legal journalism. Back to writing fiction when I could grab an hour on weekends.

"I just got the galley proofs for *Chromium Rain*," I said.

"You write at night. That won't stop."

"But . . . the biography. That would be a big project."

"You aren't going to write that. Jax and Tim's files have been sitting in your safe-deposit box for six months."

And those files were just about all I had in the bank right now.

"I'll think about it," I said.

But instead I thought about Jesse. We had postponed our marriage shortly before the wedding. Traumatic events had driven a wedge between us: the hit-and-run driver was fighting, violently, to keep from going to prison. I'd discovered parts of Jesse's past that I didn't want to face. And he began to fear that because of his spinal cord injury I saw myself as a self-congratulating martyr, staying with him out of pity. We got angry. So we decided to step back from the brink and start over.

I had felt tangible relief and a new lightness of heart. But all his losses slammed down and tipped him into an emotional crash dive. He seemed to be sliding away not just from me but from everything. And I didn't think my working alongside him could solve that problem.

He wrapped his hands around the coffee mug. "It's a job, not a jail sentence."

"Of course it is."

"So why do you look as if you're about to make a run for the border?"

See—starting over wasn't truly possible, because he knew me too well. I was about to make a smart remark when a shadow crossed his face and he dug his knuckles into his lower back. He bit his lip, trying to ride it out. I waited. There was nothing I could do.

"So what's your news?" he said.

My dad has a saying: *God save me from people with good intentions.* In the days that followed I would repeat it to myself again and again, but right then, watching Jesse lose his fight with the pain, I decided to be kind.

"It'll keep."

The bartender took her break at midnight, stepping into the alley behind the club. The rain had stopped. Her ears were zinging from the music. Propping the door open a few inches with a brick, she lit a cigarette and tipped her face up to the night sky. The sound leaked through the crack in the door, but out here at least she could hear herself breathe.

She could also hear a man at the pay phone inside the door.

"It's Merlin," he said. "She's at Chaco's. And she ain't alone."

The bartender took a drag from her Winston, watching the tip redden.

"She banged on apartment doors in Isla Vista, then drove downtown. When I come in the club she's standing at the bar drinking a Heineken."

The bartender paused, the cigarette an inch from her lips. Private investigator? she wondered.

"She was waiting for this dude on crutches. He called her Rowan," the man said. "I don't know what's wrong with him; he coulda got kneecapped." Pause. " 'Cause of stuff the Rowan woman said to him. Listen, they weirded me out big-time. Talking some crazy shit."

The bartender took a drag.

"Yeah, but only 'cause she started talking to me first. Wanting me to dance with her. But . . . No. Course not. . . . 'Cause of this guy with her, didn't I just say that? He comes on like a major badass. I think, like, he could be made."

The bartender lowered the cigarette to her side and stood very still.

"Oh, sure, I'm imagining it. It's all just a mind-fuck. Hello, are you here? Did this dude get in your face?" Quiet for a moment. "Whatever. We'll take care of it tomorrow. I'm going home. My eyes itch."

The phone clanged down on the receiver. The bartender dropped her cigarette and ground it out with the toe of her shoe. The night felt clammy.

She counted to fifty, slowly, before pulling the door open. The hall inside was empty. Good. All she needed was Mr. Easily Bamboozled to start jawing her ear off. She knew who he'd been talking to, and, if he was that stupid, he could mess his own nest.

Bartending. The stuff you heard.

Gray. Sky, light, water. By five a.m. the rain had stopped, but wind and tide had the surf running high. It roared onto the beach, almost to the cliffs. The sand was heaped with kelp. Visibility was poor. To the west, the Goleta Pier stuck into the waves. Beyond, the university campus faded into the mist.

On the cliff above the beach, eucalyptus trees creaked in the wind and millionaires' lawns eroded, inch after inch, into the Pacific. The rough weather kept the morning empty. Nobody was looking down at the beach when it washed ashore. It rolled on the waves, a limp thing rising and dropping with the swell of the breakers. Flotsam, like the driftwood that littered the sand.

Riding the gray surf to shore, it came to rest in a tangle of seaweed. Snared and heedless. Against the leaden day, the only object on the beach that shone was the bracelet, its silver charms gleaming on a wrist pale with death.

3

The garden gate had swollen overnight from the rain, and stuck when I tried to open it. It was about eight a.m., and I was coming back from the gym. I had the car keys in my teeth, coffee in one hand and sack of bagels in the other. I planted a shoe against the gate and pushed. Water sprayed from the ivy that cascaded over the fence. The gate juddered open.

I headed along the flagstone path toward my cottage. Branches were down all over the yard. Next to Nikki and Carl Vincent's house, a swath of red bougainvillea lay across the lawn like a slain dragon.

Nikki was my best buddy, my former college roommate. She ran a small art gallery, while Carl was a software executive. They were surrogates for my family, which was scattered across the country.

From the Vincents' house came the sound of pounding. At a living room window Thea, their toddler, stood on a chair slapping her hand against the glass. Her sturdy little frame was swaddled in pink pajamas. She smiled, stuck her mouth on the window, and blew like Louis Armstrong. I made a kissy face back.

My place is a small adobe house, originally the guest cottage on the property. Outside the French doors, star jasmine glistened wet silver. I fumbled with the key, hearing the phone ring. I got in and picked up to hear the gritty voice of Lavonne Marks.

"Whatever you have going this morning, put it on the back burner."

Saturday at eight was early, even for her. "Okay. What's—"

"Come to the office, pronto. Is Jesse with you?"

"No."

He was doing what he did every Saturday: coaching a kids' swim team, the Blazers. After that he would go to the office, bury himself in work, and continue running himself down. Anything to keep his mind off the pain, and the memory of violent death.

"I just got back from the gym; let me—"

"Now." She hung up.

Sanchez Marks filled the top floor of a Spanish-style building near the courthouse. Walking into the lobby, I looked out the full-length window at clouds hanging over the city, torn gray pressing on red tile roofs and sodden palm trees. A flock of sparrows darted past. Down the hall, the lights were on in Lavonne's office. I finger-combed my hair, trying to look presentable. Jesse could carry off the scruffy-with-the-boss act, but he already had the job. I called her name.

"Door's open," she called back.

She stood at her office window, arms crossed. She was wearing black, from her slacks to her turtleneck. Her unruly dark curls and half-glasses completed the look: urban, eastern, as un–Santa Barbaran as she could possibly get. She'd only lived here for twenty-five years.

I smoothed my track bottoms. "Excuse my getup. I was . . ." What, punching the bag? Hurling weights? Eating iron filings? "What's urgent?"

She turned from the window. What could possibly make her so anxious to bring me on board today? And what was I going to say, yes or no?

She took off her glasses. "I need to ask you a question. I want a frank answer."

Uh-oh. Did she consider Jesse and me too combusti-
ble to work near each other? I tried to gauge her
expression. She had only a few soft spots—for her
bookish husband, for the zaftig daughters whose faces
laughed from the photos on her desk, and for Jesse.
She admired the way he lived his life. Fearlessly, dog-
gedly. Throttle up. If it came to a choice between my
boyfriend and me, I stood no chance with her.

"Certainly," I said.

"Have you seen these before?"

She handed me a piece of paper. Confusion bit. It
was a photocopy of three checks. With many digits,
totaling almost five thousand dollars. Made out to
Evan Delaney.

"Did you cash those checks?" Lavonne said.

My pulse thudded. "No."

My gaze jumped over the photocopy. That was
definitely my name, on the line that said, *Pay to*. Then
I saw the account the checks had been drawn against,
and nausea skated through me. *Datura Incorporated*.

"What's going on?" I said.

"Those checks were stolen from Datura."

Datura was an important client. This was bad news.
Very bad.

"I didn't take them, Lavonne."

Her shoulders lowered. "Then explain how they
came to have your name on them."

My legs felt like linguine. "I can't."

Datura Incorporated was the company set up to
handle the business dealings of Karen Jimson and her
husband Ricky—known in his day as Slink, front man
for a band called Jimsonweed. They were hard-rock
millionaires. They lived on a cloistered spread in Montecito, where Karen invested Ricky's money, and Ricky
planned his next comeback tour.

The landslide had just slipped a few more feet. This
wasn't coincidence.

"Karen called me at home an hour ago," Lavonne

said. "They're giving me a chance to clean up this mess without involving the police. So if you have anything to say to me, say it now. She and Ricky are on their way over."

I forced myself to breathe quietly. "Good. Let's straighten this out right here." But my lips felt numb. The last person I wanted to see at eight on a Saturday morning was Karen Jimson, the Iron Pixie.

"You were out at the property three weeks ago, weren't you?" Lavonne said.

"That's right. With the draft contracts for the Embarcadero syndication." I tried to look at the date on the checks, but my vision was pulsing. "Is that when they were stolen?"

In the lobby, the elevator chimed. A moment later we heard a heated soprano voice.

"Where is everybody?" Boot heels clacked on the hardwood floor in the hall.

Lavonne put her glasses on. "Here."

Karen appeared at the door. When she saw me, she crossed her arms and leaned against the frame, one hip jutting out.

"Talk about chutzpah."

She stalked in, chewing gum. "Tell you, it's a hell of a way to start the weekend, getting those checks back from the bank yesterday."

I turned to her. "I didn't steal them."

"Deny, deny, yada yada. Bay at some other moon, girl."

Karen Jimson was five-foot-zilch of hard body. Kitten nose, gamine hairdo, fawn's eyes, and a white drill instructor's T-shirt, cut short to reveal her six-pack. She wore a sapphire ring the size of a Gummi Bear. Working with her was like wrestling a crowbar.

"Let me lay it out," she said. "Evan came to the house on January twentieth. Those checks are dated January twenty-first. Don't know 'bout you, but I can count."

"Wait," I said. "I was at the house for all of ten minutes, getting your signatures on the Embarcadero contracts. And I was with you or Ricky the whole time."

"Sleight of hand." She mimed a pickpocket. "Finger magic."

"Good point. Have you taken steps to preserve the fingerprints on the checks?"

She scoffed. "At this stage? There's gonna be too many to count. Mine, Ricky's, the bank teller's, whoever stuffed them back in the envelopes to mail to us . . ."

"But not mine."

"Honey, come off it. In thirty seconds you could have scoped it out."

"Karen—"

"So here's the deal. You return the money." She turned to Lavonne. "And Sanchez Marks severs its relationship with her. Permanently." The gum snapped in her teeth. "Meet those conditions and this all goes away. It never happened." She looked at me. "By Monday afternoon."

I opened my mouth, but nothing came out. Karen chewed.

Lavonne said, "Give me a minute with Evan."

"Yeah, I'll bet. Where's your coffeepot? I need a hit."

She left, and Lavonne shut the door. "Monday afternoon. Got that?"

"I can't."

"Karen's giving you a pass. She's turning her back and counting to ten, and if everything is put back in its place, they won't call the police. Or the state bar."

"Lavonne, I didn't steal the money. You can't actually believe that I did."

She stood motionless, so hot that she was practically crackling. "Belief is useless without proof."

It was an opening. "What do you want?"

"Evidence." She tossed her glasses on the desk. "By

Monday morning. Do that, and I'll present it to the Jimsons."

I stormed out of Lavonne's office into the hallway, clutching the photocopy. I was cussing rapid-fire. I rounded the corner into the lobby.

Ricky Jimson stood by the window, talking on a cell phone.

"Sloppy, man, I'm telling you the track's a mess," he said.

His arms were rope-thin. His jeans sagged across the butt. Up close I could see gray hair threading his blond mane.

"The drum's lagging, and the rhythm guitar's flat," he said. "Hey, I'm listening to it in my car, and I can hear it going south over the fuckin' freeway traffic. We gotta fix it."

"Ricky," I said.

He turned, his attention still on the phone call. In his prime he had been likened to a cobra. Now he looked like a python that had swallowed a Christmas ham. But his face was still handsome, rakish and bright-eyed, if pumped smooth with beer fat.

"No," he said into the phone. "Call the studio and tell them we'll be in this afternoon. We're Jimsonweed, dude. You don't ask; you tell 'em we're coming."

I raised the photocopy to face level. "You have a problem."

His eyes crinkled with curiosity. Scratching his chin beard, he leaned forward to peer at the text. His brow creased. "Hang on, man."

"I'm not the person who ripped you off. So think— who else knows where Karen keeps the Datura checkbook?"

Her voice ice-picked from behind me. "What do you think you're doing?" She was stalking along the hall, wagging her finger. "No. You talk to me, Evan. Me."

Ricky's gaze ping-ponged between us. He pressed the phone hard to his ear.

Karen raised her hand as if to soothe him. "I've got this."

Ricky returned to his call. She turned her gaze on me.

"You have a problem with boundaries?" she said.

"Do you keep the Datura checkbook locked up?"

"I told you what to do. Start doing it. Don't jump the fence and drag my husband into this." She chewed her gum. "He has bigger fish to fry. He's finishing an album and planning the tour. He doesn't need you turning him hectic."

"How many people work for you? Who comes out to the house?"

"Plenty of folks. But you're the one whose name ended up on those checks."

"Which is why this whole thing is bizarre and stupid. If I had actually stolen those checks, I would have written them out to *cash,* not to myself. Not ever."

The gum-chewing slowed. Her fawn eyes blinked.

"Cash. Good point. That's how I want the money." She crossed her arms. "Monday. Get to it."

I stormed out of the building. The wind caught me, raising tears in my eyes. How the hell was I supposed to find proof that I was in the clear? I stalked toward the parking lot. Rounding the corner of the building, I heard rap music reverberating from a car stereo. A BMW four-by-four, a big black X5, was emitting the boom. Its tinted windows vibrated with every thud. Its license plate read, JMSNWD. It was parked in a disabled spot.

No, it was parked in two disabled spots.

My scalp tingled with anger. The audacity. And Karen dared to lecture me about crossing boundaries? I beelined toward it, ready to lay into the chauffeur, bodyguard, whoever had parked here. I was ten feet from it when a shriek of laughter cut through the funk. In the backseat, a woman's arm arced up. Her wrist was spangled with silver bracelets. Her palm slapped against the window. I slowed.

The hand slid across the glass.

The top of a head appeared in the backseat. Dark tangles. A man, looking down. The woman raised a leg and jammed her foot against the headrest of the driver's seat. She wore black Caterpillar boots. Silver eyelets seemed to wink at me. I stopped.

The man looked up, just for a second. He held poised, his features striped by light reflecting off the window. The woman's hand pulled him back down. Before he disappeared, he grinned at me.

4

I don't remember starting my car or driving the first mile through downtown. Or anything, until I heard Toby Keith on the radio, that blue-collar Oklahoma baritone singing that he was going to kick somebody's ass. I felt my palms, sweaty on the steering wheel, and my teeth, biting my cheek. I saw that I was flooring it up State Street toward the mountains, past empty sidewalks, store windows reflecting the sooty sky, blue banners whipping on lampposts.

At the edge of my vision burned a gold corona of anger. And fear. Why didn't I tell them? Why didn't I say anything?

Because the suspicion was only half-formed.

Why didn't I insist that they go ahead and call the police?

Because when you do that, you surrender control to a machine that has power to seize your liberty. And because it was an inside job. And though I'd been in the Jimsons' house, there was someone else who was inside plenty more than I.

P. J. Blackburn.

P.J. worked as Ricky Jimson's gofer. I looked again at the photocopied checks, fearing in the pit of my stomach that P.J. had stolen them. His life had gone disastrously awry, and because of him I was in trouble.

I drove out to Isla Vista and gave his apartment one more try. Nobody was home. I left him a note.

Heading back to town, I cut through the university. When I reached the eastern edge of campus, I parked along the cliff overlooking the beach. The promontory had a grand view of the coastline, the Goleta Valley, and the mountains disappearing into the clouds. I locked my purse in the glove compartment and stuck some change in the parking meter. Burrowing into my sweatshirt, I walked to the fence at the edge of the cliff.

P.J. had always had problems. But two disastrous problems in less than twelve hours? The stars said this was not chance. And I had a bad feeling that P.J.'s troubles were tied in with Ricky's.

Ricky Jimson, Missouri farm boy, had driven the hard road to stardom. He sang with abandon, golden hair flying. And with agility, frequently ending up spread-eagled on the stage, groping the microphone stand. But mostly he sang about death.

Superficially the songs were about women, or sex, or gettin' it on, or, as one hit put it, "Ridin' the Sausage." But they were really about grief, emptiness, the grave. Because Ricky Jimson, who built a huge career in music and lived to tell about it, was convinced that death stalked him.

Or at least stalked his friends and family. His parents died trying to outrun a Kansas tornado in a '68 Cadillac. A girlfriend choked to death on a wad of chewing tobacco in his hotel room. Jimsonweed's tour bus crashed after swerving to avoid a cow on a snowy highway. And then there was Arrowhead Stadium in Kansas City, where Jimsonweed played to fifty thousand fans as thunderheads boiled overhead, and Baz Herrera strutted forward, erupted into his guitar solo, and was struck by lightning.

Ricky didn't go outside for two years afterward. According to the tabloids, there was a year when he didn't even get out of his bathrobe, unless it fell off as he staggered to the liquor cabinet for a fresh bottle of Cuervo.

Karen changed all that. Karen Herrera was Baz's widow, who poured a bucket of ice water onto Ricky, put his house in the Hollywood hills up for sale, packed him up, and moved with him and her daughter to Montecito. They married, and she began investing Ricky's songwriting royalties, running the business as Datura Incorporated. From *Datura stramonium*, the botanical name for jimsonweed, the hallucinogenic plant that gave the band its name.

But twenty-five years in the music industry, not to mention Ricky's inner Nero, had taken their toll. These days he was sober, more or less, and lucid, more or less. But he needed a helping hand.

Enter P. J. Blackburn.

Ricky had needed a gofer, and Karen asked around the law firm for a name. Jesse recommended P.J., who said one word: "Cool." So for the past couple of years, he'd been making Ricky ice-cream sundaes. He ran down to the newsstand for ciggies and *Rolling Stone*. He tossed a football to him in the backyard. He became part of Ricky's continual renewal and relaunch.

Because Ricky didn't want to become one of Santa Barbara's retired rock legends. Oh, he danced the dance. He sat in at local clubs, and judged the annual chili cook-off at Oak Park. He endorsed a hair dryer with the motto "Always ready to blow." He appeared as a judge on a reality TV show called *Rock House*. But his ultimate buzz was performing, and he couldn't give it up. That's why he was recording a new album, and Jimsonweed was planning to go on tour in a few weeks.

I didn't think it was coincidence that the checks had been stolen from Datura now. And I knew in my gut that P.J. was involved.

Below me the ocean thrashed. The surf was violent, the color of gunmetal. Nobody was out. I walked down a wooden staircase to the sand.

To clear my name, I knew, I had to call the police. Alone, I didn't have the authority to gain access to Datura's goings-on. If an investigation led to P.J., it led to P.J. So be it.

I hiked up the beach. Driftwood lay jumbled on the sand. Heaps of kelp trailed green vines back into the water. I tried to discern shapes within their tangled form. The breakers crashed.

The tide was out, exposing the rocks at Campus Point. I clambered up and across them, taking care not to slip, and hopped down on the other side. In the channel I could see oil platforms, and a container ship steaming south. Ahead of me, the beach stretched in a dirty line west to Isla Vista. The houses of Del Playa Drive lined the cliff above the sand. I picked up a stick of driftwood and threw it into the waves.

Who was I kidding? Even if she was real, I wasn't going to find her. Santa Barbara County has one hundred and twenty miles of coastline, with coves, piers, rocks, refineries, as well as sandy beaches. Time to head home and do the hard stuff, beginning with telling Jesse. I turned around.

At the point, two men were picking their way across the rocks. When they saw me, they sped up.

I'm not generally mistrustful of strangers. But a mouse of warning told me to give these two a wide berth. I looked around for another way back. They clattered across the rocks in my direction.

"Hold up," one shouted. "Stop. Yeah, you. Rowan."

It was Gopher, from the bar at Chaco's. His dirty hair ruffled in the wind.

"Thought you'd have some fun with me last night, huh?"

He teetered toward me across the wet rocks. The

second man followed him. He was Gopher's taller, balder, fitter double. Same mustache; Santa Barbara was where Pancho Villa was making his last stand.

"Playing with my head, making me feel small. That what you're into, making men feel small?"

I had left my phone in the car. How stupid was that? And the beach was empty. But on campus, past the lagoon, sat the marine science lab, and somebody had to be there.

Gopher shoved his glasses up his nose. "How about we play a new game?" He turned to his double. "Whatcha think, Murphy?"

How far was the marine lab, maybe four hundred meters? I took two running steps and Murphy jumped down in front of me, blocking my path. His head was shaved, and he was as pale as a glazed doughnut. Despite the weather he wore a sleeveless T-shirt. He seemed heedless of the cold. The studded dog collar and matching leather wristbands couldn't be keeping him warm.

"We'll play Truth or Dare." He walked toward me. "I'll start. You're a liar and a cheat."

I put my arms up, backing toward the breakers. "Stop this. I don't know you."

Gopher fumbled his way across the rocks. "Make her take the dare, Murph. She's big on challenging guys; see how she likes getting some back."

Murphy picked up a stick of driftwood about a yard long. He broke it across his knee and aimed the shattered ends at me like skewers.

"Merlin, your turn. Truth or dare?" he said.

Gopher finally reached the edge of the rocks and slipped down to the sand. "Truth."

Murphy poked the driftwood sticks at me, backing me toward the water. "So tell me, is she lying, or does she know?"

"She knows. Else she wouldn't be trying to get away."

"That's what I think."

"So we agree," Gopher said. "You got the money. Question is now, how you going to get it to us, and how quick?"

Murphy smiled. "And how you like your nose—plain broken, or with these sticks jammed so far up it, you'll be breathing out the top of your head?"

5

Money? What money? The waves foamed around my ankles. The cold was bone bending.

"We know you got it," Murphy said. "And the boss knows it, too."

"What the hell are you . . ." Wait. The boss. I bridled. "Did Karen send you?" I said.

Murphy frowned. "What?"

Anger displaced my alarm. "Dammit. If she thinks she can muscle me—"

"Who the fuck's Karen? Mr. Price sent us."

Change anger to confusion. And fright. Murphy poked me backward into the water.

"You played us all," he said. "But you didn't pull it off, and now it's time to come through. Either work the deal or give the money back."

Gopher—Merlin—twitched his shoulders. "Right now, Rowan."

"Stop calling me that. It's not my name," I said.

"Yeah, right. You're really Evan Delaney."

He guffawed. Murphy snorted.

"The games stop here," Murphy said. "We know you got the money in a safe place. Show her, Merlin."

Merlin held up a sheet of paper. My heart sank. It was the photocopy of the stolen checks. Only one way they could have gotten it from my car. Smash and grab. The water was over my knees now.

Gopher smiled. "You look scared, honey. Don't she,

Murphy? What's wrong, Tiny Tim ain't here to protect you? He can't come out of the woodwork and off me?"

"You think he was just messing with you last night?" I said.

"Course he was," Gopher said.

"Next time he won't be. And the last man who tried to mess with me ended up dead."

He put two fingers against his temple. "Bang-bang, huh?"

"Single shot to the throat. Nine-millimeter hollow-point round."

They looked at each other. And laughed out loud.

"Go on, scare us some more," Murphy said.

He trudged through the water at me. "You have a choice. Refund the boss's money, with interest. Merlin, what's the juice on the investment?"

"At a point a week?" Gopher said. "Let me think a minute."

"Never mind. We'll send you a bill. So get things together for when we come to collect."

Collect? Crap, they were repo men. Or loan sharks. And they had me down for somebody else's bad debt.

He gave me a chilly smile and tossed the driftwood sticks aside. "Oh. Yeah, your choice. Wet or dry?"

"What?"

"Wet it is."

With three lumbering steps he charged, brought up an elbow, and whammed into me. I pitched backward into the waves.

"Nice day for a swim," he said. They walked away laughing.

By the time I hiked back to the stairs I was shivering. Seagulls cried on the wind. I jogged up, stiff with cold, afraid of what I was going to find. And yep, jackpot. My car window was smashed.

Heat prickled up my neck. Unlocking the car, I peered inside. Glass lay in beads all over the seat, but

I breathed a sigh of minor relief. The glove compartment hadn't been broken into. My purse, with my wallet and cell phone, was still there.

I called the campus police. My voice sounded pale. A break-in, I said. And I had been menaced on the beach. Documents had been stolen.

But I saw that I had a replacement on the windshield. A parking ticket.

When I trudged up the street toward my house it was past noon. The garden gate was still swollen shut. My face was chapped, my feet tired, my patience gone. I whacked the latch and kicked. The wood groaned but this time the gate didn't budge.

A voice called from the garden, "Hold on, I'm coming."

The gate screeched open. Nikki Vincent stood on the path.

She wore overalls and leather gardening gloves, and held a pair of shears in her hands. She was cleaning up the red bougainvillea that had fallen in the storm. Perspiration sheened on her molasses skin.

"Oh, my God." She dropped the shears. "Where have you been?"

A caffeine jolt hit me. "Is anything—"

She grabbed me and crushed me against her chest. "Why didn't you answer your phone?"

My pulse had jumped into overdrive. "What's wrong?"

"God. You don't know."

"Nikki, you're scaring me."

"Come on." She pulled me across the lawn toward her house. "We have to stop Carl."

"From what?"

She broke into a jog. "He's on his way to the morgue."

My stride faltered.

"Come on." She tugged my arm. "Jesse—"

White noise, white air, everywhere, that's all I heard

and saw. My knees buckled and I dropped to the grass like a marionette.

I felt water soaking through my sweats. I heard Nikki saying, "Girl, oh, damn." I smelled wet grass and jasmine so sweet it could have choked me.

She gripped my shoulders. "No," she was saying. "Evan, no."

My mouth was gaping open and Nikki was fizzing in and out through the fog. The car, Jesus, tell me he didn't wreck the car.

"Carl's on his way to the morgue with Jesse," she said.

She had a hand on my elbow. I slapped it away.

"Don't do that." I heard myself. I was crying. "Don't do that to me."

She helped me to my feet. She looked disturbed at the force of my reaction. Drawing myself up straight, I climbed the porch steps.

"Why are they going to the morgue?" I said. "Who's dead?"

She opened the kitchen door. "You are."

6

Nikki gripped the steering wheel. "It's going to be all right."

"We can catch them if you'll go faster than twenty-five miles an hour."

We were crawling along Hollister Avenue through Goleta. With Thea squirming in her car seat, Nikki refused to exceed the speed limit. But Jesse's phone was off, and when I called the morgue I reached an automated message system.

"Evan, chill down. You're alive."

"He doesn't know that."

At the roadside, eucalyptus trees moaned in the wind. Inside my head the white noise and air had dispersed into bright pebbles of confusion.

"Explain it again. Maybe this time it'll make sense," I said.

She exhaled. "Jesse got a call asking him to go to the morgue."

"To identify my body."

"Yes."

"That's stupid-ass crazy."

"Hon, he was barely coherent."

Traffic slowed for a red light. My knee jittered up and down. "Keep going."

"He was at the bottom of the back steps, throwing rocks at the kitchen window to get our attention.

Shouting, 'Where the hell's Evan?'" Her mouth crimped. "The look on his face. I never want to see it again."

I felt colder than I could have imagined, and hollow. I dug my fists into the pockets of my sweatshirt. The light turned green, but the car in front of us didn't move. I reached over and hit the horn.

Nikki scowled at me. "Ease off. He's going to be okay."

"Just get there."

I felt Nikki's eyes on me. It seemed as though she were peering through my skin, down to the secret depths where I hid my worst thoughts. And she was seeing the fear I had swallowed: that, negligently or recklessly, Jesse might harm himself.

"I know it's somebody else. But I don't want him to see it. I don't want him even to set foot in the morgue. After all that's happened, it's too much to ask of him."

Thea, seeming to sense our tension, rattled the car seat. "Out. Get out."

"Has he been that depressed?" Nikki said.

Not depressed; ragged with grief. His friend Isaac Sandoval had been killed when the hit-and-run driver ran them down. And only a few months ago Isaac's brother, Adam, had died before Jesse's eyes, trying to put the driver in prison. Against evidence and reason, Jesse thought their deaths were his fault. That guilt was what pulled him down beneath the surface of a black river he swam, upstream, in his own heart.

I pointed at the cross street. "This is it."

We turned the corner. The morgue was part of the county sheriff's complex, a low building designed to be nondescript. Jesse's black Mustang was parked outside. Nikki swung in next to it. I had the door open before the car finished rolling.

I rushed inside and found Carl pacing back and

forth in the lobby. He was his usual immaculate self, with creases ironed into his blue jeans, but behind round-rimmed glasses his face looked drawn.

Seeing me, he stopped still. "My God."

"Where's Jesse?"

He pointed at a door. I ran through it and down a hall, pushed through another door, and found myself in the cold-storage room. In chilly air, rows of body lockers shone along the far wall. One was open. An attendant from the sheriff's office was sliding out a tray, on which lay a corpse covered with a sheet.

Jesse was watching. Sitting in the wheelchair, he was going to be eye-to-eye with the body. The morgue attendant reached to fold the sheet back.

"Don't," I said.

The attendant turned, her round face prickling in surprise. "You're not allowed in here."

Jesse didn't move. I walked toward them.

The attendant raised her hand. "Turn yourself around and march right back where you came from."

Jesse sat motionless, gripping his push-rims. The attendant stepped to block the corpse with her own body. I walked past her.

"Jess, it's me."

His head dropped. He covered his eyes with one hand. I fell to my knees at his side and wrapped my arms around him. He held as still as stone. He felt cold, his whole body knotted.

"Breathe," I said.

He buried his face against my shoulder. His fingers snaked into my hair. I felt his lips on my neck, and when he finally drew air it was through a kiss, fierce on my skin.

"Ma'am." The morgue attendant's voice had softened.

Jesse found my cheek, and my mouth. He kissed me twice, three times, stroking my hair, holding my face close to his.

"If you don't mind," said the attendant, "who are you?"

I looked up, seeing a name badge that read, AGUILAR. "Evan Delaney."

Surprise kinked on her face. She nodded at the sheet. "This is Evan Delaney."

"I vehemently doubt that." I stood up. "And I'm in serious need of an explanation."

Jesse turned his back on the sheet. He pulled out his phone and punched a number. Aguilar's mouth pinched.

"Sir, please. Not now."

"This can't wait." He spoke into the phone. "It's me. Here."

He handed it to me. Putting it to my ear, I said hello.

"Ev? Sweet Christ."

My brother's voice sounded brittle. I began to understand how far the bad news had spread.

"I'm okay, Bri. Mom and Dad?" I said.

"Negative. I was waiting for verification before I called them. Jesus God, how did they make this mistake? Evan, you have no idea."

From his end came the noise of traffic. "Where are you?"

"Going like a Tomahawk missile down Highway Fourteen. I'll be in Santa Barbara in a few hours."

I felt myself choking up, and fought it. "You mean you thought I was dead, and you decided to *drive*?"

He let out a hard sound that wasn't really a laugh. "The navy hates it when I borrow their Hornets for personal flights." His voice sobered again. "We'll be there in three."

We meant Luke, my nephew. I said, "Can't wait," and handed the phone back.

Aguilar said, "Ma'am, may I see some identification?"

I showed her my driver's license. She scowled.

"Kathleen Evan Delaney. Same as all the credit cards on the deceased."

"Oh, brother." I glanced at the sheet, and at Jesse. "Hear that?"

He hung up the phone. "Stolen ID. Or counterfeit. You know what that means."

"Cherry Lopez. That last kick in the pants she loved to give people."

I explained to Aguilar. "My purse was stolen last summer. The thief was into online credit card fraud. This could be connected."

Damn, had Lopez sold my credit information online? Or was the woman under the sheet a professional thief?

"It's identity theft." Jesse's face was severe. "This is not good."

"Not in any way."

Aguilar gestured to the door. "Let's discuss this elsewhere."

Jesse didn't move. "Not until you tell me why you contacted next of kin before investigating this young woman's identity."

Beneath Jesse's voice I heard Gopher's words. *Yeah, right. You're really Evan Delaney.* Laughing, because he didn't believe that. I ran my knuckles across my forehead. Something bad was unspooling all around me, and at the end of the line lay a dead woman on a slab.

"You didn't check fingerprints? Identifying marks? Missing persons reports?" he said.

I stared at the sheet, becoming aware of what I'd been consciously ignoring amidst the metallic sterility and cool of the room: a scent. Like a stagnant pond.

"Did you take even a cursory look at her before calling Evan's brother and telling him she was dead?" Jesse said.

Aguilar's cheeks were turning pink. "She had a pocketful of plastic giving us a name. And if you'll allow me to correct you, we have not identified this body. That, sir, is what you came here to do."

"She drowned?" I said.

"We haven't determined cause of death yet," Aguilar said.

The smell augured through me. It was the scent of the ocean.

"Did she wash up on the beach?" I said.

"Below More Mesa." She gave the sheet a dispassionate look. "Near the black sands."

"Jericho Point," Jesse said.

I nodded distractedly. Jericho Point was what we called the beach below the eroding cliffs, because the walls collapsed and came tumbling down on hapless beachcombers. People died there with depressing regularity. And it was where the current could have carried someone who fell into the water in Isla Vista.

"Let me see the body," I said.

Jesse gave me an incredulous look. "You don't want to do that."

"I do. You go out to the lobby." I looked at Aguilar. "Please."

Jesse took my wrist. "No, you truly don't want to do that."

"I can handle it."

His eyes were arctic. "Nobody's told you."

"What?" I looked from him to the sheet.

"She didn't drown, Evan. She was murdered."

At once I felt disconnected, as if the buzzing lights and chill air were biting at my face.

"I don't understand," I said.

Aguilar looked somber. "The deceased was the apparent victim of a homicide. Viewing the body may be difficult."

My skin tingled. I couldn't stop staring at the sheet. "I need to know."

"Perhaps there's another way," Aguilar said.

Stepping to the tray, she lifted a section of the sheet and exposed one of the dead woman's arms. I saw a delicate wrist wearing a silver charm bracelet. And a grayish hand twisted stiff with rigor mortis.

"Does this look familiar?"

She gestured to the charms hanging on the bracelet. A shamrock, a koala, a dolphin, a Chinese character. I shook my head.

"May I presume that you can give us a negative on the ID? Mr. Blackburn—can you confirm that this is not Kathleen Evan Delaney?"

Jesse was pale. "Jesus." He pushed closer to the tray, staring at that wrist.

"Sir?"

He lifted a hand to pull the sheet off, only to stop himself. "Show me."

I put a hand on his shoulder. "What are you doing?"

"Take off the sheet." Sparks in his eyes. "Do it, just do it, come on."

Aguilar looked uncertain. But with practiced formality she stepped to the side of the locker tray and folded back the sheet.

"Oh." The cry escaped my lips as I staggered backward. "God."

I had seen the dead before, but not this. "Shit. Oh, God."

If I force myself, I can see her blond hair, with one streak of blue, matted and packed with sand. A purple blouse, dried and wrinkled. Paper-gray skin. But then I smell the smell, and I start to swim, and I see her face.

"Fuck. Damn, fucking hell."

Jesse said it, or I said it, stumbling away from that tray.

"Do you recognize her?" Aguilar said. "Mr. Blackburn?"

I banged into Jesse and kept going backward. "Stop it, make it stop."

The corpse was staring at me. Right at me, shit, with bloodshot huge eyes that bulged out of her eye sockets.

She was willow thin, with flawless skin, and from the neck down her body looked perfect. She couldn't have been more than twenty-one. She could have been me at that age. Sand crabs were crawling in and out of her mouth.

It was her, I knew, the girl who had gone off the balcony at the party. She had been garroted. With wire. Through the gore, I saw a bloody, shining strand embedded in her throat. Her head had almost been sawed off. Her face was bloated. Her tongue looked like a sea slug protruding through swollen lips.

The lights spun. The door hit the wall when I threw it open. I fought to bring air into my lungs, shoved my way through the lobby and outside into the wind.

Nikki stood next to the car, bouncing Thea on one hip, talking to Carl. I lurched past. Carl called my name. I felt covered in filth. My clothes stank with the smell of the corpse. I pulled my sweatshirt over my head and threw it to the ground. I yanked off my shoes and socks and tore off the track bottoms and stood there in my shorts, shivering. I still smelled it.

"Ma'am." Aguilar was calling to me. "Ma'am. I'm sorry about that."

I paced in a circle, shuddering. "And you haven't determined the cause of death? Jesus Christ."

"As a formality, can you tell me whether you recognize the deceased?"

"Where's Jesse?"

"He said he needed to wash his face. The deceased, ma'am."

That girl hadn't fallen off of any balcony. P.J.'s story was a lie.

"I've never seen her." I sat down on the sidewalk and leaned my head on my knees. "But I think I know where she died."

I gave her a short summary. Jesse came out, looking ashen. Aguilar went over and spoke briefly to him before going inside. I sat on the sidewalk. Jesse was talking to the Vincents. Nikki put a hand over her mouth and turned away with Thea. Carl shook his head. Jesse headed for the Mustang, jerking his head for me to join him.

I stood up, gathered my things, and wandered over like a zombie. Jesse was trying to put the car key in the door lock. He kept missing.

I covered his hand with my own. "Think I'm in better shape than you. I'll drive."

"It's not that." He lowered his hand to his lap. "Did you see her charm bracelet?"

"Yeah. It brought her no luck, did it?"

The wind raked his hair. He looked up at me.

"It belongs to my mother."

7

The Mustang fired up with a roar. Jesse threw it into reverse and spun the tires backing up. I braced my hands against the dashboard. This car.

Jesse had bought it from my brother. He painted it black and installed hand controls. And he kept Brian's bumper sticker: MY OTHER CAR IS AN F/A-18. It was a load of V-8 menace.

I buckled up. "You're positive about the bracelet."

"I got the *Xi* in Beijing, the shamrock in Dublin. The koala in Sydney, when I swam Pan Pacifics. It's all stuff I picked up competing on the U.S. team." He flung the wheel and bounced out onto the street. "The dolphin was a birthday gift from P.J."

"Did you tell Aguilar?"

"I had to."

"Do you know who that girl is?"

"No." He turned onto Hollister and let the car growl. "Do you?"

I stared out the windshield. We had come to it.

"This isn't straight-out identity theft, is it?" he said.

"No. And it has nothing to do with Cherry Lopez snatching my purse."

"Spill."

"Pull over."

He gave me a canny look and stopped the car along the curb. His gaze cooled on me.

"It has to do with your brother," I said.

For a long second he continued looking at me. Then he jammed the car in gear, spun the wheel, and slewed into a U-turn across traffic. The car did what Mustangs tend to do, with the big engine up front and the short back end. The wheels got light and started sliding across the slick roadway.

I grabbed the door. "Christ."

Horns blared around us. He steered into the skid, straightened out, and slammed it toward Goleta, full throttle. My blood rushed in my ears.

"That girl's dead, and P.J.'s involved. Fuck," he said.

"Pull the hell over."

He didn't even look my way. We raced along, barreling through puddles, flinging up water. At the roadside trees thrashed in the wind.

"You're in trouble, aren't you?" he said. "P.J.'s done something that's going to boomerang on you."

"I'm in big trouble. But I don't know how P.J. fits in."

"Don't lie to me. And damn well don't lie to yourself."

We boomed past the broad lawns and playing fields of San Marcos High School. His face was severe.

"Tell me everything. And don't talk to the sheriffs unless I'm with you. I'm your attorney right now; got that?"

I sank in my seat. I felt as though everything was caving in at once.

"Evan. That young woman was murdered. And . . ." He gripped the wheel, staring dead ahead. "The wire around her throat. I think I know what it is."

We ran a red light.

"It's a guitar string," he said. "I think it's from P.J.'s guitar."

Bitch. The more he thought about it, the more it bothered him. He had missed his chance.

It had been perfect, yeah, every time he reran it in his head, he came to that judgment. Capital-P Perfect. Except for the woman. And now he'd seen her again, which made him a little jumpy, but not too bad, not yet. Bad things came in threes, and she was just a two right now. Ballbuster. Pussy whipper.

But last night . . . The problem was, it had been improvised. He had to perform at the last minute, and he was brilliant. Open-air, too. His performance had been—well, almost cinematic. She walked right into it. And everything had been right at hand. And nobody saw.

That was the kick in the ass. His hottest performance, an improv at that, and nobody saw. That was the pisser about this kind of gig. Which was why it ate at him that he didn't get it on tape. If it were on tape, it would be there for him to replay. Rewind, appreciate, critique, improve upon. Forever. If only.

But this wasn't like laying down tracks or doing a video. You performed live, ha, so to speak, and you only got the one chance. You couldn't rewind.

But you could always do it again.

Keith and Patsy Blackburn lived on a well-kept street in north Goleta. Jesse's old elementary school was at the end of the road, its playing fields dark green from the rain. The house was designed in the Taco Bell school of architecture, with stucco arches around the front door, a red tile roof, and a pint-sized Spanish fountain out front.

When we coasted into the driveway, the car was as silent as the cold-storage room. I had told Jesse everything I'd kept from him the previous night, and he was seething.

Not solely at me, of course. The destruction we'd seen at the morgue had nauseated him. It had also planted a seed of fear. He turned off the engine.

"P.J. could not have done that to her," I said.

"I don't want to think so. But that guitar string—heavy-gauge with the blue thread on the end. It's what he uses."

"It's impossible. He couldn't hurt a fly."

His eyes were weary beyond all age. "He's on drugs. Don't be naive."

His mother's Honda sat in the driveway. I nodded at it.

"Are you going to tell her?"

He looked as if he'd rather set his hair on fire. "I have to. The cops are going to come asking about the bracelet." He opened the door and pulled his wheels and frame from the backseat. We got out and headed for the house.

At the front porch he turned around. He could make it down the two porch steps with a double bounce, but not up, which meant that I got to play forklift. I went behind him and grabbed the frame of the wheelchair. He rocked back, pulled hard, and I hauled him up.

It was a moment, I think, that he quietly hated. Not because he'd thundered around this house growing up and now needed his girlfriend to help him move sixteen vertical inches. That, he was coming to believe, we could both take in stride. But each trip home reminded him that, more than three years after the crash, his parents had not built a ramp. And that he took as a message.

But they wouldn't talk about it. His parents maintained a well-honed silence, a mental version of sticking their fingers in their ears and singing, "La-la-la I can't hear you. . . ." Suppression, a cappella. It was a song the Blackburn family was good at singing. They had lots of verses. Disability was just the latest addition to the lyric sheet.

He crossed the small entryway. The sunken living room, with its wall of mirrored tiles, was empty.

"Anybody home?" He shifted his weight and bounced down the step from the entry to the hallway. "P.J.?"

"Back here, Jess," a woman called. "I'm on the phone."

We found his mom in the family room. A college basketball game was on TV. She had the phone pressed to her ear, and was stubbing out a Marlboro.

"Your aunt Deedee," she whispered. "The wedding."

Patsy wore cutoffs and a fuchsia blouse. Her shapely legs were draped across the arm of her easy chair. She cupped her hand over the receiver.

"This'll take a while." She rolled her eyes. "A bride eruption."

Patsy had always reminded me of Liz Taylor playing Maggie the Cat. She had the barracuda smoothness and overt sexuality. The pout came easily. The swirling cigarette smoke added a retro aura of fifties dissolution.

"I have to talk to P.J.," Jesse said.

She turned a cheek toward him and squeezed her lips, asking for a kiss. He held still. She gave me a tight little ain't-he-a-stinker smile and tapped her cheek. Stiffly he crossed to the chair and stretched to give her a peck.

"He's at work," she said.

"Which job, the shelter? Jimson's?"

She shrugged, making sympathetic sounds into the phone. The wedding of her sister's son was a nuptial typhoon that had sucked everyone into its maw, including me. I had been drafted as a ninth-inning bridesmaid.

"The girl's hypersensitive. Give her a Valium, Deedee."

Jesse rubbed a palm against his leg. I knew he was one step from breaking down and shouting, but his mother lived her life one step from breaking down herself, day in and day out, so he held back, saying nothing about the murder.

She glanced up. "Yes, he and Evan just came in. I don't know, I can't imagine why he . . ."

She scowled at him, and reached for a highball glass

that sat on the coffee table. Jesse watched her take a sip. His expression smoothed into a mask. Turning, he headed to the door into the garage. He opened it.

"Mom, his Suzuki's here. Are you sure he isn't upstairs?"

Embarrassed for them, I looked away. Framed photos cluttered the mantel. It was the P.J. show, a collection of photos in which he invariably looked winsome and happy. The only shot of Jesse was in one corner of a family portrait, which hung like a rebuke to all that had happened since then. Keith seemed less beaten down, spiffy in his cheap suit. Patsy smiled proudly. The house appeared less dog-eared. P.J. was impish. And Jesse looked as though he might be able to take flight. His grin and stance radiated confidence that anything was possible and just around the corner.

As it had been.

"Mom," he said.

"Hang on." Patsy put the phone against her stomach and frowned at him. "You skipped David's bachelor party?"

Keeping his face blank, he headed to the stairs and craned his neck. "P.J. Come down." He turned to me. "Go up and haul his ass out of bed."

I gave him a sour look. This wasn't my house. And I didn't like being ordered around, though I knew it cost him to ask, because it emphasized that he hadn't gone up these stairs in years.

Patsy stage-whispered at him, "Would it have killed you to spend one evening having fun with your cousin? He's included you and Evan in the wedding party. Do you know how this makes us look?"

Jesse spun. "Hang up the phone."

"Bad enough you two called off your wedding. Now you're going to embarrass me in front of my sister?"

He wasn't quick, but she wasn't sober. He grabbed the phone out of her hand.

"Aunt Deedee, she'll call you back." He hung up.

Patsy punched to her feet. "Jesse, this wedding is the biggest—"

"P.J. is in deep shit. Next time it won't be me at the door. It'll be the cops."

She didn't exactly sway, but her posture eroded. Her gaze broke from his and, seeking a new target, lit on me.

"Less than a week to the ceremony. Can't you get him to think about the family for six lousy days?"

I spoke softly. "Does P.J. know any girls with a blue streak in their hair?"

"He has a dozen girlfriends. I don't know." She put up her hands. "You work it out with him, Jess."

"You're not listening. This isn't about us," he said.

Crossing to the kitchen, she opened the fridge and took out a pitcher of iced tea. I saw confirmation that P.J. had been here recently: a pizza box, bottles of Corona beer, and Tupperware containers labeled *Patrick's*—specialties Patsy cooked to mollify his food allergies, which was what P.J. claimed made him averse to early mornings and schoolwork and a steady job. Such as his work at the animal shelter, which had been imposed as community service after a DUI arrest.

"Dad drove him before I got up. I don't know where," she said.

She poured herself a refill from the pitcher. I couldn't smell the vodka, but of course that's why it was her drink of choice.

Jesse watched. "Take it easy. Please?"

"It's Saturday. Cut the world some slack."

Bang, slam that door right in his face. He leaned back. Then cut a sharp turn and headed down the hallway for the door.

She thumped the highball glass onto the counter. "He's my sister's only son, Jess. And you're standing up for him. This is just . . . it's the country club, and your uncle's colleagues are flying out from New York; it's so—"

"Whatever."

I followed him. "You have to tell her."

Her voice trailed us. "Honey, wait. I'm sorry." She came down the hallway. "I didn't mean it. You know that, sweetheart."

At the step into the entryway he popped his front wheels up and held out a hand. The rise was too high for him to manage on his own. I pulled him up. Patsy watched, her face stricken.

She looked away, blinking. "I'll see you at the rehearsal. Okay?"

He made for the door, but I stood in front of it.

"Patrick's going to be all right. You'll see to that, won't you?" she said.

I crossed my arms. He had to tell her. His shoulders dropped.

"No, he's not." He waited for her to look at him. "P.J. took your charm bracelet, and it ended up on a girl who's dead."

Her hand went to her throat. "Why would you say a thing like that?"

"She was murdered. The police are going to be coming around to question him."

"No." She waved him off. "Don't do this."

The phone rang.

"That's Deedee. I have to get it," she said.

Without a word, she hurried back down the hall.

Blowback took longer than I expected—twenty minutes. I walked out of the animal shelter, where a canine sonata racked the air, and saw Jesse on the phone. The wind shivered across pewter puddles. I got in the car, shaking my head. P.J. wasn't there.

"Playing head games is the last thing I'm doing. This is extremely serious, and if she . . ." Hand through his hair. "No, Dad. I can't help it if— Fine. Yes. Soon as I can."

He hung up. "I have to go back to their house."

He started the car. "P.J.'s at the Jimsons'." Can you go? We have to talk to him before Mom gets riled up and starts calling him every two minutes. He'll rabbit."

As Patsy lost count of her drinks, she lost control of her tongue. But it meant a potential run-in with the Iron Pixie.

"Sure."

He shot me a glance. "Don't let her scare you."

"I won't."

I lied. But P.J. was going to tell me the truth.

Santa Barbara believes it escaped the Fall. The bumper sticker says so: ANOTHER DAY IN PARADISE. We find proof everywhere—in the sunshine, the beaches, the relative infrequency of gang wars. And, of course, the celebrities.

We're a straight shot up the freeway from Hollywood, so stars seeking a haven from L.A. land here constantly, like space debris. It convinces us we're hot stuff. Sight an Oscar winner buying taquitos at La Super-Rica, and we coast on it for weeks.

Montecito, the tony suburb that styles itself a village, draws the biggest names, and has the most pretensions. Quiet and lush, it's a place where old money needn't speak, rock gods don't raise their heads, and if your house can be seen from the street, you plain ain't rich. Granted, Jesse had a village address—but in the neighborhood that surf rats call Baja. Lower Montecito, where you get fog, and train whistles at midnight.

Karen Jimson, on the other hand, had installed her family on a Spanish-style spread with a pool, tennis court, gym with sauna, and Japanese rock garden. They called it Green Dragons, after a slang term for jimsonweed.

I followed the winding drive up to the house. The sun was spearing the clouds, gold light through the gray. Parked in front of the garage was the BMW four-by-four I'd seen that morning outside Sanchez Marks, with the JMSNWD tags. Oaks arched over the house. The adobe walls had a creamy heft. Inside, music was thundering. I rang the bell, bracing myself for Karen.

The door opened and gangsta rap rained down on me, lyrics hitting the air like buckshot. A young woman stood in the doorway. Early twenties, Karen-sized. Her long hair flashed like black water. Sunlight kicked against her silver earrings and bracelets, and the eyelets of her steel-toed Caterpillar boots. Not to mention the diamond stud in her nose.

She jerked her head, nodding me in.

She wore fatigue pants and a ribbed white under-shirt. She was eating Ben & Jerry's straight from the carton, licking a mound of chocolate ice cream from the spoon, and she was chilly. Her nipples protruded like rivets through the clingy undershirt. She was, I surmised, the Jimsons' daughter. Without a word she turned and walked off.

After a few seconds, realizing that she wasn't coming back, I followed.

Ricky's gold records formed a receiving line along the walls of the entry hall. To the left, a cavernous living room sported leather furniture and six-foot cacti. Above the mantel hung an original Georgia O'Keeffe. A white flower filled the canvas like the bell of a trumpet, green leaves spiraling behind it. Jimsonweed.

The rap music hammered the floor. The young woman kept walking.

"Excuse me," I called.

She was passing the kitchen, which led to another wing of the house. Spinning around, she pointed with her ice-cream spoon. "Ricky's in the sauna."

"I'm looking for P.J."

She kept spinning and walked away.

Though she dressed like a welder, her carriage was pure princess. It was the sway of her hips, the thrust of her chin, the cut of her hair—like Pharaoh's daughter, with black bangs cut straight across her forehead. World at her feet, her walk seemed to say, and it had been there for aeons. Top of the karmic heap.

She disappeared into a back room. I followed. It was an entertainment room, and P.J. was slouched on a sofa, his back to me, watching TV. Beyond him, outside the windows, the mountains shone green in the patchy sunlight. Clouds shredded on the peaks.

"Peej." The girl sat down on the arm of the sofa, swinging her feet onto the cushions. "That was the doorbell. You should have answered it."

He straightened. "Didn't hear it, sorry. Who was it?"

"Pizza girl." She licked the spoon. "Give her a tip."

He stood up, looked around at me, and did a double take. "Hey." He lifted his chin in greeting.

"Let's talk," I said.

He looked rough. His skin was pasty, his eyes grimy blue. His khakis sagged low on his hips, showing off four inches of his frayed plaid boxers. Nothing looked clean.

The girl gazed at him with sleepy eyes. "Stepping out on me?"

She might have poked him with a cattle prod. "No, this is Jesse's girlfriend."

"Hi, Jesse's girlfriend." She slid down onto the sofa, arching her back so that her frosty rivets protruded. "I'm Sin."

Right. "I'm deadly, myself. Evan Delaney."

Her eyes slid my way, and her mouth ticked up into a smile. "Sinsemilla. Or Sinsa."

"Jimson?" I said.

"Check my driver's license."

"That's okay. I saw the plates on your X5 this morning, outside Sanchez Marks. In a disabled spot."

She turned her bottomless black gaze on me. "Really?"

"You were playing the same rap album. Enjoying the lyrics—that line about spanking the bitch's ass with both hands. You were laughing."

"We'd just picked up a friend of mine at the airport." She shrugged. "Nobody was parked there."

"There never is, when you pull in."

"Bad me." She slapped herself on the wrist. "Boyfriend. Long time no see. We were in a hurry." She dug a new spoonful of ice cream from the carton and glanced at P.J. He was watching her as though hypnotized. "Nah, I'm kidding. And P.J. and I aren't together. We're fuck buddies, is all."

Okay, now I knew exactly what it took to make me feel like a starched shirt. P.J.'s color flooded back. His foot began jittering.

"Excuse us, would you?" I nodded toward the door. "P.J. Outside."

He winced at the sight of trees swaying in the wind, and wiped his nose on his sleeve. He was monstrously hungover.

"In my car," I said.

He followed me along the hall to the front door, through the thud of the music, gesturing to the living room. "Can't we talk in there?"

"I'd rather not bump into Karen," I said.

"She ran to the store."

I shook my head, opening the door. I didn't want to be overheard. He bent to avoid the wind and hurried to the Explorer, huddling into the passenger seat and tucking his hands into his armpits to warm them.

He blinked as though his eyes felt gritty. "You okay? You look kind of zapped."

I turned to face him. "They found her. She washed up at Jericho Point."

"Who?"

I gaped at him. "P.J., don't. I saw her body at the morgue two hours ago."

"The morgue."

"She didn't fall off the balcony. She was murdered."

He shook his head as though trying to clear it. "What are you talking about?"

"The party last night. She was garroted and dumped off the cliff into the surf."

"Party." He shrank back toward the door. "Stop. You're scaring me."

I stared at him, hard. "Christ."

He was used to fibbing his way out of tight corners. But right now he wasn't giving me sweet talk or a smile. He was gasping, as though he couldn't get oxygen.

"Don't you remember?" I said.

He shook his head. Was he lying?

"She's blond with a blue streak in her hair. Wearing your mother's charm bracelet."

He went stone still, not even blinking. Until he grabbed the door handle. I slammed the power lock button.

"Tell me her name," I said.

His fingers dug for the handle. "Let me out. I'm going to be sick."

"Then be sick. Tell me her name."

He glanced at me in panic, and away. "Brittany Gaines. Open the door; I'm gonna heave."

I unlocked it. He hurtled from the car and fell to all fours on the wet brickwork. He spewed with an awful horking sound. I counted to ten, got out, and walked around to him. His head was hanging low.

At the front door, Sinsa leaned against the jamb, pursing her lips. "Wow, Deadly. You have a helluva way with men."

8

Ignoring Sinsa, I crouched down to face him. "They thought it was me. She had credit cards with my name on them."

He moaned. "This is unreal."

"You mean fake? Counterfeit? Like the ID you helped her steal from me?"

"This has to be a mistake," he said.

"Whose idea was it, yours or Brittany's?"

"You can't be serious." He climbed to his feet.

"Do you need the money to support your habit?"

"I don't have a habit."

"What do you spend per day?" I nudged him against the car. "A hundred bucks? Two hundred?"

He put his hands up to ward me off. "Stop it."

I cupped his cheeks and forced him to look at me. "It was brutal, P.J."

He pressed his lips together, looking like an obstinate toddler, and squirmed. I braced to stop him from bolting.

He started to cry.

His chest gulped in and out. He slid down the side of the car and buried his head against his knees. If I ever thought he'd had a hand in the young woman's death, I didn't now. I waited it out. Looking at the house, I saw no sign of Sinsa. After a minute P.J.'s tears subsided.

"Who was she?" I said.

"My neighbor. The apartment next door."

I pictured the Don Quixote Arms, and the curtains twitching on the window next door to P.J.'s place.

"Did you take her to the party?"

"No. No way."

"You sound sure of that," I said.

"I was trying to cool things with her. That's the last thing I would have done."

"So, you were buddies? The same kind as you and Sinsa?"

"Now and then. It was nothing heavy."

I clenched and unclenched my fists. This had just turned ten times worse.

"Get real. You gave her your mom's bracelet. It was more than that."

He flushed. "It's not like Mom ever wore it anymore. I gave her that dolphin charm, but she wouldn't wear it. Not after Jesse . . ."

He didn't say the rest. Red spots mottled his face.

"Jesse's ballistic, isn't he?"

"We all are," I said. "What do you remember about last night?"

"Jamming with some guys at the party. Then . . ." His gaze lengthened. "This morning. Dad woke me up."

"What was Brittany doing at the party?"

"I don't remember her there." His eyes were red. He wiped his nose on his sleeve. "How come you came out there last night?"

I told him. With each detail he seemed to shrink.

He pressed the heels of his palms against his eyes. "I tried to stop you from calling search and rescue? What the fuck is wrong with me?"

With a shard of wind, the rain came again. Sinsa appeared in the front doorway. P.J. furtively wiped his eyes.

"You're melting," she said. "Come in."

I shook my head, but P.J. clambered to his feet,

holding his stomach, and trotted inside. I found him at the fridge, drinking milk from the carton. The kitchen was an echo chamber of chrome and hanging copper kettles.

"You know, that was scary," he said.

"What?"

"In your car, you locking the doors. I've never seen you mad before."

"You still haven't."

He gave me a guarded look. I took the milk carton and set it on the counter.

"You have serious problems to contend with," I said.

He hung his head. "You don't have to tell me. I'm a shithead."

"That's a long-term issue. I'm talking about this afternoon. You should talk to a lawyer."

"I'm talking to you."

"I mean you should retain legal counsel, officially."

"What for?"

"You said you were jamming at the party. Where's your guitar?"

"The Stratocaster? It's . . . ." His lips stayed open. "Crap, I must have left it there. Why?"

From the far wing of the house Ricky came padding toward us, whistling. He was dressed in psychedelic green swim trunks and glistening with sweat. His blond locks were pulled off his forehead into a samurai ponytail. A white gym towel was draped around his neck.

He waved at P.J. "Calistoga."

P.J. got a two-liter water bottle from the fridge and handed it to him. Ricky glugged half of it down, splashed a swig on his face, and stood there letting water drip onto the stone floor. He burped and broke out a Cheshire cat grin.

"Saunas, man, they revive you." He pointed the bottle at me. "You weren't here before."

"No."

"You work for Vonnie Marks."

"On and off."

"Check this out." He slid his hand up and down his stomach. "I'm down twenty pounds since October." He slapped a hand against the belly. "Listen to that. Solid."

Sinsa walked in. "Twenty more to go, Slink."

"Spandex is forgiving." He scowled. "Crap, Sin, put a sweater on. I've seen smaller teats on a dairy farm."

He should talk. He had the biggest tits in the room. No way could I have gotten a nipple ring that size through mine.

He squinted at P.J. "You look strung out."

Sinsa hopped up to sit on the counter. "He came from the animal shelter. Putting puppies down."

"I don't do that," P.J. said.

She mimed a dog being held by the scruff of the neck, with a syringe aimed at it. "Here, Spot. Head toward the light."

He blushed a deeper shade of red. "That's not funny."

"I'm teasing." She hopped off the counter. "Don't be a sourpuss."

She jammed her hands in the back pockets of her fatigues, so that her nipples stretched the undershirt like explosive bolts. Her silver jewelry sang in the light. She passed P.J., managing to brush his arm with her breast.

His heel stopped bouncing. He leaned against the counter and crossed his legs.

Ricky swigged from the water bottle. "We laid down vocals for the new track. Come up and listen after I shower."

P.J. squeezed his knees together. "Great."

Ricky cocked his head. "That's the garage door. Go help Mom carry the groceries."

Sinsa pouted. "It's all stuff she buys for your Mick Jagger diet."

Ricky put a hand on her back and walked her out of the kitchen. "And change this shit music. Pick a rapper who samples my tunes, not Steven Tyler's."

P.J. waited, trying to calm down enough to follow. I glanced toward the garage, wanting to leave.

"You need to understand how serious the situation is," I said. "You may have witnessed a murder last night, and the authorities know it. You need to talk to the sheriffs, asap."

"But I don't remember anything."

"Listen to me. Your ex-girlfriend was strangled."

"She wasn't my ex—"

"Shut up. She's dead, and you were at the scene. The cops will suspect you."

His face went blank. "You mean . . ."

"They'll look at you and see motive and opportunity. And possibly means. You said you left your electric guitar at the party."

"It's probably gone now."

"Brittany Gaines was garroted. Jesse thinks it may have been with a guitar string."

"Shit." He pressed his palm against an eye, and stopped. His head jerked up. "Wait, Jesse thinks it's a string from my Strat?"

"P.J., last night you gave me a story that was a bunch of bullshit. You need to remember the truth. And you need to tell me what Brittany was doing with my ID."

The color had leached from his face again. "Shit. Jesse thinks it was me."

Abruptly the stereo shut down. Boots knocked along the hallway. Grocery bags rustled.

I heard Karen's sharp voice. "There's barf outside on the driveway." She walked in, arms full, and saw me. "And guess what, it's in here too. Talk about balls."

"I'm going," I said.

"Did you bring me my money?"

Sinsa brought more bags. "She walked straight in. I found her going through your desk."

I whirled on her. "Knock it off."

"Lighten up." She rolled her eyes. "Where's your sense of humor?"

P.J. was looking ill. Karen nodded at him.

"Go hose down the driveway." She set the groceries on the counter. "Sin, put on a bra."

He stalked out of the kitchen, looking bleak. Sinsa ran after him. I made to follow, and Karen stopped me. I heard the front door slam.

"You. Set foot on our property again, I'll treat it as a robbery," she said. "I don't mean I'll have you arrested. I mean we'll fill your ass full of buckshot." Her nostrils flared. "Am I clear?"

"As ice."

"Good. Get out."

It was a long walk to the door, and I felt the skin tighten on my cheeks. Outside, I looked around for P.J.

The black X5 went roaring by. He was in the passenger seat. They raced down the wet driveway before I could shout.

9

By the time I got home I was pissed off, hungry, and chafed. My track bottoms were full of sand. The day had been horrible.

It was about to get worse.

I phoned the morgue and gave Aguilar the name Brittany Gaines. Then, sitting down at my desk, I went online and checked my credit report. It confirmed my fears.

Allied Pacific Bank. Credit card. Amount past due: $3,758.
Delta One Visa. Credit card. Amount past due: $2,241.
Americredit Financial Services. Auto lease. Ninety days past due. Status: Involuntary Repossession.

I counted ten fraudulent entries, racking up twenty thousand dollars' worth of bad debts in my name. I was going to be thoroughly, painfully reamed. This was bleeding-ulcer territory. And not all the bad debts were listed by the credit agency—such as the one that the Pancho Villa mustaches wanted to collect.

Had a bad debt gotten Brittany Gaines killed?

I phoned the credit agencies and put a fraud alert on my account. Then I phoned my bank. And each company that had issued a fraudulent card in my name.

One of the fake cards had been issued by Allied
Pacific Bank, the bank where the stolen Datura checks
had been cashed. That made me think somebody had
opened an account there in the name of K. E. Delaney. But I couldn't check that out until Monday. I
printed everything. Karen Jimson would need to see
this.

I flopped back in my desk chair, nerves jangling. I
knew what I had to do next: file a crime report. The
police department had forms online. While it printed,
I went to the kitchen for a glass of water.

Filing a crime report meant exposing P.J. to a harsh
wind. But I had no doubt that he had taken the checks
from the Jimsons, and helped Brittany forge my
identity.

What was wrong with him? Stealing from the Jimsons? He loved working for Ricky. He didn't have to
do anything. He watched TV. He had Sinsa to wind
him up like a top. Why would he sabotage his ideal
job by stealing checks from their business account?

Some E. And maybe a few lines. I set my water glass
down so hard it cracked.

Outside came the sound of light feet running. "Aunt
Evvie. We're here."

My anxieties fell away. I let out a whoop. "Luke."

He was sprinting along the flagstone path, so nimble
he might have been weightless. His black hair bounced
up and down. His eyes were alight, his face split by a
smile. I ran out and he leaped into my arms.

I spun him around. He smelled like fresh air. He
felt as light as a melody, but I said, "Wow, you're
so heavy."

"I'm not little anymore."

No, he wasn't. My nephew was seven years old and
the toughest, purest soul I knew. I kissed him and he
kissed me back. At that moment, I could have died
happy.

At the front of the garden, the gate scraped the walk. My brother's name was on my lips. But he wasn't the man standing there.

"Marc," I said.

In the wintry light, Commander Marcus Dupree looked like a crag of basalt. Black jeans and turtleneck, bitter-chocolate skin, aviator shades. He tipped his head and strolled toward us.

"Evan. Delighted to see you." His voice was velvet: Barry White minus two hundred pounds. "The drive certainly ended better than it started."

His smile was melancholy. I knew then how desolate my brother had felt until he found out it was all a mistake. For Marc to drive two hundred miles with him . . .

"You're a pal, Dupree," I said.

Behind him Brian appeared, carrying a duffel bag. He slung it to the ground and swooped me into his arms.

"Nine lives, kid." He kissed the top of my head. "You may still have 'em, but you knocked a few off of my count today."

He couldn't afford to squander any more. I leaned back to get a good look at him. "Didn't help. You're still the ugly child."

In truth, he was looking good. Angular as always, black hair and eyes shining, implacable cool in place, though I knew it hid a well of concern.

We headed for the door and he said, "Explain this balls-up today. Jesse didn't give me much info."

"He couldn't talk. We were in the cold room at the morgue."

I said it without thinking. Luke turned round eyes on me. Brian put a hand on the back of my neck and nudged me onward, telling me unmistakably to shut up. He didn't want to talk about death in front of Luke. But we couldn't avoid it. That was why they had come.

"Credit card fraud. She had my ID on her," I said.

Luke hopped up and down, tugging at my shirt. "Where's Jesse?"

I pointed inside. "Give him a call."

Brian's hand tightened on my neck. Wonderful. Jesse wasn't even here yet, and Brian was acting annoyed about him. Add a couple of actual Blackburn wisecracks and they'd be celebrating the annual Rub Each Other Wrong Festival.

Family. Kill me now.

"Let me get this straight." Brian sat on a kitchen stool, peeling the label from a bottle of Dos Equis. "In the past twenty-four hours your ID gets stolen, Slink Jimson gets ripped off, two shylocks play Beach Blanket Bingo with you, and the thief washes up, stiff. Santa Barbara has more action than Bangkok."

"It's been going on for months. I only found out about it in the last twenty-four hours."

"The way a blocked sewer backs up until it blows. The question is, what kicked off the explosion?"

Outside the French doors, Luke paced up and down the path. He looked our way and said, "How much longer?"

I shrugged and smiled at him. "It's only been fifteen minutes."

He continued pacing. Across the living room, Marc finished a phone conversation, saying, "Love you, too."

Though I pretended not to listen, I was struck by the warmth in his voice. I knew him as the cool hand on my brother's shoulder: half sensei, half guardian angel. He had been, ever since Brian separated from his wife but couldn't stop loving her, even through the crazed days that ended in her death. But usually I saw Marc in the cockpit, opening the throttles on an F/A-18. Slinging a Hornet across the desert sky, screaming past the airfield with Brian on his wing, he was one mean son of a bitch.

He sauntered to the counter. "The girls are fine. Ball game and the ballet recital were both wins." He raised his beer. *"Salud."*

He'd been divorced about a year. He and Brian, friends from Naval Academy days, were now bound by their singledom as well. At sea on dry land.

"And there's no problem with canceling the reservation in Palm Springs," he said. "I got two rooms at the Fiesta Coast Motel here instead."

"Sorry to throw a wrench into your vacation," I said.

"No problem. Santa Barbara has golf courses. We'll spend the week here." He clinked beer bottles with Brian.

Outside, I heard Jesse. "Hey, little dude."

Luke leaped and came down sprinting for the gate. He ran out of sight beyond a trellis of jasmine, saying, *"Yes."*

Jesse laughed. The sound made my weekend. A moment later they came along the path. Luke was kneeling on Jesse's lap, hands on his shoulders.

"And I can almost do an ollie. There's a skate park by the lake. The teenagers don't like second graders skateboarding there, but I did the quarter pipe once. It rocked."

"That must be how you knocked out your front teeth, huh?" Jesse said.

"No, I wiggled them loose. Silly." He pushed against Jesse's chest.

Brian hopped off the stool. "Careful there."

From experience, I could see that Luke's weight was balanced on Jesse's knees. They weren't going to fall over. Also from experience, I knew not to intervene. But Brian was halfway across the room, hands out.

"Better hop down," he said.

Jesse came through the door. "We're fine." He extended his hand. "Brian."

They shook. I introduced Marc, who smiled and

sought for anyplace to rest his gaze besides wheels. Jesse came into the living room, keeping up his stream of chatter with Luke. What's up at school? Science. Chicken pox. Hot lunch. One reason he got such a kick out of Luke, and from kids generally, was that they quickly treated him as a regular person. They might stare and ask blatant questions, but then they added his circumstances to their view of the world. Whereas adults sang from the Hymnal of Inane Remarks, at the liturgy of Avoiding the Obvious. *Let us now cloak our discomfort. And twist our tongues, Amen.* However, Jesse dealt with that in his own way.

"Got any more beer?" he said. "I need at least three before I can skateboard."

But then, guns blazing was his standard personality setting. Marc smiled so tightly that a corkscrew couldn't have pried through his lips. I brought Jesse a Dos Equis.

Brian turned a chair around and straddled it. "How's my pony?"

"Full of fight." Jesse tilted the bottle to his lips.

"You letting her out? You know how she likes to run."

I rolled my eyes. "And she looks great in black. But she's staying in the barn tonight." They didn't need to brag about how fast the Mustang could go, or soon they'd take it out and find an empty stretch of freeway. I put a hand on Jesse's shoulder. "Things okay with your folks?"

"Mom's upset, and so I'm in the doghouse. Find P.J.?"

I glanced briefly at Brian. "He doesn't remember anything. He blacked out."

Jesse eased Luke off his lap. "Don't tell me you believe that."

"When I told him, he broke down. It was pathetic."

"He can be extremely convincing. Don't let him play you."

"It wasn't an act. He's that bad, Jesse."

"Great." He pinched the bridge of his nose. "That's just great."

Brian leaned on the back of the chair. "What's the deal with your boss? She can't honestly believe this crap about Ev stealing checks from a client."

"Officially? She's reserving judgment," Jesse said.

"Dammit." I felt cut to the quick.

"Unofficially, she thinks it's a gambit. Karen's hoping the firm will simply cover the loss."

"Not at my expense," I said.

Brian nodded at Jesse. "And what are you doing about it?"

Jesse gave him an unhurried look. "I'm working on it."

Luke tensed around the mouth. I pulled him to me and kissed his hair. He fidgeted.

And pointed at the door. "Who's that?"

The knock brought all our heads around. A man and woman stood outside in the dwindling light.

"Jehovah's Witnesses," Brian said.

I shook my head. They looked too cynical. "It's the police."

The woman held up a badge. "Sheriffs."

She had a boxer's stance, as though she was used to holding her ground. "We have some questions about Brittany Gaines."

I sensed Brian and Marc falling in behind me, acting as my wingmen. That felt good. But patriotic gal though I am, who chokes up at the thought of navy pilots launching off the carrier deck, I knew that Brian and Marc couldn't do a damn thing to keep the police off my back.

But Jesse said the magic words. "Talk to me. I'm Ms. Delaney's lawyer."

The woman flipped open a notebook. "Your name?"

Jesse handed her his card.

"Detective Lilia Rodriguez." She handed the card to the man. "Gary Zelinski."

They were young. Rodriguez had a Peter Pan haircut and a kid's restlessness. And big, wary eyes. She looked as though she ran full tilt, watchful for all the bad things that racked the world.

"Any relation to Judge Rodriguez?" I said.

"I'm her daughter."

Zelinski did a slow strut, taking in my Navajo rugs and Yosemite prints and the martial hostility radiating from the pilots. He had perfect cop features. Bland, like a sponge. Just right for soaking up information.

He eyed Brian and Marc. "Who are these gentlemen?"

"My pallbearers," I said.

Jesse shot me a shut-up look.

Luke walked to Brian's side and leaned against him. Brian glanced at Marc and said, "We'll take a walk." Finding their jackets, the three of them headed out the door.

Jesse pulled out a chair for me at the dining table. He wanted to get us all on equal footing, with the cops at eye level with him.

Rodriguez sat down. "I talked to Jenny Aguilar, over at the morgue. She says neither of you could identify Miss Gaines's remains."

"That's right," he said.

She tapped her pen against the notebook and looked at me. "But last night you got search and rescue out looking for her."

"Evan did the right thing last night," Jesse said.

"Your name's in our paperwork too, Mr. Blackburn." Rodriguez wet her thumb and flipped through the notebook. "The deputy took it down from a man at the house. Were you at the party last night?"

"No."

"Because there's some confusion about the identity—"

"Lots of that going around."

Again she tapped the pen against her notepad. "Ms. Delaney, why don't you explain everything that happened last night."

Standard procedure with lawyers is to stonewall, but sometimes the best way to get out of trouble with the police is to explain yourself.

"Lay it out," Jesse said.

I told them everything. The crazed atmosphere at the party. The confusion over P.J.'s name. My 911 call. And this morning, going to the beach in a vain attempt to see if it had been true.

"How did your ID end up on Miss Gaines's body?" Rodriguez said.

"I don't know. The ID's fake."

"And your credit cards?"

"Fraudulent. My identity's been stolen."

"You haven't reported this alleged identity theft to the police."

Alleged. My warning board lit up. *Incoming*. Jesse laid a hand on my arm. The gesture seemed casual, but he was radiating heat. I got it loud and clear: *Down, girl.*

"Because I didn't know about it until the thief washed up on the beach." I grabbed my credit report off the printer and handed it to her. "I called in a fraud alert to the credit agencies half an hour ago."

She scanned the report. "Mind if I keep this?"

"Be my guest."

She handed it to Zelinski. Smiled at me. "You got a parking ticket this morning."

"Expired meter." I disliked that smile. "I also got my car burglarized."

Zelinski looked up from the credit report. "And all they took was documents. Didn't touch the stereo, your phone, your wallet." He read some more. "Must have been important stuff."

Documents that incriminated me in grand theft. Shit and more shit. "Yes."

"Related to this identity theft?" he said.

"Yes." I glanced at Jesse. He was grim. "I was harassed by a couple of repo men on the beach. I told this to the campus police this morning."

Zelinski lowered the report. "And all this happened at Campus Point, virtually in sight of the spot where Brittany's body washed up."

Rodriguez scanned me with those alert brown eyes. "Did you know Brittany Gaines?"

"No."

"Did you see her at the party last night?"

"No."

"I think you did."

Jesse straightened. "We're done."

Rodriguez looked at me. "Ms. Delaney?"

"We're done," I said.

She capped her pen, closed her notebook, and stood up. "We'll be in touch."

They left. I flexed and unflexed my hands, watching them cross the storm-tousled yard. The sky was furrowed yellow, sunlight cutting through black clouds.

"How did I do?" I said.

"Better than I expected."

"Thanks, Coach."

"And things are much worse than I thought."

10

Sunday morning the rain came in batches, broken by cold sunshine. Dew glimmered on the grass. There was a picture of Brittany Gaines in the paper.

Alive, she'd had eyes that looked luminous. The blue streak in her hair seemed playful. She didn't look like a coldhearted thief. Her smile was crooked. No sand crabs were crawling out of her mouth. After seeing it, I had to throw away my bagel and pour my coffee down the drain.

I double-checked the crime report I'd written up, and drove down to police headquarters to file it. I had duct-taped plastic sheeting over the broken window, and it vibrated in the wind. Jesse's assessment of the murder investigation dripped over me like chill water.

"They think P.J. killed her," he had said, after the sheriff's detectives left my house. "And that you helped him."

"Bullshit."

"What really twists their nuts is you going to the beach. They figure you went looking for the body, so if it washed up you could get rid of it." He was dour. "They probably guess you were running a scam with her."

"Faking my own fake ID? And then what happened, she went wild in the Saks shoe department, so I had P.J. strangle her? That's idiotic."

"People pull stupid scams all the time. They run up

crazy debts and blame pickpockets. They burn down
their own businesses to get the insurance. They kidnap
themselves for ransom."

"I get the picture."

And it had my face in the center of a bull's-eye.

The Santa Barbara Police Department's main station was a Spanish-style building across from the
courthouse. I was speaking to the desk officer when I
spotted Lieutenant Clayton Rome pouring himself a
cup of coffee. I waved. He came over, smoothing his
black hair and extending his hand.

"Miss Delaney. Just a friendly visit, I hope?"

Rome and I had an acquaintanceship that could be
called contentious. He thought me reckless, hot-
tempered, and pigheaded. I found him aggressive, hot-
tempered, and pigheaded. Plus, I had to admit, a solid
cop. He kept himself tanned, toned, and as polished
as a police motorcycle.

"Identity theft." I showed him the report.

He shook his head. "I tell you, it's a damn epidemic.
We're averaging a report a day like this."

"Great, a popular crime. I'm finally one of the cool
kids."

"They're like rats, these thieves. They paw through
your trash, they steal your mail—they're clever and
persistent and devious as hell."

He ran a finger alongside his nose, frowning on my
behalf. He knew too well what could happen when
your identity was stolen: credit and reputation ruined,
jobs lost, wages docked and paid to creditors for bad
debts that weren't yours, getting arrested for crimes
the thieves committed.

He perused the report. "You able to provide any
leads?"

My cheeks felt prickly. "The woman who washed
ashore at Jericho Point was carrying counterfeit ID in
my name."

He glanced up sharply. "A pro? She part of a ring?"

"I don't know."

"You talk to the sheriff's detectives?"

"Lilia Rodriguez."

"The judge's kid. Lily's thorough. Good investigator." He flicked his finger against the report. "Stay on top of this. And . . . keep your eyes open. This one may be at a different level than most."

He gave the report a few more seconds, and handed it back. "Jesse doing all right?"

"It's been tough."

"Even when you get 'em, it isn't painless, is it?"

Justice never is.

Late morning I went to Mass at the Old Mission. Afterward, while Brian and Marc went to play golf, I took Luke to meet Jesse at the movies. When I drove into the underground garage at Paseo Nuevo, I saw the Mustang parked and Jesse waiting for the elevator. I let Luke out and the two of them went up to get the tickets. I circled the garage and found a slot.

I was reaching into the backseat for my coat when there was a shredding sound at the window. A knife was gashing through the plastic sheeting. A hand ripped it wide-open and garbage came pouring in.

I shouted, recoiling from cigarette butts and KFC leftovers. Outside the car, a glazed skull shone under the lights. Murphy dumped the rest of the greasy garbage bag onto me.

"You give us trash, this is how you get repaid," he said.

Agh. I turned to climb over the gearshift, and outside the passenger window Merlin appeared. His gopher shoulders were hunched inside his aloha shirt. He pressed a small rectangle of paper against the window.

"Now you're bouncing checks. This came back marked Insufficient Funds."

I batted a wet ribbon of gauze off of my skirt. "It wasn't me. A girl named Brittany Gaines did this."

"It's signed K. E. Delaney."

Something viscous was dripping down my cheek. The smell of grease was overpowering. I couldn't tell if it was Murphy or the chicken leg lodged in the collar of my blouse.

"A thief stole my ID. She's the one who's been ripping people off."

Merlin held up the photocopy of the stolen Datura checks.

"This shows you put plenty of money in the account." He waved the bad check. "And this tells us you took it out and hid it someplace else."

"Listen to me," I said.

"You pay it back, this week, with twenty percent interest. That's fifteen, plus three for the juice."

Did he mean *thousands*? "You—"

Murphy reached in the window and palmed my head. His hands were hot. His leather wristbands smelled of musk and dirt.

"If you don't pay, the boss gets angry. And when he gets angry he takes it out on us. Which pisses us off, so we take it out on you."

And then he won the World Grossness Challenge. He leaned in the window, said, "Mmm, special sauce," and licked off whatever was dribbling down my cheek, with his flat, rough tongue.

He shoved me loose. "That's just a taster."

Merlin leaned close to the glass. "We'll be seeing you."

They hopped into a grubby red van and pulled away. Blue exhaust hung in the air behind them.

I jumped out of the car. Ignoring the chicken bone and the cigarette ash on my neck, I grabbed a piece of paper and wiped my cheek. Scrubbing, trying to eradicate the sensation of tongue. I wondered if I

should get a skin graft. After I burned the piece of
paper, in a biohazard containment facility. And *blech*,
I realized it had come from the garbage sack. I
dropped it and saw something worse. It was a printed
flyer. I'd been wiping my face with a photo of Merlin
and Murphy.

I nudged it with my boot and read the blurb: *Party
down with the Party Kings—Avalon! The best party
band in Santa Barbara. All occasions. Christmas par-
ties! Senior prom! Seventies nite!*

The road to hell was paved with disco balls. Burn,
baby, burn.

Jesse pinched the flyer between his thumb and fore-
finger, touching it as minimally as possible. "Avalon.
I dig the photo of the band, in their platform shoes.
And check out Murphy and Merlin's last name."

"Ming. They're the Party Dynasty." I squeezed the
steering wheel. "Except the band must be lousy, if
they're loan-sharking as a sideline."

The big rig ahead of me on the freeway cast spray
on the Explorer. We had dropped Luke off with the
Vincents, and were heading for P.J.'s apartment. I had
showered and was wearing fresh clothes. The ripped
plastic chattered on the window.

"It's not necessarily money lending. Could be drugs,
or stolen property," Jesse said.

"Yeah." What had they said to me on the beach?
Work the deal, or give the money back. That implied
a transaction, possibly fraudulent from the start.

"Twice now they've talked about their boss," I said.
"Take a look at the back of the flyer."

He flipped it over. " 'For booking, contact Tibbetts Price.' "

"Shall we?"

"Call him? No."

"He thinks I have his money. Perhaps I can dis-
suade him."

"Let me put that another way. No."

Fields and lemon orchards shone green in the setting sun, wet with rainwater. Spray freckled the windshield. He pulled his red Blazers cap low on his head.

"We're dealing with pond scum. For guys like these, fifteen grand is plenty of money to kill people over." He looked at me. "It may be why Brittany Gaines is dead. And now they're after you."

I didn't want to deal with that thought. Los Carneros Road came up. I pulled off the freeway and headed toward the beach. From the overpass we could see the university riding the promontory above the ocean. The sea was a blue smear between land and sky.

"So," I said. "You agree that P.J. couldn't have done it."

He sighed. "Cut it out."

"What out?"

He pulled himself up in the seat. "Stop protecting him."

I glanced over, taken aback. "That's not what I'm doing."

"Of course it is. You're feeling sorry for him, so you want to save him."

"You're exaggerating."

His laugh was sardonic. "Evan. It's in your bones. You're drawn to wounded things."

Oh, boy. Instant heat, from my belly to the center of my skull.

"Jesse, you—"

"Don't get me wrong. It's an unselfish impulse," he said. "It's not like you're watching for us to fall behind the herd so you can strike. You want to help."

Puddles shone yellow with the reflected sunset. "That's . . ." My palms tingled. "Christ, you—"

"But you can't stop P.J. from wrecking himself, any more than you could coach me to high jump."

"Damn, I . . . you can't . . ."

"That stutter's getting worse. Bang your head against the door frame, see if you can get rid of it."

I forced myself to slow down. We curved along the road through a landscaped business park.

"If—"

"There is no *if*. There's only the way it is."

I stopped at a red light. Ahead, Isla Vista's crammed apartment blocks formed a beige rampart. Cars lined the curbs. Students zigzagged along the street on clunker bicycles.

"You should come with a warning label," I said.

"Danger, in sight." He put his hand across the back of my neck. "I love you. But you need to get your head completely clear. You have too much at stake here to mess around trying to rescue my brother."

A horn honked. In the next lane a woman was waving at us. Correction—at Jesse. She smiled and blew a kiss. The light changed and she turned the corner.

I crossed the intersection. "Somebody you know?"

"No clue."

He peered after the car. I eyed him with mock suspicion.

"Seriously," he said.

I slowed, turned down P.J.'s street, and pulled up in front of the Don Quixote Arms. "Fine, Blackburn. No rescues. So what are we here for?"

"A reckoning." He unbuckled his seat belt. "Let's do it."

I hopped out, and his cell phone rang. I heard him say, "Right here." His tone of voice told me it was work.

"I know she did." A glance at me. "Lavonne, I asked her to. My brother was working over at the Jimsons' house."

I winced. She was irked that I'd gone over there. Jesse indicated for me to go ahead.

"Impolitic?" he said. "That wasn't my foremost concern."

The Don Quixote Arms was quiet. A soccer ball lay on a patch of grass in front of the building, but nobody was out. Word about Brittany Gaines had spread. P.J.'s roommate answered my knock, still wearing the *If I gave a shit* T-shirt and the zombified look. It was apparently his natural state.

He scratched his cheek. "He went to the library."

And I had hatched full-grown from the forehead of Zeus. "I'll wait."

I walked in before he could think about why P.J. wouldn't want me to do that. I strolled through the living room, checked the kitchen, and walked back toward the bedrooms. The apartment smelled like pepperoni and bong water. A draft was blowing from under a bedroom door.

I opened it. P.J. froze like a chipmunk in the high beams.

"Forget your library card?" I said.

"This isn't what it looks like."

"Get down."

He was standing on his bed with one leg out the window. His Suzuki was parked in the alley behind the building. When I walked in he gripped the windowsill.

"I'm going back to Mom and Dad's," he said.

"And a force field prevents you from using the door."

"Brittany's father is next door." He lowered his voice, glancing in the direction of her apartment. "I can't deal with him."

"You mean you're avoiding the sheriffs."

"He's a gorilla. And he's looking for somebody's head to rip off."

"Yours? She must have made you out to be a prince."

He hiked himself farther onto the windowsill.

"Hey." I knelt on the bed and grabbed his arm. "Okay, two-minute warning. You're coming close."

"To what?"

"Seeing me get mad."

His blue eyes were pleading. "You don't understand. She was hanging onto me, way overboard. Like, obsessing."

"Obsessing about what? Your credit card scam?"

"No, following me. Popping up everywhere. Like I'd open the door and she'd be right outside. Or at the Laundromat I turn around and, boo, she's behind me. Wanting to *talk*. It was freaking me out."

"Did you lift my wallet?" I said.

"You're trippin'."

"It had to be a few months ago, because that's when the unauthorized purchases began."

"But that's when your purse was stolen. That woman, Cherry whatsit?"

"Good answer." I let go of him. "Almost like you'd rehearsed it."

He hesitated, just long enough. "No."

I sighed and stood up off the bed. "So you figured what—I'd chalk it up to Cherry Lopez, and the card companies would eat the bills?"

"You have this totally wrong."

"Go ahead, explain it. I'm at ninety seconds to mad, and counting down."

His eyes skipped around. He brought his leg in.

"I made a mistake. I told her how your purse got stolen. Britt, she . . ." He looked pained. "She had a problem. She took things. Big-time. I don't know why; she had plenty of money. Her dad's rolling in bucks."

"How did she get hold of all my information?"

"It was at my gig, the one you came to with Jesse. The Battle of the Bands." He sat on the windowsill. "She got your wallet from your backpack. Took down your driver's license, Social Security number, and the rest, and put the wallet back without you knowing."

"And you set me up. You pointed me out to a kleptomaniac."

"I made a bad choice. I know that. I'm sorry."

He had the face of an angel. And he was full of crap.

"Only one problem with your story," I said. "Karen Jimson wants to pump my butt full of buckshot for stealing checks from Datura. How are you going to blame that on Brittany?"

His pained look sharpened. "I would never steal from the Jimsons."

"Who killed her, P.J.?"

"I don't know."

I held up the Avalon flyer. "Know these guys?"

He jumped like a startled monkey.

"I thought so. The one in the pimp hat turned my car into a Dumpster today."

Through the thin walls, we heard voices in the apartment next door. Before I could stop him he scrambled out the window. I climbed onto the bed and clambered out after him, but he was already loping down the alley, pushing his bike. By the time I dropped to the ground, he was jumping on. He started it up and gunned it out of sight.

I wasn't about to climb back in the window wearing a skirt and boots. I walked down the alley. Passing Brittany's apartment, I caught a look through the bedroom window. Her roommate was dabbing her eyes with a tissue, talking to a man in his fifties. He was a tree trunk, with grizzled hair and arms that hung like clubs from his shoulders. Brittany's father. Behind him another man paced the shadows. Taller, younger. I heard them say "coroner" and "autopsy."

I walked around to the front of the building. In the car, Jesse was still talking on the phone. Lavonne must have been giving him an earful.

The door to Brittany's apartment opened. Holding

the doorknob was the younger man I'd seen through the window. "Come here."

Sculpt a Greek god with a delinquent's slouch, and this would have been him. He was mid-twenties, wearing tangled hair and a Limp Bizkit T-shirt. His eyes were sea green, pale and wild, and his gaze felt familiar.

I slowed. "Can I help you?"

"Eavesdropping on private conversations isn't cool."

I stopped. "I meant no offense."

"What are you, press?"

"No." Not at the moment.

I was getting a weird vibe. He was a beefy slab of handsome, and those pale green eyes could have sold teen magazines by the truckload. But the slouch gave him a Napoleonic whiff. Chip on an arrogant shoulder.

"Have we met?" I said.

His mouth creased, seemingly with scorn. "*Rock House*. I'm Shaun Kutner."

Yes. *Rock House*—the reality show. Hopefuls singing to industry big shots for a chance at a recording contract. Every week the hapless and half-assed belted their guts out, and every week the judges told them precisely how hapless and half-assed they were. It was a cavalcade of schadenfreude. Jesse found it appalling. I loved it. Of course I knew Shaun Kutner. He was infamous.

He saw it on my face, and his expression soured. "The one and only."

Twenty-six million people had watched it, live. Bright lights, raucous audience, the camera swooping across the stage. Shaun attacking a rock classic with angry authority. He worked the song, and worked himself up, and finished wet with perspiration. Not damp—sopping. With rings darkening his armpits, his shirt clinging to him like a leech, and rivulets streaming down his face and neck.

The judges weren't shy. "Great vocal. But what's with the sweating?"

Curious now, I walked toward the door. He was the first tabloid headline I'd ever met: Sweaty Shaun Voted Off.

He raised his hands. "This isn't the time. I'm jet-lagged, and we're all grieving."

Jesus wept. He thought I wanted an autograph. The weird vibe returned, stronger.

"Britt was my best buddy in *Rock House* prelims. This is devastating."

"I didn't know she was a contestant," I said.

He jammed his hands into his pockets. "She got knocked out early, but she was my strongest backer. Before and after."

Inside the apartment voices approached, and a man said, "Who is it, Shaun?"

His jade gaze held mine. "It's Snoopy. From the alley."

The vibe twanged again, and I realized I'd seen him before, in person. But before I could say anything, a hand pulled the door wide. The tree trunk stood there. The muscles in his jaw were popping.

"You want to talk about my daughter? You speak to me. Ted Gaines."

He had seen her body, I could tell. Though he was stump-solid, he looked as though a daisy cutter had torn up his insides. How he was still standing, I couldn't imagine.

"I'm so sorry for your loss," I said.

"You a friend of Brittany's?"

Behind him, the roommate dabbed at her nose with the tissue. "She came by Friday night. Around midnight, looking for P.J."

Gaines and Shaun shifted, seeming to fill the doorway. Shaun took his hands out of his pockets. Gaines's eyes cooled.

"What do you want with him?" he said.

Shaun said, "I bet she's his lookout."

"Not at all," I said.

"Yeah, you're hanging around here so you can tell him when the coast is clear." His gaze lengthened, past me, to the street. "Oh, man. It's him."

Gaines stepped into the doorway. "Where?"

"The shithead. There." He pushed out the door past me.

I turned. If P.J. had come back, he was in for it. But I saw no sign of him—and with awful certainty I understood. Shaun was charging toward my car.

Jesse had the phone pressed to his ear, baseball cap pulled low on his head. With sunset reflecting off the window, it was easy to make the mistake.

I moved. Gaines wrapped a hand around my arm. "No, you don't."

"That's not P.J." I tried to pull free.

"He has to answer for this."

Shaun pounded down the walkway. I shouted Jesse's name. Shaun steamed up to the car, yanked open the door, and grabbed Jesse by the arm. He heaved him out of the Explorer.

I saw Jesse slam to the ground. Then things flared solar white, and I was shoving Ted Gaines into the wall and running for the car. Shaun was standing over Jesse, his face crimson, shouting. "Bastard. Cocksucker." He drew his leg back and kicked him in the ribs.

Blue light shot my vision. I felt Ted Gaines running behind me. Jesse was on his back on the dirt, and I saw that his leg was jammed between the door and the frame of the car. He couldn't go anywhere and couldn't get up. Shaun kept shouting. "Shit for brains. She's dead on account of you." He swung his foot again.

Jesse gritted his teeth. The kick connected. And he swept an arm out, locked his elbow behind Shaun's leg, and rolled against him.

"I'll break your knee," Jesse said.

Spittle flew from Shaun's mouth. "Fuckhead. She only went to that party because of you. And now she's dead."

"Five more pounds of pressure. You'll hear it crack."

Shaun wrenched back and forth, but Jesse had too much upper-body strength. Shaun was caught. He grabbed the car door. His eyes were glazed, his cheeks burning. I saw what he was going to do.

Jesse saw it too: slam the door and snap his leg. He popped Shaun's knee at about the same moment I bodychecked Shaun into the side of the Explorer. After that, Ted Gaines had me in a wrestling hold. Shaun was barking in pain, limping in a circle.

Gaines pushed me against the car. "You ain't gonna interfere."

I pointed through the window of the car at the wheelchair. "That's his. You understand?"

Gaines stared at it. "What?"

Shaun limped. "Dickhead. I'll kick your face in."

Jesse's face was pure fury. He struggled to sit up, flinching and putting a hand against his ribs where Shaun had kicked him. Gaines took in the fact that he hadn't tried to stand up. His hands fell away from me. He looked horrified.

Shaun broke for Jesse. Gaines blocked him.

"No. The guy's in a wheelchair. It's not Blackburn."

"The hell it's not."

Gaines held him back. Shaun glared at Jesse. Uncertainty spread across his face. He threw up his hands and backed off.

Gaines reached down. "God, son, I'm sorry. Let me give you a hand."

"No."

Jesse's leg was still jammed in the door. He pushed and pulled, trying to free it. I stepped toward him.

"I'm fine." He looked at Shaun. "The hell's wrong with you?"

Shaun rubbed his leg. "You broke my knee."

"If I had, you'd be on the ground, screaming." Jesse wrenched his leg loose and sat up. "She altered the angle with that body slam. You lucked out."

"It hurts. I oughta sue your ass."

"Bring it on. I love shooting fish in a barrel."

"You making fun of me?" He wiped his forehead with the back of his hand. "Know what? Screw this."

He limped away. I went after him.

"Hey. Come back here."

He headed for the apartment, daubing his forehead. "He was sitting right there in your car. What else was I supposed to think?"

"That's it? That's all you have to say?"

"My best friend's dead and now my knee's fucked. So yeah." His shirt was dampening under the arms. He wiped his upper lip, and stopped. "Get off your high horse. If P.J. didn't kill Britt, one of his hophead buddies did. Tell him he's on notice. I see him, I take him apart."

He walked away.

Next to the car, Jesse sat on the curb beside Ted Gaines. The back of his Blazers Swimming shirt was muddy.

"You okay?" I said.

He nodded.

Gaines rubbed his forehead. "You got no idea how sorry I am about that. But Shaun's taking it hard." He sagged. "We all are. God." His shoulders huffed. "God, my girl."

Covering his eyes, he lumbered to his feet and halted toward the apartment.

When he closed the door, the dimming light and the wet street and the empty evening spread out around us again. The wind blew cold over our backs.

"Fuck this whole day," Jesse said.

He slid along the curb and jacked himself up to sit in the door frame. His face looked strung with pain.

"Sure you're all right?" I said.

Grabbing the handhold above the door, he pulled up onto the seat. "Getting in this car's going to bust my shoulders someday. Big high SUV—it's like rock climbing."

Ping, right between the eyes. "Oh."

He slammed the door.

On the drive home he leaned back against his seat, staring out the window. He didn't want to talk. The black river had risen on him again. Outside my house he headed straight for his car, parked down the street.

"Shall I come over?" I said.

"Your family's here. Stay."

Ivy spilled over the fence, dark in the twilight. He stopped on the sidewalk by the Mustang. In the fading light he looked far older than twenty-eight. I brushed a lock of his hair back behind his ear.

"I know. I'm acting like an open sore," he said. "Sorry for getting snarky about the Explorer back there."

"No problem. Sorry I kept you from breaking the guy's knee."

"Yeah, it would have made a good headline. 'Sweaty Shaun Gets Bent.' "

"I didn't know you recognized him," I said.

"Not every day I get kicked by a reality-show reject." He arced around to face me. "You know Ricky Jimson was the judge who called him Sweaty Shaun, right?"

"I remember. And I know where I've seen him before. Yesterday, in the Jimsons' four-by-four outside Sanchez Marks. Banging the gong with Sinsa."

He thought about it. "I just got stomped by a jealous boyfriend. This keeps getting worse and worse."

I held out my hand. When he took it, I hitched up

my skirt and straddled his lap. He wrapped his arms around me. My feet dangled behind him.

"Wish I had a wand I could wave," I said.

"Nothing to be done. You play the hand you're dealt." He breathed. "Though sometimes I think an ordinary deal would have been good."

He never admitted that the hit-and-run had ravaged his life. He coped and kept going. He had survived. And if his legs didn't work right anymore, then he'd use the wheelchair, or crutches, and do the things he could. So the wreckage didn't always seem that bad. But at times like this tenacity didn't cut it. I could have cried.

But I didn't. I laughed. "Boy, you are a riot."

"I am?"

"Jesse Matthew Hotshot, Wiseass, National Champion, Cut 'Em Off at the Knees in Cross-examination Blackburn. As if you really wanted to be ordinary. Fat chance."

He tried to keep the long face, but I'd caught him out. He rolled his eyes.

"Once a year, that's all I ask," he said. "Ignore my moping for five minutes."

"Maybe on your birthday."

Headlights caught us. Marc Dupree's silver Ford truck pulled up, pinning us like teenagers caught breaking curfew. I hopped off Jesse's lap and smoothed my skirt down. Jesse shook his hair out of his eyes.

Marc parked and cut the lights. Brian got out and walked past us, poker-faced, whistling. Marc followed. His gaze was cool.

Jesse watched him. "Officer, I swear she looked eighteen."

Marc snickered and walked through the gate. Jesse got out his car keys. The moment was gone.

When I went inside, Brian was foraging through the fridge. He pulled out a hunk of cheese, sniffed it, and started cutting off the blue bits.

"Things okay?" he said.

"That's Roquefort. It's supposed to be that color."
I didn't want a go-round about the afternoon's events,
much less my love life.

"Jesse doesn't look so hot."

"Long day."

He continued cutting. "How much weight has he
lost?"

I leaned back against the counter, saying nothing.

"Ev. Is he all right?"

I couldn't hide it. He put down the knife. He pulled
me against his chest and hugged me.

"I'm scared," I said.

11

Monday morning broke gently. The storm had passed, and the sky spread satin blue above the mountains. When I stepped outside, the air tasted crisp. I drove out to Goleta, where Allied Pacific Bank sat at the corner of an undistinguished strip mall. I walked in and asked to speak to the manager.

Bianca Nestor had a brisk stride crimped short by her skirt. I handed her the SBPD crime report.

"I think the thief opened a checking account here, under my name," I said.

"Nasty business." She peered at the police report. "We'll check into it, and all pertinent information will be provided to you. It usually takes ten working days."

Karen Jimson wanted my blood this afternoon.

"Could you check right now? Please. I'm in hot water over this."

She drummed her fingers on the desk, turned to her keyboard, and typed, staring at her computer screen. After a minute her face pinched.

"I'm right," I said. "You have an account in the name of Evan Delaney."

"No." She read the computer screen. "It was closed this morning."

We stood up simultaneously. Going behind the counter, she questioned each teller. Finally a balding young man nodded to her. Nestor came back around, heels ticking.

"I just missed her, didn't I?" I said.

"Nope. Mr. Evan Delaney closed his checking account twenty-five minutes before you walked in."

A man. Blame my parents for sticking me with a boy's name. Defrauding me can be a gender free-for-all.

"What did he look like?" I said.

"Twenties, white. Scruffy hair, according to my teller."

P.J.

She glanced at me sharply. "Do you know who did this?"

How I could still feel disappointed in P.J., I didn't know. But I did. "Possibly."

Nestor walked me to the door. "We'll have him on surveillance tape. Leave things in my hands. I'll be in touch."

I headed out into the chill sunshine. Det. Lilia Rodriguez was leaning against my car.

"A word, if you don't mind?"

I'm a rotten liar. That's why I'm not an undercover agent, or writing *The Seven Secrets of Weight Loss*. The problem is, I get shamefaced, at least when fibbing to people I respect. Once I faked it during sex, and Jesse said, "You just blew up the polygraph machine."

But I didn't need to lie to Rodriguez. I needed to convince her that I was Little Miss Honest Citizen. Which was just as bad, because nobody can answer police questions without anxiety. *Are those your toes sticking out from the ends of your feet?* Gag. Stammer. *Mine? Yes. They're not toes smuggled in from South America. God, no.* Panic-stricken laughter.

I also needed to get across town so I could convince Lavonne Marks that I hadn't committed grand theft.

Rodriguez was dressed in a blue blazer and khaki skirt. Her hair was suffering a cowlick. Sticking up like that, it made her look like one of the Little Rascals.

"Bad checks?" she said.

"How'd you guess?"

"Lieutenant Rome sent me a copy of the crime report you filed."

I made a mental note to send Rome a bouquet of weeds.

She opened her notebook. "Friday night, at the party. The fire captain describes you as 'agitated' when they couldn't locate Miss Gaines's body. Were you expecting them to spot it?"

"I was hoping they'd find a live girl, not a corpse."

She ran her index finger down the torn plastic sheeting on my car window. "This doesn't look street legal."

"If you want to find out who's behind all this, check out some guys in a band called Avalon."

"And where would I find them?"

"Bar mitzvahs, the veterans' hall, maybe the policeman's ball." I gave her a rundown.

"Right. Disco." Her cowlick waved in the breeze. "Blame it on the boogie."

She closed the notebook. "Covering your tracks on the fly doesn't work. It leaves a messy trail." She nodded at the car. "Get that fixed."

Nuts. It was driving him nuts. The more he thought about it, the more he knew. This was the one, the big kahuna, the performance that should be getting top billing in his collection.

Hey, sweet stuff, come in here for a minute; I got something for you.

Dumb as a stump, the girl, she always had been. And upset like she was, she was easily distracted.

Yeah, it's awesome to see you, too. Ssh, close the door; it's too loud out there. Go on and lock it. No, leave the lights off. Little surprise here for you.

But she was crying, and over P.J., of all people.

Why do you let him get to you this way, girl? He's not worth it.

Chicks.

In trouble? Hon, a dickhead like him is always in trouble.

Okay, right there his line could have been better, but that was the tricky thing about live performance.

No, you're right, he's not a dickhead. I shouldn't have said that. I just get hot, seeing how you worry over him.

Taking her eyes off the prize. That had always been her problem, now that he thought of it. Getting distracted, falling in woo-hoo love. Which was why she was never going to make it. As anything.

Hush, girl, don't cry. Tell me what he did to make you so upset.

And she did. Just spewed it right on out. Telling him all the details, and what she planned to do about it, which would have blown everything sky-fucking-high. Idiot. Writing her own ending, right there.

Well, I have something to make you feel better. Turn around and close your eyes; it's a surprise.

Drumroll.

Okay, I'll give you a hint. It's a necklace.

Pause the memory. Shit, was that not the best line, or what? A necklace. He smiled, and turned to the mirror, and watched himself smile. A necklace. An E-string necklace, you fucking moron. Let's see how it fits.

Hot, hot. He was hot. Except . . .

He didn't get to see her reaction. And that was always the best part—audience appreciation. The silence at the end of this show left him feeling . . . dissatisfied. But what the hell. He had more good lines.

Jesse met me in the lobby at Sanchez Marks. "Got your body armor on?"

"Chain mail, crucifix, garlic. Let's go."

In her office, Lavonne pointed me to a chair.

"I've boxed three rounds with Jesse over this. He won't stand by and let you be accused of stealing from a client. And he can't represent you because it puts the firm in an impossible position." She crossed her arms. "So give me something that renders this argument moot."

I handed her a folder. She put on her glasses and sat down at her desk.

She read the crime report and my credit agency file. Jesse scrawled on a legal pad. The sunlight showed how pale he was. I told Lavonne about the fake checking account at the bank. She listened, like a stone.

"Is there anything else?" she said.

"Yeah." Jesse tossed the legal pad on the desk.

In black ink, he had written, *EVAN WOULD NEVER FUCKING DO THIS*. She stared at it. In spite of myself, I smiled.

"Pithy as always, Mr. Blackburn," she said.

"Karen Jimson's looking in the wrong direction," he said.

"I agree."

I felt an electric sense of relief. "You believe me."

"Yes. I'll talk to Karen." She closed the folder. Her face turned rueful. "And you know which direction she will have to look."

"My brother's going to have to deal with it," Jesse said.

"My regrets."

Her disorderly curls gleamed in the sunlight. She looked pensive.

"Something bothers me, deeply, about all of this," she said. "The stolen checks and the identity theft. I think it's possible that someone close to the Jimsons is involved in both. And I don't mean your brother, Jesse."

"Then who?" he said.

She leaned forward. "Watch out for Karen's daughter."

Outside, traffic rolled past. Cars honked. Lavonne looked exceedingly serious.

"I say this not as an attorney, but as a parent." She nodded at the photos of her daughters, Yael and Devorah. "The girls went to high school with Sin. And I go way back with Ricky."

"Way back?" he said.

"Before Karen, or Charlie."

She nodded at a photo of her husband, Charlie Goldman: glasses, bow tie, and a gently distracted smile. He was a professor of classics at the university. Jesse and I gawped at her.

"Pull your jaws off your laps. I didn't always look like a warmed-over burrito. I was a hot chick," she said. "My point is that Sin has been a handful since the day Ricky married Karen."

We continued gawping.

"She made parents nervous. The teasing, the sexually provocative poses. The bitter-teen persona. And she leveraged the hell out of her position as Ricky's stepdaughter."

I was still straining to imagine Lavonne as a hot chick. I brought myself back. "The rock heiress come to call?"

"You know the story, that Karen dragged Ricky up here to save him from his appetites. In truth they were desperate to get Sin away from Hollywood. The girl was out of control," she said. "Of course, she resented moving, as she puts it, to East Buttfuck. She's never forgiven them."

"For moving to a mansion in Montecito? Then why doesn't she get herself a job and move out?" I said.

"Gilded cage. She gains control of a trust fund when she turns twenty-five. She loses it if she steps out of line, and the leash is short. Trust me, she is a miserable young woman."

She tapped her fingers on her desk. "She's an instigator. Expert at manipulating . . . softer people to do her bidding."

I thought of P.J., her windup toy. I scooted forward on my seat.

"You think Sinsa stole the checks."

The phone rang. She grabbed the receiver, said, "Not now," and hung up.

"I don't know a thing about Brittany Gaines. But I know that this sort of thing is right up Sinsa's alley," she said.

Jesse gave me a glance. "If she stole the checks, she's behind the bad debt to the Mings."

"How do we find out?" I said.

Lavonne shook her head. "You don't. The police do. You stay away from her."

Her face was hot. I had never seen her this way.

"Lavonne, did she do something to your family?" I said.

"There were incidents. Felonious. Devorah was lucky not to have been injured or arrested. Let's leave it at that."

Her daughter was now, as far as I knew, a straight-A student at City College. I left it.

"Perhaps it comes down to this: Her eyes don't reflect the light. It's spooky. She seems to draw in other people's energy and crush it."

We sat for a minute, listening to traffic. Jesse said, "Maybe her parents shouldn't have named her after a strain of cannabis."

"Her parents named her Cynthia. Calling herself Sinsemilla was her own idea."

With a knock on the door, the receptionist stuck her head in.

"Sorry. Jesse, you really need to come out here. Your brother dropped something off for you."

In the lobby, a cardboard box sat on the receptionist's desk. A mewling sound was coming from inside it.

"Oh, God," Jesse said. "Tell me that's not a baby."

The receptionist reached into the box. "I'd say about nine and a half pounds."

She lifted out a puppy.

At sunset that evening, scarlet embers of light ticked across the ocean. Off of Isla Vista Beach, a surfer lay on his board, waiting for one last wave. When it came, he paddled like hell and stood up to ride it toward the cliffs. In the angled light, he caught sight of an object lodged in the sand. For an eerie second it looked like an arm reaching up out of the water, and he cut a turn away from it. But when he went closer, he saw that it wasn't an arm. It was the neck of an electric guitar, sticking out of the sand.

12

In Jesse's kitchen that evening, I stared at the puppy. "Cute."

"Yeah, he should be on a calendar."

Sunset reddened the house, throwing long shadows across the big space that comprised the living room, dining room, and kitchen. Wood and glass shone pale below the high ceiling. Beyond the wall of windows, surf churned the beach. The dog lay curled on a blanket inside the cardboard box with its tail tucked between its legs. It was skinny, all scruff and brown fur, with a white patch around one eye.

Jesse was mopping up its latest mess. A whiff reached me.

"Gah." I opened a window. Salty air rushed in, dispersing the odor.

I am not a pet person. To my mind they're all blood-letters, including hamsters and goldfish. The puppy gazed at me with the eyes of a Dickens waif. *Not buying it, buster.* I stayed by the window.

"So here's the story." Jesse slapped the mop onto the floor. "P.J. rescued him from the animal shelter."

"Why'd he give him to you?"

"He's an apology."

"Most people send flowers."

The puppy wobbled to its feet, wagging its tail. But that's how they break down your defenses—they feign adorableness, right before they chew through your tibia. It whimpered at me.

Dammit, this was too much. I crouched down next to the box. Tentatively I stroked him. The tiny thing was soft and trembling.

"Poor little guy," I said.

"Know anybody who wants him?"

"You don't?" I sounded palpably relieved.

"I work. I'm not home." He jammed the mop into the bucket and stopped. "There's no way I can take care of him."

I felt like a match had been lit against my head. How could P.J. be any more clueless, doing something that actually made Jesse feel worse than before?

"Call your idiot brother," I said.

"He won't take him."

"Then he can return him to the shelter."

"They'll put him down. He'd never let that happen." The puppy whined.

"Then I'll take him," I said.

He gave me a disbelieving look. "Right."

"I'm serious. I'll find him a new home."

"Delaney, you wouldn't have a dog in your house if it wore a French maid's outfit and served you caviar in bed."

"Just for a day or two. Until somebody adopts him."

I picked the puppy up. He didn't rip out my carotid artery. He was warm in my arms.

"Forty-eight hours, max. Piece of cake."

The puppy licked my hand. And peed on my blouse.

I rinsed the blouse in the bathroom sink. I wrung it out, held it up, and spotted, on the shelf beside the towel rack, the manuscript for my new novel.

The first chapter, anyway. Back in the kitchen, I found Jesse putting away the bucket and mop. He looked tired. I had to do something about this situation.

"What do you think of my new story?" I said.

If he'd been a gecko, he would have scurried up the wall and through a crack. "It's awesome."

Turning on my heel, I strolled to his bedroom. Books were stacked on the nightstand.

"Let's see what we have. *Band of Brothers*. The *California Bar Journal*. The new FDR biography."

He came in behind me. "I'm reading your manuscript."

"*Warrior Politics: Why Leadership Demands a Pagan Ethos*. Oh, and a DVD. *Beavis and Butt-Head Do America*." I put a hand on my hip. "You haven't read past page nineteen."

"Sure I have."

"That's what's in the bathroom."

"No, really. That part with the soldiers dying."

I walked toward him. He backed up.

"Rowan's men. Her lovers. They all get killed; it's terrible," he said.

I kept walking. "How?"

"How what?"

He had that *Honey-does-this-dress-make-me-look-fat?* expression on his face: *Just hand me the seppuku knife, now.* He kept backing up.

"How do they die?" I said. "Come on, the medicos explain it."

"Um." He backed into a corner and had to stop. "Too much woman?"

I gave him the black stare. He held his breath.

I erupted in laughter.

He relaxed, almost smiling, and I walked back to the kitchen and got the cardboard box. "Come on, dog. We'll go to my place, where people appreciate fine literature."

On my kitchen floor the puppy quivered in the box, looking small. Luke knelt, stroking him. His face was bright.

"What's his name?" he said.

Give them a name, next thing you're putting their photo on your Christmas cards wearing an elf's hat.

"What do you think we should call him?" I said.

He tilted his head, thinking. "Ollie."

As in the skateboard move. Or as in Ollie, short for apology.

I nodded. "That's it, then."

Luke lifted the puppy's ears. I smiled at Brian, ever so hopefully.

"No way, no how. I need a dog like I need a root canal," he said.

I dropped the gooey smile. "Fine. Then do something else for me."

"What?"

"We need to threaten P.J. Metaphorically speaking."

"Metaphorical Threat, that's my middle name."

"I thought Death from Above was your middle name."

"No, that's my rap handle."

"Excellent. Because I want P.J. to be Scared into Talking."

When Patsy Blackburn opened the door, I heard laughter inside, overlaid with boisterous voices. Patsy wore a skintight turtleneck with six strands of gold chain around her neck. Her eyes had a fluid glow.

"Come join the party. It's the family of the groom," she said.

Right—her nephew's wedding, coming up that weekend. Though I was in the wedding party, I hadn't met the blushing couple. The remains of a lasagna dinner cluttered the dining room table. The too-bright talk faded when we walked in. Keith Blackburn stood up, extending his hand to Brian.

"Commander Delaney, I thought you were still at the Pentagon."

Keith had given his sons their strong looks and their

height, though he seemed to be eroding with time. He
was a neat and courteous man who worked on his feet
all day at Office Depot, selling staplers and printer
paper.

He introduced us. The parents of the groom, Patsy's
sister, Deedee, and her husband, Chuck Dornan, had
an air of insouciant Manhattan sophistication. Santa
Barbara was where they kept their winter home. Their
son, David, gave us a killer smile that struck me as
pure frat-boy bravado. And Caroline Peel, the bride,
vibrated like a pink cashmere espresso bean. She
hadn't eaten a bite of her lasagna. Only when Keith
introduced me as Jesse's girlfriend did she stop gripping David's arm like a claw hammer.

"You're my sub," she said. "Terrific."

"Emergency replacement bridesmaid, reporting for
duty," I said.

She eyed me up and down. "Have you tried on the
dress yet?"

Caroline had asked me to join the lineup for one
simple reason: I fit the uniform. Her first-string bridesmaid was laid up, having been thrown by her polo
pony the week before.

"My fitting's Friday," I said.

David leaned his chair back on two legs. "You a
Pi Phi?"

I smiled. "I'm more sci-fi."

Two blank stares.

Brian said, "My sis wasn't sorority material."

Patsy laughed, loudly. "Evan writes *books*. Science
fiction. I hear they're kind of like *The Jetsons* but with
guns and group sex."

Seven blank stares, including mine. Patsy's cocktail
tumbler was empty. She'd hit round three: past sentimental and surly, onto spill-the-beans.

In the family room, I heard P.J.'s guitar. Through
the door I saw him sitting on the floor. He was picking
out a blues line, and had a melancholy look on his

face. His guitar strings were wound with blue thread at the ends.

"Excuse us."

I left as if being chased by bees, heading into the family room with Brian following. P.J. looked up, and his eyes went wary. The guitar fell silent.

"Sweaty Shaun Kutner," I said.

"Aw, do we have to do this?"

"You sent Jesse a puppy-gram to make up for Shaun. Yes, we do."

"Doesn't Jesse like the puppy?"

"Shaun seems to hate you, supposedly because of Brittany. But he's also Sinsa's boyfriend, so I think he wants to whomp your butt to keep you away from her."

"He just got in from the Caribbean; he only sees her because she's going to produce an album for him."

Stop. Reset. "Sinsa is a record producer?"

"Shaun's her first big artist. She sort of took pity on him after the *Rock House* thing. Ricky felt bad about mentioning the sweating, but what can you do? It came out of his mouth and he couldn't put it back."

"So this recording project is her way of making it up to him?" I said.

"No, but it'll create a buzz. An irony kind of thing. And Sin needs a buzz, something to put her own stamp on things. It's tough for her."

Brian faked ignorance. "Because she's so young?"

"Mainly 'cause of her folks. The Hollywood dudes hear 'Jimson' and think showbiz brat, riding her dad's coattails."

Brian nodded. "Like Frank Sinatra Junior. Or Ringo's kid."

"Right. Coming along behind a star, you have to climb out from under their footprint."

"How many artists has she produced?" I said.

He shrugged. "Five or ten. Demos, not whole albums. I mean, she doesn't run a record company. She takes the demos to the A and R people to get her artists signed."

"And is she getting her artists signed to record deals?"

"It takes time. You have to know who to know."

I nodded. "Who's putting up the money for Shaun's record project?"

He shrugged.

"Me?"

He pulled the guitar against him, as though trying to hide behind it.

"Excuse me, I mean is *Evan Delaney* putting up the money? You know, the man who opened a fraudulent checking account at Allied Pacific Bank?"

He shook his head.

"The person who ripped off some lowlifes from a group called Avalon, and told them I had the money ready to pay back?"

"I don't know what you're—"

"Don't tell me you went to such trouble on Shaun's behalf."

He didn't say anything.

"Did Sinsa ask you nicely? Explain it all, how she needed extra money, some safe way of getting cash?" I walked toward him. "The thing is, I think that all of this ties in somehow to Brittany's death."

He pressed his lips together, shaking his head.

"A police lieutenant downtown thought Brittany might be part of a ring of thieves. Looks like that involves you and Miss Jimson."

He kept shaking his head.

I stopped. "Hold it. Sinsa's not producing an album for the Mings, is she?"

Patsy walked in, a Marlboro in her hand. "Patrick? I heard you talking about that poor girl." She looked at Brian. "Patrick's been so upset."

P.J. stood up. "Evan, let's go outside."

"Don't you want dessert?" Patsy said.

P.J. headed for the front door. As we went along behind him, Brian nodded at all the family photos and leaned close to my ear. "No question who's the favored son, is there?"

I shushed him.

"It's like Jesse barely exists. Are they ashamed of him?"

Outside, P.J. tucked his hands into his armpits and paced in a circle on the driveway.

"Jesse put you up to this, didn't he?" he said.

"Do you have cotton stuffed in your skull? This is not about Jesse."

"I'm sorry Shaun got into it with him, but don't let that color what you think. You have this thing all wrong."

"Then tell me how to get it right."

"Sin's working seriously hard on this. Songwriter-producer, it's a big thing to tackle. Hiring musicians, writing songs, booking studio time, that stuff."

Like a drip from a faucet, repetitive and insistent, an idea was forming about Sinsa's new production company. It was producing nothing but promises, and it was exacting them at a high price. And instead of working on record deals, she was spending the money on herself, and on Sweaty Shaun.

Wait. Musicians. "Is she hiring musicians to play on Shaun's album?"

He nodded, looking walleyed with love. "Putting it together. Don't say anything, but looks like I'll be playing lead guitar."

I somehow kept my face from spasming. "Wow."

"It's going to be great. Her stuff's amazing."

He was still nodding, with all the oblivious eagerness of the puppy, when the unmarked sheriff's car pulled up and detectives Zelinski and Rodriguez stepped out.

Rodriguez strode up the driveway. "Patrick John Blackburn?"

P.J. didn't answer. He didn't move. He had the frozen-chipmunk look again. Rodriguez walked toward him.

"We'd like to ask you some questions," she said.

He bolted.

He ran for the porch, aiming to get in the house, and he was fast. But the detectives were faster. They caught him in the entryway, and ten seconds later they had him handcuffed and were leading him to their car. The noise brought the dinner party to the door.

Patsy put a hand to her chest. "Oh, my God."

Rodriguez was giving him the Miranda warning, telling him he could have an attorney present during questioning. "Do you understand?"

"Yeah." He walked to their car, head down, hair hanging over his eyes. "Evan's my attorney. Can she come to the jail with me?"

My face went numb. "P.J., I can't be your lawyer."

Patsy was wringing her hands. Behind her in the doorway Deedee and Chuck and David and Caroline jostled for staring space.

Keith pushed through the crowd. "What's this all about?"

P.J. tossed his hair out of his eyes. "Evan, you said. Please—I want you present during questioning." He looked at the detectives. "Let her come with me."

Dammit. "No, P.J."

Zelinski let go of P.J.'s arm and came toward me. "But I insist."

"Excuse me?"

"You're coming to the station with us for questioning."

If there's any worse impulse than running from the cops, it's challenging them. But that's what Brian did, straight in Zelinski's face.

"You can't take my sister in."

"Bri, don't," I said.

His fuse was lit. "On what charge, Deputy Dawg?"

I jumped between him and Zelinski. But outrage and momentum did the rest. Brian knocked into me. My elbow ended up in Zelinski's ribs. And *boom*, I found my hands on the hood of my car, my feet spread, and Zelinski patting me down.

He brought out the cuffs. "You're under arrest for assaulting an officer."

Brian spread his arms. "You can't do this. Get your hands off of her."

"Bri, stop." I looked at him. "Call Jesse."

Zelinski snapped on the cuffs and led me toward the car. Brian raked his hands through his hair, spun, and kicked the wheel well of my car. Keith Blackburn stood impotently on the driveway. Patsy clutched her sweater.

"You heard her," she said. "Call Jesse. He'll know what to do. Call Jesse."

13

At the county jail, Zelinski unlocked the handcuffs
and gave them my name. "She's an attorney." The
shine on his face said, *Bagged one.* "Her client's coming in with Lily."

"He's not my client," I said.

The booking officer was happy to show me in. "This
way, Counselor."

He took my mug shot, and my fingerprints, and my
shoelaces, and stuck me in a holding cell. With the
proud winner of a knife fight. She weighed in at two-
twenty and had *Marie* and *Nolinda* tattooed on her
biceps, which could have been either her name or a
list of defeated opponents. Her wrists were as thick
as Murphy Ming's; the two of them would have made
good dance partners. I kept my back against the wall
for an hour, until a jailer unlocked the door and led
me out for questioning.

The county sheriff's office was next door to the jail.
The detectives were waiting in an interview room. Zelinski uncuffed my hands. Rodriguez gestured me to
a plastic chair.

"You and your brother always get so hot?" she said.

"No. May I apologize on his behalf?" Assaulting an
officer. It was ludicrous and they knew it. "I didn't
intend to knock into Detective Zelinski."

Zelinski leaned against the wall in the corner, snick-
ering. I figured I had one more sentence, max, before

my eyes glowed red and my lizard tongue shot across the table and gored them both. I saved my words.

"What went wrong?" Rodriguez said. "Did Brittany get greedy?"

"I don't know what you mean."

She opened a file folder. "Don't know if you've checked, but your credit report's been updated. More bills have come in. Somebody went on a spree a couple of weeks back." She ran her fingers down the page. "On Rodeo Drive, no less. Prada, Hugo Boss, Manolo Blahnik . . . Day Spa at someplace called the Retreat. Goodness, Gary, did you know you can blow a grand on aromatherapeutic massage and a honey-cucumber body scrub?"

"Go on, tell me what the total bill was," I said.

"Just under twelve thousand."

A headache started behind my right eye.

"Did Brittany have a habit of spending too much?" she said.

"I didn't know Brittany Gaines. I never met her. I never spoke to her. The only time I ever saw her was at the morgue."

Zelinski walked to the table. "That's funny. Her roommate says you came by their apartment twice in the space of a day."

"I did. The first time, I was—"

"And the second time you became violent with a visitor."

"Shaun Kutner? Sweaty Shaun? That's baloney."

"She describes an altercation between you, Mr. Kutner, and Jesse Blackburn. Brittany's father had to break it up. Is that correct?"

"That is incorrect."

Zelinski ran his fingers alongside his nose. "Ted Gaines didn't have to wade in and stop your brawl?"

"I wasn't brawling. Shaun attacked Jesse without provocation. He had him on the ground."

He hesitated, assessing that. "Jesse may have been

helpless, but you certainly weren't. Mr. Kutner has a torn cruciate ligament in his knee."

Don't cheer. Applause, victory yells, spiking an imaginary football would not be taken well. I laid my hands flat on the table.

"Did you kill Brittany Gaines?" Rodriguez said.

The headache leaped on me. The lights felt sharp and had a buzz.

"No."

"Did you set it up with P. J. Blackburn?"

"No."

Zelinski sat down. "Here's how it lays out. You set yourself up as the victim of an identity theft. Created your own mirror image."

"No."

"You had good cover because your wallet was stolen last summer, but things got out of hand. P.J. gave extra credit cards to his girlfriend, or she had a shopping addiction that slipped the leash. Brittany was spending too much, and maybe threatening to turn you and P.J. in if you reined her back. You two killed her and threw her body off the balcony into the water."

"No."

Zelinski leaned his elbows on the table. "You tried to cover it by calling nine-one-one and reporting an accident. You knew nobody would find the body in the storm. It made you look like the good guy."

"No."

Rodriguez smoothed her cowlick down. "How much do you know about guitars?"

My mouth was still open.

"Did you know each string is a different weight? The bottom E string, I found out today, is the heaviest."

She turned to a new page in the folder. I saw a photo of Brittany's body. Close-up on the wire that had sawed through her throat. I turned my head away.

"We found P. J. Blackburn's guitar on the beach

below the Del Playa house. A Fender Stratocaster. The neck was broken and the strings sprung. The bottom E string was missing."

She tossed the morgue photo across the table.

"That's it. Willie Johnson brand, custom gauge, nickel-wound guitar string. It's what garroted her."

I tried to get away from the photo by shoving my seat back, but the chair was bolted to the floor. My head was splitting.

"Remember what I mentioned," Rodriguez said. "Covering your tracks on the fly leaves a messy trail."

"You have it wrong," I said.

Zelinski leaned toward me. "You're going away."

There was a rap on the door. A deputy stuck his head in.

"Her attorney's here."

All I wanted was to grab Jesse's hand and let him take the pilot's seat. But it was Lavonne Marks who walked into the room.

"Has Ms. Delaney been charged?" she said.

"Assaulting an officer," Zelinski said.

"Don't play games, Detective." She looked at Rodriguez. "Anything else?"

"That's under advisement."

"In other words, no."

"As of the present, she isn't being charged. But she's a material witness, and a suspect in the death of Brittany Gaines."

"This is rank speculation. You don't have probable cause. It's time to cut her loose."

And that, when it came down to brass tacks, was that.

Lavonne gestured to me. "Come on, Evan."

Zelinski stood up. "She'll have to make bail on the assault charge."

"You're really going to do this? Fine." She put a hand on my back. "It won't be long."

I said, "I'd like to speak privately to Ms. Marks."

Rodriguez gathered her things. "As long as you'd like." She and Zelinski left.

"Thank you." I leaned on the table, massaging my eye. "Where's Jesse?"

"Arranging your bond. We suspected Zelinski might play hardball over the assault charge. He has that whiff of authoritarian glee about him."

"They want to charge me with murder," I said.

"They're fishing."

"Yeah, with a harpoon gun."

She put her hand on my arm. "Hang tight. It will be a few hours before you make bail. Is there anything I can do for you?"

I thought about returning to the holding cell, and almost asked her to call Vegas and put a hundred bucks on my cellmate in her next knife fight. But no.

"Want a puppy?" I said.

The cell door slid open at eleven p.m. Big Knifey was snoring in the corner. In the lobby I was surprised to see Marc Dupree waiting with Jesse. I managed a weak smile, feeling enervated and grateful. Marc patted me on the shoulder. I crossed the lobby to Jesse.

"You're my hero." I took his face in my hands and kissed him.

He brushed a lock of hair off my forehead. "Brian's groveling. Insists he'll pay me back for the bondsman's premium in the morning."

"He ought to."

"This isn't on Brian, or on you, Ev. It was Zelinski's call. He owns this."

"I'll accept that." I bent and kissed him again. "Thank you."

The door opened with a gust of wind, and in walked Jesse's parents. Strutting beside them was a man who had the flash of a cheap sports car, and a blond haircut that screamed *suave*. They angled toward the front desk.

Patsy said, "Well, isn't this a picture?"

Jesse's shoulders sagged. I felt the headache spiking into me.

The blond lifted his chin in greeting. Under the fluorescent lights, his fake tan was the color of pumpkin pie.

"Skip," Jesse said.

He mock-saluted. "Jester. Don't worry, amigo, I've got this covered."

Jesse watched him walk past. "Go on home, Ev. I've got work to do here."

I hesitated for a second, and squeezed his hand. Marc held the door for me. As it swung shut I heard Jesse saying, "Mom, you hired Skip Hinkel to represent P.J.?"

"You didn't give us much choice, did you?" Patsy said.

I turned to go back in. Skip Hinkel was the kind of lawyer who gives lawyers a bad name. Devious, bullying, and effective. Seeing him here was like having a pint of motor oil poured down my throat. But Marc set his hand against the middle of my back and nudged me toward his truck.

"Know when to retreat. You can't win this dogfight," he said.

"Afraid I'm one of the bones of contention."

"You've been chewed up enough for one night. Jesse's going to have to hold his own."

14

The next morning, the only thing that made me happy was seeing that my name was not in the paper. Yet. I poured myself a cup of coffee and phoned Jesse.

"P.J.'s out," he said.

"They didn't charge him?"

"For Brittany, no. For possession of marijuana and eight hundred bucks in unpaid traffic tickets, yes."

"No wonder he bolted." I stirred my coffee. "What's the situation with P.J.'s legal representation?"

"You mean Skip the Wonder Lawyer? They're thinking of adopting him."

Despite my mood, I had a full day of work to do. I walked Ollie around the yard, fed him and fluffed his blanket, and went over to the law library down at the courthouse. I came home at lunch and took the puppy out again, and went back downtown. Piece of cake, did I say? When will I learn not to boast?

When I finished at the courthouse in the late afternoon, I hiked down the spiral staircase and out into the sunken garden. The air felt crisp. The walls of the courthouse towered white against the blue sky. My cell phone rang as soon as I switched it on. It was Ted Gaines.

"I got something to show you."

I agreed to meet him at a café across from the courthouse. When he came in I was at a table, drinking a cup of coffee. He looked like a husk. Gray stubble bristled on his cheeks. His tailored shirt was rank with BO.

"I want you to see what he destroyed," he said.

He opened a briefcase on the table. It was packed with mementos of Brittany. I felt as if a giant fist were squeezing me. He handed me a photo album.

"This was her dream," he said. "What she could have been."

The album was full of pictures of Brittany performing—singing in community theater productions, in college choirs, in garage bands. She looked shy, almost anxious, as though people might tease her about projecting a rock-'n'-roll persona. Gaines watched me, waiting for me to understand.

"I don't come from a flashy background," he said. "I made my money in auto parts. But Brittany, she had this passion for singing. And when your kid has that passion, you back her two hundred percent."

I turned the page and found photos taken backstage at the taping of *Rock House*—Brittany with the host, with other contestants, and crossing her fingers before going onstage. There were a few with Shaun Kutner. In all of them Brittany was under his arm, looking up at him, seeming at the periphery of the photo.

"You smeared her," he said. "You told the cops she was a thief."

"I didn't need to tell the cops anything. Sir, I'm sorry, but she—"

"The credit cards. Yeah. Fuck 'em, pardon my French. Somebody planted those on her."

This was pointless. "Mr. Gaines—"

"My girl wasn't no thief. Understand?"

He took a CD from the briefcase. "This was my girl."

He pressed it on me. "Listen to it. You'll see. What a heart she had."

I looked at the CD. "A demo?"

"And now it's all there's gonna be. No point in sending it to the record company after all." His eyes were red. "Listen to it. You'll see. This was my baby."

Driving home, I put the CD into the car stereo. When the slender voice reached me through the speakers, I had to pull over.

This was Brittany Gaines. Breathy, tentative, hopeful. The songs were dark but her voice sounded sunny. I felt that she was a breathing presence slipping around me in the car. I looked at the CD cover. The photo was professionally done. Expensive lighting, plus hair, makeup, and clothes. She'd paid to look good, and was going to be like a million other hopefuls: nowhere. I felt ineffably saddened.

I read the song titles. "Accelerant." "Bone in the Box." "Hobbled."

Why was I not surprised to see that they were all written and produced by Sinsemilla Jimson?

How much had Brittany paid Sinsa to come up with this? Or rather, how much had Ted Gaines paid, and I? I drew a little diagram in my head. Sinsa—Shaun—Brittany—P.J. The fab four. Taking my name, and other people's money, to finance dreams of glory.

At home, I got the mail from the mailbox and sorted through it on the way along the walk. Bills, magazines, and—uh-oh, something from Card Services, with FINAL NOTICE in red letters. I ripped it open.

Well, goody. Evan Delaney had been on a fabulous getaway to San Francisco. Staying at the Fairmont Hotel, racking up purchases at Prada and Tiffany. This was fantasy tourism at its most grotesque: no trip, just the bill. And I knew this was only the start. I went inside, throwing my backpack on my desk. My sympathy for Brittany faded away. She might have been a vocal lightweight, a rock star wannabe, and Ted Gaines's precious, passionate girl. But she'd also had hot credit cards, and he had given me not one iota of evidence that they had been planted on her.

I got my blood pressure back down with a box of Junior Mints. Followed by a hot dog. I opened the rest of my mail.

Knock me out with a hammer. I had a hand-delivered letter from Skip Hinkel, attorney-at-law. It notified me to cease and desist my legal representation of one Patrick John Blackburn, and demanded that I transfer all files and correspondence to Hinkel's office immediately. A substitution-of-attorney form was included, directing me to consent.

I couldn't consent, because I hadn't been P.J.'s attorney to begin with. And if I sent anything to Skip, it would be hair I pulled out of the shower drain. And maybe the puppy, along with all the wet newspapers he left on my floor. No, I couldn't do that to the dog.

But that wasn't the real problem. The letter also stated that all communication between me and P.J. regarding Brittany Gaines fell under attorney–client privilege. It ordered me to refrain from revealing any information I had received from P.J. It mentioned obtaining a restraining order. Skip was trying to gag me. And if he succeeded, if I couldn't use the things P.J. had told me to exculpate myself, I could end up in jail.

Needless to say, P.J. had gone to ground. Not at his apartment, his parents' house, the animal shelter, or the Jimsons'." My stomach was aching. The hot dog and Junior Mints were laughing at me. I changed and went for a run.

Coming back, I found a tow truck cruising the street. The potatohead behind the wheel had a clipboard, and was looking at the license plates of cars parked at the curb. He stopped in front of the Vincents' house and put down his window.

"Hey. Looking for . . ." Eyes on the clipboard. "K. E. Delaney."

"Did he call you about a breakdown?" I said.

"Not exactly."

He was looking to repossess a car. Well, he wasn't getting mine.

"Sorry, can't help you. What's he driving?"

"Alfa Romeo." The clipboard again. "Red."

Like I was seeing. And if I found P.J. driving it, red would be the color of his butt after I whipped it raw.

15

At ten Thursday night, I walked into Chaco's to hear Ricky Jimson play. It was an impromptu gig: no publicity, just Ricky and his guitar player working the kinks out of new material. Brian and Marc were with me. Jesse was already there, sitting at a table against the wall. P.J., we bet, would be there with Ricky, and we were going to have it out with him. It was an ambush.

Chaco's on a weeknight felt like a coffee bar. The lights were low. Onstage a trio was swinging through Latin funk. Jesse had one empty Carlsberg in front of him and a second in his hand, half gone. His crutches were leaning against the brick wall behind him.

"No sign of Ricky yet," he said.

I took drink requests. A few minutes later I was standing at the bar when I felt a tap on my shoulder.

"I take it back."

Karen Jimson was chewing her gum. Her fawn eyes looked contrite. "I shouldn't have dissed you."

Dis seemed a gentle euphemism for claiming I'd stolen five grand. "Thanks. From me, and from my butt."

In the mirror behind the bar I saw Ricky walk past, chatting to his guitar player. "Gotta grow it down your back, dude. Otherwise you're just wasting money renting the wind machine."

The economics of hair rock. The guitar player wore

his like a Cherokee brave, and Ricky had done some back-combing tonight, adding a couple of inches to his height. Karen winked at me and strolled off with him, just as P.J. came in.

That confirmed my suspicion: Karen didn't think P.J. had stolen her money either, or she would have fired him. Which suggested to me that Sinsa had to be the one, and her mother probably knew it.

P.J. was riding Ricky's backwash, proud to be the entire entourage tonight, but when he saw me his strut slowed.

"I know you're bent out of shape. I know it's my fault," he said.

"How's the Alfa Romeo?"

He went on by, turning and walking backward away from me. "What about the Alfa?"

My anger flared gold. "We need to talk about Sinsa and her record production company."

A jagged light skipped across his gaze.

I paced him. "She's been talking rich wannabes into paying her big bucks to produce their stuff, hasn't she? Promising them the moon and delivering nothing. It's a scam."

He looked Ricky's way, anxious. "You can't do this here. Her folks."

"Bud, you're out of choices."

"Peej." At the far end of the bar, Ricky beckoned.

P.J. turned and sped up, saying, "Gotta work," but I followed him. Ricky was leaning back on a bar stool, and smiled when I approached. "Hey, thanks for coming."

"I brought a cheering section. Mind if P.J. joins us? He hasn't seen his brother in way too long."

P.J. gazed at Jesse, deflating. "No, that's okay. I don't want to slack off."

"Nah, go on, Peej. Your brother's a kick." Ricky craned his neck to see our table. "I ever phone Sanchez Marks, we talk about karma."

"Karma. Jesse," I said.

"You know, with him landing on wheels, does it mean he's going up to a higher plane next time around."

"Karma. Jesse. What does he tell you?"

"Maybe not. In his last life he was Jimi Hendrix, and now he can't play guitar for shit." He laughed. "He's cool. Just wait till I start the set, okay?"

P.J. looked bereft.

I got our drinks and carried them to the table. Marc stood and pulled out a chair for me. Jesse was talking to Brian.

"Cave kayaking—I have to say Luke's too young. You can boogie board, but this time of year you need to watch the current."

Marc said, "You know the coast pretty well?"

"Grew up here."

Brian said, "Jesse was a lifeguard. He knows it like the back of his hand."

"Yeah?" Marc said.

"In college," Jesse said. "All winter, the riptides run right off the beach. Even strong swimmers can get in trouble."

Marc smiled. "*Baywatch*, huh?"

Jesse gave him a detached look. "Yeah, thong swimsuit, silicone implants, all of it."

Brian shook his head. "To be certified in open-water rescue you have to know CPR, first aid, have the swimming background, scuba training. It's no picnic."

I gawked at Brian. What was he doing?

"Did you perform a lot of rescues?" Brian said.

Jeeminy. I'd told him Jesse was depressed, and this was how he tried to buck him up—by singing from the Up with People songbook.

"My share," Jesse said.

Marc was smiling. "It's not just surfboards and guitars around the bonfire?"

"Afraid not."

A woman walked past us toward the door. She gave a frilly wave. Jesse glanced over idly, and she smiled at him. Me, she gave a challenging gaze.

"Hi, Jesse," she said, opening the door. "Bye, Jesse."

He watched her go. "Who was that?"

"If you don't know, I certainly don't," I said.

She passed by the window outside. On the street, pinpoint white lights twinkled in the trees. She leaned up to the window, cupped her breasts against the glass, and ran off laughing. Jesse's mouth was half-open.

Marc set down his bottle. "No, lifeguarding's all serious. No fun at all. Is she somebody you resuscitated? In an extra-special way?"

"That was truly weird."

Brian was still waving the pom-poms. "Hey, CPR's no joke."

Marc nodded. "Sure. Sorry. You ever perform no-joke CPR?"

Jesse's color drained, and his eyes went blank. "Successfully? No."

The music subsided. The trio onstage had finished their set. The crowd applauded, but Jesse seemed to be staring through the table. Damn.

The door opened and Sinsa Jimson came in. Shaun Kutner was with her. Even with his arm over her shoulder, he managed to slouch.

"This could be trouble," I said.

Jesse put the beer bottle to his lips, tilted his head back, and emptied it. Shaun and Sinsa headed to a table across the club, in the back. Shaun's sea green eyes shone in the low light. He was wearing fabulous accessories: enough hair gel to turn his tangles completely ratty, and a blue knee brace. His limp was pronounced but sporadic. If he had actually torn a ligament, he was the world's fastest healer. Sinsa was cold again. Her shirt had writing across the bust, and her right nipple was dotting the i in *diva*.

Brian watched her. "Whoa. Keep my pants on."

I set my beer down. "Shaun wouldn't start something with P.J. tonight. Not in public, at Ricky's show."

Jesse finally glanced across the room. His voice was flat. "Why not? He thinks Ricky cost him a shot at *Rock House*."

Shaun's hands began reading Sinsa like a Braille book. She seemed beyond noticing it.

Applause rose from the crowd. Ricky was taking the stage. The guitarist thumbed a chord and adjusted a tuning peg. Ricky leaned into his mike and said, "Me and Tiger got some tunes for you."

He counted off the beat. Tiger hit a ringing minor chord, and Ricky launched. "Baby, you're the thorn in my crown . . ." He grabbed the mike stand. "The thorn in my side . . ."

His voice sounded rich, that famous bell-like tenor with the burnt edges. Brian and Marc listened. Jesse peeled the label off his empty beer bottle. Shaun gave Sinsa a long, sloppy kiss.

P.J. stood at the bar, watching them.

Ricky sang. "You're the thumb in my eye . . ." Sinsa stood up. Shaun grabbed her by the belt loops, pulled her backward, and bit her on the rump. She slapped his hand.

Karen, sitting on a bar stool, scowled. Ricky stroked the mike, mouth close to it. "You're the light when I die."

Sinsa sat back down, flipping her hair over her shoulder. Shaun nuzzled her neck but she pushed him away. He mouthed a word that I could lip-read. One syllable, rhymed with *kitsch*. He stood up. And headed for P.J.

"Here we go," I said.

Shaun sidled up to the bar and elbowed next to P.J. P.J. was hunched over, silent, staring at his beer bottle. Shaun talked. And then he took the beer bottle and stuck it upside down inside the neck of P.J.'s shirt.

I stood up.

Jesse rubbed his forehead. "Don't."

"If P.J. gets his teeth knocked out, he'll never be able to tell us the straight story."

"You aren't the Eighty-second Airborne."

Marc pushed his chair back. "No, we're Strike Fighter Squadron One-fifty-one."

Brian was on his feet as well, heading for the bar before I said anything. They cut between tables, smooth and quiet, with me behind them. P.J. pulled the bottle out of his collar but his back was drenched with beer. Shaun shoved him. Karen was coming down the bar. Ricky and Tiger went into the chorus, trying to ignore it.

Brian and Marc stepped up on either side of Shaun. They took his arms and Shaun bunched, ready to fight. Brian set a twenty-dollar bill on the bar, put his face to Shaun's ear, and spit words at him.

Shaun's head whipped around. He stared at Brian, his face stark. Then he shook loose and stormed out the door.

The bartender threw P.J. a towel. He wiped his neck. I let out a breath.

Brian put a hand on P.J.'s shoulder. "Come over to our table."

P.J. threw the towel on the bar. "No, I'm outta here."

Brian's hand was insistent. "You aren't going out there yet. That guy has *lying in wait* written all over him."

Reluctantly P.J. walked to the table with us. He shot a glance at Sinsa. Karen was at her table, hands on hips, giving her an earful. Sinsa stood up and started bitching back. Mighty Mites in battle. A moment later Karen took Sinsa by the elbow and walked her out of the bar. Ricky's song finished and the crowd applauded.

I spoke into Brian's ear. "What did you say to Shaun?"

"That I was paying for his drinks."

"And?"

"If he left right now, I'd leave the money on the bar. But if he stuck around, I'd shove it up his large intestine with a pool cue."

Ricky gazed past the stage lights, trying to see where his family had gone. He tried to act cool, but when he put his Evian bottle down he missed the stool and spilled it. I had a feeling this was the effect Sinsa had hoped for. We approached the table. Jesse's face was unreadable. P.J. looked like a whipped dog.

He lifted his chin in greeting. "Go on. Say whatever it is you're gonna say."

Jesse stared. And stared. "No, I don't think I will."

Marc and Brian sat down, but P.J. stood by the table. His eyes came up to about my navel.

"And I get your point about the Alfa Romeo," he said.

"What's that?" I said.

"Shaun supposedly needs it for his image. But I'm being played for a sucker."

Simultaneously Jesse and I said, "*What?*"

"Sorry I can't measure up. Yet again," he said.

Jesse grabbed his crutches, balanced, and pushed to his feet. I felt Brian and Marc shift, surprised. They weren't used to seeing him so tall. It unsettled people who only knew him sitting down.

Jesse looked pale. "And you're screwing Evan over for those two? What is wrong with you?"

P.J. glared at him. "Know what, Jesse? I'm a shit-head, but at least I admit it. I don't claim to be a saint and then take out my frustrations on everybody else."

I flinched. It was an ambush, all right.

Onstage, Ricky said, "How about something happier?" He spoke over his shoulder to Tiger.

Jesse leaned on his arms. He looked away from his brother.

From the stage came a flash, and sparks misted the air. The amplifier exploded. Tiger came flying into the audience in a cloud of smoke, his guitar shrieking with feedback.

Marc drove Brian and me back to my house. We rode in the truck, listening to the radio, digesting the mayhem from the club. The paramedics and fire department were there when we left. Jesse wasn't. He had gone home without saying good-bye.

While Brian went to get Luke from Carl and Nikki's, Marc walked me to my door. Amber light flowed from the Vincents' windows. The live oaks leaned above us and ivy poured over the fence, gleaming in the moonlight.

I sought for something innocuous to say. "Luke's going to be a rag doll when Brian carries him out."

Marc's breath shone in the dim air. "You're good with Luke."

"It's easy to be good with such a great kid."

"Brian's thrilled for you to spend time with him. It's hard, Luke not having his mom."

This wasn't as innocuous as I'd planned. "You miss your girls, don't you?"

"Like I've had my lungs yanked out."

His rich voice tapered off. It was as much as he was going to say. But I knew the basics: that his wife had come home one day and told him their marriage was dead. She took the kids and headed home to Greenville, South Carolina.

He pulled out his wallet. "Here. Take a look."

He handed me a dozen photos to look at under my porch light. His daughters looked very much like him, with serious eyes, enigmatic smiles. They had pigtails done up with plentiful hair doodads.

He pointed. "Here's Lauren, and this is Hope."

"They're perfect."

He slid the photos back into his wallet. We stood under the porch light.

"So," he said.

He drew out the word, almost begging for permission to speak.

"Marc, you're practically family. Just act like the rest of my relatives and ask nosy questions. Let's have it."

"You and Jesse."

The cold prickled on my face. My fingers were growing numb.

"Tonight dredged up some bad memories. Don't judge him by tonight."

He gazed at the vast winter sky. Above the black silhouette of the mountains, the polar star watched us spin.

"You two seem to chuck a lot of rocks at each other," he said.

God, another big brother. I stepped out from under the light. "Let me explain something. Jesse and I are both lawyers. We argue for a living. We're good at it."

"So you actually enjoy battle?"

"Says the man who gets paid to dogfight other airplanes."

"Touché. Still, that can make life tense, day to day."

"Did you and Brian plan ahead to double-team me? Look. Jesse got upset tonight because—"

"Double-team you? You think Brian wants to ride you over this stuff?"

I snorted. "Tonight was an exceptional performance on Brian's part. Usually Jesse gets under his skin like a bad rash."

"He has nothing but praise for Jesse."

I stopped. "Really?"

"If it wasn't for Jesse, he'd be dead. Surely you know how thankful he is."

I nodded, feeling an unexpected sense of warmth.

"But," he said, "I see that Jesse's hard on you. People with high expectations of themselves often are. Take my word, I know from sad experience."

I took that not merely as a reference to his failed marriage, but as an opening. In the cold night air I felt a homey bond of kid talk and school photos between us. So I jumped—into a well of deep, irreparable stupidity.

"Between us? I don't want Brian worrying about this."

He nodded.

"Jesse's everything to me. But sometimes . . ." I hesitated. "You nailed it—he's hard on himself. He judges himself ruthlessly. That's one reason why he got so upset at the club." I stared into the night. "Which makes me worry. What if I can't live up to his standards?"

He seemed like a solid wall beside me. "If that's so, he's a fool. Because you're flawless just the way you are."

Straight out of the Buck Up the Kid Sister handbook. "Do you always know the right thing to say?"

"Hardly. But I'm working on it."

Inside my house, the puppy barked.

"You know . . ." I smiled. "You can never say anything wrong to a dog."

"Good try. But that would be too easy." He smiled back. "And I like a challenge."

Ricky needed a few drinks to unscrew his head. The paramedics took Tiger away on the stretcher, his hands bandaged. The club still smelled like fried hair.

The firefighters said water on the floor and a bad connection between the guitar and the amp was what caused the explosion. But Ricky stared vacantly at the stage.

"It's close," he said. "Death. I can smell it."

"That's Tiger's guitar. Or else his boots," P.J. said. "They both melted."

After a couple more whiskeys, P.J. led Ricky out of the club. When they got to the parking garage Ricky gave him the keys to the four-by-four. P.J.'d had only a few beers. And hadn't felt the Reaper reach down onto the stage and miss him by inches.

P.J. turned the key in the ignition, but the engine wouldn't start. That wasn't right. Not with a Beemer. He tried again, pumping the gas pedal, but still nothing. The lights on the dash were flipping out. And he smelled a smell. Coming from the vents.

Ricky opened his door. "Shit. It's smoke. The Reaper's in here, fucking chasing me, man." He jumped out. "He wanted me back there. He got Tiger by mistake."

P.J. didn't bother to point out that Tiger wasn't dead, just slightly scorched. But he did smell the smoke. He got out and put up the hood.

He stumbled back. "Fuck."

"What is it? Is it . . . what is it?" Ricky said.

"Ravens."

"What?"

P.J. put the back of his hand against his nose to block the stench. "Dead ravens. Jammed down on the engine block."

They smelled like decay and gasoline. Dried blood coated their feathers.

"What are they doing there? Get rid of 'em, Peej."

P.J. wasn't about to touch them. "Ricky, they can't hurt you."

They burst into flames.

Lying awake in bed at five a.m., watching the trees outside dipping in the wind, I finally admitted that Jesse wasn't going to call. I'd left him six messages after leaving Chaco's. I got dressed and drove out to his house.

The freeway was empty. My tires droned on the road. When I reached San Ysidro I headed for the beach, across the train tracks and down the road through the Monterey pines. His Mustang was in the driveway. The morning star hung above the ocean. Beyond the mountains the sky was hinting blue.

Unlocking the door, I crossed the entryway. In the living room a single lamp was on, low. The morning twilight was pushing shadows across the house. The tide was out, and the ocean lay deep blue. Waves shimmered up the sand.

I saw the wheelchair, near the windows, disassembled. One wheel was off the frame, the tire was off the rim, and a repair kit lay on the table.

"Jesse?"

I heard a rustling sound, the noise of hands sorting through small, hard objects. I walked around the end of the kitchen counter.

He was sitting on the kitchen floor. As cold as it was, he was barefoot, in nothing but jeans. He had his kitchen junk drawer on his lap. He was rifling through it, pawing pencils and rubber bands and nuts and bolts.

"Get a flat?" I said.

"You don't miss a trick."

His shoulders were tight. His mahogany hair was falling over his face. He picked up a package, saw it was batteries, tossed it aside.

"What are you doing?" I said.

"Choosing a new shade of nail polish."

I saw a tumbler broken on the floor, and a jar of pills spilled amid the shards of glass, looked like diazepam.

"Jess."

He sifted junk through his fingers. "I'm trying to find a tire patch. Which I need because I ran over the broken glass and got a flat. Which I need to fix, because the tire goes on the wheelchair. Which I need

to be in working condition, because . . ." He looked
in the drawer. "Which . . ."

He heaved the drawer across the room. Junk flew.
The drawer crashed against the plate-glass window
and clattered to the floor.

Junk freckled the wood. A coin rolled across the floor
and tipped over, ringing. Jesse's hands fell to his lap.

"Don't say anything," he said.

I took a step toward the kitchen.

"Leave it," he said.

I stood, hands limp at my sides. "Jess, Marc didn't
know."

"Leave it."

I knelt down. "Babe, there's nothing you could have
done for Adam. CPR wasn't successful, but you didn't
fail. Nobody could have saved him."

"There it is." Leaning sideways, he reached for an
object near the refrigerator. He grabbed the pack of
patches he'd been looking for.

"Jesse." I stretched my hand out but he wouldn't
even look at me. "You can't go on like this."

He put the patches between his teeth and started
pulling backward toward the wheelchair. He kept his
eyes trained on his feet.

I stood up, blood rushing in my ears. He reached
the kitchen table, pulled up onto a chair, and tore
open the pack of patches. I picked my way through
junk and broken glass to the broom closet.

"I'll get it," he said. He picked up the tire. "I'm
going to fix this, and head in to work. I'll talk to
you later."

Behind him, outside the plate-glass windows, the
sky was cobalt. A crescent moon skimmed the horizon, so thin it seemed illusory. But I knew it was real.
All of this. And it wasn't going away.

Ravens feast on the dead.
They eat carrion. He'd looked it up.

People used to think ravens could smell death on a person who was going to croak. That was why the birds were omens: *Time's up, sucker.* And that's why Ricky Jimson had been afraid tonight. You could see that from the photos.

The pix were lousy quality, because of the tiny camera in the cell phone. Still, when he downloaded them from the phone to disk he got that rush again. The one he'd felt when he shot the ravens. The one he'd felt when the birds caught fire on the engine block while P.J. tried to work the fire extinguisher and Ricky tripped and fell running away. They never saw him in the corner of the parking garage, behind his car. Losers.

He edited the photos and added them to his collection. It was good stuff.

So why did he feel that gnawing sensation in his stomach?

Because there were three problems with tonight's pictures. One, they were still footage. Two, they had no audio. And three, he wasn't in them.

Shit.

No, calm down. Tonight was a head fuck. Toying with them. Don't sweat it.

To cool off, he watched the greatest-hits video. That always put him in a good place. Sure, the video was incomplete—the early stuff was missing, the home burglaries, but back in school it hadn't occurred to him to film them. Doing robberies was what gave him the idea. He always scoped a job out ahead of time, photographing the place he planned to hit. Then a flash of genius told him to take the camera with him on the boost. People's faces, man, they were priceless. And when he got a girlfriend to tape him in action, the highlights video was born.

He fast-forwarded. Yeah, this one was good, the old Lebanese guy cowering behind the counter at the minimart. And this one, the fat chick at Jolly Time

Liquors, crying as he whipped an electrical cord across that lard ass of hers.

He felt so frustrated. Pix without him in them—that just didn't cut it.

He fast-forwarded to his favorite performance: hitting the 7-Eleven. That was the jackpot, because the CCTV footage made national television. *America's Most Wanted* ran it. He watched himself pistol-whipping the store clerk. The blood, the screams, the perfect arc as he swung the butt of the gun down on the guy's forehead. He looked great. Confident. Powerful. Too bad about the ski mask; you couldn't see his face.

Fuck.

Screw this. He stood up and went to wash his face with cold water. Looked in the mirror. Took cleansing breaths, watching his chest rise and fall. He needed to plan his next performance. That would fix things. Solve his problems. Fuck all these losers who were interfering with his life. Like Ricky. And P.J. And that nutcracker Evan Delaney. He gazed in the mirror. His eyes grew serene.

16

When I got home I worked for six hours straight, staring absently at the draft of an appellate brief. Then I ran for an hour through bracing sunshine. I showered, and told myself that things would even out. Eventually. They had to, because I couldn't stand to think of any other outcome. I sat on my bed running a comb through my hair, and looked at the clock.

Holy moly. I was due for the fitting of my bridesmaid's dress.

I threw on some clothes, took Ollie outside to relieve himself, poured him fresh water, and shut him in the kitchen behind the baby gate Nikki had lent me. I ran out. Wait—fancy shoes. I ran back in. I found one under the coffee table and the other in Ollie's box. Drooly. *Blech*. I dashed to the car and peeled out for the dress shop.

The boutique was in Montecito, between an art gallery and an Italian restaurant in an elegant arcade. It was presided over by a crone named Madame Kornelia, who would have fit in at the kaiser's table with the other monocles, cracking a riding crop against her hip. She was the size of a porcupine, smoked like an exhaust pipe, and had a reputation for poking contentious brides with straight pins. But she had a knack. She made women beautiful. She could turn brides made of sauerbraten into wisps of confectionery— sugarplum fairies, ready to float to the altar.

And she charged for it.

This wasn't, I add, where I purchased my own wedding dress. The one that hung in the back of the closet, looking perplexed, wondering when I planned to put it on. But that was an unfinished story between me and Mr. Blackburn.

A bell tinkled when I opened the door.

"Ah, Miss Delaney. Five minutes ago your appointment was."

Madame Kornelia shuffled across the shop toward me. She had mastered the art of walking without lifting her feet off the floor. She wore a tape measure around her neck and a pincushion on her wrist. She had my bridesmaid's dress on a hanger.

Shoving it into my hands, she shooed me around the corner into a dressing room by the back door. I pulled off my cords and blouse. Seeing myself in the mirror, I knew I should have worn better underwear. The safety pin in the bra strap didn't cut it, much less the *Star Trek* panties.

The dress. Yes.

On the hanger it looked spooky. For starters, the color gave me qualms. Madame Kornelia called it crème de menthe, but any tomboy knows pus when she sees it. Then there was the hemline. It frothed, putting me in mind of mint juleps exploding from a blender. I held it up, trying to figure out which side was the front.

"Knock, knock." Madame Kornelia pulled open the door. "Let me see how you look."

Too late. I stood there while her gaze lingered on the *Trek* panties. They said, *Resistance is futile.*

Her expression didn't change. It remained exactly as arch as before. She bustled in, took the dress, and unzipped it. "Deep breath." She flipped the dress over my head. It rustled and she grunted and I squirmed, and when my head popped out again she said, "Suck in," and wrestled the zipper up my back. I squeaked.

She stepped back, stared, and pressed teeny fists to her hips. "Will do."

"Does it come with an oxygen tank?"

She made a spinning gesture with her index finger. Turning, I saw myself in the mirror.

"Oh, my."

She fluffed the hem and straightened the seams, her knuckles digging into my ribs. I felt dizzy.

"Is okay, I think."

"Okay isn't the word."

Grammar deserted me. This was a double negative turning into a positive. My sprinter's legs and meager chest were juxtaposed against the strict bodice and green lather of the hem—and, inexplicably, it worked. I looked timeless.

"It's exquisite," I said.

"Come over to the light; we let out that seam."

I slipped into my dress shoes. I rustled when I walked, which made me forget the dog drool. Out in the shop she pinned up the bodice while I savored the view in the mirror. My every move seemed elegant, every gesture polished. I felt like Grace Kelly. Until Madame Kornelia handed me the bill.

My eyes had gone bad. I prayed they had.

"Your credit card will cover?"

"Yes." If I sold a kidney.

It was impossible. And it was the day before the wedding, and I'd promised Jesse. He and his cousin and the jittery bride and his fretful mother were all counting on me to do this. And I was almost out of work, and should be saving up for my criminal appeal.

"I just need to call the credit card company. Can you put the dress on hold?" I said.

She gave me a look like a piece of broken glass. "Very so."

I went to the dressing room to change, but ended up twirling helplessly, trying to reach the zipper. I went back out. And saw, cruising past in the parking lot, the red van that Merlin and Murphy Ming drove.

I ducked behind a clothing rack. The van rattled away, spewing blue fumes.

Madame Kornelia huffed. "For some reason you think people should not see you in my dress?"

I scuttled to the counter. "Unzip me."

Clucking her tongue, she gave the zipper a tiny tug, three inches at best. I hurried back toward the dressing room, around the corner, and stopped. The back door of the shop was open. Had the wind blown it open?

Outside, in the alley behind the arcade, the red van cruised past. I hissed and jumped inside the dressing room, trying to get out of sight.

Murphy Ming was waiting for me inside.

He grabbed me and swept his hand across my mouth.

"Rowan," he crooned.

He smelled like cooking grease. The drooping mustache gave him a lazy look, but agitation vexed his eyes. I pawed behind me for the doorknob.

"You look wicked in this dress."

I found the knob. As soon as I turned it, Murphy lifted me off my feet, swung me around as if we were waltzing, and pinned me against the mirror. He flattened himself along me like an enormous flank of meat. He brushed my neck with his lips.

"The money."

His breath was humid on my skin. His mustache licked my neck, silken and stubbly, like a hairy insect.

"You're close to getting hurt," he breathed.

He leaned against me, the studs on his dog collar scraping my collarbone. I couldn't move. His thighs were warm. And oh, crap, I felt his crotch against my thigh. The big worm was wriggling awake.

"But I don't have to do it. Getting hurt's up to you.
Understand?"

I nodded.

"I'm gonna give you a choice. People always get a
choice. You act of your own free will."

There was a tap on the door. I writhed and moaned.

Merlin hissed from outside the door. "Murph, cut
it out. You ain't supposed to mess with her."

Murphy's face was two inches from mine. His skull
shone as if it were varnished.

Merlin tapped again. "The hag's gonna see. Let's
go."

Murphy breathed against my throat. "Here it is.
You can come with us and fix the money issue this
afternoon. Or you can scream, in which case the old
lady ends up with sewing scissors through her eye
socket. And she will; don't even think about doubting
it. Then we'd have to come back another time to sort
things out. And that'll be far worse, believe me."

I didn't doubt it for a second. And I knew this
wasn't really a choice. But I also knew that they
wanted money I didn't have, and if I could convince
them they'd been lied to—if I could clarify that to
them—I could get out of this. Once and for all.

"I'm taking my hand off your mouth. You decide
which it is." He pulled his hand away.

"I'll come with you."

The red van was parked next to a Dumpster in the
alley. They shoveled me into the back to sit among
keyboards, drums, and sound equipment. And a clothing rack on which hung what looked like the Bee
Gees' closet, circa 1978.

"Where are you taking me?" I said.

"To meet the boss."

They pulled me out of the van at the harbor. It was
a glittering winter day. On the beach, tourists braved
the brisk air. Kids with pails and shovels sprinted

toward the water, kicking up soft sand. Seagulls screeched overhead.

Murphy held my biceps. "Keep your mouth shut. Just walk."

"And if people ask me when the bride's tossing the bouquet?"

"Shut up."

They led me toward the marina. The ocean was sapphire spread with gold sparks. Sailboats lazed at their moorings, halyards clanging against masts. Merlin's eyes jerked back and forth and up to the sky, as if a gull might mistake him for a burrowing rodent and carry him off.

I had a plan: talk, straight, about the money. This boss of theirs, their manager, Tibbetts Price, may have been ripped off. I needed to explain that nobody had ever given me their money. I didn't have it, knew nothing about it, couldn't get it.

I'd tell him to take it up with Sinsemilla Jimson.

We went through a gate and out onto the dock. We passed a long row of sailboats. I heard radios and televisions, and saw an occasional sailor working on deck. We walked to the end of the dock to a sleek white boat.

Navy brat though I am, I had no idea what class of boat it was, except expensive. Merlin grunted and hopped aboard. Murphy and I followed. It had been years since I'd been on a boat, and, wearing high heels, I felt myself pitching. Merlin walked down a set of steps and opened the cabin door.

"Boss, it's us."

Murphy stood behind me, one moist hand gripping my arm. His other hand crept to the center of my back and began unzipping the bridesmaid's dress.

I pulled away. "Stop it."

He pulled me back. "You want to play hard to get?" His hand went to his own zipper. "Okay, me first."

Merlin called into the cabin, "We got her."

A voice spat back from belowdecks. "Hey. Hey. Haul it right back up the steps, Merle."

"But—"

"You need to request permission to come aboard. Do I have to tattoo that on your forehead?"

Merlin bungled backward, pushing his little glasses up his nose.

Murphy called out, "Permission to come aboard, Skipper?"

His answer was a whistle from the cabin. He zipped up and pushed me down the steps ahead of him. I ducked my head and went inside, getting a Jonah-versus-whale feeling.

The cabin was beautiful. Teak paneling, brass fixtures, sconces on the walls. Like something out of *The Great Gatsby*, aside from the empty pizza boxes, bags of tortilla chips and popcorn, the half-eaten tubs of cake frosting on the coffee table, MTV droning from a television, and the roaches in the ashtray.

"You wait topside, Murphy."

He left, climbing the stairs to the deck. I stood, trying to find my sea legs, facing their boss, who leaned back in a green canvas director's chair, reading the *Wall Street Journal*. He wore horn-rimmed half-glasses. A .44 lay by his feet.

He nodded at a bench built into the wall. "Sit."

I rustled over and sat, tamping down my green hem. My hands were cold and trembling.

"Murphy behave himself?" he said.

"He likes unzipping in public."

"He's a musician. Busy hands."

"Quite. Hello, Toby."

He thumped the chair down onto all four legs. "It's Mr. Price. But I'll let that slide, since I did ask you to call me Toby the other night."

In the daylight his hair was streaked with gray, his

tan dark and weathered. His T-shirt wilted across his beef-jerky frame.

"And what should I call you?" He folded the newspaper neatly and set it down. "Kathleen Delaney? Rowan Larkin?"

"Evan."

I could barely hear myself. I could barely think. I squeezed my hands between my knees so he wouldn't see them shaking.

He was the one who'd phoned me to come to the party where Brittany Gaines was murdered. His flunkies had been dogging me ever since. They were the ones, I thought. They had killed her.

He took off his glasses. "You messed my evening up, calling nine-one-one like that. I ask you to deal with one kid having a bad trip, and next thing I know the house is full of uniforms."

He stared at me intently but his eyes didn't lock on, as though a hive of bees were loose in his brain.

"I looked you up," he said. "Kathleen Evan Delaney."

He stood and went to the back of the cabin. Opening the boat's first-aid kit, he took out bandages, a flare gun, and a silver cigarette case. He got himself a prerolled joint and offered the case to me.

"No, thank you."

He lit up, holding the smoke in his lungs. Exhaled.

"Merlin went to the courthouse, checked out property records. The place you live is owned by people named Vincent. But there's a K. E. Delaney listed in the phone book. So we know she's for real. And we know she has credit cards. And a bank account." He took another toke. "That she writes bad checks on."

The smoke began to sweeten the air. He set the joint in the ashtray and rooted around in the debris on the coffee table, knocking popcorn and a bag of Oreos to the polished wood floor. He came up with a well-thumbed paperback. It was my novel *Lithium Sunset*.

"And weirdest of all, here's a book by Evan Delaney. No photo on the jacket. Could be you, could be some hack the publisher hires. But the book's about this guerrilla babe called Rowan Larkin."

Sitting back down, he opened the book. He had highlighted passages in yellow marker and written in the margins, tiny reams of commentary. My skin shrank. The only people I knew who did that were unmedicated compulsives or survivalists parsing the Bible for signs of the Apocalypse.

"Some extreme stuff here. This Rowan chick, she cooks a guy's brain inside his head just by staring at him." His gaze swarmed over me. "That your message? Men gotta toe the line, or women'll fry their minds?"

He took a drag from the joint.

"You've been playing with my head. You were supposed to be the silent partner, the go-between who was gonna make the payoff. Instead you kept the money for yourself and left me twisting in the wind."

Silent partner. God. Was the other partner Brittany Gaines—now silent forever? This wasn't about mistaken identity or money. I smelled the fetid ocean smell of the morgue, and saw Brittany's torn throat. I had to get out of here. Alive.

"I—"

"Do not interrupt me."

"Just—"

"Not one fucking word."

No amount of identification, and no explanation, was going to satisfy him. Not when he had done this . . . research.

"You told Merlin you were Rowan, which is obviously an alias. You may be Delaney. Or that may be a nom de plume." He pinched the joint between his fingers. "What I do know is, you're in entertainment."

He turned my book over and peered at the spine. "Arcturus."

He squinted at me like a law professor demanding an answer.

"That's the publisher," I said.

"A subdivision of Spillhouse Media."

"Yes."

"Which in turn is owned by the VZG Group."

Why did this matter? Where was he going with it?

"Which owns radio stations in the U.S. and Canada and is a minority stakeholder in film production companies and record labels headquartered in Hollywood and Nashville."

This was news to me. I felt my knees jouncing. I glanced at the *Wall Street Journal*, and the zing in his eyes.

"It's one of North America's largest entertainment conglomerates. Did you think I wouldn't find out? I have a degree in business economics, for fucksake. I ran the dope business for half of Isla Vista from my fraternity house when I was nineteen."

He knocked more junk around the coffee table, finally coming up with a CD. He tossed it at me like a Frisbee. I caught it clumsily. It was Jimsonweed's last album.

"And Jimsonweed records on the Black Watch label, which is owned by the same conglomerate that owns your publisher. I do my homework, bitch-hole."

I stared helplessly, thinking: *So what?* "I—"

"No excuses. The deal didn't go through, so you're going to get me my money back. Do you fucking dig?"

"I don't have that power."

The beehive awoke behind his eyes, and he leaped off the director's chair. He was on me in a second, grabbing my hair with one hand and planting his knee between my legs.

"Don't fuck with me, woman."

The joint was pinched between his fingers, aimed at my cheek.

"Representations were made to me. I was promised face time."

"With whom?"

"You're insulting my intelligence. With Slink's producer. And the execs at the label, who were doing the deal. Three albums, a spot on the tour. *Access.*" The joint wavered back and forth in front of my face. "Fifteen K in pay-fuckin'-ola, and I got jack shit."

He flicked the joint at me. I put up my hands. It stung my palm and fell to my dress. I swept it off and ground it out on the floor.

He loomed above me. "I'm not going to dink around Santa Barbara forever, booking bands to gig at the Elks lodge and the county fair. I have real singers, acts who can put me on the map in the industry. And I paid real money to get them signed. And you fucked me up the ass."

He pointed at me. "You wrecked my deal. And instead of me, who's VZG paying? You." He grabbed my novel. "For your publishing deal. So to make up my losses, you're going to donate your book money to me."

He flipped pages. "Shitty paperback, I'll lowball the estimate, figure seven grand. Add it to the original fifteen, plus the three in interest, that makes your bill twenty-five thousand."

He threw the paperback at me. I batted it aside and pressed my fists into the seat, trying not to scream or wet my pants.

I didn't know who had sold him fool's gold. Almost certainly Sinsa. But right now that didn't matter. I had to get out of here in one piece and get to the police. I smoothed the skirt of the dress, brushing away ash. I exhaled, slowly, and prayed to God to put lies in my mouth.

"Mom always told me only easy girls say yes right away. You've got to say no, or the boys think you're a slut."

He gave me a crooked stare. I cleared my throat and continued, stronger.

"Don't blame a girl for trying." Before he could respond I put up my hands as if in apology. "We'll make an arrangement."

He sank back onto the director's chair. "That's better." He reached again for the silver cigarette case. "The Mings will take you by the bank on your way back to . . ." He blinked and widened his eyes, as if assessing my getup for the first time. "Wherever it is you came from."

"That won't work."

"Make it work."

"The money is safe, but I can't get it today."

He pressed his fingertips to either side of his skull. "I'm getting a sensation here like you're trying to barbecue my brain."

"Allied Pacific Bank is under surveillance. Didn't the party kings tell you what happened the last time I went in?"

His forehead creased. "What?"

"The cops were waiting when I came out."

He looked frustrated, perhaps displeased that the Mings hadn't reported this detail. "So do it inside the bank. Ask for a private room. Get the cash and give it to the boys behind a closed door."

"With surveillance cameras filming the whole thing? The account is flagged, Toby. There's been too much cash flowing in and out of it, plus some checks that bounced. They're watching it."

"That's your problem, not mine."

"It's not a problem. It's a matter of timing."

"How?"

"Think about it."

The beehive decelerated behind his eyes. I balled the fabric of my skirt between my fingers. He was thinking. He believed me.

"Time-lock vault?" he said.

That worked. "In part. Safe-deposit box."

"So go get the key."

"It's not that simple. There are several accounts involved, and other banks, and travel time."

He reached for the tub of chocolate frosting on the coffee table. A butter knife was stuck into it. He swirled a gob onto the end and poked it into his mouth to lick it off.

"Tomorrow," he said.

"Afternoon."

"Don't fuck—"

"Wouldn't dare." I stood up.

He stabbed another gob of frosting onto the knife. He licked it, taking his time.

"Have it here tomorrow at five p.m." Finally he looked at me. "Now get out."

The red van chugged into the alley behind the bridal boutique. Murphy slid open the door and climbed out with me.

"Tomorrow. Dress in something else," he said.

I took a step, and he put an arm out to block me. "Remember, I said I always give you a choice?"

Merlin moaned from the van. "Naw, Murph."

A new light was playing in Murphy's eyes, what in a normal man would be amusement. His hand went to his mustache, smoothing it. His greasy body scent filled my nose.

The thought slapped me. Did he give Brittany a choice? I backed against the van.

He leaned his face close to mine. "Naked or not?"

I felt myself jerk. "What?"

"Murph," Merlin said. "We ain't got time for this shit. The boss won't like it."

Murphy smiled. "How do you want to go back in the wedding shop? Naked or not?"

"Not," I said.

"Fine."

Grunting, he heaved me off my feet and pitched me into the Dumpster.

I landed on my back in soggy lettuce and veal gristle and wet cardboard. I looked up to see Murphy slamming the lid shut. Dark and stink enclosed me.

He banged on the side of the Dumpster. "Tomorrow. Don't fuck us."

I heard the van drive off. Gingerly I sat up. Every inch I moved brought new sucking, sliming, crackling noises from beneath me. They mixed with another sound. Myself, crying with relief.

The lid cracked open. Madame Kornelia peered in.

"You will pay for this dress. Now," she said. "In cash, fräulein."

17

An hour later I met Detective Rodriguez at the International House of Pancakes, off the freeway near the sheriff's station in Goleta. The restaurant was busy with truckers and deputies and the usual crowd of retirees eating dinner at five p.m. Rodriguez was sitting in a bright blue booth near the counter, digging into bacon, eggs, and a short stack of pancakes. I slid into the booth, across from her.

She wiped her mouth on a napkin. "Tibbetts Price. Known as Tokin' Toby, or Toby Price-Is-Right."

"You checked out what I told you?" I said.

Her nose wrinkled. "What's with the garlic?"

"It's eau de Dumpster."

"You're here without your lawyer. You must be feeling brave."

"Feeling scared."

Too scared to put off this meeting until I could get someone to come with me from Sanchez Marks. Jesse was in court, and Lavonne had gone to Ventura for a deposition. I needed Rodriguez's help, right now.

"Tell me about Toby," I said.

"Local boy makes bad. He's smooth, he's rich, and, for a drug dealer, he's smarter than the average bear. As he'll tell you."

"Degree in business economics. Reads the *Wall Street Journal*."

"Bred in the bone. He's a stockbroker's kid. Got

his start selling to his classmates at Lassen Academy, then moved his trade to the frat house at UCSB. Now he runs a tidy organization. Under the umbrella of his music promotion business. He does a lot of his business in international waters."

"He can actually sail that boat, then."

"Grew up sailing it, and inherited it from his father. The slip, rumor has, he got as payment in a drug deal."

I didn't bother laughing at how absurd it was—Toby Price, drug runner, expecting fame in the music industry. People with worse reputations, people who'd done prison time for homicide, ran record labels and hosted radio shows in L.A.

"And the Mings?" I said.

"Merlin's clean. No arrests, not even a parking ticket."

"What about Murphy?"

She poured maple syrup onto her pancakes, taking her time, drawing a spiral.

"Detective?" I said.

"Murphy Ming has a longer jacket."

She had that wide-eyed face, and the cowlick sticking up. And, despite being a tough gal who wore a holster on her belt, she looked reluctant to say anything cruel.

"Auto theft, assault. Robbery. And he did three years for sexual battery."

His greasy presence asserted itself. I felt a phantom sensation, his mouth against my skin.

"He raped somebody?" I said.

"The robbery victim. Though he claimed he was settling a debt, and that the victim consented."

"I know what he claimed. He claimed that he gave her a choice," I said.

"Him." She put down her fork. "Gave *him* a choice."

I leaned my forehead on my palms. "What was the choice?"

"The victim could get it, or his sister could. And it was penetration with a foreign object."

"What object?"

"A curling iron."

A feeling of slime and blood and dirty seawater was rising in me.

"Murphy killed Brittany Gaines," I said.

"You have no evidence to support that."

"She died. Toby Price was there at the party; I saw him. Murphy was too, I'll bet anything."

"I reread the deputy's report. He got three names at the Del Playa house—you, P. J. Blackburn, and somebody called Bill Smithers."

"It was Toby Price. I don't care what he called himself. Describe him to the deputy; he'll confirm it."

"Even if he does, what does that prove?"

"Toby's probably thirty-five years old. What was he doing at a college party? And don't say he was dealing coke. He's the boss, not a snow-cone vendor. Besides, he acted like he owned the place."

"So?"

"He lured me there. What if he lured Brittany there too?"

"This is all frightened speculation."

"Lily, help me."

She gave me a conflicted look. I spread my palms flat on the table.

"These guys are after me. They're going to hurt me."

"Evan, calm down."

"I think they killed Brittany because they thought she was me," I said. "The ID. They thought she was Evan Delaney."

She scrunched her mouth like a kid working on math homework, biting her lip.

"What are you suggesting? That they demanded the fifteen thousand from her, and killed her when she didn't pay up?"

"Maybe." I searched her face, trying to tell whether she believed me.

She shook her head. "We have a suspect in Brittany's killing."

"Give me a break. There's P. J. Blackburn, who gets *scared* when he's stoned, and who rescues puppies from the animal shelter. Or there's Murphy Ming, who was pawing me up and down today and who sodomized some poor bastard with a curling iron." My voice rose uncontrollably. "Did he rape her? Brittany—Jesus, did he rape her before he killed her?"

The truckers, the waiter with the coffeepot, and the grandparents in the next booth all stared. I put my head in my hands, forcing my mouth closed.

After a moment I managed to speak quietly. "Murphy did it. Bring him in. Because he's going to be coming after me tomorrow."

"Evan, from what you've described the only crime anyone committed against you today is misdemeanor battery, for tossing you in the Dumpster."

"So arrest him."

"He'll be out in two hours. Then what?"

Encase them in cement up to their necks and drop a bag of hammers on them. From a roof.

"Can't you get them for extortion, or trafficking, or . . ."

I looked down. I had ripped my place mat into curlicues. This wasn't working. I needed to turn my head in a new direction.

"They expect me to get this money for them. When it's time to deliver, what if you're waiting for them?"

She lowered her fork, pondering. "You're suggesting a sting."

"Call it what you want."

"That would involve you. You're supposed to deliver the money."

Not a chance in hell did I want to do that. "You'd

back me up. When they show, you swoop in and arrest them.''

"*For what?* You agreed to pay them.''

"Under duress. To get off that boat alive.''

"At any point today did Toby Price or Merlin or Murphy Ming threaten you with bodily harm?''

I clutched the rim of the table. "You're crazy. You know the threat was implicit. Why are you doing this?''

"So that I'll have a persuasive argument when I take it to my lieutenant and try to talk him into it.''

I reached across the table and squeezed her hand.

"I'll have to think about how to handle this. I'm with Crimes Against Persons. Extortion is Crimes Against Property, our other detective unit.''

"What do I do?''

"Sit tight. I have to kick this up the chain of command.'' She signaled the waiter for the check. "You have someplace you can go tonight?''

"Other than home, you mean?''

"You said the Mings have been dogging you. Think they're really just going to leave you to your lonesome until you show up at Price's boat tomorrow afternoon?''

"Crap.'' I ran my hands through my hair. A toothpick fell out. "Yeah, I can find someplace to go.''

I gave her my cell phone number so she could reach me. The waiter put the check on the table. She took some bills from her wallet.

"Understand, though. No guarantees. On anything,'' she said. "I'll call you. Just lie low.''

And my brain screeched to a halt. *Wedding rehearsal.*

She stopped counting dollar bills. "What's wrong?''

"I have to be somewhere.''

"Don't go.''

"I know.'' Slowly, slowly I leaned forward and put my forehead on the table. "I know.''

*   *   *

"Damn." I hung up my cell phone again.

No Nikki. No Jesse. No Brian—he had taken Luke whale watching. The puppy had been alone all afternoon, without food, possibly out of water by now. I couldn't leave him by himself any longer. I had to go by my place and get him.

Playing it wary, I parked a block away and circled toward the house from a side street. On the western horizon, twilight glowed pink. In the east above the mountains, stars spattered an indigo sky. I slipped into the garden through a break in the back hedge.

When I flipped on a light Ollie yapped, a happy sound, and stood up in his box wagging his tail. I scratched his ears.

"We're going for a ride. Let's get your gear."

His tail wagged frantically.

I found his dog food and his leash. Into a gym bag I threw jeans, a shirt, running shoes, and my laptop. And, acting on hope, I added panty hose, wedding-worthy underwear, and makeup. I was going to miss the rehearsal, but maybe, just maybe, everything would work out and I could make the wedding.

Yes, and Santa's going to bring me that pony next Christmas. I was zipping the gym bag when the phone rang. The machine got it and Nikki came on.

"Ev, pick up."

I grabbed the phone. "Where are you?"

"I just walked in the door. Are you expecting company?"

"No." I twirled, looking outside, seeing the lights on in Nikki's living room but nobody outside.

"Two men are out front. They have a red van and a bad vibe."

"What are they doing?"

"Standing on the sidewalk, staring at my house. Do you know them?"

"Lock your front door."

"Shit." I heard her footsteps as she ran down the hall. "Should I call the police?"

"Yes."

"What are you going to do?"

I stood frozen in the living room. If the Mings wanted me badly enough, they could get to me before Nikki finished talking to the police dispatcher.

"I'm going to split. If I'm not here, they'll go away."

"Then split. Now." Her voice pulled away from the receiver. "Thea, baby, get down. Come here."

I looked out the French doors and across the lawn at her windows. Thea was standing on the chair, little hands pressed to the glass. Nikki came into view and swept her under one arm. On the phone she drew a sharp breath.

"They're heading toward the gate."

I ran to the door and flipped the dead bolt. Grabbing the leash, I rushed to Ollie's box and clipped it to his collar.

"Listen, Ev, I drove past your car, and—"

"You spotted my car?"

"So did these guys. Hard to miss the white Explorer with the broken window. One of them was out of the van, looking at it."

I stopped. "Did he do anything to it?"

"He touched the hood. Like he was checking whether the engine was warm." Her voice stretched with tension. "They're coming down the path."

Holding the gym bag and Ollie's leash, I backed into my bedroom. The puppy fumbled happily around my feet. "Where's Carl?"

"In San Jose on business. They're coming to your door. Oh, Ev . . ."

I pushed open my bedroom window and tossed the gym bag outside. "I'm going out the back window."

"Hurry."

I bent to pick up Ollie. "Just have to get the puppy."

"What? Leave it."

He wriggled under my arm. "They might hurt him."

"Screw the puppy."

"But—"

"Shit, woman, I'll get the frickin' puppy. Go."

I heard the knob turning on my front door, the glass rattling. I gave Ollie a long look and set him on the floor.

"He's in my room," I said.

"They're peering through the French doors."

I climbed out the window and dropped onto the grass outside.

"Uh-oh, they're walking around the side of the house," Nikki said.

"Which side?"

"Right."

I ran left. Heading around to the garden, I aimed toward the break in the back hedge. Behind me I heard murmuring as the Mings circled the house. I squeezed sideways into the hedge, trying not to rustle.

"Get going," Nikki said.

"I'm gone. Call the police."

I hung up, set the phone on the ground, and inched my way through the hedge. I was breaking free on the far side when I heard Murphy say, "Fuck it, she's not here."

"Bet she switched cars. She's being sly," Merlin said.

"Then we keep an eye on her lawyer. She won't stray far from him."

I took off running, with that thought pounding in my ears.

18

Twelve knocks, no answer, but I kept pounding anyway. Brian might have been putting Luke in the tub. The doors at the Fiesta Coast Motel were thin, and eventually he would hear me. I glanced over the railing at the courtyard below. Green and blue lights illuminated the pool and palm trees and the pure sixties decor of the motel. I knocked again.

The door to the room next door cracked open and I heard a voice like cream.

"They're not back yet." Marc stood in the doorway. "Come in."

"Man, I'm glad to see you. I thought you went with them."

"Small boats make me seasick. I drove out to Sandpiper and scrounged together a foursome."

He closed the door behind me. We faced each other in the faux-Spanish room, and the awkwardness switch flipped on. He had obviously jumped out of the shower to answer the door. His hair shone wet, and a line of water was gleaming its way down his bare chest. He grabbed a white polo shirt.

"Everything all right?" he said. "You look upset."

He wrangled the shirt over his head. The planes of his back reminded me of a Shona wood carving, dark and burled and sleek.

"Is it Jesse?" he said.

I rubbed my eyes. "Jesse doesn't know he's upset with me yet."

My cell phone started ringing. I read the display.

"But he's going to go nuclear in about ten seconds." The phone kept ringing. "Listen in; it's going to be a laugh fest."

"Can I do anything?"

"Bust open the minibar and keep those tiny bottles coming. I'm paying."

"Run that by me again. Slowly," Jesse said. "Because I think you just told me that you're trying to set up a sting that might get you killed."

"And I have to miss the wedding rehearsal."

"We've figured that out. Caroline's pulling out her eyelashes. Give me Detective Rodriguez's number; I want to get on her ass, have her commander arrange protection for you."

I gave it to him. "I'm sorry about this. Caroline isn't throwing things, is she?"

"A shoe, but Evan, forget the rehearsal. Where are you?"

I procrastinated, twisting the top off a one-sip bottle of Famous Grouse. Marc sat on the bed, looking pensive.

I tossed back the tiny bottle, draining it. "You have to stay away."

Through the phone I heard voices jousting in the background. And a penetrating complaint about the flowers, which must have come from Brideasaurus Rex.

"Stay away?" Jesse lowered his voice. "Explain that. Please."

"The Ming brothers are watching you. I heard them say they would find me by tailing my lawyer."

"Fuck. So don't—"

More voices, now talking at him. He apologized for his language. I screwed the top off another wee bottle.

He came back on the line. "So don't go home."

"And I won't go to your place. And you're not going to see me until this is done. In fact, I'd rather not even tell you where I am."

The silence on the other end was painful. "This isn't *The Terminator*, Delaney. Mutso and Moonie won't track you down through a phone call."

"I'm okay, Jesse."

"You think they'll hurt me to get to you."

"They'll hurt you, me, anybody they feel like. Maybe you shouldn't go home tonight either."

"Get real. Where am I going to sleep, my parents' couch? Or how about with you? Wait—I can't, because I *don't know where you are*."

There was a long, scraping quiet. "I'm at the motel."

"Good." The relief in his voice was tangible. "Brian will stick to you like gum."

I looked at Marc, and didn't correct Jesse.

"Ev, there's no way these shitheads can tail me tonight. By the time they even got the idea to follow me I was long gone from work. They have no idea where I am."

"But this is how we're going to play it. I'll see you tomorrow."

His voice was grudging. "Okay."

In the background, music struck up. "I have to go. They're practicing the processional." He forced his voice back toward normalcy. "Evan. This is serious stuff."

"I know."

"The cops will try to use you. Make no mistake about that. Watch your back."

"You too."

I set the phone down and pulled my feet up on the chair, hugging my knees.

Marc scanned my face. Without a word he stood and began packing his bag. "I'll stay with Brian and Luke tonight. You take this room."

"Stop. You don't have to leave."

He lifted an eyebrow.

"No, I mean *I'll* stay with Brian and Luke tonight."

He smiled not so enigmatically. "Dang."

I wagged my finger at him. I was flushing. "Pilots. You think everything's a launch signal."

Still smiling, he zipped the bag. "I'll go. You need space and quiet and a hot shower. But I'll stick around until they get back." He picked up the room phone. "What do you want from room service?"

I ran my hands through my hair, smelling the Dumpster. "Anything but Italian."

Rodriguez phoned midevening. I was in Brian's room, playing cards with Luke and the guys. Clouds had blown in, and raindrops pocked the swimming pool. Rodriguez didn't have good news.

"My lieutenant is annoyed that I agreed to the whole thing," she said. "But on the bright side, the commander's now on my butt, thanks to Jesse Blackburn."

"Remind me to give Jesse a big fat kiss," I said.

"I knew he was more than your attorney."

"So where are we on this, Detective?"

"In limbo. Sorry I can't do better than that right now."

"In twenty hours Toby expects me to turn up with twenty-five thousand bucks. Don't let this get buried in administrative haggling."

"I'm working this. Is there anything else you can give me?" she said.

"Would your commander like a puppy?"

"I'll talk to you tomorrow."

I put my cell phone down. Luke was peering at me like a gunslinger playing poker in an Old West saloon.

Brian fanned the cards in his hand. "What do you need me to do?"

"Nothing yet."

"Is this Rodriguez likely to get her act together?"

"That remains to be seen." I nodded to Marc and said, "Hit me."

He dealt me the queen of hearts. Luke, trying to sound cool, said, "Hit me too." Marc dealt him an ace. Luke was fidgeting, scratching at bug bites on his arm. That put me in mind of squirmin' Merlin Ming. I looked at Marc and said, "Again."

He dealt. "Black jack on the red queen."

"This isn't solitaire. The lady's on top."

"Whatever you say. Either way, you win."

"Got that right. Twenty-one." I laid my cards faceup on the table. "Maybe it's an omen."

He gathered up the cards. "We can hope."

Later, lying in bed, I listened to the rain patter on the roof. It was after midnight when the room phone rang on the nightstand. I started. My heart was thumping when I picked it up.

"You're a hard woman to track down."

I sank back onto the pillow. "You startled me."

"I called your cell first," Jesse said.

"I didn't hear it."

"Because it's next door. Commander Marc answered."

I slapped my forehead mentally. I'd left it on the table after the card game.

"Gentlemanly of him to give you a place for the night."

It came out *genlaminly*. I listened to him breathing.

"Jesse, are you okay?"

"The rehearsal dinner was a real piss in the pants. You missed all the fireworks. It was a top-ten evening, total Blackburn classic."

He sounded slick, like he was skating across a glib surface but not getting traction on his thoughts.

"Where are you?" I said.

"The restaurant. Aunt Deedee started crying about

her baby boy getting all growned up and leaving the next."

"Get somebody to drive you home."

"Caroline is wired to her eyeballs. I think P.J. gave her Whites to use for diet pills."

"Is your dad there? Get your dad on the line."

"Sure." The sound went muffled and he said, "Dad, the woman you plan to stone out of town wants to talk to you."

Keith came on. "My son insists you have a good excuse for tonight. But you're going to make the wedding tomorrow. Right?"

"Keith, you need to drive Jesse home."

"Jesse's fine. You worry about getting yourself to the country club by ten a.m."

I ran a hand through my hair. Jesse came back on.

"I'm good, sugar. I'm not drowsy or operating heavy machinery. I'm A-okay."

"How about one of your cousins? I'm dead serious here. Could David drive you home?"

"No prob." His voice veered away again. "David—can I hitch a ride? Evan thinks I'm blasted." I heard laughter and voices joshing with him. "They want me to walk a straight line."

I let my head fall back against the headboard.

"I flunk. All set. Evan, just be careful. I love you."

The phone went dead.

Losers, losers, everywhere. Screwing up his life and thinking they could get away with it. Keeping him down, robbing him of the success he deserved. The hits, the applause—and now the money too. The money, he had a bad feeling, was gone. *His* money, money for *him*.

The Allied Pacific account was fucked; he knew that much. And he hated to think so, but it probably had been even before Brittany. His big moment, and it was starting to look like it was all for nothing.

He was going to fix that. He was going to show

them. It was going to be a blockbuster, and the audience was gonna go nuts. He even had the title track: that song of Slink's. He sang it to himself, watching his reflection.

You're the thorn in my crown
The thorn in my side.

That was going to be him. A sharp fucking thorn.

You're the thumb in my eye.

Absolutely. They just didn't know it yet.

You're the light when I die.

In a blaze of glory. His theme song.

19

Marc knocked on the door shortly after seven the next morning. "You awake? Phone call for you."

I stumbled into my jeans and pushed my hair down, blinking at the cheap motel painting of children in sombreros with sad eyes the size of saucers. When I opened the door, the sun made me squint.

Marc was put together in a button-down shirt and khakis. He handed me my cell phone and a take-out cup of coffee.

"We're on," said Lilia Rodriguez.

I snagged Marc's arm before he got out of reach and gave him a thumbs-up.

"We're still working out the logistics. We'll meet you this afternoon to go over it." She sounded revved up. "Will you be on this number?"

"Yes."

"I'll call. Evan, you're going to be okay."

"Thanks, Lily."

I leaned against the door frame, shaking with nerves and relief. Marc had that laid-back expression pilots get, as if nothing ruffles them, even as they fly fully loaded across a hostile coastline a hundred feet off the deck.

"She's going to work it out," I said.

He glanced past the roof of the motel at the mountains and the sharp morning light, as if absorbing the sky.

"No, we're going to work it out," he said.

"Define *we*."

"You, of course. And your brother and I." His smile was languid, and anything but relaxed. "You know. You've seen what's painted on my tail."

Indeed I had. His fighter squadron's emblem was a red-eyed death's-head with a flaming dagger between its teeth.

"The deputies may claim they have you covered," he said. "But the Vigilantes will have your back."

By eight, things were taking shape. Lavonne met me downstairs in the coffee shop, where she turned on her sternest glower.

"What you've agreed to do is dangerous. Even with the sheriffs nearby," she said.

"I understand."

"You aren't doing it unless you get something big in return."

"I'm getting the Ming brothers and Toby Price locked up."

"I mean from the sheriffs. You don't go near Price's boat unless they drop the assault charge and grant you immunity from prosecution for Brittany Gaines."

"Drop the charge, yes. Immunity, no."

"Yes to both."

"Demanding immunity makes it look like I was involved in Brittany's murder. I've just about managed to convince Lily that I'm on the level. Don't even mention immunity."

She stirred sugar into her coffee. "Lily?"

"Detective Rodriguez."

"Don't get cozy with the cops."

"She's on the up-and-up."

"I agree. But she is not your friend, not in this matter. Be clear about that."

I picked at my bagel.

"Later you can be friends. But today it has to be business and you have to watch out for yourself."

"Yes, ma'am."

"We'll meet the detectives here at three. They're going to want you to wear a wire."

"I presumed as much."

"They'll want you to coax Toby and the Mings into incriminating themselves."

"To confess to murdering Brittany Gaines?"

She nodded.

"I don't know if I can do that."

"What do you doubt, your cunning or your courage?"

"Both."

She drank her coffee, and set the cup down. "I should tell you something. Before this fiasco began, I was planning to offer you a job."

My cheeks felt warm. "Jesse told me."

"Two of my reasons for doing that are your quick mind and your moxie."

"Not my punctuality and perfect spelling?"

She leaned forward. "You can do this. Yesterday on Price's boat you dug deep and held your nerve. Today you'll have armed officers backing you up."

"Thanks for the vote of confidence." I gave her a sly look. "Was that a job offer?"

"Stop talking to cops without my permission, and we'll see."

I felt buoyed, despite everything. I ate a bit of the bagel and decided I could keep it down. So I told her the hard part.

"I'm going to this wedding."

The dress didn't look too bad, really. Pellegrino had lifted out the marinara sauce, and the minty green fabric actually complemented the remaining Dumpster stain: cold-pressed extra-virgin olive oil. Bottled in

Tuscany. Probably by a farmer who could trace his
lineage back to the poet Virgil, so try to tell me I'm
not up to social snuff, Miss Sorority Bride, just try.
Go ahead, bring it on.

I stopped stabbing the eyeliner brush at my image
in the bathroom mirror. Put it down. Good. That's it,
both hands on the counter where we can see them.

Wetting a washcloth with cold water, I pressed it to
my face. Jesse's relatives weren't a pack of jackals.
They wouldn't go for my hamstrings. That would come
later, when I met Toby and the Mings.

Jesse's family would simply go for the jugular.

They already had him halfway to the ground, I
knew, because when he drank it wasn't for pleasure
but erasure. *Walk a straight line.* Sophomoric bozos.
Come here, Hilarious. You too, Sidesplitting. Let's
have you walk a straight line. While I beat you on the
head with the heel of my shoe. Like that? Yeah,
pointy, isn't it?

I ran the water hard over my hands and splashed it
on my face.

I managed mascara and lipstick before my vigilantes
knocked on the door. I called, "Almost ready," jamming a foot into a shoe, twisting my earrings into
place. "Coming, Bri." I turned the doorknob and
hopped around the room looking for my other shoe.
"Can you zip me?"

"I think I know how to do that."

It was Marc. I spun around, embarrassed.

"Sorry. I thought . . ."

"Not a problem."

He was wearing not only a crisp navy blue jacket
and tie but his aviator sunglasses, so that I couldn't
judge his expression. And it was only the last inch of
the zipper. I stood still and felt his fingers grasp the
pull.

"It's been a while since I've done this." He paused.
"Up?"

When did it get so warm in here? "Isn't that the direction the arrow's drawn on my back?"

He tugged it up. When I turned around I saw traces of a smile.

"Thanks. Where's Brian?" I said.

"He can't come."

My nerves popped. "Why not?"

"Luke's sick."

I headed out the door and straight for his room. "What's wrong?"

"Chicken pox."

"No way."

"Those bug bites he was scratching last night? They weren't bug bites."

In Brian's room Luke lay cuddled under the covers. His cheeks were hot and his eyes glowed with fever. Red spots were breaking out across his chest. I sat on the edge of the bed and stroked his hair.

"Hey, champ. I'm sorry you're not feeling well."

"It's all itchy. Can I have a Seven-Up?" he said.

"You bet."

Brian hung up the phone. "That was Nikki. She's got Luke an appointment with her pediatrician in an hour."

I poured Luke's soda into a glass and gave it to him. Brian stepped outside with Marc and me.

"Sis, I have to get him to the doctor. This is a bitch; I'm sorry."

"No apology necessary. I'll be fine. You just take care of him."

He caught Marc's eye. "It's you three, then." He put a hand on my arm. "Be careful. I mean that."

Jogging down the stairs, Marc took my elbow.

"What did Brian mean, you three?" I said.

He smoothed his tie. "Me and my companions. Heckler and Koch."

20

The Cold Springs Country Club adorned a Montecito knoll, draped across the hem of the mountains like an emerald stole. We could see the clubhouse from a couple of miles away, beyond the jackhammers and traffic cones, shimmering on the hillside like a dream. Cruising up the glen past live oaks, we glimpsed the velvety fairways of the golf course. Marc drank them in.

"Jesse's family's loaded, huh?" he said.

"Not the way you're thinking."

I should have kept the edge from my voice. Marc's eyes were still hidden behind the reflection of his aviator shades, but his wide mouth creased in curiosity. I sidestepped.

"His aunt married money, and now their son's marrying money as well."

The clubhouse was modeled after a Medici palace. Red tiles, more arches than a Roman aqueduct, columns that may have been scrounged from Pompeii. Plus fountains and lush landscaping and an eager young man in a red waistcoat and bow tie, trotting toward us to take Marc's keys and park the truck. Marc shoved his semiautomatic pistol securely into the small of his back beneath his belt, and reached for his jacket.

"Idle curiosity," I said. "Are you licensed to carry concealed?"

The valet opened the door for me. "Good morning, ma'am."

Marc adjusted his sunglasses. "Yes. And what's mine stays with me. Not in the glove compartment, where it would be worse than useless." He opened his door and slipped into the coat before the valet could see the gun. His serene facade didn't waver. "Brian warned me you'd get legal."

I climbed out into air that felt richer than down where I lived, and sunlight that landed soft and dappled on my arms. Marc came around the car.

"Any objections I have aren't legal; they're visceral," I said. "Packing at a marriage ceremony just seems out of line."

"Really? The phrase 'shotgun wedding' has no resonance with you?"

"My parents should get so lucky."

They'd scream hallelujah at any event that involved me taking vows, period. Marriage, becoming a nun, joining a coven, whatever. We walked toward the entrance, past waist-high terra-cotta urns overflowing with orange bougainvillea.

Marc held the door for me. "In all seriousness, remember that no matter how bad things get today, you won't, under any circumstances, be allowed to wrest the gun from my hands and shoot the bride."

I felt myself relaxing. Beneath his offhand manner, he radiated confidence.

"How about if I just brandish it at her?" I said.

I went through the door. Inside the foyer the Italianate motif continued. A few members of the wedding party were there, chatting, waiting for directions. Across the room, at the foot of a curving marble staircase, I saw Jesse talking with two young men who had a Blackburn look to them. They were tall and rangy and had gregarious smiles.

Jesse was wearing his best black suit with a silver tie that highlighted his blue eyes, and he looked knock-me-flat handsome. He spotted me coming and, though he continued talking for a moment, his face smoothed with wonderment. He mouthed, *Wow*, and his cousins turned their heads and conversation ceased. They watched me walk toward them across the entryway, looking like they'd been stunned with a Taser. Slowly, thoroughly, Jesse smiled. It was an unguarded, spellbound, plain old lovestruck smile, and though I tried to give it that Grace Kelly cool, I knew I was smiling back.

And I couldn't be sure that these were his cousins Hilarious and Sidesplitting, who thought it cute to crack wise with the crip jokes, but good chance they were. I walked straight up to Jesse and said, "Something knocked this crooked," and, running my fingers around his silver tie, I leaned in and kissed him. I closed my eyes and felt his hands slide up my arms. I looked at him, smoothed the tie, and wiped a smudge of lipstick from his mouth with my thumb. His cousins hadn't moved an eyelash.

Every woman should get such a moment once in her life.

He managed to get out the words *Evan* and *cousins* and *New York*. They pumped my hand like maniacs. Jesse gazed past my shoulder.

"Marc?"

"Good morning." He removed his sunglasses. "Brian couldn't make it. I don't want to step on toes—I'm just going to blend into the woodwork and keep an eye on Evan."

The cousins glanced at each other.

Jesse touched his forehead. "Sorry." His smile had drifted. "Commander Marc Dupree, U.S. Navy."

With a flurry of noise, the bridal herd came through the entrance. Their girlish voices bounced off the atrium ceiling. Caroline led the pack, hair in curlers, bridal gown in a bag over her shoulder. She was surrounded by her mother and Patsy Blackburn and the other bridesmaids, who were giggling at a pitch that suggested they'd already been drinking mimosas.

Patsy wore stilettos and her ice-pink suit. She raised an eyebrow at me. "You're here, and without handcuffs. Wonders never cease."

Caroline's eyes widened. "Huh, the dress looks good on you. It isn't too young at all."

I had the receipt from the bridal boutique in my purse. But Jesse was holding my hand, which kept me from stuffing it down her throat.

Then the swarm descended, dousing me with X chromosomes and perfume and champagne giggles. Had I been this fizzy straight out of college?

Patsy turned her gaze on Jesse. Her mouth contracted to a crimson marble, as if her girdle had suddenly shrunk. "I see I have no sway over you."

She thumbed his earring, tut-tutted, and clipped away. I gave him a what's-with-that? glance. He leaned one hand on a push-rim, looking fatigued.

"The earring isn't the accessory she's tweaked about. Forget it," he said.

Caroline looked at Marc and broke off the giggles. "Excuse me, we haven't met."

Jesse said, "This is Evan's Secret Service agent."

It was going to be a long day.

"Back, back, no, behind Kristi, come on, we're doing this by height. Jesus, Caitlin, did you comb your hair with a Weedwacker? It's too tall for this."

Did I call Caroline an espresso bean? I meant machine gun, set on autofire.

She snapped her fingers at me. "Evan, you're between Lou-Lou and Kelli. Come *on*, ladies."

Her gown was cinched around her with Elizabethan severity. Stick a pin in her, she would have popped and flown around the hallway like a deflating balloon. We were lined up outside the Pavilion Room at the Cold Springs clubhouse, waiting to go in. I could hear music inside, something baroque played on piano and violin.

The girl behind me, Lou-Lou, an ample blonde with a thick New York accent, leaned in and murmured. "He's gorgeous."

"Who?"

"Your Secret Service agent."

My headache was returning.

"Do you work at the White House?" she said.

Caroline stalked around us. "Kelli, chin up. Up."

She was biting her nails. Either that or she was eating the bouquet. Her father milled nearby. We were at T-minus two minutes and counting.

"Hey, there. Don't start without me."

P.J. came sauntering toward us, smiling brilliantly, waving to Caroline. He wore a well-cut charcoal suit, and my first thought was, *All grown up*. Sinsa Jimson was on his arm.

The bridesmaids, the bride, and her father did a double take. The slinkiness factor had jumped by a significant digit. Sinsa wore an iridescent dress that swirled as she walked. The fabric must have been a nanotechnology experiment, because it was submicroscopic. I'm talking uncertainty-principle small. But bare skin was the point of the outfit, and hers was bronzed and smooth, a perfect playing field for her jewelry. An ornate ruby cross hung between her breasts. Her Egyptian hair streamed across her shoulders. The father of the bride, I thought, was about to step on his tongue.

P.J. smiled with such goofball happiness that I almost felt touched. He squeezed Caroline's arm.

Sinsa passed by, greeting me with those sleepy eyes. "Hello, Deadly."

"Hello, Inside Job."

P.J. pulled her along into the Pavilion Room, but her gaze lingered on me.

Caroline leaned toward us. "Do you know who that

was? That's Ricky Jimson's daughter. From Jimson-weed."

The replies came as a crème de menthe chorus. "Oh, my God."

"At *my* wedding." She beamed. "That's going to be in the newspaper."

She stopped, and her eyes went round. She was staring at my dress. "Holy shit, what's that stain?"

With that, the music inside paused and the pianist struck up a new tune. Caroline glared at me. Her father said, "This is it, sweetheart," and urged us forward.

We processed through the door. The Pavilion Room gushed with gardenias and pink roses. From the corner of my eye I saw Marc standing at parade rest by the back wall. I clutched my little bridesmaid's bouquet as if it were a grenade. Mention the stain again, the bride's side gets it. I'll pull the pin, I swear.

I paced, paced, at an even tempo, up the aisle. The other bridesmaids were doing a cagey two-step. Damn Toby Price for making me miss the rehearsal. The bridesmaids' shimmy had a sort of Motown groove, and now that I listened, the tune the violinist was playing sounded like "Chain of Fools." *Chai-chai-chain* . . . Over the heads of the girls ahead of me, I saw the judge, dignified in his black robe. And David, bedazzled and terrified. *Chai-chai-chain* . . .

Jesse was down the line from him. Well, the groomsmen weren't going by height, because Jesse was taller than all of them. You just couldn't tell because he was sitting down. I lost the Motown beat. This explained Patsy's tiff. Jesse was standing up for his cousin—without standing up. She thought he looked out of place. Sheesh. It didn't bother him a bit, or David, but was driving her bananas. Was she embarrassed by him? Embarrassed for him? *Chai-chai-chai-ai-ai-ai-ai-ain* . . . I listened for the beat, and braked to keep from running into Kelli. Kristi. Bambi?

Jesse gave me a bemused smile.

At the end of the aisle we fanned out and took our places. Jesse tossed his head, chasing his hair from his eyes. People forgot his height, how physically imposing he was. And there were times, I knew, when he missed being tall. But walking with the crutches took all his focus and energy. It tied up his hands and kept him from going very far. The paradox of his life was that the crutches could put him back on his feet, but the wheelchair gave him freedom.

The music paused. The pianist broke into "The Ride of the Valkyries." I mean, "Here Comes the Bride." Caroline launched down the aisle. Three hundred guests stood up. Women dabbed their eyes. Caroline approached, and her father kissed her cheek, and David smiled. Funny, he looked happy about being fitted with the nose ring.

The judge gave them a sentimental smile and began. I gazed at Jesse. He took his time gazing back, giving me a wry look. He was good at that look. It was shorthand for, *What about us, Delaney?*

The judge was efficient. For better or worse? Check. Richer or poorer? Check. Till death, cellulite, monster truck rallies, the pool boy, or Internet porn do you part? Check. He pronounced them, and Caroline lifted her veil to seal the deal.

I had tears in my eyes.

I wiped them away, trying not to smear my makeup. It's a terrible secret of mine. I always cry at weddings. And when they play "The Star-Spangled Banner." And at the end of *Armageddon,* when Bruce Willis nukes the comet. The guests were applauding. Jesse was staring at me, baffled.

The ballroom faced gardens and the swimming pool, with the mountains forest green beyond. Light gleamed through the windows. It illuminated the beads on Caroline's wedding dress and the adoration on David's face.

They stood with their parents on the dance floor, greeting guests coming through the receiving line. I caught up with Jesse at the buffet table, where a cornucopia poured out around an ice sculpture of two leaping dolphins.

"Coming down with a cold?" he said. "You looked sniffly back there."

"Recessive gene. It causes nuptial dementia." I hesitated, and decided to bring it up. "Your mom wanted you to park your ride and walk to the ceremony, didn't she?"

"The photos would have looked so much more . . . well. Like she wishes things were. Ah, never mind, they can doctor them, like the Kremlin used to do. Besides, Mom and Dad were already fuming at me."

"Over P.J.'s bail?"

"And that I didn't leap to defend him."

My cheeks felt warm. *But you're defending Evan*, his parents would have said.

"Did you get a load of his date?" I looked around the room but didn't see him; just Keith and Patsy at the bar.

"Sinsa. He's begging for trouble." He made a face. "I'll talk to him."

His hair was falling in his eyes again. He tossed his head but it did no good. I brushed it clear with my fingertips. A crazy thought rushed toward my lips. I'm going to catch the bouquet. Period. If I have to lob grenades at every other woman here.

"Evan."

Marc's bass voice rolled over us. He strode up, his face alert, eyes scanning the room. "What's the schedule like from this point? Food, cake, dancing . . . figure we need to be out of here by two, and it's noon now."

"I'm just going with the flow. Jess, is there a schedule?"

"You didn't get the Eyes Only briefing papers?" he said.

"Missed that," Marc said. "But seriously."

"Limbo competition at four, bridesmaids falling into the pool at five. Sorry you'll be gone."

Someone called Jesse's name. Across the room, David and the other groomsmen were gathering with the photographer, waving him over.

"Excuse me," Jesse said. "The politburo's assembling for photos."

He headed off. I watched him, saying nothing. Marc put a hand on my back.

"Everything all right?" he said.

"Dandy. I need a drink."

The room was filling with guests, the conversational temperature rising. The rest of the bridesmaids were huddling in a pack that giggled and lurched its way around the room. I headed to the bar.

"Champagne," I told the bartender.

P.J. and Sinsa strolled up next to me. Their eyes were bright for each other, their hands loose and familiar. She whispered in his ear and he flushed.

"Two vodka tonics," he said, and smiled at me. "Having fun?"

If Sinsa had a cold drink wearing that dress, she'd get hypothermia. She leaned on the bar and tilted her head toward me.

"Your date's hot."

I took the champagne from the bartender. "Marc's not my date."

"Then why is he scaring off every man who comes within ten feet of you?"

From a bowl on the bar she took a green olive on a toothpick. She put it to her lips and sucked the pimiento out. P.J.'s trousers were about to spontaneously combust. She turned away from him.

She acted as though nothing could touch her. She was showing me, right now, that P.J. was her tool. Flip on, flip off. Did she think she had that much power and protection? She undoubtedly knew that I was onto her record production scam. And she was beyond cool. Which put me beyond uneasy.

But challenging her right now would serve no purpose. I was going to be good.

Well, halfway good. "Marc's a strike fighter pilot with half a dozen kills to his credit. I'd stay out of his way."

"If you say so."

Their drinks came. They clinked glasses.

I nodded at P.J. "Jesse wants to talk to you."

"I'm not hiding from him." He shook his glass, rattling ice cubes. "Evan, I shouldn't really be talking to you. My lawyer says."

Sinsa was giving me a sleepy look and sucking another olive through scarlet lips. P.J. scanned my face. He looked pained.

"I'm sorry. Really," he said.

One of the other bridesmaids, Weedwacker Hair, came up, gushing at Sinsa. "Your dress is *so* gorgeous. Is it Versace?"

"Kasja Benko," Sinsa said.

From Weedwacker's gasp, I guessed that meant it contained remnants of the True Cross. I turned away. Marc was going through the buffet line, but keeping an eye on me. Jesse finished the photo shoot. I asked the bartender for another glass of champagne and headed his way.

I held the glass out to him. "Cheers."

He just looked at me. "Is this an approved departure from your schedule?"

"I have two hours of wedding hilarity left. I'd like to enjoy it with you."

He turned to face me. "You know, I'm going with you to talk to the sheriffs at three. And I'm going to ride along when you meet Toby Price. Did you think I wouldn't?"

I hadn't thought at all, I realized.

"So let's reset the radar to stop painting me as a

hostile blip." He looked past me. "Yup, bandits at twelve o'clock, here comes your wingman."

Marc strolled up with two heaped plates. He held one out to me. "This is some spread. Jesse, your family's generous to let me barge in on the day like this."

"Not a problem."

P.J. walked by.

"Wait up," Jesse said.

P.J. lifted his chin in greeting but kept going. Jesse exhaled, annoyed. I shrugged.

For a moment it looked as if Jesse was going to let it go. Then he frowned. "No, I should do this now, while he's not attached to Sinsa like a tick." He nodded at the plates Marc held. "Don't eat all the hot wings."

He pushed toward the buffet table, where P.J. was munching on tiger prawns. Marc handed me a plate. His face was neutral. I pointed at him with a carrot stick.

"I didn't say a thing," he said.

"Good policy."

"I'm no fool."

Spinning, I headed for empty seats at a table where an elderly couple was chatting with David's friends. I sat and Marc sat next to me, being solicitously silent. I stabbed at crab claws with a salad fork.

The chair next to me scraped backward and the dress from beyond the laws of physics sat down. From the corner of my eye I saw Sinsa's crow hair swing down off her shoulders.

She had an asparagus spear in her fingers. "They couldn't be more different, could they?"

My eyes bugged.

She nodded at the buffet table. "P.J. and Jesse."

They were talking. Sunlight refracted through the dolphin ice sculpture, shining on their faces.

"Brothers often are different," I said.

"It's funny. They look so much alike, have the same

mannerisms. You must wish their situations were reversed."

I put down my fork. "No, I don't. Not ever. Are you baiting me?"

Marc shifted in his seat.

Sinsa reached past me, offering him her hand. "Hi. Sin Jimson."

My head was humming. Be good, I told myself. I lowered my voice so that David's friends and the elderly couple across the table wouldn't hear.

"Are you picking a fight with me?"

"Tell me you don't think about it. Taking P.J. for one night, just to remember what it was like," she said.

My glue was loosening. "Fine, you want to do this here? Now? Go ahead, I'm up for it."

"Meow. Did you miss your kitty treats this morning?"

"You took fifteen K from Toby Price, for payola. He wants me to pay it back to him with interest and penalties. And I'm not going to let you get away with it."

She flipped her hair again. She didn't keep her voice down. "P.J. goes all night long, like a cordless drill. Tell me that's not what you're missing."

The entire table shut up and stared at her.

She bit into the asparagus. "Jesus, I'm teasing. He's my handyman."

Somewhere behind me, the dance band started tuning their instruments. But even the New York Philharmonic couldn't have overcome the dazed silence that hung across the table. Which was why I heard, suddenly and clearly, Jesse and P.J. arguing.

"You didn't back me. That's the bottom line," P.J. said.

"This has nothing to do with whether I believed you or not," Jesse said.

"It has everything to do with that. Mom and Dad had to take out a loan to cover my bail. You could

have done it out of the cash in your pocket, man."
P.J. put his plate down on the table. "But that's no
surprise. You care more about Evan than your own
family."

I was on my feet.

Jesse pointed at him. "Don't talk about Evan. She
went to bat for you from the moment you turned up
wasted in a bathtub, and what does she get for thanks?
She gets thrown in jail. She gets Skip Hinkel jamming
her up."

P.J. raised his hands. "You aren't laying this on me.
I have to do what my lawyer tells me."

He took a step away. Jesse swung out and blocked
his path. I was heading toward them.

"Get out of my way," P.J. said.

"Don't be an asshole."

"No, *you* don't be an asshole."

P.J. turned away. Jesse grabbed his arm. I walked
faster, but it unfolded in front of me with excruciat-
ing clarity.

P.J. tried to pull free. Jesse held on. P.J. seized
Jesse's tie. Jesse grabbed P.J.'s lapel. P.J. pulled Jesse's
hair.

Across the room, Patsy yelled, "Stop it."

Too late. Neither one of them would let go. Jesse
chucked P.J. off his feet, and went flying along with
him.

They hit the buffet table. Plates broke, a waitress
shrieked, the table shuddered. The band stopped tuning up. The ice dolphins dove from their pedestal and
shattered on the floor.

Patsy waded through the crowd, shouting, "Stop it.
Stop it."

I stood six feet away. They lay tangled on the
ground. P.J. was shouting and flailing. Jesse had him
in a headlock.

Marc pushed past me. He hauled P.J. to his feet
with a skill that told me he'd broken up fights before.

He bear-hugged him away from Jesse, saying, "It's over, man. It's finished."

Caroline and David pushed through the edge of the crowd. She gasped at the crushed ice sculpture. P.J. thrashed in Marc's arms.

His face was mottled. "He started it. He grabbed me."

Marc squeezed him. "No pride in this. You win nothing for fighting with him."

Patsy burst through the throng with Keith at her shoulder. She tottered on her stilettos, gaping at the mayhem.

"What have you done?" She clawed at her suit. "What is wrong with you? Goddammit, Jesse."

The guests glared, watching Jesse work himself to a sitting position. Patsy turned and stumbled back through the crowd. David and Caroline stared at the ruined table. Caroline covered her mouth. She turned her head and David led her away.

Jesse leaned on his arms, closed his eyes, and hung his head. Marc was holding tight to P.J., calming him down, until finally P.J. sagged and held up his hands.

"I'm cool. Let me go," he said.

Marc waited a few seconds and released him. P.J. stalked off, slammed open the patio door, and stormed out to the veranda. After a moment Sinsa ran after him.

The crowd dribbled away in embarrassment. Jesse reached for the wheelchair and flipped it upright. Waiters and the maître d' bustled in from the periphery to clean up. Jesse hoisted himself into the chair. A busboy with a broom and dustpan started sweeping up broken plates.

Jesse looked at him. "I'm sorry."

He peered around and spotted David and Caroline. She was hunched under her father's arm, shuddering with tears. Jesse took a breath and headed toward them.

Marc touched my elbow. "You all right?"

"Hell, no."

Outside, P.J. had sunk onto a bench near the pool. Sinsa sat by his side, cradling him. His hands sawed the air. He spit words, staccato and inaudible. Across the ballroom, Jesse was apologizing to Caroline and her parents. They couldn't have looked more unforgiving.

From the bandstand, a guitarist picked at a chord. "All right. Let's get this celebration into swing." The keyboard began an arpeggio. "Come on, this time everybody hits the dance floor. We're Avalon, and we're here to party."

My heart hopped. I turned and looked at the stage. Merlin Ming stood at the microphone with a guitar in his hands.

21

What a big band. They were bigger than I'd thought. Drums and bass and keyboards, guitars, sax. Murph on the kit, and Merlin playing lead, counting off, one, two.

He turned and spotted me.

They hit the opening chord of the song, and swung straight into it. Merlin was strumming with vigor, catching all the chord changes, and his eyes were pinned on me.

"Marc," I said.

His face was severe. "Is that them?"

I was backing up. "What the hell are they doing here?"

His hand wrapped around mine. "Easy does it. We're going to leave, but we're not going to run."

My legs wanted to jackrabbit. Merlin cut his eyes away from me to his guitar, his fingers sliding up the neck. His round little shoulders hunched to the beat. His leisure suit was powder blue. He turned his face from the mike and mouthed something. Murphy, pounding on the drums, lifted his face and looked out across the crowd.

"Now," I said. "I want to get out of here."

Marc's hand steadied me. "We're cool. These guys just hit the first chorus. They're not going to interrupt the song to come after you. So let's just stroll on out of here."

People were taking to the dance floor. We wound our way among them, walking toward the door. The only thing that kept me from bolting was Marc's hand, clasping mine.

I leaned toward him to be heard over the music. "I have to warn Jesse."

I scanned the crowd. Jesse was across the room near the door, by himself, looking drawn. Looking, I saw for the first time, like his father. Beaten down.

I tried to speed up and Marc held me back. Jesse caught sight of me. For a second he looked relieved. But he blinked, and his expression clouded. Without a word he pushed back, hard, out of the room into the hall. He turned and was gone.

I knew what he'd seen: me, on the dance floor, hand in hand with Marc Dupree.

Shit. Shit. I wrenched loose and pushed my way past dancing couples. The bridesmaids were doing a group squiggle in the center of the floor. I reached the far side of the room, near the bar. The song was hitting its final chorus.

Marc reached for me. "Maintain, Evan."

Sinsa brushed past me, going to the bar. "Gotta hand it to you. You're alpha."

"What?" I said.

"You managed to set all the dogs against each other. You're top bitch."

Up on the bandstand Avalon was swinging. Murphy rode the beat, right foot kicking the bass pedal, drumsticks hitting the cymbals, shaven skull bobbing in time. His gaze slid my way. Behind his drooping mustache, he wet his lips with his tongue.

I pulled Marc from the ballroom into the hall. The music dimmed.

"Don't run," he said.

"I have to find Jesse. And I have to talk to him, alone."

He was nowhere in sight. I headed for the entrance.

Marc jogged to keep up. "No can do. The Secret Service doesn't work that way."

No Jesse in the atrium. In the ballroom Avalon's song echoed to an end. There was a smattering of applause, and the band switched gears into a Bee Gees tune, too fast. I headed out the door into the sunshine. Across the drive, Jesse was slamming the door of the Mustang.

I walked past the urns with the orange bougainvillea. Marc shadowed me.

I stopped. "Wait. Here. Please."

He shook his head, frowning. The Mustang fired up.

I put a hand on his chest. "If the Mings come out, shoot their disco boots off. But let me talk to my boyfriend alone."

It sounded adolescent and insufficient. *Boyfriend.* I should have said *lover.* Meant to say, *my heart.* Knew the word I needed was *husband.*

Jesse backed out of the parking slot, turned the wheel, and saw me. I ran into the driveway in front of him and put both hands on the hood.

"Wait."

The engine idled. It felt churlish and powerful, rattling through my hands and up my arms. Jesse's face was exhausted and remote. The stereo was up high. Springsteen, *The Rising.* It sounded dark and harsh.

Jesse put down the window. "I don't want to do this, Evan."

"I'm getting in."

"No. I'm done. I'll have Lavonne go with you this afternoon."

"The Mings are here. That's them inside, butchering 'Stayin' Alive.' "

He glanced at the clubhouse, and at Marc fuming outside the door.

"They saw me," I said. "They may have seen you, too."

His shoulders rose and fell. He looked at me. "I'm going."

"I'm with you."

I ran around the car and got in. Shut the door. Marc marched toward us. Jesse gripped the gearshift. He was waiting for me to say something. One word. I was that close to getting tossed out. I gave Marc an apologetic glance, and held my tongue.

"Okay then." He floored it.

We thundered down the driveway. Gold light and green shadow strobed across us. I checked the wing mirror and saw Marc running behind the car, sprinting but losing ground. After a dozen strides he gave up. He changed tack, waving to the parking valet.

"Do you see the Mings?" Jesse said.

"No, but that doesn't mean they aren't coming."

"We're gone. They won't catch us."

We roared out onto the main road. The Mustang's engine sounded raw. "Worlds Apart" coursed from the stereo, a hard melody of loss and anger. I watched the live oaks streak past.

"I know I'm an idiot," I said. "I blew it, big-time."

The road curved. He took the bend hard, and I pushed my feet against the floor, but I had no brake pedal. He straightened the wheel and the car leaped down the road.

"Where does he get off, telling P.J. there's no pride in taking me on?" he said.

"Jesse, you—"

"And don't say it. Just don't. That was the stupidest, rudest thing I've ever done in public, and I'm dogshit in my family for the next century." He checked the mirror. "I had P.J. He was done."

"I know. And thank you for taking my corner."

"It was a fight. Straight up. I didn't need Roger Ramjet wading in and saving my ass."

"I get the feeling he's pulled people out of fights before. He meant no disrespect."

"Right, strutting around with his lock-and-load attitude. Wearing those fuck-me shades."

"All right, enough." My shoulders tightened. "This isn't about the U.S. Navy."

"No? Then what is it about?"

The white line on the road was a blur. The stereo was hurting my ears. I turned it down.

He turned it back up. The car heaved over a rise in the road.

"You're going too fast," I said.

No response.

I reached for the stereo and hit the eject button, put down the window, and threw the CD out. His mouth opened in astonishment. But he didn't stop.

Her. It was her, Evan Delaney, here at this la-di-da Montecito wedding. Her and her little friend. He watched her run out of the room, and he wanted to run after her, but they were in the middle of the song, so he kept playing, and shit, they had to do something, now.

He turned, keeping the beat. Murph was steady on the kit, but looked like he had a plan. Murph always had a plan, made them up right on the spot. That got them into trouble sometimes, with Toby. Got *him* into trouble, 'cause even Toby was scared of Murph and wouldn't yell at him. So he got his ass chewed instead.

Final chorus. They ritarded. Murph did a little roll and fade. Merlin worked his shoulders. Shit, stuff like this made him itch.

The next song on their set list was "Isn't She Lovely," but Murph stood up and told the guys, " 'You Spin Me Round.' Acoustic." Murph pointed at him with his drumsticks. "Come on." Merlin's nerves jumped.

The guys slid into the Dead or Alive shit, no questions asked. He and Murph hopped off the bandstand and went out into the hall. Murph pulled him toward the entrance.

"You saw Delaney?" Merlin said. "She shouldn't be here, middle of the day. She's supposed to be getting the money. What's she pulling?"

Murph stuck his drumsticks in his back pocket. He was thinking. Hard, Merlin could tell. They came to the entrance and looked outside.

"Don't know," Murph said, "but we're going to find out."

They saw him in the sun, the black dude. Looking pissed off. Standing at the parking valet's podium, while the valet phoned to have his car brought around.

"Yeah," Murph said. "We're going to find out right now. Come on."

Jesse gaped at the rearview mirror, watching the CD spin across the asphalt behind us. "Why'd you do that?"

"That album makes you angry and depressed. And it was giving me a headache."

"You're blaming the E Street Band?"

We were coming down the glen, back toward city traffic. My stomach was cramping. He had the Mustang running flat out.

"You're in danger. It's because of my brother. How could you think I would let you face it alone?" He stared out the windshield. "Do you want me on your team?"

"Don't say that. You and I *are* the team."

"I'm not blind, Evan."

I felt two inches tall. "I know."

"And I will not play second string. Not with you."

"That's not what's going on."

He looked at me. "Delaney. You came to the wedding with another man."

I saw it ahead, where the road curved left—the line of orange traffic cones Marc and I had passed driving to the wedding earlier. The job site was now empty.

I saw the sunlight turning through the canopy of the
live oaks. I felt the car going into the bend. Late.

"Jesse."

He braked. The tires grabbed for the road and
missed. He threw the wheel, but the back end of the
car danced to the right and swung out from under us.
We skidded sideways into the cones, flying down the
line. They spewed around us one after another, *bam
bam bam,* flying up like bright scattershot. The view
out the windshield panned to trees and the golf course
and the road back where we'd been. Jesse hung onto
the wheel but we were gone.

22

We spun, tires screaming, off the asphalt onto the shoulder. Dirt blew over the car and in my window. The air went brown, stinging my eyes, and I felt Jesse hanging on and trying to stop the car, but we were slaves to acceleration. The trees were coming at us through the flying dust.

I prayed. God, please. We were going backward, loose and helpless, bouncing over the dirt. I waited for it.

And without a sound, we came to rest on the shoulder. Dirty and stunned and unscathed. The engine guttered, ready to rumble some more.

The dust settled outside like a brown veil, clicking onto the roof and hood, clearing to a view of light glowing through the trees, and strewn orange cones, and skid marks. Jesse gripped the wheel, breathing hard.

"You okay?" he said.

I listened to the engine and the dust shirring down.

"Evan." He clutched my arm. "Are you all right?"

I saw him. He wasn't hurt. But he wasn't okay.

I opened the door. I tried to get out but couldn't stand up. I looked down and unbuckled my seat belt.

I got out of the Mustang and stood by the roadside. My legs felt like a newborn foal's, ready to buckle. The air seemed to be knocking me around. Looking back in the car, I saw Jesse leaning across to my side, his face dazed.

He wasn't anywhere close to okay. He was only close to the edge. And I could see only one way to get him back.

"Go home," I said.

"Did you hit your head? Are you hurt?"

I walked away from the car, heading down the glen toward town.

He called my name. I walked. The light was intensely bright. Where the trees shaded the roadside, puddles lingered. The engine dropped into gear. He pulled alongside.

"Please get in," he said.

I shook my head. The Mustang inched alongside me.

"Please. I'll drive slow. You can drive. We won't drive; we'll just talk. Please."

The engine growled. It sounded as if it were ready to eat me.

"I'm not getting back in this car. Nothing you say can make me."

"Evan, I'm sorry."

I didn't look at him. "You're going to kill yourself. I can't be with you when you do it."

A raw silence bled around me. Jesse's voice was empty. "Marc's going to be here in a minute. Go with him."

I nodded. He kept pace, until finally I said, "Go."

"When I see his truck coming."

I stepped in a puddle without meaning to. After a minute we heard a vehicle coming down the road from the direction of the country club. It was Marc's truck.

"Ev."

"Just go."

He pulled away.

The silence in the glen felt sharp. I waited, and as Marc's truck drew nearer I hugged myself, because I was about to lose it. I hated the thought of unraveling in front of Marc, every bit as much as I wanted to cry on his shoulder. The truck slowed and stopped. I walked toward it.

The doors opened, and the Mings stepped out.

Two beats, count 'em, I stood by the road. What had they done to Marc?

Didn't matter. They were going to do it to me too. I ran like a stone flung from a slingshot.

Murphy ran too, with real linebacker speed. He clipped me from behind with a low tackle that threw me off my feet. I landed flat, splashing in a puddle. The breath clapped out of me. My elbows scraped open on muddy gravel. I got to my knees to crawl but the skirt of the dress tangled around my legs. Murphy jammed his foot between my shoulder blades and stomped me down again.

"Where's the money?"

I writhed but he put weight on his leg.

Gut check. I couldn't lose it. "The money's all set."

Merlin paced back and forth. He was a powder blue rodent. "She's lying."

"What's your problem? I'm not supposed to pay Toby until five o'clock."

Murphy dropped onto my back, straddling me. It was like having a two-hundred-pound mattress draped across me. I could hardly breathe.

"You said you needed till five to get the money transferred. Instead you dicked around, coming to this froufrou wedding." He waved at Merlin. "Check her purse. See if it's in there."

Merlin grabbed my small purse and dumped out the contents. He kicked my lipstick and cell phone into the puddle.

"Nothing."

I turned my head toward him. "I couldn't fit twenty-five grand into that tiny purse. Give me a break. You know how big a wad that much cash makes."

He kicked my key ring, picked up my wallet, and pulled out all the cash I had, sixty-four bucks.

"You haven't done jack," he said. "Lying bitch. You played us again."

He threw the wallet at me. And he threw the money at me. He spun in a circle, little hands pawing his thinning hair.

"Toby's gonna kill us, Murph. We are so fucked."

Murphy's hip bones pressed on my ribs. "Calm down."

"We were supposed to keep tabs on her, make sure she was doing what she was supposed to," Merlin said.

"Shut up," Murphy said.

"What we gonna tell the boss, we saw her at our gig? Right, keeping tabs on her, we catch her all prettied up partying with her pals, having a good laugh at us?"

I looked at him. "The money's ready to go."

"We seen you there, talking with your partner." He stalked in a circle.

"If you mean Sinsa Jimson, you're—"

"You were figuring how to hose us up the ass." Without warning he changed direction and slapped me hard across the face.

My head snapped sideways. He slapped me back the other way and my vision fireworked white. The pain caught up with the shock and drove my thoughts away to the edge.

Murphy said, "Jesus, chill down."

But Merlin had sprung a valve. "We're screwed. So screwed."

He squatted down in front of me, grabbed me by the hair, and shoved me facedown into the puddle.

Straight through cold brown water and down into the mud and pebbles at the bottom. Eyes, nose, mouth shoved under. Panic hit me.

He yanked me up by the hair. "Screwed. 'Cause of you."

Air. I inhaled, choked, coughed. "No. I'll—"

He shoved my face back down. I heard a splash this time before my nose and mouth hit the mud and sank in.

My right arm was free. I swung wildly and tried to lever myself up, but Merlin had plenty more leverage to keep me under, and Murphy was on my back. I clawed my fingers into the water by my mouth, into the mud, trying to scoop it away. It was too deep. I grabbed dirt and pebbles into my hand and flung them blindly, trying to hit Merlin. My lungs burned. I grabbed again, fingers catching on my key ring. I closed my fist around it and swung, trying to stab him with a key, something.

They were too strong. I was drowning in an inch of water. Jesus Christ, it hurt.

Merlin's hand jerked off my head.

I pulled my face out of the puddle and gulped air. Mud was caked in my nose and mouth. I spit it out, coughing. Had I hurt him? I blinked, tossing my head back and forth to clear the mud from my eyes, and saw him sitting on his butt in front of me. I breathed, frantically.

Merlin's shoulders were chugging up and down. His face was red. Maybe I got him in the nuts.

Murphy was pointing at him. "Not that way."

No, I hadn't hurt Merlin—Murphy had knocked him down. Murphy's hand settled on the back of my neck. It was hot, and the size of a catcher's mitt.

He leaned close to my ear. "I'm going to give you a choice."

In dreams, I try to run but my legs stick, as if the air is glue. At that moment the nightmare broke the bounds of sleep. I couldn't make my limbs move. Murphy leaned close to my face. He had two drumsticks clenched in his hand.

"How do you want it?" he said.

This was no dream. I fought.

I kicked, I thrashed, I bucked my head back. Murphy said, "Hold her down." Merlin got to his haunches and pinned me by the shoulders. Murphy unzipped my dress. Cool air pricked my skin, and I felt Murphy's clammy hand running up and down my back.

He lay on top of me. I sounded like an animal, groaning and thrashing beneath him. The hand with the drumsticks slid down my ribs and past my thigh and rustled beneath the fabric of my skirt. I screamed through my teeth.

His mouth touched my ear. "You fucked us, we fuck you. How do you want it?"

His hand climbed up my thigh under the skirt. The drumsticks traced a line along my leg. I clawed the dirt, trying to pull out from under him with my fingernails alone, but he covered me like a flesh blanket.

I squeezed the words through my teeth. "The money. I'll get it."

"What?"

"The bank. I'll take you."

His mustache dragged across the back of my neck. His lips were moist. "That's not your choice."

The drumsticks rode along my skin. Murphy grunted. His breath was damp on my neck, and his crotch was hard.

Don't cry. Don't cry. Weakness won't win.

I needed time. We were by the side of a road, for God's sake. A car had to come by soon. Shit, in this Montecito glen where privacy and isolation went for seven frickin' figures. But if I could stay alive, somebody would come along.

But not before he raped me with the drumsticks. They stroked the edge of my panties. Don't cry.

One chance, that was all I had. That they feared Toby more than anything else.

"*Your* choice," I said.

"What?"

My mouth was full of mud. I spit. "We get the money, or not. *Not* makes Toby mad."

Murphy laughed. He sounded incredulous. "You don't get to give out the choices."

"Yes. We get the money. We take it to Toby. We finish this. Or he'll be on all our backs. Bad."

Merlin stopped pacing. Murphy lay still. But he was hard, and his hand was between my legs.

"Let me get it," I said.

They seemed to be thinking about it.

"Think. If you . . ." My voice faltered.

Don't say *rape*. Don't say *beat*. Don't say *kill*. Don't give them ideas.

"If you mess me up then I can't get the money, and he'll be mad at *you*. It'll be your fault."

I let my face sink to the ground. My ears were ringing. Their voices ping-ponged, whining. They were talking about it. So much noise, like a drill in my head.

Murphy shifted on my back. "Which bank?"

Think of one. "Wells Fargo. Downtown."

Merlin's feet scuffled near my head. I was drooling. Just don't cry.

"It won't work," he said. "If she goes in looking like this, they call the cops. We're hosed."

"And whose fault is that?" Murphy said.

"If we go in with her, we're on film. We wait outside, she calls the manager," Merlin said. "She's shining us on."

"No," I said. "We end this. Today."

Murphy inched the drumsticks under the lace and ripped my panties. I squeezed my eyes shut.

"Prove it. How do we know the money's there?" he said.

I needed something tangible, any kind of proof. My keys were in my hand. I held them up. "Safe-deposit key."

It was my little bike lock key, mixed in with the

rest, but it looked odd enough that it just might convince them.

Merlin yanked the key ring from my hand. "It's been in a safe-deposit box the whole time?"

"Put it there this morning."

"What's the number?"

"I'm not telling you."

Murphy inched the drumsticks between my legs. Don't cry. Don't.

"We all go together," I said. "I'm not an idiot."

Merlin jangled the keys in his hand. "I don't know."

Murphy thought about it. "Yeah. We do it."

Don't cry. Not yet. Not out yet.

From up the road I heard the sound of an engine. Finally. Coming from the direction of the country club.

Murphy still lay on my back. "Let's go. Get her in the truck."

I strained to hear the engine. How far away was it? Could be a mile. A minute, ninety seconds away.

I went limp. Let them drag me. Let whoever was coming see that.

Murphy grabbed my left arm and stood up, trying to pull me up with him. I drooped, making myself deadweight. The engine drew closer.

"Hurry," Merlin said.

I hung from Murphy's hand. Moving just a little, pretending to comply.

Murphy smacked me in the face. I moved faster. He looked up the road. The car was coming, weaving past the scattered traffic cones. The lights flashed and the horn honked.

"Who's that?" Merlin said.

Don't cry, not yet. I crawled to my knees. "Vigilante."

"Fuck. Fuck."

It had to be Marc. It was the bride and groom's getaway car, with tin cans tied to the bumper and *Just Married* written on the windshield in shaving cream.

Merlin flailed his hands. "She screwed us. I told you."

Murphy held me by the wrist. "We aren't done with this."

The wedding mobile knocked through the toppled cones. Two hundred meters and closing. Marc extended his arm out the window, gun in his hand. I was okay now, scared to death, but dizzy with relief.

Merlin waved his arms. "Murph, let's book."

Murphy looked down at me. "Fuck you."

He hit me in the jaw, a huge punch. The lights split inside my head. He struck me again. I felt myself land on the dirt. Then he unleashed blow after blow. I tried to raise a hand but he held on to my arm and kicked me in the ribs, kicked me in the stomach. He wrenched my arm, getting leverage for another blow, and I heard a loud pop. I felt pain and uselessness.

I heard a gunshot. Again. Again. Murphy dropped me.

I fell on my side, head flopping in the puddle. Shoes scuffled away. Heard car doors slamming. Truck engine, roaring off, gravel and dust spewing in my eyes.

I lay on the ground, one side of my face in the water. I didn't move. Breathing was agony. It felt like a hot iron bar had been run through the bones of my arm and shoulder.

I heard, dimly, the wedding car braking to a halt. Feet running toward me. Felt a new hand touching my hip.

"Don't move." Marc's voice was a blanket of calm. "Can you hear me?"

I moved my lips. All I could see was red and yellow light. The world tasted like mud.

"Can you feel your arms and legs?" he said.

I could. But when I tried to shift my arm, it just hung. "Uh-huh."

"Hang on."

I felt him gather me up and lift me off the ground.

I crumpled against him, head on his shoulder. He carried me to the car and lowered me in. I still couldn't see his face, or much of anything. But I felt his hand touch my cheek.

"Motherfucking bastards," he said.

I cried.

23

The ER doctor said, "Take a deep breath." But breathing killed. I held still instead, sitting on the examination table with the nurse bracing herself against me and the doctor maneuvering my arm, getting ready to pop my shoulder back into the joint. His touch was torment.

He yanked. It went loud and quick, with a crack and a flashing sensation through my whole body. He lowered my arm and felt the shoulder and the elbow.

"Got 'em. That reduced both dislocations."

The nurse helped me lie down. I curled onto my side and she draped me with a blanket. Still, I shivered. The lights in the treatment room seemed cold. Remarkably, the pain in my shoulder was diminishing. But my arm felt useless. I felt useless.

The nurse's voice was quiet. "The police are here to talk to you."

"Okay."

She put her hand on mine. "When we took off your dress, we saw that your panties are ripped. Did the men who attacked you—"

"No."

The dress was smeared with muck. Looking at it made me feel slutty. The nurse's hand rested on mine, cool and insistent.

"They didn't," I said.

Two SBPD officers interviewed me. They were polite, but their blue uniforms crowded the room. I lay on my side with my knees pulled up. I could talk if I kept my teeth together.

They were about to leave when I asked whether Marc was in trouble. "Commander Dupree. About the wedding car."

"Ma'am?"

Outside the country club, the Mings had jumped Marc from behind. They wrapped a phone cord around his neck, tethered him to the parking valet's podium, then hopped in his truck and took off after me. Marc fought his way loose and forced the parking valet to give him the keys to the wedding car. At gunpoint.

"Afraid I don't know anything about it, ma'am."

The next hour passed in a haze. The doctor brought X-rays. I had broken ribs and extensive internal bruising. They admitted me for observation overnight. They taped my ribs and immobilized my shoulder, and took me upstairs to a room. Getting into bed hurt worse than having the dislocations reduced. They gave me heavy-duty painkillers.

Eventually Brian came. One glance at his face told me how bad I looked. His eyes were so black they practically glowed. His voice was barely a whisper.

"Those fucks are going away. Make no mistake."

I blinked. The drugs hadn't reached the pain yet, and talking hurt.

"I should have gone with you," he said. "If I'd been there, none of this would have happened."

"No. My fault."

"Absolutely not." He stared at the bruises and cuts on my face. He took his time. "Marc saw you leave with Jesse."

"Don't."

"Why shouldn't I?"

His voice was rising. The old fight was once again in front of me, and I had no strength left for battle.

"What happened? Where is he?" Brian said.

I gaped. What did he mean, where was Jesse? "Doesn't he know?"

"Marc tried and couldn't get him," he said. "Evan, did he leave you there alone?"

"No."

"Don't cover for him."

Behind him in the doorway, Marc appeared. "Delaney."

Brian hated to disengage. From the heat in his eyes I knew he had his target in sight and wanted to lock on. He stood by the bed, clasping the rail with both hands.

Marc walked to the bedside. "This is neither the time nor the place."

He had removed his jacket and tie, and his white shirt was blemished red with blood where my face had lain against it.

I looked at Brian. "I got out of the car." I shifted, wincing. "Jesse begged me to get back in. I wouldn't."

"Why?" Brian said.

"None of your business." As if they couldn't guess that we'd argued. "We saw Marc's truck coming. We thought it was safe."

"He should have—"

"Stop," I said.

Marc put a hand on Brian's shoulder. "Take five."

Brian looked ready to resist, but Marc's hand was firm. Brian nodded, gave me a reluctant look, and left. Marc exhaled.

"Thank you," I said.

"I don't deserve it. I was a lousy bodyguard."

"You showed up. That's enough."

Carefully, he brushed a lock of hair off my forehead with his index finger. His face was solemn. The pain in his eyes embarrassed me. I didn't want this attention, people's sad stares.

"You were tough out there today," he said.

"No, scared shitless."

"That's what bravery is. Keeping your head and executing when it's scarier than shit. And you did, which is why you're alive."

I couldn't stand hearing this. I had different words to describe myself. Foolish. Cocky. I had misjudged the risk and overestimated my abilities. Leg speed and fast talk counted for nothing with people as brutal as the Mings. Nothing I did could stop them. I had tried everything, and they beat me to hell anyway.

Like a wave the tears rose again. They stung my eyes and face where my cheek was cut.

"Damn. Ow."

I blotted at them with my good hand. Marc took out a handkerchief and dabbed my face. He smoothed my hair.

"You have nothing to be ashamed of. Hear me? You were overmatched, and you got out."

"Great. Next time I won't fight as a heavyweight."

His brown eyes refocused, taken by surprise. He smiled and shook his head. He covered my hand with his, stroking it.

"Do you not know that you are amazing?" he said.

He lifted my hand to his lips. He kissed my palm. He kissed my wrist. He kissed each of my fingers in turn, his lips lingering on my skin.

It was incredibly touching, and sexy, and emotionally bewildering. I didn't pull away.

He looked at me. "That's just because you deserve it."

I felt thrilled and wrong and frighteningly at peace, all at once. Marc's gaze steadied on my face. He lowered my hand to the bed.

"You rest. Brian and I will be right outside all night."

When he was gone I lay silently, focusing on nothing for a long time. I could feel the drugs taking effect. Dulling the pain, dulling my brain, until I didn't care about broken and dislocated bones, only about the drowsiness luring me. I knew I was going out. I held on a minute, thinking, and the nurse came in. She asked if there was anything I needed. There was.

I couldn't reach the phone. I asked her to dial Jesse's number for me.

Jesse sat on the beach. It was cold. Too cold to swim, but being near the water cleared his head. The breakers rolled white in the reddening light. The sun was halfway down. He'd been out here for a long time.

He watched the sun thin to a gold lacquer on the ocean. Dusk came, chill and blue in a sky that emptied to infinity.

He saw two choices. One led to his life emptying out like the sky, blue to black to absolute zero. The other led he didn't know where. Maybe to the sun coming up. Maybe right back to this place he'd been for so long, a chronic twilight where the pain stripped him bare and ghosts beseeched him deep at night. He didn't know which choice was harder.

The breakers rolled, on and on. Finally, when nightfall swallowed his shadow, he headed back to the house.

I couldn't reach him. His home phone just rang and his cell was switched off. The drugs were hauling me toward sleep, and I couldn't last any longer. I asked the nurse to have my brother keep trying both numbers. I drained into the darkness.

24

The phone rang, and he ignored it. It stopped. He turned on a lamp. It brought up his reflection in the plate-glass windows. His hair was wrecked with wind. His eyes looked sooty. What a picture, to quote his mom.

The phone rang again. Persistently. Fifteen, twenty rings. People knew that it could take him a while to pick up, but usually nobody insisted like this. Finally he answered it.

Lilia Rodriguez sounded ticked off. "Evan didn't show for our meeting today."

It knocked him on his ass. "That's not possible."

"She didn't show at the harbor, either. And unless she's with you, we're looking at a world of trouble," she said. "Because the Mings did show at the harbor. And we've got a one-eighty-seven."

"Say that again?"

"You heard me."

The walls went crooked. One-eighty-seven. That was the California Penal Code section for murder.

Not at home, not at Nikki's house, not at Lavonne's. Her cell phone was out of service. Where was she?

He phoned the Fiesta Coast Motel, both Brian's room and Marc Dupree's. He called everyone. She was nowhere. He grabbed his car keys.

He drove to the motel. The rooms were upstairs,

and it took him five minutes to find the fucking elevator. He pounded the doors so hard and shouted so loud that other guests began poking their heads out to see who the wacko was. He went back down to the parking lot.

The hole started forming in his stomach.

He tried her phone again. He got back in his car and jammed the key in the ignition. He stopped, trying to slow down his heart.

But the thought devoured him. One man was dead, and Evan had vanished somewhere between Cold Springs and the harbor. And the Mings had been driving Marc's truck, Rodriguez said—the truck he'd seen in his rearview mirror as he drove away from her. God. Fuck. Fucking hell.

He could phone Rodriguez and tell her to check the hospitals. But once he did that, he knew where else she'd check, and he couldn't face that thought.

He had a single option left. He had to retrace their path, starting back on the road where he'd spun out. He fired up the engine. He dropped it into drive and went ripping out of the parking lot. One last time.

Late that evening I roused from thorny dreams, hearing voices in the hallway. I squinted at the door. My eyes were swollen nearly shut, and I couldn't focus.

I swam back to sleep, but when a nurse came in I said, "What's going on?"

"Checking your blood pressure."

I thought about the voices and said, "Lily Rodriguez is here."

She wrapped the blood-pressure cuff around my arm. "The sheriff's detective? Honey, that was three hours ago."

"Oh." I closed my eyes. "Did Brian get Jesse?"

She ripped off the cuff, taking a long while to answer. "Everything will keep till morning."

Her gentle tone unaccountably disturbed me. "What's wrong?"

"Nothing. Let's get your pain medication."

But something was amiss. I swallowed the painkillers. I tried to unravel my sense of foreboding, but my mind and spirits were tangled by the drugs. A vision swept past, of a black wing cutting through my life and cracking open the sky.

"You sleep," said the nurse.

The specter fled. I lay in the dark, feeling my heart pound.

I knew what the phantom was. It was death. Only when I woke in the morning did I learn how close it was.

25

Light was creeping through the window. Outside the door the breakfast cart trundled down the hall. The television was on, with the sound muted. That was odd enough. It took me half a minute to focus my eyes sufficiently to see that the local news was reporting a murder.

I fumbled awake. On the TV I saw a shot of the marina. Sailboat masts and last night's sunset. By the gate a sheet covered a body. The camera zoomed out, and I saw a slick of blood trailing back to a truck. Marc's truck.

I moved, and my body groaned. The pain had drilled to the core and spread wide. I blinked at the television. A reporter was interviewing a witness on the dock. The woman talked and pointed toward the body. I groped for the remote control. I mashed my palm against the buttons and the sound jerked on.

"—moaning and shouting," she said. "I came up on deck and saw the one guy on the ground and the other running past my boat, screaming at somebody."

She pointed to the far end of the dock, where Toby Price moored his boat.

"Then the police drove up, with all the lights and sirens. And he dove off the dock in his clothes and everything."

A reporter came on, thin and brusque. "Police continue to search for the dead man's companion. The victim's name is being withheld pending notification of the next of kin."

My head thudded. I exhaled.

"It was Merlin Ming."

I turned. Jesse was sitting in the easy chair beside the bed.

"Murphy's the one who dove into the marina. The Harbor Patrol hasn't found him. And Toby's boat is gone." He rubbed his eyes. "I hate having to tell you this."

From the state of his clothes and the way he was slouched in the chair, I guessed that he'd been there most of the night. A couple of pillows were shoved behind his back, and his feet were propped up on the seat of the wheelchair.

"Merlin?" I said.

"Bled to death from a gunshot wound."

Along with shock, I had a spooky sense that Jesse was here only by providence. The black wing and broken sky sliced through my thoughts so sharply that I felt pain.

He straightened up. "And the news has it wrong. It isn't a murder."

"No?" I glanced at the TV, showing the slick of blood. "Don't tell me it's suicide."

I didn't like the look that crossed his face when I said that word. He pulled his feet down, reached over, and lowered the rail on the bed.

"No." He swung over to sit by me. "It's justifiable homicide. Marc shot him."

I let my head fall back on the pillow, remembering gunfire as Marc drove up in the wedding car.

"They haven't arrested him, have they?" I said.

"No, but he's at the station answering questions." As if to soothe me, he added, "Lavonne's with him."

He was being magnanimous. Very much so. I closed my eyes.

"Marc's going to come out of this okay," he said.

"The DA may give him a rough ride, but Marc had cause. The best cause."

"Murphy." My throat felt tight. "He said it wasn't finished. And now—"

"There's a police officer guarding your room. Rodriguez badgered SBPD into sending him."

My nerves began vibrating. My eyes stung yet again. I squeezed back tears.

"Okay."

He put his hand on the blanket near mine. "Toby's running. And Murphy may have drowned."

"Do you believe that?"

"Toby's gone and isn't coming back. He'll be arrested as soon as he runs out of weed and Oreos and sails into port someplace to resupply."

"But Murphy."

Jesse never sweetened things for my benefit. "I don't know."

I drew a painful breath, getting a good look at him. He seemed far beyond exhaustion. His voice was calm, but jarringly so, like the eerie quiet at the eye of a hurricane. I couldn't bring myself to start the conversation we needed to have.

"How'd you convince the nurses to let you in the room overnight?" I said.

"Georgia knows me. From when I was here."

What an understatement. "When he was here" encompassed critical internal injuries, a broken pelvis, compound fractures of both legs, and crushed spinal vertebra. He came in that evening with a paramedic riding the stretcher on top of him, pressing on his femoral artery so he wouldn't bleed out. He faced multiple surgeries, weeks in ICU, followed by a long stretch in the Rehabilitation Institute.

I felt like a sissy.

Jesse had borne more than I could stand to consider, and I had never seen him cry about what happened to him. I was going to walk out of here this

morning, and I was close to mewling. I tried to blank
my face and herd the tears back down my throat. I
failed.

I covered my eyes with my good hand. Jesse shut
off the TV and eased my hand away from my face,
leaving me no choice but to look him in the eye.

"Yesterday was a cascade failure," he said. "One
thing slamming into the next until, boom."

"I wish we could erase yesterday."

"We can't."

The urge to cry was growing. His hand lay on mine.
I held intensely still so that I wouldn't sputter. He
kept my gaze.

"And coping with yesterday is going to absorb your
strength, and fear, and anger, for a long time," he said.

I breathed.

"Tell me what you want me to do," he said. "Do
you want me to leave?"

"No." I took hold of his arm. "God, no."

Relief seemed to flicker behind his eyes. It was the
first expression I'd been able to identify on his face.

He held on to my arm. "Then I want to get you
out of here, and get you mending. Everything else will
wait till you're up to it."

"You don't have to baby me."

"Ev. You took care of me. Let me take care of
you."

I squeezed his arm. The impenetrable mix of fatigue, sorrow, and distance on his face was still giving
me pause.

"We have to talk," I said.

"I know."

"Are you angry?"

"I'm so far past furious that not even light could
catch up with me," he said. "But not at you. At the
men who did this to you."

He let go of my arm. He reached for the wheelchair
and hopped on.

"Let's find out when you can blow this joint." He pressed the call button for the nurse and took out his phone. "Shall I see if Nikki can bring you some clean clothes?"

"Please."

Staying busy was how he kept his mind off of things. Working, coaching, swimming—noise and motion were his hiding places. And at that moment I was glad for it.

Or not. The nurse came in, and through the open door I saw the uniformed officer outside the room. The nurse smiled, and we talked, and she patted Jesse on the shoulder and asked if I wanted breakfast. Surprisingly, I did. She bustled out, and Jesse spoke on the phone to Nikki.

"She'll be over soon," he said.

I gazed at the door, fretful.

He looked up at me. "If my car . . . Nikki can drive you home. I don't have to."

"That's not it," I said. "Are the police going to put a guard on my house?"

"For a few days."

"But not beyond that."

"No."

I knotted the blanket in my hands. I felt an urge to lock the door and jam a chair under the knob. Jesse leaned on his knees, focused now.

"Brian and I are working on it," he said.

I almost remarked about the unlikelihood that they could work together on anything, but his expression stopped me. Finally a look I recognized: pure ferocity. I knew he had given Brian that look when he arrived. Brian would have stepped aside when he saw it. Without a word.

"He's doing T and E," he said.

Test and evaluation. With Brian's job, that involved air combat maneuvers and studies of weapons lethality.

"What's he evaluating?" I said.

"Recoil. I need something that won't dump me flat on my back when I fire."

He was buying a gun. I didn't say anything, but he felt the need to reassure me.

"Evan. These guys are not going to get you. Not while I'm alive."

That was what worried me.

26

Monday morning the alarm clock rang at seven. Jesse
turned it off and lay for a few seconds, rubbing his
eyes. The sun was shining through the shutters in my
bedroom. He caught me watching him, pulled closer
to me, and propped himself up on an elbow. He
stroked my good shoulder, one of the few places on
my body that didn't ache.

It was all the touching I could stand. Almost every
other inch of me howled. My shoulder and elbow had
improved, but seemed to lack any strength.

Jesse had been here since bringing me home from
the hospital. He hadn't left my side. And we still
hadn't talked. Not about the spinout, the attack, us,
anything. I brushed the back of my hand across his
face. He looked half-asleep.

"I'll make coffee," he said.

He got out of bed, careful not to jostle me. Before
heading to the kitchen he came around to my side
and pulled the quilt over my shoulders.

"Thanks," I said.

A minute later I heard the coffeepot turn on, and
the television news. He returned to the bedroom and
set the morning paper on the bed within my reach.
Soon enough the hot water ran in the bathroom, and
through the open door I saw him shaving. He was
getting ready for work. I pulled my knees up and huddled deeper into the quilt.

Nikki would be going to work today, too.

Brian and Luke would be over soon, but Brian had to return to duty. They were going home this morning.

A uniformed police officer was parked outside my house in a patrol car, and would be for another twenty-four hours. The sun was shining. If I opened the windows, I could hear the birds singing in the trees. But I didn't want to open the windows.

Jesse had bought a handgun, a Glock nine-millimeter, but couldn't get it until a background check went through. Damn laws. Damn lawyers, abiding by them.

Marc had to stay in town until the police finished their investigation into the shooting death of Merlin Ming. His gun lay beyond reach in the evidence locker at police headquarters.

I wanted protection.

I cringed my way out of bed and padded into the bathroom to brush my teeth. Seeing myself in the mirror no longer horrified me. I was black and purple ripening to green, with a cut through my eyebrow and a busted lower lip. I was hideous, but I was used to it now.

Jesse looked at my reflection. "I can drive you to your dentist's appointment."

"That's okay. I need to give driving a try."

I grimaced in the mirror. Five chipped teeth, including the top front. I looked like a hillbilly. I put a hand on his shoulder, squeezing in next to him at the sink. His skin was cool, and under my hand his collarbone was prominent. I realized again that he was too thin.

Thin, and tired, and unnaturally composed. He was here, supporting me, virtually carrying me. But he wasn't all here. His turbulence was gone, and I didn't know where, or why, or if it would return. Its absence left me ill at ease.

He was knotting his tie when Lilia Rodriguez knocked on the door. Monday mornings agreed with her. She was fresh cheeked, wearing a cheap brown suit, and the cowlick was asserting itself. I was still dressed in one of Jesse's Blazers Swimming T-shirts and pajama bottoms.

"Good news," she said. "The assault charge is going away, Evan."

"About time," Jesse said.

"In light of what's happened, especially with your brother, it's—"

"What about my brother?" he said.

"Exculpation." She caught herself. "I assumed he'd told you."

He hadn't spoken to his family since the wedding. The cold war was on.

"P.J.'s in the clear over the murder?" he said.

"The crime lab found evidence that's taking us in another direction."

"What was it?"

"That I won't say."

They must have recovered evidence from the scene, or from Brittany Gaines's body, belonging to the killer. Fibers, hairs, DNA—and it didn't match P.J.'s.

I said, "Have you put out a warrant on Murphy?"

"All kinds. But none for murder yet."

Jesse and I exchanged a glance. Either they had insufficient evidence to get the warrant, or they didn't think it was Murphy.

"What about Sinsa?" I said.

"Cynthia Jimson? Nothing."

"Have you checked out what I told you?"

"There's no evidence to tie her to the murder. Nothing to tie her to the stolen checks, or to the fake Evan Delaney bank account, or to the ID theft."

"Lily, she's involved."

"Granted, she knew Brittany Gaines. But we can only draw a business connection. She was producing Brittany's demo. Not a thing connects her to Toby. *Nada*."

"That's it? You have nothing else?"

"She caught the bouquet."

Jesse and I both stared.

"At the wedding. Oh, and there is one weird tidbit going around. Not about Cynthia but the car she drives, the BMW four-by-four. And this is wicked weird. Somebody put dead ravens on the engine block."

She described it. I wondered whether Shaun Kutner had put them there, or the Mings. Or Sinsa herself.

Lily patted my arm. "I have to go. I really just wanted to check in and see that you're doing okay."

"I'm splendid. Stick a tiara on my head and call me Miss Universe."

Nobody laughed.

"Any leads on Toby and Murphy?" I said.

"There's a statewide BOLO." Be on the lookout. "They'll turn up."

"On my doorstep, I'm afraid."

"You have my card. Call me anytime."

We said good-bye and I watched her go, thinking, *Anytime?* When Murphy came through my bedroom window, a business card would be worth jack. My skin felt the memory of him. Tongue, sweat, meat.

Jesse put a hand on my back. Wholly without volition, I shrank from his touch.

"Sorry, didn't mean to hit a sore spot," he said.

"Not your fault." I ran my hands up and down my arms. "I'm going to take a bath."

"Need a hand?"

"No." I needed to hurry. I needed to get clean.

Bending over to turn on the faucet proved too painful just then. But I was having to bathe rather than shower, because I was supposed to keep the tape around my ribs dry. I squatted down next to the tub and tried to stretch, but my balance was shaky.

Jesse angled into the bathroom. "Let me."

I sat on the edge of the tub. The bathroom was barely big enough for the two of us, and he had to lean around the sink to reach the taps. He checked the temperature and watched the tub fill. I huddled on my perch.

"Want me to help you get the shirt off?"

I shook my head.

His gaze lay lightly on me. "I know you're a modest Catholic girl. But, sugar, I've been making you scream for a while now."

I had to make the effort. I scooted toward him. And he was right; I needed help. I managed to get one sleeve off, but couldn't raise my injured arm high enough to do the other side. Even though this was a big shirt, one of his, plenty loose across the chest.

He teased the neck of the shirt over my head and eased it down my arm. Every brush of his hands against me was like hitting a nerve. I kept shying from him.

He bunched the shirt on his lap. "If it's this painful, you should see an orthopedist."

"That's not it."

He turned off the water.

"I feel disgusting," I said.

His voice was quiet. "Why?"

The water dripped. The way water had dripped from my face into the mud puddle while Merlin held me by the hair, while Murphy lay on my back. I yanked the shirt from Jesse's lap and fought my way back into it. I had to be covered. I had to be dry.

He looked bewildered. "What's wrong?"

"Murphy."

I hadn't told him, hadn't told anybody, but he saw it on my face. He went ungodly still.

"Evan."

The water was dripping. "Turn that off. Please. I can't stand it."

"What did he do to you?"

I looked away. He tightened the faucet.

"Did he touch you?"

He put his hand to my cheek and turned my head back. I stared at his chest.

"Yes," I said.

His hand stayed steady on my cheek. I kept my eyes on his shirt. And I told him. The hand like a catcher's mitt. The drumsticks. The ripped panties. Murphy.

I waited for him to smash something, or to back out of the bathroom in revulsion. At length I looked at his face. I saw pain, as though he had taken a physical blow. And anger that he pushed away. Compassion came into his eyes.

"Whatever you need," he said. "Whatever you want me to do."

Finally, for a moment, I felt safe. Not safe from everything lurking outside my front door, but safe with him. I pulled him close and laid my head across his lap. He put a hand on my back. I let go.

How long I stayed there I don't know. Finally I said, "You're going to be late for work."

"It's okay. Do you want to get back in bed?"

"I want to take this bath."

He added hot water and held my arm while I got in the tub.

"If you don't want me to touch someplace, shout," he said.

He wet a washcloth and stroked it across my back. He smoothed the soap along my arms and legs, taking care not to dampen the tape. I held my damaged arm against my side. When he was done, he clasped my hand and helped me out of the tub. I felt better.

He wrapped me in a towel, and asked if I needed help getting dressed. I told him I could manage it. I dried off and put on some sweats. I went out to the living room and found him with Brian. Jesse was holding a semiautomatic pistol in his hand, loading the clip into the butt of the gun.

*　　*　　*

They paused, looking like schoolkids caught smoking in the boys' room. Outside, Luke was playing with his fingerboard, practicing skateboard skills on a three-inch version of the real thing. He was covered with red chicken pox spots, but his fever had broken and he looked perkier. I walked over to Jesse and Brian.

"Great," I said.

Brian jammed his hands in the pockets of his jeans. "It's mine. I have a permit. I'm merely lending it to Jesse until he gets through the background check and—"

"Excellent," I said. "Do you have more ammunition?"

They exchanged a glance.

"This box," Brian said.

"That's only twenty rounds," I said. "Jess, can you pick up some more? At lunchtime?"

"I guess," he said.

"You're leaving it with me today, right?"

"Okay."

He cleared the chamber, clicked the safety, and set it down on the table. I rested my hand on it. It felt solid, and warm where Jesse had held it. I would have taken it straight up to the firing range and spent the day practicing head shots, if not for the fact that I didn't want to step outside the door.

They swapped looks again, and Jesse held out a hand to me.

"Call me. For anything," he said. "I'm fifteen minutes away." He looked outside, and a wistful expression came over him. He called to Luke. "Hey, polka-dot dude. Have to tell you good-bye."

Brian walked him to his car. When he returned, I had the sense that they'd been discussing things. Such as me. Brian stared surreptitiously, as though I had grown a third, beady eye. With a gunsight attached.

"If there's any way I could stay, I would," he said.

"I know."

He refilled my coffee cup. I warmed my hands on the mug.

"How long does Marc think he'll be in town?" I said.

"Few days at least. He hasn't been by?"

With Jesse staying here? Ha. I shrugged and drank my coffee.

Brian leaned against the kitchen counter. "You want to tell me what's going on?"

"Nothing."

"Sis. Dupree's a cool customer, but he's blatantly crazy for you."

I felt miserable all over again. "Marc saved my life."

"Marc's a hell of a guy. And he's not after gratitude," he said. "And the way you were flirting with him the other night at the motel, you let him think he's going to get what he is after."

I ducked his gaze, looking outside at Luke. He had earphones on and was listening to a tiny audio player.

I waved at him. "Hey, where'd you get that?"

"Jesse gave it to me."

I recognized it. It had Hendrix, Clapton, Creedence— Jesse was starting Luke's indoctrination.

"Turn it up," I said.

Brian pulled out a chair and sat down at the table next to me. "I have to hit the road in ten minutes. We don't have time for evasive maneuvers. So I'm going to fire this at you, head-on."

I pulled my knees up. "Watch out. Let me activate my cloaking device."

"Why don't you marry Jesse?" he said.

"Oh, brother."

"Do you love the guy?"

"Yes."

"So what's stopping you from getting hitched?"

"When did you become my yenta?"

"I have nine minutes left."

"He drives you bonkers half the time," I said.

"I'd take that as a glass-half-full scenario, if I were you."

I slumped back in my seat.

"Let's cut to the chase. Are you waiting for him to get his legs back?" he said.

"No." I looked at my hands. "That's not going to happen."

"Then are you afraid of what it would be like to be married to him?"

"His disability isn't an issue."

He weighed that, nodding. "Shall I tell you what I think?"

"As if I could stop you."

He pulled his chair closer to mine. "I think you're allergic to permanence."

My eyebrows jumped up toward my hair. It hurt. "What?"

"Look at how you've structured your life. You do freelance work. You live alone. You hop from job to job."

"You think I'm some kind of emotional gypsy?"

"Blame our itinerant childhood, or Mom and Dad getting divorced. And me as well."

"I don't like your nine-minute love diagnostic."

"My point is, you always plan an escape route, so that at any time you can blow. Eject, eject, eject."

"That's ridiculous."

"Really? You picked the one man you'll always be able to outrun."

I stood up. "You're a son of a bitch."

"And when you turn around, who do you line up with?"

"I'm not listening to you anymore." I walked into the kitchen.

"A pilot who goes out of sight at Mach two."

I leaned on the counter and let my head drop. Brian came over to me.

"I may be a son of a bitch. But I'm a smart one."

He put his arm around my shoulder. "Things are crazy enough right now. You don't need more excitement in your life. You need to cool things down."

I tried to resist his hug, but gave in, putting my head against him.

"But I can't cool things down as long as Avalon's still around." I laughed without humor. "Don't you get it? I'm being pursued by a wedding band."

At three I stepped outside to go to my dentist's appointment. The garden was still. Sun was gentling on the hibiscus. Playground noise roiled from the school up the street. It emphasized Luke's absence. And beneath it I seemed to hear whispers—the voices of Merlin and Murphy, slinking around the side of my house in the dark, saying, *She's pulling something sly*.

I set the burglar alarm and struggled with my house keys. With my left arm in a sling, I had to lock the door single-handed. The garden gate swung open, and I jumped, adrenaline slamming my heart. The keys fell from my hands. I picked them up and stabbed them at the lock, frantically trying to open the door.

The police officer who was guarding the house came through the gate. He was carrying a spectacular flower arrangement.

"Hope you don't mind," he said. "The florist was delivering these. I took the liberty of intercepting him."

I stood shaking like a paint mixer. "No. Great."

The flowers were extravagant—red snapdragons, white lilies, yellow roses in a vase wrapped with a velvet bow. I couldn't carry them with one arm. I couldn't even see straight. The officer brought them in for me and set them on the dining table. I thanked him and locked the door.

The snapdragons looked sinister. The lilies made me

think of death. My nerves were vibrating all the way up in the register only dogs can hear. What if Toby had sent the flowers, as a warning?

I called the dentist and canceled my appointment. Then I took Brian's gun into my room, set it on the nightstand, wrapped up in my quilt, and lay on the bed, listening. I was still there when Jesse turned his key in the front door at six thirty.

"Ev?"

"Back here."

He leaned through the doorway, face half shadowed by the bedside lamp.

"Gorgeous flowers. Who sent them?" he said.

"I didn't look."

His gaze lingered. "I'll check."

That got me out of bed fast, ouch, ouch. When I got to the living room he had the card envelope in his fingers. He raised an eyebrow, asking permission. I nodded.

He opened it, read the card, and his mouth skewed. "We're safe." He handed it to me.

Feel better soon. Love, P.J.

The next morning the officer guarding my house went off duty. He told me good-bye. I heard him start the engine of the patrol car. And drive away.

I straightened up the living room, and made my bed, and put on another pot of coffee. Listening. Keep the stereo and television off, that was the thing to do. Don't make any noise that could obscure the sound of people approaching.

Breathing, for instance. Breathing was noisy. Just hold your breath, Delaney.

Nikki stopped by at lunchtime, bringing me my mail. She had the puppy on a leash. He strained at it and wound around her legs. She looked unusually whimsical.

"That's because I have news that will cheer you up. We're going to keep the pooch." She smiled and bent to scratch Ollie's ears.

"You're a pal," I said.

"I'm going to go whole-hog. Enter him in dog shows. Knit him a little tartan blanket and Tam o' Shanter." The fanciful smile remained. "Nah, Thea loves him. Thanks, Ev."

After she left, I went through the mail. Bracing myself for unwanted bills, screaming demands for repayment, and, of course, offers to sign up for new credit cards. I sorted through the envelopes. Mine, mine, junk, junk. And a manila envelope. Addressed to Rowan Larkin. I felt it, making sure there weren't any wires attached, and ripped it open.

It was the paperback of my novel, the one Toby had deconstructed. It was now physically deconstructed. The cover artwork had been defaced. My name had been scratched out with a knife. Most of the pages had been ripped out. But one chunk remained: the chapter where Rowan's soldiers were massacred. The page describing their deaths had been circled in fat red marker. An arrow was pointing to the worst atrocity. An angry hand had written, *YOU, BITCH.*

Motion at the door, and a knock. I leaped, practically clawing my fingers into the ceiling.

Marc stood outside. He was holding a bouquet of purple iris. Beneath his aviator shades he wore his enigmatic smile. When I opened the door, it vanished.

"What's the matter?" he said.

I handed him the manila envelope and paperback. I balled my hands and pressed them against my forehead. He hung his shades in the collar of his polo shirt, his demeanor stiffening, and read the envelope.

"Postmarked Los Angeles."

My fists were knocking against my forehead. "Jesus, Jesus, Jesus."

He led me to the sofa and sat me down. I heard him on the phone, calling the police. Then he sat down beside me.

I squeezed my hands between my knees. "It isn't over. Murphy said that it wasn't, and he's making sure I know."

He put an arm around my shoulder. I felt his strength and chill heat. His brown eyes held a merciless calm; he was wearing his game face.

"I'm going to cover your six. Twenty-four by seven," he said.

I felt relief and thankfulness and a yearning for him that came on like fever. That was as scary as anything. "Thank you. But I need something else."

"Tell me."

"Target practice."

He nodded. Clasping my hand, he stood. "Come on."

He took me to the firing range up in the mountains off West Camino Cielo. When we checked in and went out to the range he laid out Brian's gun, the magazine, and a box of nine-millimeter ammunition.

"Have you ever fired a gun?" he said.

"Of course. I'm a military brat. I want to be sure I can hit a moving target. In the dark. Fifty times in a fricking row."

He picked up the gun. "This is your weapon. A Beretta semiautomatic pistol." He put it in my hand. "Hold it. Get used to the weight."

I had been carrying it back and forth from the living room to the bedroom, so I wasn't surprised by the weight, a couple of pounds. And the cool. The metal felt good in my hand.

"Okay," Marc said. "Can you get by without the sling for the next hour?"

I took it off.

He led me through it. Loading the clip. Racking the slide to chamber a round. Safety on, and off. Adopting a stance, feet shoulder-width apart, knees slightly flexed. Two-handed grip, left hand bracing the right.

He put a hand on my injured elbow. "Arm all right?"

"Fine."

"Hold it," he said. "Feel the weight. After only a short time it can affect your aim. And if you're in a situation to fire, you won't be calm. Patience." I knew all this, but having him run me through it calmed me.

"The main point is commitment," he said. "If you draw your weapon, that means you're in a life-or-death situation. You shoot to kill. Not to wound, or wing, or frighten. Do you understand?"

"Absolutely."

"Do you? You can't falter. You have to commit. Sometimes women . . ." He put up his hands. "Don't take offense at what I'm going to say. My ex took a self-defense course, and this is the point the instructor drilled home to the gals in the class. Women can let compassion trip them up. They'll hesitate, pulling back at the last second, not wanting to inflict the fatal blow."

"That won't be my problem."

I held the pistol out. He steadied my arm. He radiated a blue-star intensity that went through me like a burn.

"Marc, I . . ."

Eyes on me.

I didn't know what to say. I didn't know what I felt. I remembered Brian's warning to cool things down.

His eyes held mine. "What?"

I adjusted my grip on the pistol. "Anything else your ex gleaned from the class?"

He held quiet for one beat, then two. His hand slipped off my arm. "Beyond ten feet, most shooters won't hit you. If you're unarmed, your best option is escape."

"I'm planning to be armed."

"Then plan to get within ten feet of your target, so you'll have a chance of hitting it."

"Gotcha."

He pointed at the paper target out on the range, and stepped back. "Take your shot."

I aimed at the silhouette of a human form. Exhaled. Squeezed the trigger. Again, and again, and again. But it was just a target. No resolution. With anybody.

27

I don't believe in luck. I believe in chance, but I think we make our own luck, good or bad. And I was about to live the luckiest day of my life.

By the end of that week I was improving physically. Ibuprofen was keeping the ache in my broken ribs under control. I could straighten my arm without pain, though I was still using the sling when I was up and about. My face had mellowed to green and brown. I hadn't received any more threats from Murphy. I had scrounged together enough courage to go out in the yard by myself. But I still didn't want to drive more than a block from my house.

But my time and energy were tied up with keeping ahead of the identity theft. More bills were coming in. More checks had bounced. And though I wasn't liable for any of it, I was constantly contacting new batches of creditors with affidavits proving my innocence. It looked as though I was going to have to go to court to get an official declaration that I was not involved with the fraud.

I was chasing the debts. The thieves—presumably Brittany, P.J., Sin, and Shaun, the fab four—had been opening new accounts one after another, simply running up charges to the limit, then abandoning the account and signing up for new credit cards in my name. The only way I could keep up was by checking my credit report every day.

The fraudulent accounts were being shut down once I notified the credit agency. But each time new charges were posted, I enjoyed the pleasure of reading them on-screen like a bill. It was infuriating. Until Monday. That was when I got the hit I'd been looking for.

Proof. Purchases made *after* Brittany Gaines died.

Outside, the live oaks flickered under a cool wind. I leaned toward my computer, scrolling down the screen. Another thousand for the Beverly Hills Day Spa. Two grand at a men's clothing store on Rodeo Drive. A hundred bucks from an outfit called Bloomsberry. Three hundred at Coast Medical. Twenty-eight hundred at Collezioni Benko, also Beverly Hills. And the biggie, the one that gagged me: eleven thousand–plus dollars to Tropical Holidays World Travel. The thieves liked to travel. First-class, apparently. To Barbados. I saw sugar-white beaches and orchids dripping from the ceiling and sweet cocktails with fruit and little umbrellas in them. Now laid at my doorstep. I ground my jaw and stopped, feeling my broken, yokel teeth.

Calming down, I went through each of the charges in detail. I looked at the bills from the Beverly Hills clothing stores. One men's, one women's. My head began throbbing. I got on the phone and called up the shops. They confirmed my suspicions.

One man's suit, charcoal gray, hand-tailored and guaranteed to make you look all grown-up. One Kasja Benko dress, designed to suspend the laws of physics. They were the clothes P.J. and Sinsa had worn to the wedding.

I felt excited. Here was the first bit of evidence tying Sinsa to the identity theft. Of course, she could claim that P.J. bought the dress for her and that she had no idea the purchase was squirrelly. I thought back to the wedding, Sinsa's effusiveness and affection toward P.J. Perhaps it was because he had found a way to become her sugar daddy. But I doubted that P.J. was in this alone. I read further through the new credit card charges, feeling a niggle at the back of my mind.

"Oh, no."

From the dining table I got the card that had come with the flowers. I snarled. *Bloomsberry.*

And I had written him a damned thank-you note. I returned to the computer, continuing to read the expenses listed. Tropical Holidays World Travel. P.J. hadn't been out of town recently—had he? I didn't know. But, staring at the computer screen, I got a sick feeling about the rest of the bill. It couldn't be, I thought. Tell me no.

But when I phoned Coast Medical, they told me yes. I grabbed my car keys.

P.J.'s roommate didn't expect me to kick their apartment door open when he tried to close it in my face. Neither, frankly, did I. He backed away from me, blinking. I stalked in after him.

"I said, where is he?"

"Honest, I have no clue."

I picked up the bong from the coffee table. Stinking water sloshed in its base.

"If you don't want me to baptize you, you'll tell me."

He kept backing away. "All right, all right. He went out to some fancy restaurant."

"Which one? Think about it. Hard. Now."

The stud in his bottom lip juddered, and a thought seemed to click into place behind his eyes. "He called to double-check the reservation." He pointed to the phone on the kitchen counter. "Push redial."

And my, my, was I surprised when the maître d' answered at the San Ysidro Ranch. P.J. was going so far upscale he'd shot off the chart. And probably on an Evan Delaney credit card.

"Confirming a reservation," I said. "The name's Blackburn."

"Party of two? Yes, one o'clock," he said.

I hung up, unplugged the phone cord, and stuffed it in my purse.

"Hey," said the roommate.

"P.J.'s lunch is not going to be disturbed."

Not by the roomie, that is.

The San Ysidro Ranch is tucked into the greenery of the Montecito hills, and, pulling in, I knew my clothes were all wrong. Jeans, cowboy boots, and an old denim shirt I'd grabbed from Jesse: yeehaw. But the Ranch hasn't worked cattle since the 1800s. Nowadays it works celebrities and power players. It's where Vivien Leigh and Laurence Olivier were married, and JFK and Jackie spent their honeymoon. Guests come expecting foie gras and ayurvedic massages, and the Stonehouse Restaurant has a reputation as one of California's best. It's a classy place, which was why the hostess managed not to gape when I walked in looking like an extra from a John Ford western, with my bruised face and my arm hanging in the sling.

"May I help you?" she said.

"I'm joining Mr. Blackburn."

A look of pity and understanding came into her eyes. She led me into the restaurant.

Across the crowded room P.J. sat at a corner table by the windows. His back was to me. Sycamores shaded the view beyond him. I didn't recognize the young woman sitting across from him, a big-boned girl with Raphaelite curls and a lively light in her eyes. But I recognized P.J.'s charcoal gray suit. And I recognized his ride, the Quickie wheelchair he'd rented from Coast Medical.

He was pouring white wine into the young woman's glass. She was listening to him, nodding intently.

"Booking the studio time," he said, "and hiring the band. I know you're tight with the guys you've been gigging with, but for this you need pros, session players from L.A."

She bit her lip with apparent excitement. She was beaming at him like a mystic having a vision. He was basking in it.

My temples were thudding, my black eye throbbing, but for the first time since the beating I felt no pain. Only heat. I pulled out the chair next to him and sat down.

"And the producer won't come cheap, but is he ever sweet. He's—"

"Boo," I said.

I saw shock on his face, and a streak of fear that went away when he inhaled. So. Game on.

"Nice suit," I said. "Aren't you going to introduce me?"

He paused just long enough that I knew he was calculating. Warily he gestured at the young lady across the table from him. "This is Devi."

I extended my hand to her. "Howdy. Kathleen."

She had a guileless face, and didn't suppress her surprise at my appearance. "Wow, what happened?"

"Didn't he tell you? No, but he wouldn't. He's a sensitive person." I set a hand on P.J.'s arm. "And he respects attorney–client privilege."

She nodded. P.J.'s arm was tense under my hand. I gave it a squeeze.

His index finger jittered. "Why don't we go outside? It's more . . . confidential."

"I won't be a minute. I don't want to interrupt your date," I said.

"This isn't a date."

Devi sat straighter, shaking her head. "No, no. This is a business meeting." But her cheeks glowed pink. "Jesse's helping me with my record deal."

I nodded. "Jesse's a helpful guy."

She gave him a bashful look. It was full of longing.

And full of sadness, as if she felt pain at the thought of his tragic life. Romantic pain. I'd seen women look that way at Jesse, and it made me want to scalp them. P.J. was eating it up.

I'd seen Devi somewhere as well. I wondered if she sang in local clubs, or did musical theater around town.

"Let me guess," I said. "You're signing with Black Watch Records."

"Right," she said. "Are you signed to them, too?"

"I'm not a musician. But I know that Black Watch is Jimsonweed's label, and Jesse's tight with Ricky Jimson."

She smiled. "I know. That's why Sin recommended him."

Bingo.

P.J. squirmed. I lowered my hand to my lap and eased it under the table to pat him on the knee. His mouth tightened.

He gave me what I presume was his most attorneylike look. "Why don't we go outside, so you don't have to worry about, ah, revealing . . . lawyer, stuff. Details."

"That's okay. I'm not embarrassed. She can hear the whole thing." I squeezed his leg.

His knee jumped, and he worked to keep a straight face.

A waiter came to the table, asking if I'd like a drink. I ordered a double shot of Bacardi 151. P.J. squinted at me uncertainly.

I smiled at the girl. "Devi. That's Indian, isn't it—the name of a Hindu goddess?"

She flushed, seemingly with pleasure. "Goddess . . ." Laughing, embarrassed. "Not me, hardly. It's short for Devorah. Goldman. Hundred percent Jewish."

It took a second, but the switches flipped. I knew where I'd seen her photo. In a frame on a credenza, next to the photo of her dad the classics professor, Charlie Goldman.

She was Lavonne's daughter.

She was Sinsa's high school buddy, now in college. Which meant that P.J. was either incredibly ballsy, or incredibly ignorant. Casually I put my hand back on the table, covering my fork. I gave Devi an earnest look.

"And you're old friends with Sinsa? That's why she sent you to Jesse's firm?" I set my hand in my lap, with the fork.

"She said Jesse's the man to go to for entertainment law. And she should know."

I poked P.J. in the thigh with the fork. His shoulder twitched.

"What about your mom?" I said.

Bemusement. "She does litigation, not entertainment. You know my mom?"

"Sure. Lavonne Marks—she's top-notch."

P.J.'s face drained of blood. Ignorance it was. He had no idea that Devi was related to Jesse's boss. I jabbed him again, harder. His eyes crossed.

Devi's face had also paled, but for another reason. "Mom doesn't . . . She wouldn't . . . I mean . . . I'm doing this on my own."

"She doesn't know you're signing a recording contract?"

"Not yet."

"Because she'd rather you study law than sing in a rock band," I said.

"You see." Her shoulders relaxed.

The waiter brought my drink. The fumes from the rum could have peeled the paint from the walls.

"Who's fronting the money for the record deal?" I said.

She looked at P.J., as if waiting for a cue. The thudding in my temples deepened.

"Let me guess. College fund?" I said.

Back to the fork. I gave him two hard jabs.

He inhaled sharply. "Kathleen, I don't want to keep you. Why don't I see you to your car?"

He pushed back from the table, moving unevenly in the wheelchair. Okay. Pedal to the metal.

"Got a light?" I said.

He turned, laboring at it, and looked at me with suspicion. "Why?"

"Devi? How about you?" I said.

"Sure." She took a lighter from her purse and handed it to me.

I pushed my chair back as though to stand, and hindered P.J.'s way. "Hang on—I almost forgot to tell you what happened to me."

"Right." Devi leaned forward on her elbows. "If it's not too personal."

P.J. was beginning to sweat. "It is."

"Not at all," I said.

He nudged forward. "No, you shouldn't put yourself through it again."

"On the contrary, I need to vent." I leaned toward Devi. "It was a screwup. On the set."

Her eyes pinged. "Set—like, for a TV show?"

"Like that. Have you heard of *Mistaken Identity*?"

Her expression turned vague. "It sounds familiar."

"It's a genre we call extreme reality. Your identity is assumed by another person without your knowledge. Then we see who gets into bigger trouble, you or the impostor."

"That does sound extreme," she said.

"Hilarity ensues," I assured her.

P.J. wiped his nose nervously. "Ev—"

I settled a stare on him.

His eyes bugged. "Uh." The *oh, shit*, was all over his face. "Ev . . . everything's going to be all right, Kathleen. But I think it's time for your medication."

I turned back to Devi. "The thing about *Mistaken Identity* is, the participants can't predict when they're going to get hit with the consequences. That's why we don't stick to the studio. We go on location."

She nodded, intrigued.

"Because you never know what might trip up an impostor." I gestured to P.J. "Right?"

"Kathleen, you're looking awfully pale. I think I'd better get you home."

"For example. Where's your center of gravity?" I said.

"I don't—"

"Knees, butt, axle of the rear wheel?"

He leaned back, raising his hands, before apparently realizing that this was a fact he should know. "Hip level. Middle of the seat."

I nodded, smiling, looking from him to Devi. "See?" I stood up. "This is why we do the show live."

I walked around behind him, so that I was at the window and he faced the restaurant as he would an audience. He sensed trouble too late. I grabbed his shoulder and flipped him over backward.

He pitched to the floor. Devi shrieked. Someone shouted, "Oh, my God." Silverware clattered and conversation died.

"A man's center of gravity is chest level," I said. "Lean back, you can tip over."

Devi leaped to her feet. P.J. lay splayed on the floor beside the wheelchair, shocked and scared. He knew he'd better move—but there was the rub.

"What is wrong with you?" Devi said.

"Nuptial dementia. Call the police."

Devi looked across the restaurant, where the maître d' was stalking toward us, and cried, "Call the police—"

P.J.'s arms shot into the air like a faith healer's. "No! No police."

She ran around the table and dropped to his side, touching his chest gingerly, as though he might disintegrate. "Are you hurt?"

"Not yet," I said, "but he's coming close. Twenty. Nineteen. Eighteen."

He reached for the wheelchair. I righted it and pulled it toward me, backing against the window, out of his reach.

Devi's fingers hovered above him, fluttering. "What should I do?"

I said, "You'll have to pick him up. Seventeen. Or I might just blow, you know—out loud, shouting all kinds of things."

He shot me a crazed look. "No, I can do it myself. Everybody just back off."

Several patrons and the maître d' were closing on me. The maître d' gave me a supercilious little two-fingered wave. "Madam, you must leave. Come with me."

"Back off, Pierre."

I fended them off with the wheelchair. P.J. waved his arms.

"Don't touch her."

Devi's hand was at her throat. "He's paralyzed. Leave him alone."

"Remember, I gave you a two-minute warning about me getting mad. You're down to sixteen seconds."

He pushed himself up to a sitting position. "Kathleen, you need help. Let me take you somewhere safe."

"Fifteen. Credit card fraud. Fourteen. Practicing law without a license."

"Jesse, what should I do?" Devi said.

"He's not Jesse," I said. "Thirteen."

"What do you mean? Of course he's Jesse." She looked on in horror as he pulled himself along the floor, trying to reach the chair.

P.J. had broken out in a full sweat. "Everybody just . . . go back to eating. Please, for God's sake. Give me some dignity."

The maître d' stepped back. I picked up my double Bacardi shot.

"Twelve, P.J. Eleven."

"P.J.? Who's P.J.?" Devi said.

"He is. Ten. Grand theft. Nine. That suit. Eight. Sinsa's dress. Six. The flowers you sent me. Five."

He kept dragging himself backward. "What happened to seven?"

I pulled the chair out of his reach. "Four. First-class airfare to Barbados. Tell her who you are."

"Ev—Kathleen . . ."

"Three. Faking paralysis, when you're perfectly able-bodied." Heads turned. The maître d', the waiters, and every diner in the room were watching. "And doing it to con this girl out of her money."

"No."

"Two. Breaking your—" My voice caught. "Breaking your brother's heart."

"I haven't done that."

"You're doing it right now. One. Blaming everything on Brittany Gaines."

He backed into the table and stared at me, breathing hard, saying nothing.

"Zero." I threw the rum in his face.

More gasps, and a "Hell, what a bitch."

"Now I'm mad," I said.

From the sling I pulled out Devi's lighter. I held it up, thumb on the striking wheel. P.J.'s face went blank.

"Ever hear of a drink called a Flaming Asshole?" I said.

"Plain Bacardi isn't a . . ."

"No. You are."

I flicked the lighter. The flame jumped alive. So did P.J., leaping to his feet and dashing for the door.

28

A quarter of a mile down the road from the Ranch, I caught up with P.J. He was walking along the shoulder with his thumb out. Hearing an engine approach, he looked over his shoulder expectantly. He did a double take, jumped, and broke into a run.

"Oh, please," I said.

We were going downhill through wooded countryside, heading toward Montecito village. I gave him a head start before pacing him, close enough for the motor to sound threatening. Ten miles an hour; he could do better. I put the car in neutral and gunned the engine.

He burst into a wild sprint. Nineteen mph—now we were talking.

But after seventy yards his form disintegrated and he began staggering. When he floundered to a walk, I pulled alongside him and rolled down the window.

"How long do you want to do this? I have a full tank," I said.

He was grabbing for breath, mouth hanging wide. His glare crumbled with defeat. He faltered toward some boulders off the shoulder and flopped down. I stopped and got out.

"I paid your lunch bill," I said.

He was panting. "Great."

"Otherwise Devi would have been stuck with it. But you're going to pay me back. For a lot of things."

He stared at his feet, shaking his head. "Save it, all right? One Jesse in my life is plenty."

If my ribs hadn't been broken, I would have collapsed with hysterical laughter. "You're not even being ironic, are you?"

"The big nagging finger, wagging in my face. Always perfect, always smarter than everybody else. And off-limits from being criticized, because of everything."

"Oh, P.J."

He slid off the rock slowly, his coat riding up, his hands raking his hair. Dropping to the ground, he wrapped his elbows around his knees and put his head down.

"You're going to tell him, aren't you?" he said.

Did he really think Jesse was his big problem? Well, duh.

"How long have you been doing this? How many people have you scammed?" I said.

He sat with his head on his arms, his knee beginning to jitter. "I'm so screwed."

"Did Brittany take part in any of it?" I said.

He rocked back and forth. "No."

He said it softly, but it felt like a punch in the gut.

"P.J., why?" When he didn't respond, I touched his face and turned it so he had to look at me. "Why did you do this to me?"

"I didn't think it would hurt you."

I searched his face. His handsome, stupid, pain-stricken face. The air was cool and the sun thin. His blue eyes squinted against the light. Traffic sped past, rocking us with noise.

"You knew it would hurt me," I said.

"No, you're not liable for anything. You're not responsible financially. That's the law. The banks and stuff can't come after you."

"The banks didn't. Merlin and Murphy did."

"I didn't know they were going to get involved. Honest."

"What did you think was going to happen?"

"I don't know." He dug his heel into the dirt.

"What you told me about Brittany being a klepto-maniac—"

"That wasn't fair of me."

"She wasn't the kleptomaniac. Sinsa is. Right?"

He leaned his head back against the rock.

"You have to stop protecting her," I said.

"You've gotta understand. To the outside world it looks like Sin has everything, but she's trapped. She has nothing of her own. Unless she does everything her folks tell her, she gets cut off without a dime."

He pulled off his tie and undid the top button on his shirt. "I know you don't understand. But not all of us have the kind of resources you and Jesse do."

"Are you crazy?"

"Look at this suit I'm wearing. Jesse could have bought it without breaking a sweat. I've just never caught a break like everyone else. Is it so wrong to want that?"

I stared at him, speechless.

"Sin needed help. She just needed enough cash to jump-start her project. And her parents wouldn't give it to her. What was she supposed to do?"

"Get a job?" I held up my hands. "Rhetorical question. And Sinsa convinced you to play Jesse?"

"It was the clincher. I mean, he works for the firm that represents her parents' business, what's—"

"How many times, P.J.?" I gritted my teeth, amending that. "How many *women*?"

"He should thank me. They all love him. I mean, they all think he's just the most lovable guy."

My hands drew into balls. "You've given him a reputation as a stud?"

"They think he's a teddy bear. And they're so happy that they can . . . I mean, he's so grateful. . . ."

I boxed his ear.

He clapped a hand against the side of his head. "What was that for?"

"Jesus, are you trying to get me counting down into negative numbers?"

This explained the woman blowing kisses at Jesse, and the gal shaking her boobs at him outside Chaco's.

"Please tell me you didn't sleep with them. Please," I said.

He looked affronted. "That wouldn't be professional. I just made out a few times."

I boxed his other ear. "Did you want to impress Sinsa? Buy her love?"

He rubbed his ears. "I didn't know how else to help her. And before I knew it, I was doing more and more to help her get the project going."

"Did you hook Brittany up with her, to produce the demo?" I said.

"Yeah. But Britt already knew Sin, through me, and from doing that *Rock House* show with Shaun Kutner."

"And Brittany got her dad to stump up the money for the project, because she was so desperate, and her dad didn't know anything about the music industry to know that—"

"No, no—Britt knew that once she signed a recording contract, the record company would pay her an advance to record an album. She just paid for the demo."

"You mean Ted Gaines paid Sinsa. Way above the real cost of the recording."

"Producers get paid, Evan. It was legit." He wiped his nose.

A rusty soda can lay on the ground. I kicked it. "How did Toby Price get involved?"

"I didn't have anything to do with him, never. He's bad news."

"Did he know Brittany?"

"He wanted Brittany to sign him as her manager."

"Did she?" My heart was thumping.

He shook his head.

"What happened the night Brittany died?" I said.

"I don't know."

I crossed my arms.

"She was crying. I was jamming with some guys and she tried to pull me away from the party."

"Why?"

He shrugged. "I was pretty toasted. I—"

I stepped closer. He put his hands over his ears.

"She got hold of the credit cards. You know, the Evan Delaney cards."

"How?"

"She found them in my pocket." He wiped his nose and avoided my eyes. "I left a pair of jeans in her apartment. She washed them."

"She did your *laundry*?"

And he was still sleeping with her. I pulled him to his feet. He looked abject.

"I told you, she was obsessed with hanging onto me. But she found the cards in a pocket, and a bunch of credit card receipts. She recognized my handwriting on them and figured it out."

"And that's why she came to the party?" I said.

"She thought I was gonna ruin my life, end up in prison. She wanted to stop me."

"You mean she was going to tell the police?"

"No, no. You. If I didn't cut them up, she said she'd tell you."

I rattled my head back and forth, trying to clear my thoughts. "How did she know who I was?"

"She knew everything about me. My folks, Jesse, and she'd seen you with him at the Battle of the Bands and asked who you were. So she knew."

My aches were returning. "You're telling me Brittany only had the credit cards on her to confront you? That she never used them, never participated in the scheme?"

"That's right." He squinted into the distance. "I'm sorry, Evan."

It was the first time he'd said it. I sat on the rock. A breeze riffled through my hair, and the air took on an edge.

"She was killed because she had them," I said.

He stared at the trees. "You think so?"

"Yes." I let that settle on him. "Who else knew she had them?"

He lifted his shoulders.

"Who killed her, P.J.?"

"I don't know."

"But you saw it happen."

He hunched on the rock. Though it was only mildly chilly, he had begun shivering.

"We have to clear Brittany's name," I said.

"How?"

"You need to tell the cops."

"I don't want to talk to the cops."

"You go to them, or they come to you."

He crossed his arms, sticking his hands under his armpits for warmth. "My lawyer won't let me talk to the police. No way."

My head was throbbing again. We were back to Skip Hinkel, asshole-at-law.

"P.J. *I'm* going to tell the cops. They'll take it from there."

"No. Evan, it wasn't that bad. Brittany shouldn't have died. I don't know how that happened. All the rest—Sinsa, I . . ."

I stood up. "Let's go."

I couldn't convince him that she was worse than he thought. In his eyes, Sinsa was the goddess. Huge and powerful and needing to be appeased. I walked toward my car. I heard him shuffling behind me.

"And by the way," he said. "At the restaurant, you accused me of buying expensive plane tickets. That's totally untrue."

I shook my head. "Give it a rest."

"No, seriously. It wasn't me."

I glanced at him. "You didn't take Sinsa on a nice little jaunt to Barbados recently?"

"No. I don't even have a passport."

"Shall I show you the bill? Two first-class tickets on American."

He stopped. He looked wan. "Whose names were on the tickets?"

I hadn't checked. "Let's find out."

If I was right, I might knock some sense into him.

Back at my house, I phoned the credit card company. They put me on hold. P.J. stalked the living room, scratching his nose.

"Can I grab a beer?" he said.

"No."

"Just one."

"No." Muzak burbled against my ear.

He stopped in front of the flower arrangement. "They do look nice."

"Glad you think so. After I finish this call, you're going to cut them up and eat them for lunch."

A woman came on the line.

"I need some help tracking down a thief who flew to Barbados on your dime," I said. I gave her the transaction number for the airline tickets. I heard her typing. After a minute she came back with a locator number, names on the tickets, flights, and the rest of the vacation package, which had posted since I'd last checked. I wrote it all down. She said she'd fax me a copy of the information.

P.J. drew near. "Well?"

He looked over my shoulder. All his jittering stopped. Dead.

"I'm sorry," I said, though I wasn't.

He was staring at the names I'd written down. One was Kathleen E. Delaney, which indicated that Sinsa had managed to obtain a fake passport. The other was Shaun Kutner.

"Are they sure?" P.J. said.

"It isn't a wild typo."

He stared numbly at the sheet of paper. "This other stuff, too. The day spa, that's Shaun getting his Botox treatments."

"You can't be serious."

"Not his face, his armpits. It helps stop the sweating." He shook his head. "I can't believe I'm such an idiot."

"One other thing, P.J. The checks that were stolen from Datura Inc."

"No. I told you, I would never steal from the Jimsons. I helped Sin get around their restrictions, but I would never, ever rip them off."

"Then it wasn't you who closed the fake checking account at Allied Pacific Bank?"

"No."

I made one more phone call, to the bank manager, Bianca Nestor. I described Shaun Kutner and asked if it matched the surveillance tape. The Adonis build, the slouch, and especially the pale green eyes. To a T, she said.

I told P.J., and waited for it.

I expected him to get mad, but he melted to a lump of wax. "She did it for him all along. She was using me."

"It's a tough break."

"But . . ." He was grasping, but not so hard anymore.

"She and Shaun ripped off Ricky, P.J."

"What am I going to do?" He wiped his hand over his face, like a washcloth. "And no cops. Don't even go there."

"You're done running away from this," I said.

He sighed, and surprised me. "Then let's talk to Ricky."

29

I parked on the circular driveway in front of Green Dragons and headed for the front door. Halfway there, I realized that P.J. wasn't following. He was still in the car, ducking his head, trying to get out of sight below the dashboard.

When I yanked open the passenger door he was tipping pills out of a Baggie into his palm, a colorful candy store of pharmaceuticals.

"You don't need that," I said.

He picked out a blue one and slurped it before I could stop him. "It's Valium. What's your problem? Jesse takes Valium all the time."

Diazepam. "As a muscle relaxant for chronic pain, not an anesthetic against bad love. Jeez."

"This is hard. I'm just taking the edge off, hey—"

I grabbed the Baggie from him. He closed his palm and stuffed the remaining pills into his pants pocket.

"Did you bring a sampler for the afternoon?" I stopped myself from giving the lecture. There was no point. "Just tell me none of those pills is Viagra."

I squeezed his arm and pulled him toward the front door.

P.J. went straight in. He was entourage, after all. The housekeeper was in the living room, vacuuming beneath the jimsonweed painting. He waved and asked her where Ricky was. She pointed up, indicating the studio.

We climbed the stairs, hearing music coming from a room above.

P.J. called, "Ricky?"

We approached the door. Inside, Ricky was leaning against the recording console. Behind him a sofa was piled with his old stage outfits, a sea of Day-Glo Lycra. He was wearing a blue-and-black leopard-print catsuit. He looked our way with bloodshot eyes.

"Peej. Help."

His face was scarlet. He was stuffed into the catsuit like a sausage into an intravenous line.

P.J. darted past me and into the studio. "Ricky, shit."

"I'm stuck. The zipper," he said. "Fucksake, I can't breathe."

The catsuit was zipped up to the top of Ricky's sternum. P.J. grabbed hold of the pull and yanked. Ricky yipped.

"It's caught in my chest hair."

They fought with the zipper but got nowhere. Sighing, I pulled out my key ring. It had a little Swiss army knife on it. I flipped it open and said, "I can get it."

"No. This is vintage." But he was clawing at the neckline, scraping his fingernails against the skintight fabric. P.J. thrashed with the zipper.

"It's no good, Ricky," he said.

"All right, all right."

"Turn around," I said.

He did. I slit the bodysuit up the back seam. He spilled out, gasping.

"Thank you." He drew breath. "Karen's not here, or Sin. I was desperate."

The suit flapped like a popped balloon. He slumped onto a chair.

"This is weirding me out, man. After Tiger getting burned, and the ravens on the engine. I threw away all the outfits with flame motifs. But now the animal prints too . . ."

I felt for him, but enough was enough. "Ricky, you have bigger problems."

He looked at me. "Gal, you don't look so good."

"I have bad news," I said.

He looked at P.J. "You either, dude. What is it?"

P.J. walked to the bay window and thumped down on the window seat. Outside, La Cumbre peak shoved into view, teal and gold against the sky.

"It's about Sinsa," I said.

Ricky frowned.

"Where's Karen?" I said.

"Up in the valley, checking out that vineyard where we're doing the gig next week. She won't be back till tonight." He looked from me to P.J. "What's wrong?"

"P.J.'s going to tell you," I said.

Perhaps it was the Valium kicking in, or the bloodlessness of his broken heart, or the desire for revenge. P.J.'s voice went flat.

"She's ruined me, man. She's ruined us all."

Ricky sat leaning his elbows on his knees, blond hair hanging, bodysuit looking like a tattered latex glove. Cigarette smoke trailed from the Winston in his fingers.

"You don't seem surprised," I said.

"Are you sure about all this? Sure, sure, sure?"

I gave him copies of the bills for the Kasja Benko dress, and the full details of the trip to Barbados. The cigarette hung between his fingers, the ash growing.

"It says Kathleen Delaney took the trip," he said.

"You think I took a tropical vacation with Sweaty Shaun? Check Sinsa's stuff. You'll find a K. E. Delaney passport alongside that designer dress."

He shook his head. "I don't need to." The ash dropped to the floor. "She said she was staying with a girlfriend down south." He looked at P.J. "Devi Goldman, you know her?"

P.J. nodded. He was moving like syrup. The Valium had apparently taken the edge way, way off. I wondered how many he had snarfed before I grabbed the Baggie.

"It's because of Shaun," Ricky said. "Fucking Sweaty Shaun Kutner. How I wish I'd never said that word on national TV."

"If you hadn't done it, the press would have," I said.

"He blames me, you know. He hides it, but he thinks his career would have taken off if I'd just kept my mouth shut. And Sin plays into it." He smoked. "She wanted me to produce an album for him. I said no. That's what this is about. Getting back at me for Shaun." He looked at P.J. "I'm disappointed in you."

P.J. hunched on the window seat.

"Get out, Peej. I don't want to see you around here no more."

P.J. blushed a hard red. His eyes ducked Ricky's gaze, and he swallowed. "Can I just say—"

"No. You're out of here."

For a second he stared at Ricky. Pulling himself to his feet, he hurried from the room.

Ricky stabbed out the cigarette in an ashtray. "Jesus, that makes me feel like a prick." He looked at the receipt for the Barbados tickets. "How am I gonna tell Karen?"

"The direct approach would be good."

"I have to finesse it. Or she might think I'm stabbing Sin in the back." His eyes dropped. He looked a thousand years old. "You don't have kids, do you?" He grabbed another cigarette and lit it. "Sin's not my natural daughter."

"I know."

"She's Baz Herrera's kid. She was nine when he died. I legally adopted her, but she's never been totally mine. You get it?"

Unfortunately, I did. I nodded.

He gazed again at the Barbados itinerary. He got a perplexed look on his face. "What's with these dates?"

There were two locator numbers, one for K. E. Delaney and one for S. Kutner. I saw what I hadn't before: They had flown outbound on the same flights, but had returned on different dates. Sinsa returned on a Sunday. Shaun came back three days later, Wednesday. Barbados—Miami—LAX—Santa Barbara.

Wednesday.

"That's wrong," Ricky said. "We picked him up on a Saturday morning."

"I remember."

It was the Saturday morning when I saw Shaun and Sinsa romping in the BMW four-by-four. The day after Brittany was murdered. But the airline records showed that Shaun had flown home several days before that.

"What do you make of it?" he said.

"Not sure yet." But I had a bad thought: Shaun wasn't really out of the country when Brittany died.

He stubbed out the cigarette. "No point in hiding from what I gotta do. Let me talk to my daughter. Maybe I can convince her to come clean. That would be the best thing all around. If she and I tell Karen together."

I stood up. "Where is she?"

"Shopping. She'll be back soon." He looked up at me. He seemed sad, and strangely hopeful. "Can you just give me today—hold off on going to the cops until tomorrow?"

"I'm going to tell Jesse. After that I'm going to the sheriffs. However long that takes, it takes."

"Might be a couple hours, right?"

"It might."

"Thanks."

I did it because he was trying to do the right thing. Good intentions, big mistake.

*　　*　　*

P.J. wasn't in my car. The housekeeper said she'd seen him heading around the side of the house to Sinsa's apartment above the garage. Then she clucked. *He* was allowed in Sinsa's apartment, but *she* hadn't been allowed in for weeks—because the girl liked to sleep late. She shook her head. *Princess,* she seemed to be thinking.

I climbed the exterior stairs to the apartment, knocked, and went in.

"Leave me alone," P.J. said.

I leaned against the door frame, exhausted by the sight of him.

The apartment was minimalist modern in design, a loft with grand windows overlooking the mountains. But the furnishings were pure Sinsa: combination Santeria sacrificial altar and Paddington Bear. Candles, incense, Thai silk, stuffed animals three feet deep. And a skinned Tickle Me Elmo, its pelt nailed to the wall above her bed.

Which was where P.J. lay, facedown, hugging a three-foot stuffed Tigger.

Two suitcases lay open on the floor, erupting with men's clothing. I checked the name tags; they were Shaun's.

P.J. curled on his side. "She did it all for him."

"Sorry. It's a bitch."

I looked around. The wastebasket was in the corner, and lucky for me the housekeeper hadn't been up there yet. I picked through it.

"That's not your stuff," P.J. said.

"As if you didn't come up here without permission to recover your stash." I pulled out a Baggie with half a dozen tiny brown seeds inside. "Looking for this?"

"That's probably Shaun's. He takes herbal remedies to control his sweating." He clutched Tigger more tightly. "Shit, I can't believe she wants that clammy pig instead of me. She's gonna get tired of it; she has to."

I dug, and voilà. I found the airline baggage tags. They confirmed that Shaun had flown in from Barbados on the Wednesday before Brittany died. I kept digging.

"What are you looking for?" P.J. said.

I peered in and pulled it out. "This."

It was a crumpled airline ticket and boarding pass. Los Angeles–Santa Barbara, one way. A twenty-minute hop on the morning after Brittany was murdered. I stood up and stuffed them into my purse.

"Let's go," I said.

He rolled onto his back. "She's going to be mad. When she finds out that I told."

"Too bad."

"So will Shaun."

"Shaun's going to be dealing with the sheriff's detectives. Don't worry," I said.

"What if he comes after me?"

"Slap him with a restraining order." I knelt a knee on the bed and pulled him up by the arm. "You've played lawyer enough; you ought to be able to figure out how to do that."

A few minutes later, Sinsa flipped the turn signal in the four-by-four and slowed for the stop sign, waiting to make the turn onto the road leading to Green Dragons. Cross traffic didn't have a stop. She waited for a pickup to speed past, and a Jaguar. And a white Explorer.

Uh-oh.

She watched it recede down the road. That had definitely been P.J. in the passenger seat. This could be bad.

When she swung up the drive at the house, she headed straight for her apartment. Lie low while she scoped it out, that was the thing to do. Call P.J. He should have been with Devi Goldman, not the Delaney woman. Charming the socks off her. And then the clothes. And then the money. If he'd fucked this up . . .

She trotted up the stairs to the apartment and unlocked the door.

Ricky sat on a chair in the center of the room, waiting for her.

"Daddy."

"Baby. Sit down. Let's talk."

30

I dropped P.J. off at his apartment. He paused before getting out of the car, as though wanting to say something. But all that emerged was a sigh.

I knew he might pack up and gun his motorcycle straight out of town. But the disappearing act didn't have to be physical. He was more likely to vanish into a miasma of drugs and alcohol.

"What's that look?" he said.

"You're such a jerk. And we love you. You know that, right?"

Though he looked miserable, he almost managed a smile. "I guess."

He opened the door but didn't get out.

"When you tell Jesse what I did, tell him I'm sorry. I shouldn't have pretended to be him. And what I said, about him catching the breaks—I didn't mean it. I know he's . . ." His hands lay in his lap. "I know what he's been through."

"I will."

"Do you think . . . Should I apologize to Devi?"

"That's your call. But it would be the right thing to do."

"She's a nice girl."

He was looking for a soft shoulder to cry on, I thought. I took his hand.

"I want you to give me the pills you put in your pocket."

His back started going up.

"Just for tonight," I said. "Do this for me. Just tonight. Stay sober. Don't get wasted."

"When's the last time you went through a breakup sober?" he said.

"Things will feel much worse hungover. And worst of all if Sweaty Shaun pays you a visit when you're blasted."

"Why should I do it?"

"Consider it a down payment on your redemption."

This time he tugged his mouth into a junior version of the Blackburn Wry Look. He scrounged in his pocket for the pills and gave them to me.

I handed him the phone cord, which I'd taken from his kitchen earlier. He took it, puzzled. Driving away, I saw him in the mirror, walking toward his door, head down. I wondered how long he would last.

Back home, I locked the door behind me, something I never used to do. I took the phone to the sofa and lay down, with my feet still on the floor. Afternoon light fell silently through the windows, casting a pale shine on the hardwood floor. I felt exhausted. My bones were ringing.

After a minute I lifted the phone and dialed Sanchez Marks. Recognizing my voice, the receptionist said, "Jesse had to go home."

I glanced at the clock. "At three thirty?"

"His burglar alarm went off."

I sat bolt upright. "And he went to check it out?"

"He said he was going to call the sheriffs."

I was up off the couch, heading for the door.

Jesse wouldn't wait for the sheriff's deputies. He never waited for anything. I swerved through traffic on the 101. The stupid sling was restricting my movement. I undid it and tossed it aside. Hitting speed dial on my cell phone, I tried him again. No answer. What the hell was he thinking?

I pulled off at San Ysidro and headed toward the beach, barely tapping the brake to check for trains at the railroad crossing. Down the isolated road, where houses were sparse and burglars could break in at a leisurely pace.

Except that it wouldn't be burglars.

I turned in at his drive. The Monterey pines rushed past. I punched it around the bend. A strange car was parked in front of the Mustang. The side door to the garage was open. The lock had been splintered and the window cracked. Inside, things were strewn across the floor. No cops.

I slewed to a stop and jumped out. My palms were sweating. I heard no music, no conversation, only the smothering roll of the surf. I ran to the front door. Shielding my eyes from the sun, I peered through the narrow panes of glass that flanked the door. Everything looked still. I couldn't see or hear anybody.

I didn't want to go in. Inside meant being shut in a box, where I couldn't run, couldn't jump back in the car. My heart was skipping, and I was cold with sweat. What if Murphy Ming was here? My bladder felt weak. My thigh was trembling.

If Murphy was here, he had Jesse. What was I going to do, hide on the floor of the car and wait to see if the sheriffs turned up in time to stop him? I breathed, counted to three, and dashed around the side of the house.

And gave myself a mental forehead slap.

On the edge of the deck Jesse sat cross-legged, sleeves rolled up, tie loosened at the collar. On the sand nearby lay something I hadn't seen out of the garage in years: his surfboard. Sitting on it was Ricky. He was slumped over, blond hair riffling in the breeze, and he was talking a hundred miles a minute.

"For a second she got almost panicked, and I thought she was going to own up. Then she turned ultracool, playing it like it's no big deal. Made a pot of actual fuckin' tea. But I pressed her, and then, shit. She went off on me."

Jesse gave me a look that told me to stay quiet and roll with it. I sat down beside him. His face was weary; Ricky must have told him about P.J. playing lawyer.

Ricky was holding a seashell, turning it over and over in his hands. He had extricated himself from the catsuit and was wearing jeans. His eyes were rimmed red and his face was flushed.

"She said I was abandoning her. Throwing her to the wolves."

The tide was going out, the waves breaking white over blue-gray water. Ricky turned the shell.

"Sin thinks I've ruined everything. She said I've squashed her—I'm repressive, forcing her to have a small life. You believe that? Stymied her. Me, Slink Jimson."

He looked at me. His pupils were wide, as though the shock had blown them open.

"She says what she did, stealing your ID, she did it to breathe, to live. Said it was my fault; I gave her no choice." He raised a hand. "I know; don't say it. She did it for the thrill."

His shoulders slumped further. "I tried to talk her into going to the police. Get the identity theft cleared up for you." He gave me a look of regret. "And that Gaines girl. Clear her name, you know, her memory. Give her father some peace."

He threw the shell toward the water. "It cut no ice."

Jesse said, "Will she talk to an attorney?"

"She don't want to talk, period." He squinted at the surf. "She cut me dead. Acted like I was nothing, invisible, just air."

Jesse spread his hands, seemingly searching for something to say. Ricky straightened and his face became thoughtful.

"It's no secret, I've always felt like the Reaper hovered around me. And I thought when my turn came,

I was gonna go quick. Wham, out of the blue, you know?"

Like lightning striking.

"But having Sin treat me this way—it feels like this is the end, and it's just long, slow fucking agony." He glanced at Jesse. "I mean, is this how it feels?"

"What?" Jesse said.

"Being near death."

Okey dokey. The breeze raised whitecaps on the water. Jesse's hands lay loose on his knees. He didn't have a poker face, but he knew how to play it cool. Ricky leaned forward on the surfboard.

"I know plenty of guys who've gone. And that's the thing—they're gone, so they can't describe it." He calmed. "But you survived. You can tell me."

Jesse remained chilled. "The void. All around, calling you into it. Yeah."

Ricky drew a slow breath, and let it out. From the intense look on his face, this was confirmation he'd been seeking for years.

"I won't give up," Ricky said. "I'll talk to her again."

"Do that." Jesse gazed at the surf. "But you can only do so much. She's an adult."

"She's my daughter. I won't give up on her. But I'm scared for her, man." He put a hand against his chest. "My heart's running a mile a minute just thinking about it."

"It'll be a lot easier for her if she turns herself in," Jesse said.

"Not scared of the law, dude. Scared of *him*."

Jesse shifted. "P.J.?"

Ricky's head clocked around. "Shaun. He has her under a spell."

From the cast of Jesse's mouth, he thought exactly as I did: Ricky had that backward. Sinsa was the sorceress.

Ricky stood up, brushing sand from the sagging seat of his jeans. He rubbed his chest and blinked as though his eyes hurt. This was taking a toll on him.

I stood too. "I can't wait any longer. I have to go to the sheriff's."

"I know. I'll do what I can do." He shrugged. It was a gesture of surrender. "Sorry about setting off the alarm."

"No problem," Jesse said.

"Don't know what I was thinking, except I saw the surfboard hanging on the wall in the garage and remembered how catching waves used to mellow me out."

Jesse tilted his head. "Know what? Take it."

Ricky looked at him with surprise.

"If surfing evens you out, that's great. It's yours," Jesse said.

Ricky's red eyes softened. "Thanks, man."

I said, "I'll be at the sheriff's station in an hour. You and Sinsa can meet me there."

"Hope so." He picked up the board. Putting it under his arm, he trudged off around the side of the house.

Jesse exhaled. "Jesus." He shook his head and reached for the wheelchair. "He's in a bad place."

"No kidding."

"Sinsa's turned out worse than his harshest lyrics. Jimsonweed's darkest hits come to life." He hoisted himself up.

"What happened?" I said.

"He came looking for us. Did you tell him you were here?"

"I told him I was going to talk to you."

"He jumped to conclusions." He turned toward the house, and the sun caught his eyes. "You came tearing around the corner. What did you expect to find?"

"I don't know." But I did. "Trouble."

He gave me the full-blown Look, dry as bone. "Supergirl to the rescue. Sling off, fists up, ready to rock." He pushed toward the patio doors. "Welcome back."

Flushing with embarrassment, I followed him inside. On the kitchen table lay something new: his Glock.

"You got it," I said.

"Yup."

I knew Jesse could defend himself. He was fine. I swallowed my discomfiture.

"You know about P.J.?" I said.

"I wish I didn't." He found his keys. "I don't trust Sinsa. We don't know what she might do. You should get to the sheriff's asap."

"Sure." I watched him. "You're coming, right?"

"Gotta wait for the cops. I'll catch up."

My hand was on the front doorknob when he called to me. "I didn't mean it. The Supergirl crack."

He was near the table, with the sun shining off his hair, his face tired.

"I know," I said.

"It's great to see the fight in you again."

I walked back across the house and kissed him. "Call me."

Outside, I turned the Explorer around on the driveway. The Monterey pines waltzed in the breeze. Backing up, I checked over my shoulder that I was clear of Jesse's car, and stopped. The Mustang had a For Sale sign in the back window.

I'll be damned. He was getting rid of it. I'd gotten through to him.

Feeling relieved, I pulled out. This time I slowed and looked both ways before crossing the railroad tracks. The mountains pushed toward an azure sky. I worked my injured shoulder back and forth. Even without the sling, the pain had receded to a background ache. I was mending.

Accelerating onto the freeway, I turned on the radio. Heard Mary Chapin Carpenter singing "Jubilee." She sounded tender and sad, wishing for her lover to find release, to leave pain behind like wreckage in the dust. The piano was spare, the guitar an embrace. A Gaelic flute wound through the song like heartache itself.

Letting go of the wrongs that have been inflicted on us—how do we do that?

High overhead, cirrus clouds streaked the sky. A flock of sparrows flew in front of me, swooping up to meet the blue.

The black wing sheared across my thoughts. The sky seemed to splinter.

The Explorer veered right, across the lane onto the shoulder. The tires shuddered onto the dirt. I yanked it back onto the asphalt. My throat was dry, my head pounding.

Jesse wasn't letting go of the wrong. He was just letting go.

Preparing to leave the pain behind. Giving Luke his audio player, with the music he'd taken months to program. Giving Ricky his surfboard. Selling his car.

Talking about death.

Saying he was glad that I felt stronger and could take care of myself. I jammed the pedal down, looking for an exit off the freeway. He thought I didn't need his help anymore. He could let go. *The void. All around, calling you into it.*

Tears stung my eyes. God. I swung into the fast lane. The car in front of me was dawdling. I flashed my lights. He pulled over and I barreled past. The exit, I needed the exit. I could no longer hear the music, only the blood rushing in my ears. I could see the black specter fracturing the world. I could see Jesse's calm face. I could see the sun glinting off the ocean behind him. Glinting off the windows. Off his infinitely distant blue eyes.

Off the gun.

31

Sinsa stood by the window overlooking the driveway. Thinking, *Please*. She was brushing her hair slowly, pulling the bristles through the thick rain of black. She was watching for Ricky's car to come back.

Please. It had been over an hour. Daddy, please come back.

Was he just going to leave her here? He couldn't. She worried her hair with the brush.

If he didn't come back soon, it would mean something had happened to him. Out on the road, like a car crash. If his vision got blurred, or he fainted. That couldn't happen. She had to see him. They weren't done.

He was upset, but how upset? Enough to drive off and leave her here alone. But upset enough to mess up his afternoon schedule? It was after four. Four p.m. meant a hot fudge sundae while he watched *Magnum, P.I.* He never missed *Magnum*. Then he hit the sauna.

Where the fuck was he?

She set down the brush. If he didn't come back soon, it meant she had miscalculated. The timing, and maybe the dosage.

She glanced at the table. Next to the brush, the Baggie still had a good supply of seeds. She could give him another cup of tea. The first cup hadn't been scientific. Just her best guess about what would unbalance him. Shaun always used a few seeds at a time,

to dry up the sweats. She'd given Ricky ten times that.
But if she overdosed him with the first brew, he might
not make it back.

She picked up the Baggie. Devil's Trumpet, they called
it. Mad Apple. Inferno, Locoweed, Zombie. Nightshade,
Green Dragon. *Datura stramonium.* Jimsonweed.

Ask your doctor before ingesting. All parts are toxic.
Come back, Daddy. We're not finished.

Racing along the road toward Jesse's house, slamming over potholes, I steered with one hand and
thumbed the phone with the other. Grabbing a look
at the display, and back at the road.

"Oh, Christ."

At the railroad crossing bells were clanging, lights
flashing, and the gate was swinging down. A hundred
yards up the track, a freight train steamed toward me.

I had to get across. Shit, had to. I could.

No.

I hit the brake with everything I had. The tires
shrieked. The antilock brakes kicked on and the steering wheel chattered in my hands. A horn blared from
the train. They had to see me laying rubber. I jammed
the brake to the firewall and the Explorer stopped,
snapping my head forward. The gate came down. On
the hood. Loud as hell, the train thundered past.

And past, and past. A dozen cars. Two dozen. Come
on, come on. I dialed Jesse's number. Got the machine. Tried his cell. Off.

The train clattered by, thirty cars, thirty-five, and I
still couldn't see the end of it. I phoned information
and asked for Sam Rosenberg, Jesse's neighbor. He
was unlisted. I couldn't do anything. But maybe—
maybe—the sheriff's deputies had already arrived at
Jesse's house to check out the alarm call.

Boxcars rattled past. I wrung my hands on the steering wheel.

I'd been blind. I'd told Jesse he was rash, tried to

slap him with the fact of his own recklessness, but I hadn't seen the depth of his despair. Instead, I'd misbehaved. I'd aligned myself with another man, right in his face. And when we needed to talk, I hid from it.

I prayed. God, not this. Stop this from happening. I'll do anything you want. You can have me. Just stop this.

In the rearview mirror I saw a car pull up behind me. It was a sheriff's cruiser.

Standing in the garage, Sinsa heard Ricky's car coming up the driveway. Finally. She put down the garage door, concealing the BMW four-by-four inside, and ran toward the house before Ricky drove around the corner. Sprinting toward the back door. Her silver bracelets rang on her wrists.

Inside. The maid had gone for the day. The house was empty.

Ricky would think.

She ran to the living room, where the Georgia O'Keeffe painting of jimsonweed hung above the mantel.

"He's here," she called.

She peeked out the front window.

Yeah. He was out of the car. He was rubbing his eyes. Was that a fucking *surfboard* in the backseat? Whatever. He didn't look so hot.

But he would, in just a few minutes. Real, real hot.

Behind me at the railroad crossing, the sheriff's deputy was talking into his radio, doubtless running my tags for wants and warrants before coming to question me about why I'd nearly crashed into a Southern Pacific locomotive. The train finally cleared the crossing. The lights and bells shut off. The gate lifted from the hood of the Explorer. I gunned it across the tracks.

In the mirror, I caught the cruiser's lights flashing on. Come on, then. Let's go.

I was there in under a minute. The front door cracked against the wall when I threw it open.

"Jesse."

All I heard in reply were my boots echoing on the hardwood floor. Outside the deputy pulled up, lights blazing. I called Jesse's name again. I ran to the windows. There was no sign of him outside on the beach.

A rap on the open door with a nightstick. "Ma'am? Step outside, please."

Jesse was gone. I spun around, looking at the kitchen table. So was the gun.

Sinsa charged toward the back of the house, tripping over her heavy boots, nearly falling. She caught herself and hurried to the kitchen. Was that an omen—a foreshadowing? Telling her she could trip up?

No. No doubts. She couldn't go back now. She had already thrown the dice. In the kitchen she double-checked. The note, everything.

She heard the front door open. Out of time. She raced to the gym. She saw Shaun inside, facing the wall of mirrors, pointing a finger at his reflection.

He cocked his head to one side. "What's that I see under your armpits, Ricky . . . sweat?"

She rushed in. "He's here."

He stared at himself. "They say success is one percent inspiration and ninety-nine percent perspiration."

"You hear? This is it."

"So here's to success, shithead." He gave his reflection the finger.

"Shaun, look at me." She grabbed his arm. "Forget rehearsing the punch line. You have to do this cold."

"Relax. I'm golden." He dropped his hands, rolled his head, and shook his shoulders to loosen up. "I don't need a run-through."

"You sure? 'Cause if you have any doubt, if you think it might get fucked up, we call it off."

"It's improv. I rule at improv." He took a cleansing breath. "P.J.'s the fuckup, not me."

She looked around at the exercise bike, the treadmill, the weight bench. Props. The only thing Ricky ever touched in here was the sauna. She was counting on that.

Shaun looked at himself dead-eyed in the mirror. "Now who's sweating? Huh?"

She knew he wouldn't get stage fright. The problem would be holding him back.

He wiped his forehead. "No way I have time for a shower, is there?"

Maybe this wasn't going to work.

No. No. If she did this, Mom would never have to know about any of it. Things would be all right. Mom would protect her. Except for those other two—P.J. and Evan Delaney.

"And no mess," she said.

"No guarantees."

She pinched his chin between her fingers and turned his face to hers. "Brittany was all the mess you can afford. A second one, and they start looking at us. It has to be an accident."

He nodded. His breath tingled on her fingers. Jesus, this was it, the real deal. She tried to identify what she felt. Yes. Excited.

"We should film it," Shaun said.

"No. This is business, not theater."

"But this is completion. He killed me on live television. Now the circle's closing."

What an unbelievable dumbshit. "Baby, we can't. No time."

"Fine." He turned to the mirror. "Who's sweaty now, fucker?"

Hearing a sound from the other side of the house,

Sinsa pushed him toward the patio doors. They had to get out of sight in the bushes past the pool.

Shaun cracked his knuckles. "Yeah. That's the line."

She tensed, eager. She recognized the sound she'd heard. It was the TV. *Magnum.* This was going to run like clockwork.

32

The deputy held his nightstick against the door. "Please, ma'am. Outside, now."

"We have to find the man who lives here. The one who called you," I said.

Behind me, I heard, "Ev, what's wrong?"

I turned and saw Jesse wheeling out of the bedroom. I crossed the room in four strides, fell to his side, and threw my arms around his chest.

"Sir?" the deputy said.

Jesse put his hands on my shoulders. "Evan."

Their voices warped into a hiss. I couldn't bring my arms to let go, but I was aware of Jesse untangling me from him, and him going outside with the deputy to explain about the break-in that wasn't. I knelt on the floor staring out the plate-glass windows. The wind was raising chop on the ocean. I heard the deputy start his cruiser, and Jesse close the front door. I stood up.

"Where's the Glock?" I said.

He came toward me, his face solemn. "I put it in the bedroom. Cops get twitchy if they see firearms lying around. What's wrong?"

"Give it to me."

I went to the bedroom. He followed.

"Evan." He caught me and locked a hand around my wrist. "What the hell—" He stared at my arm, snagged under his grip. "You're shaking."

He looked up, eyes questioning.

"Don't do it," I said.

And he understood what I was talking about. He didn't try to hide it. His hand fell to his lap.

"Please, God, Jesse. Don't." I couldn't stand up anymore. I dropped onto the bed. "I can see how much pain you're in. But suicide isn't the answer."

"Evan, stop."

"No. Please, babe, we'll find some way."

He rubbed his fingers across his forehead.

I clasped his arm. "Look at me."

He did.

"Your death would not even the books," I said. "And the Sandovals are not beckoning for you to join them."

He froze. I held on to him.

"Isaac and Adam—do you know how angry they'd be if you cut your life short because they died? They'd be horrified."

His gaze dropped to the floor. As if he'd been socked in the gut, he leaned forward, hands on his knees.

I covered his hand with mine. "I love you. Let me help you get through this."

"Ev, don't do this." He sat bone still, staring at nothing.

"No. I won't let you."

He closed his eyes. "Stop."

"I will not stop. If you die, I will hunt you down. From here to kingdom come, and I will whip your ragged ass until there's nothing left. You will experience pain unlike anything you imagined possible. I will ride you until the goddamned universe burns out."

He squeezed his eyes shut.

"Do you understand? I know you're fearless, but you should be afraid of me." I shook him. "Do you get it?"

"I get it." He held still for a long count. He opened his eyes and looked at me. "I told you, nobody's going to get you while I'm alive. I meant that. I'm not going anywhere."

"Truth, Blackburn."

"Truth."

I held his gaze until my vision swam and I had to wipe away the tears that were falling down my face. And then he was swinging over from the wheelchair to sit next to me on the bed, and his arm was around my shoulders.

I tightened my grip on him. "I'm so sorry. I've been so wrapped up in my own stupid problems that I didn't see what was happening to you. I know it's the pain and the grief. If I'm not the one who can help you, let's find somebody who can."

"Evan, you can stop. You already got through to me."

"I want to reinforce my point."

"Days ago. When I spun the car."

"Jesus. When I said you were going to kill yourself, I wanted to shock you. I was not giving you permission to die."

"You did shock me. You forced me to choose."

I thought of the specter sweeping over me in the hospital, my sense that death was close. I tightened my arms around him.

"And when Lily Rodriguez called and said you were missing, I went nuts. I had to find you. You mattered more than anything." He held on to me. "I'm staying. I want it to be with you."

"I want that too."

He looked so far into me that I knew I couldn't fake it. "Nothing happened with Marc Dupree. Nothing's going to." I held his eyes. "Forgive me."

"There's nothing to forgive. I've been a miserable son of a bitch. I'll think I'm all right, and then it comes out of the dark and grabs me by the throat."

"Tell me when it does. You don't have to carry it alone."

He crushed me to his chest and buried his head against my neck. We held each other.

Without more words, I took him. I pulled him down on top of me. I needed his heat, was desperate for the taste of his mouth, the feel of his skin. It had been so long. Suspending thought, wanting only sensation, closeness, and the knowledge of carrying each other. I wanted to give myself to him completely, so that he could let go in me. His mouth was on mine. And on my throat, and pulling open my blouse, kissing my breast, and I made a low sound and arched my back. He pulled himself farther onto the bed, and I fought with his shirt and tore it off, kissed his chest, his shoulder, his hand, his palm, sucked his fingers, licked his wrists and the inside of his arms, and pulled down the zipper on his trousers, slid my hand down and found him, held him, stroked him, hard, because he could feel that. I climbed out from under him and pulled his shoes and socks off, pulled his pants and boxers off, while he was trying to get my jeans down, unzipping me, slipping his hand down the back and under my panties onto my ass. We were tangled, but I didn't want to stop or think or let anything interrupt, not after so long, and break the moment. I pulled my jeans off and fell on top of him. He pushed my legs apart. Everything else was light and sensation.

33

Ricky turned up the volume with the remote. He hadn't missed too much—Magnum was up in T.C.'s helicopter. He loved episodes with the helicopter. Magnum always ended up hanging from the skids. Maybe this episode would cheer him up.

The house was quiet and the four-by-four was gone. Sin must have taken off. His heart felt bruised, and wouldn't stop racing. His eyes were blurry. Like the Jackson Browne song—maybe he'd kept them open too long, seen too much. He felt parched too. And hot. He went to the kitchen for a cold drink, and found her note.

I didn't mean what I said. I was scared. I shouldn't have lashed out at you. I'm sorry.

It melted him. He ran his fingers over the words, trying to tamp down his emotions.

I'm going to talk to a lawyer. Please don't tell Mom. I have to be the one to do that. I'm really, really sorry.

The page looked smeared. His eyes were a mess. And he felt hot. It must be from the relief, but he sure felt hot.

P.S.—I made your sundae.

*   *   *

The shutters in the bedroom were open, enough to see cirrus clouds glowing white above the ocean. The pines swayed, limbs shirring like brushes on a snare drum, shadows sliding across the ceiling. I scooted to the foot of the bed and grabbed the sheets and blankets from the floor. Pulling them around us, I sat next to Jesse, hugging my knees, watching the sky pour by.

He turned on his side and coiled against me, resting an arm along my leg. I smoothed my fingers through his hair.

"You don't have to watch me," he said. "I'm not going to change my mind."

"But I want to watch you."

"Besides, if I ever did it, you know how it would play. 'Crip Puts Self Out of Misery.' How shitty would that be, people thinking it had to be because of the injury." His hand was warm on my leg. "Fate worse than death and that crap. Well, fuck 'em. I'm sticking around."

I stroked his hair. The sun lit the clouds, tinting them pink.

"I'm going to say something," I said.

"You, talk? How novel." But the sarcasm ebbed when he saw my face. "What?"

"This sense of guilt." He rolled his eyes, but I kept stroking his hair. "You think it's unfair that you lived when your friends died."

"It is."

"Wrong. Their deaths were crimes. You surviving is a gift."

His mouth pulled down, and he started to speak.

"Hear me out. You were hurt, severely, and your life was changed. But you feel so guilty for breathing that you think it's selfish to acknowledge that."

"What do you mean, acknowledge it? I deal with it every way, every day. The point is, it hasn't ruined my life."

"I know. Babe, you suffered a hell of a blow, and

grieving for what you lost isn't petty. But you feel so bad about feeling bad that you only get more depressed. It's a vicious circle."

"Wow."

"Sorry," I said.

"No, it's okay. I'm just amazed. You never talk about this stuff with me."

"It's not fun."

"But I'm pleased. You didn't even dive headfirst through the plate-glass window. I've waited years for you to stop being scared to talk about it."

I realized he was right. I didn't want to run screaming from the room. He kissed my hip. His hand slid across my belly.

"Thought you had to go back to work," I said.

"I do."

I rolled on top of him. "When?"

"Now." His fingers raked into my hair. He pulled me into a kiss, and more.

It was intense. But it wasn't work. Not even close.

Ricky turned off the TV, thinking: *Too much sundae.* Finished the whole huge thing. He undid the button on his jeans. He needed a long sauna to work off the calories. Jesus, and after the scare with the bodysuit, he should get right to it. Tight clothes could be dangerous.

In the gym, he turned the sauna up high and shut the door. The heat was overpowering, but that had to be good. This session needed to be quick. He didn't know when Sin would be back, and he had to be ready to talk to her. This could be a breakthrough. The tang of hot cedar filled his nose. The black stones piled in the heater glowed red. He dumped water on the rocks, three dippers full. Steam powered over him and the temperature shot up. He sat down. Sweat it out, all that hazardous weight.

Except he wasn't sweating. He was plenty hot, but

dry as a bone. He poured three more dippers over the rocks. The air thickened and stung. It felt like being in a fire. He was still dry. His heart was racing like he'd taken speed. What was up?

He rubbed his chest. The walls were turning green and yellow, like fireworks. Purple, shit, emerald green again. This was way wrong.

He heard a scraping sound right outside. A metallic noise against the wood. The handle of the door jittered.

He stood. He had no coordination. His heart was zinging like a hummingbird. He reached for the door handle.

It wouldn't move.

He shook it. It wouldn't budge. He put his face near the window in the door and tried to see what was going on outside.

Shaun's face appeared on the other side of the glass.

Ricky screamed.

Shaun stared. "The ravens are here."

Ricky staggered back, screaming. The colors swooped at him.

"Die, fucker." Shaun head-butted the glass. "Die!"

Ricky tripped against the water bucket and fell back on the floor, cracking his head on the bench. His heart was jumping up and down. The heat was killing him.

That scraping sound again. The door handle jangled. And he heard another voice. His daughter's voice.

"Stop. Shaun, don't."

She was coming. Steam and the wild colors obscured Shaun through the window. But he saw Sin's arm around his neck, saw them wrestling. God love her. He tried to get up. His feet went their own way and his butt stayed down. But he had to get up, had to help Sin. Shaun would overpower her. Holding on to the bench, he tried again to stand.

The scraping sound came again, and the door swung open. Shaun stood in the doorway holding the cross-bar for the dumbbell. That was what had locked him in. Sin was pulling on Shaun's belt, trying to hold him back, punching him in the kidneys.

"No," she yelled.

Ricky staggered to his feet. He cocked his hand into a fist.

Sin begged. "Shaun, don't. You'll leave prints. You'll leave trace evidence. Let it be—the heat'll get him."

The colors jumped at Ricky. The racing in his chest stopped, bang, cold. His legs slid out from under him. He looked at Sin, undone. He was going down.

Until Shaun caught him. "Not yet. Look at me, old man. I'm the light you hoped you'd never see."

Ricky felt himself lifted off the floor. He felt the burning when Shaun swung him toward the heater. Toward the red-hot rocks.

34

When my cell phone rang, the sky had deepened to cobalt and the room lay in shadow. Jesse was stretched out facedown, with his head at the foot of the bed and one arm hanging off the side of the mattress. He was sound asleep. For the first time in months, perhaps. I was faceup, staring at the ceiling, sprawled across him with my legs splayed over his back. I had no idea where the bedclothes or pillows had gone. Or the headboard. The phone rang again. Rolling over, I found it on the floor.

"You left me an urgent message?" Lily Rodriguez said. "What's going on?"

I shook myself awake. "Sinsa Jimson."

I summarized P.J.'s confession, told her that Sinsa was behind the identity theft, and that Brittany Gaines had gotten hold of P.J.'s fake credit cards the night she died.

"And get this, Shaun Kutner wasn't in Barbados that night. He was in Santa Barbara. I found his plane ticket and boarding pass."

"You think he was building himself an alibi?" she said.

"Yes."

She went quiet. I found my jeans on the floor. Squeezing the phone against my shoulder, I worked my way into them.

"I think he killed Brittany, then drove to L.A. and

flew back here in the morning, pretending he was returning from Barbados."

Jesse raised his head, saw the sun heading down,
and said, "Oh, shit. Work." He pushed himself up,
searching for his clothes.

Lily's voice was cautious. "I'd like to see the ticket."

"That's why I got it out of the trash." I wriggled
into my shirt.

Jesse found his own shirt crumpled between the wall
and the top of the bed. He also found the headboard,
collapsed onto the floor. He pulled on the shirt to
discover the buttons torn off. I opened his dresser and
tossed him a sweater.

"I'll bring everything by the station," I said.

Jesse found his trousers, took one look at the destroyed zipper, and dropped them back on the floor.
I threw him a pair of jeans.

"If I'm not here," Lily said, "leave the tickets with
the desk. Think I'll get Zelinski and go have a talk
with Miss Jimson."

"Thanks, Lily." I hung up. "She's on it."

He was wrestling the jeans up. He nodded at the
headboard. "You have a hell of a kick."

I put on my socks and boots and went in the bathroom to wash my face. My cheeks were flushed. I
looked like a deflowered hillbilly. When I came out
Jesse was tying his high-tops.

He finger-combed his hair. "Do I look like—"

"You spent the afternoon having wild sex," I said.

"There goes my annual bonus."

A few minutes later we were outside getting ready
to leave. The clouds were glowing red with sunset and
he was locking up. My phone rang again. It was Marc.

"I'm going home. They've cut me loose," he said.

"You're clear?"

"No. But they trust me to come back for questioning and court dates. Thank Lavonne for that. She

even got forensics to finish with my truck and release it from impound. She's a bull terrier."

Silence stretched on the line. "I'd like to stop by. Brian forgot to give you back your house key. Can I drop it over?"

Jesse watched me with not-so-idle curiosity. I had no doubt he knew who it was.

"I'll be there in forty-five minutes," I said.

Marc hesitated, probably guessing where I was. "See you shortly."

I put the phone in my pocket. Jesse's gaze was soft. "Do what you need to do," he said. "I'll come over later."

I dropped Shaun's airline tickets at the sheriff's station and headed home. The sky was purple with twilight when I walked toward the garden gate. Lights sprinkled the foothills. The wind was coming up, and the air had a bite. Down the street, Nikki and Thea were walking Ollie. With the little girl holding the leash it looked more of a meander than a journey. I waved.

Inside the house, I flipped on the lights and the stereo. The thought of telling Marc good-bye in silence felt unkind. Fine, I was a coward. I wanted backup, even if it was only the Dixie Chicks.

I took five minutes to straighten up the place, wipe down the kitchen counter, and brush my hair. The Chicks warmed up the atmosphere with fiddle and slide guitar. I began closing the shutters on the French doors. Nikki was in the yard with her charges. She waved to me and strolled toward her kitchen door, letting Thea play in the yard with the puppy. I finished closing the shutters, and listened for Marc's knock.

But a few minutes later I heard a different set of sounds outside. I heard a heavy engine accelerating. I heard the screech of brakes, and I stopped still, waiting for the crunch of metal. Possibly as it plowed into my car. But the brakes let off and the vehicle roared away.

A few seconds later, I heard Nikki screaming.

Later, a neighbor identified the vehicle: a black BMW four-by-four with JMSNWD vanity tags. It had driven down the road at least twice, cruising around the block before returning and parking a hundred yards from my place.

Sinsa sat at the wheel. Shaun jogged up and jumped in. He wiped his forehead with a handkerchief.

"All her doors and windows are locked. And she has an alarm. I can see the alarm company sign." He glanced at Sinsa. "And I'm not smashing my way in. The bells go off, she'll rabbit."

"We can't come back later. We're running out of time." She stroked her hair. "We have to do this tonight. We shut this down, now, or it's all over everyplace."

"How am I supposed to make this one look like an accident?"

"Murphy Ming is after her. Everybody will blame him."

"What should we do?" he said.

She glanced around at the parked cars, the lights coming on in houses along the street, at the sparse traffic. Well, look at that. A woman with a kid and a mutt were stopping at the garden gate. The kid was yanking the mutt's leash. It was a little kid, screaming age, still uncertain on its feet. Jerking and stumbling around, with a Frankenstein walk. The mutt looked cowed. The woman opened the gate and they went through.

"Go check it out," Sinsa said.

Shaun trotted across the street and peeked over the fence. Jogging back, he hopped in the BMW and said, "The mom went in the house, but the kid and the dog are playing in the yard."

"I'll fix this," Sinsa said. "Go and open the gate,

quietly. See if you can get in the shadows inside, like behind a tree."

"What are you going to do?"

"Create a distraction that'll get Delaney out of her house."

"What should I do?"

"Count to ten and whistle."

He took a pair of leather gloves from his backpack. She put a hand on his arm.

"Shaun, *quietly*. No gunfire or screaming. You want to be long gone before anybody finds her."

"She can't scream if her windpipe's cut."

But she could watch.

He looked toward the gate. "What if the kid comes out with the dog?"

"That's not our problem."

I ran outside and saw that the yard was empty. Thea and Ollie were gone. Then I heard tires squealing around a corner, and saw the gate open. I stood as dumb as a sheet of cardboard. Outside the gate, Nikki knelt in the street.

I stumbled toward her. My tongue tasted like copper. Nikki's back was to me, but her hands hovered above the asphalt, as though afraid to touch what lay before her. From other houses, people were coming out. Helen Potts came running down her walk, one hand clutching her cardigan, the other to her lips. Nikki had gone utterly silent.

In place of her screams came a heartbreaking sound. The puppy crying in agony. My legs turned to paper. I tottered to the sidewalk.

Thea stood by the curb, thumb in her mouth. I scooped her into my arms. Baby smell. God-loving little-girl sweetness. She wriggled against me. Her face was fretful.

"Doggy," she said.

"I know, punkin."

Ollie continued whimpering, more softly. Helen Potts knelt down next to Nikki.

"What should we do?" Nikki said.

Another neighbor brought a beach towel. "Here, wrap him up. Poor thing. The bastard who did this."

Collectively we looked down the street. The car was gone. Nikki saw me holding Thea and mouthed, *Thank you.* She eased the beach towel around the puppy. From the house on the corner, Dennis Hutchinson jogged over. He was a vet. I rocked Thea, and the others huddled around the little form in the street. But Ollie wasn't crying anymore.

Hutchinson took a look and shook his head. "I'm sorry."

After talking to Nikki for a minute, he wrapped the puppy in the beach towel and carried it back to his house. Nikki stood, but made it only as far as the curb. I handed her Thea and she sank down, clutching her daughter in her arms.

I sat next to her, arm around her shoulder.

"I thought . . ." she said.

"Me too."

"That gate needs a better latch."

Thea strained in her arms, pointing after Dr. Hutchinson. "Doggy's sad?"

"Yeah, baby."

We sat there for a minute.

Nikki said, "This may be the luckiest day of my life."

"Mine too."

Life abounds with irony. Irony sucks.

Back inside, I locked the door and dropped down on the sofa. The music was too bluesy, all wrong. The air felt close. I needed a drink.

I heard the floor creak behind me. I half turned and a gloved hand covered my mouth. Silver flicked past my vision. A strong arm held me still. The blade of a serrated knife pressed against my throat.

"Keep absolutely quiet."

Shaun climbed over the back of the sofa and crouched on the cushion beside me. The blade bit at my neck. His sea green eyes were vivid. He put his face close to mine.

"You're going to stay silent and do exactly what I say."

He dropped a backpack onto my lap. "Open it."

He hadn't slit my throat, but that didn't mean he wasn't planning to. I stared at him and refused to look away.

A few hours earlier I had made a promise that if Jesse lived, God could have me. And guess what.

No. Not like this. Not now. Not if I could help it.

And, staring at Shaun, I felt with unearthly certainty that this was not my time. That God did not possess such a perverse sense of humor.

I opened the backpack.

"Get out the camcorder," he said.

I took a video camera from the pack. And I looked around for a way out. All the shutters were closed. Shaun had unplugged the phone cord, and my new cell phone was across the room on the dining table. My sense of calm persisted. It may have been shock. But I knew that Nikki was home. Marc was on his way over. If I could get somebody's attention, I could get help. Better still, if I could get hold of a weapon, I could help myself. And Brian's gun was in the bedroom.

"Stand up."

We rose together. He kept the knife at my throat.

"We're going to the kitchen together. Slowly."

Nudging me ahead, he walked me to the counter.

"Put the camera on the counter and aim it back this way."

I set it down, pointing at us. Was he planning to take a self-portrait?

"Right." Mouth next to my ear. "Today we're taping *America's Rudest Home Videos*."

It took a second, but the reference clicked. I stiffened. He was wearing the same combat pants as that night at the party in Isla Vista, when he unzipped them to piss on a parked car.

"She remembers." He sounded delighted.

I opened my mouth to speak and the knife pushed against my larynx.

"Unh-unh. You don't have any lines in this film. You only get a listing in the credits, with all the other losers who've been fucking up my life." His voice lowered. "Crying Moron—Brittany Gaines. Rock Has-been—Slink Jimson. And Ballbusting Bitch—Evan Delaney."

All my doubts evaporated. I knew he had killed Britt. And that he was here to kill me.

"Where's your duct tape?" he said.

It was in a kitchen drawer. We walked together as if doing a macabre tango, blade to my throat. He made me get the tape out and rip off a strip.

"Over your mouth," he said. I did it. "Now your hands."

I wrapped the duct tape around one wrist and then the other. Shaun tugged on the tape to see that it was secure. He didn't bother to cut it away from the rest of the roll. The spool hung below my hands, swinging like a pendulum.

There was a knock on the door.

Shaun went still. The knife pressed against my windpipe. The knock came again, and Marc's deep voice.

"Evan?"

Shaun pressed the blade harder against my throat. It wasn't cutting me yet, but I felt a strangling sensation and the desire to squirm. He held me still. His jade eyes were alight.

The knocking stopped.

Shaun spoke sotto voce. "Turn on the camera. You're going to do what I say. We get one take, so it's gotta be perfect."

Because there couldn't be any retakes. And I realized that he wanted to film himself killing me. I had to get away, right now, but the front door was deadbolted, and even if I made it there, by the time I got it open he'd have me again. Unless I slowed him down I'd never make it. I needed a weapon.

Outside, across the yard, I heard Marc's voice. He was talking to Nikki. Come on, Nik. Tell him I'm home. Send him back here.

Keeping the knife on my neck, Shaun waltzed me back a few feet. He maneuvered to center me in the lens of the camera. He slid the knife under my chin, forcing me to look up. He stepped forward and back, and flipped on a light over the stove.

He exhaled with a hiss. "Fuck. This won't work."

He gazed around the living room.

"Where's a mirror?" he said.

He pulled me out of the kitchen, peering at the walls in frustration. "Where are your mirrors?"

He looked at me, angry. I pointed at my bedroom. Where the gun was.

He grabbed the camera and we walked in lockstep toward the bedroom. How was I going to do this? How would I get the gun quickly enough?

Moot point. Shaun pushed me through the doorway and his feet tangled with mine. We stumbled past the nightstand. The knife nicked my throat. Adrenaline dumped through me. Dammit.

He marched me into the bathroom. Unrolling the spool of duct tape, he tossed it over the rod for the shower curtain, binding me there with my hands above my head like a prisoner in chains.

He set the camera on the counter by the sink and flipped on the makeup lights that surrounded the mirror.

"Oh, yeah."

The cut on my throat was burning but I forced myself to ignore it. I pulled against the strip of duct tape.

The curtain rod quivered and the spool swung back and forth. If I hung all my weight on the tape, would it break? Or would I simply dislocate my aching shoulder again?

"Perfect," Shaun said.

His jade eyes had widened. His breathing was quickening. He faced the mirror, staring at himself with the pleasure most men reserve for a lover. He rolled his neck and straightened his T-shirt and tossed his tangled hair.

This had to be fast.

I jumped, bending my elbows, doing a rope climb on the duct tape. The curtain rod broke loose from its moorings.

Shaun gaped—watching me in the mirror. He began to turn but by that time I was moving and I rammed him for all I was worth. The knife was in his hand. I grabbed the camera and smashed him in the face with it.

"Shit."

He dropped the knife and slapped a hand over his eye. I bashed him again and his head went sideways into the mirror. I heard the glass crack. He howled and put a hand to his head, which came away bloody.

I jumped past him. He grabbed for me and missed, and I blundered out into the bedroom.

From the front of the house came pounding on the door. I pulled the tape off my mouth.

"Here," I shouted.

More pounding. "Evan?"

"Marc, break down the door."

I reached the nightstand. But back in the bathroom the spool of tape was still trailing behind me, and I felt it go taut. Shaun had grabbed it. I bungled the pistol into my bound hands and swung around. Shaun stood in the doorway.

"Move and I'll blow holes in you," I yelled.

Now, unbelievably, I felt scared. This was the position I'd been in by the roadside with the Mings—seemingly out of the woods, with Marc a few seconds away. Nausea hit me.

Shaun saw it. He smirked. He didn't think I'd pull the trigger. He yanked on the tape spool, pulling me toward him in the bathroom. Hard. The gun went out of aim. I dug in with my feet, backpedaling, but my boots were slick on the wood, and when he yanked again I pitched to my knees.

He reeled me toward the bathroom, straining to haul me in. He wasn't coming out—he wanted me back in front of the mirror. The gun was aimed at my dresser. I slid closer to the bathroom, fighting to bend my hands around toward the doorway. And Shaun saw that, and believed.

He backed up and slammed the bathroom door.

I squirmed, trying to stand up, and to my horror the strip of tape continued disappearing under the door, pulling me with it. Like a slap I understood that he meant to batter my hands into the door and knock the gun loose from my grip. And then he'd have me. I twisted the barrel toward the door.

I fired.

The report shocked me. The gun popped up toward the ceiling. I brought it back down and fired again. And again. The bathroom door splintered. Out in the living room the glass cracked as Marc broke a pane on the French doors.

The strip of tape went slack. I smelled cordite. My ears were ringing. Marc burst into my room. I pulled my finger off the trigger and let the pistol hang loose.

Without a word Marc took it from me and leveled it on the door.

"Open it," I said.

He did. Shaun was gone.

35

Gone, out the window. Shaun had scaled the fence and made it to the street. Helen Potts saw him running past her house in the chill dusk, looking over his shoulder at my place.

Marc sat with me on the Vincents' back steps, while SBPD uniforms and crime scene techs went through my place.

"What do you want to do?" he said.

"Rent a bulldozer. Destroy that bathroom."

"You made a damned good start. The tile is shot to hell."

"I'm serious. This is not the first close call I've had around that shower."

He rubbed my back. "Bad soap?"

"I was attacked," I said.

Sidelong glance. "By?"

"My law school diploma." I squeezed my hands between my knees. "It's a vortex, some kind of whirlpool of evil."

"You can say if you're scared, Evan."

"Who even needs water? I might never bathe again. I'll use moist towelettes instead. I'll install a sandbox and roll in it, the way chinchillas do."

Marc put an arm around me. I let him.

"God's a lousy comedian," I said.

"You need a drink."

"Several. But no liquids, so it's a problem."

Carl came out, carrying Thea. She was wearing footsie pajamas and sucking a pacifier. He sat down beside me on the porch steps and pushed his glasses up his nose.

"He lured Ollie out the gate, didn't he? And Thea followed," he said.

"I wish I'd shot him," I said. "I should have emptied the whole magazine."

"You need a drink," Carl said.

"So I hear."

He gazed across the lawn, at the cops gathering evidence in my living room. "I don't know how to put this, Evan. But do you ever wonder why these things happen to you?"

"My shower is a vortex of evil."

"Ah." He snuggled Thea against him. "So you don't think—"

"I'll get a cement truck to plug it. Or an exorcist."

"—that you might consider changing your life, so it's less exciting?"

I pressed the heels of my hands to my eyes, and Marc tightened his grip on my shoulder. I was seriously at the end of my rope, and Carl was onto something, and I couldn't begin to deal with it right now.

Nikki pushed through the screen door, holding the phone out to me. "Jesse."

Marc's hand lifted from my shoulder, and he stood up. I put a hand on his arm. And the phone to my ear.

"You heard?" Jesse said.

"Lieutenant Rome told me."

Clayton Rome was with the uniforms in my house. He had arrived with the news that Ricky Jimson was dead.

"Karen found him. Can you imagine?" Jesse said.

Yes. I could imagine finding my man's body. I couldn't imagine anything worse.

Marc squeezed my hand and slipped out of my grasp. He walked down the stairs and out onto the lawn, hands shoved in the pockets of his jeans. His breath frosted the air.

"Are you sure you're in one piece?" Jesse said. From the noise on his end, he was in the car.

"Apparently. But listen, I tried to get hold of P.J. and he's not at his apartment."

"That's probably a good thing, considering that Shaun is still at large."

"You think he could have run?"

"Possibly. But he's more likely at Mom and Dad's."

"Right."

"Is Marc with you?"

I glanced at the lawn. He was staring at the stars. "Yes."

"Don't let him leave. I want to thank him."

"I'll ask. No guarantees." I thought: Jesse knows he's in no jeopardy with me. And so does Marc.

"What's that silence?" he said. "Oh. You're right. I would not be anywhere this noble in defeat."

My laugh was feeble.

"Ev. I'm so sorry. Hang on; I'll be there as soon as I can."

Setting down the phone, I walked out to the middle of the lawn. Marc continued gazing up.

I crossed my arms against the chill breeze. "Some vacation you're having here."

He snorted. "I drove into Santa Barbara thinking you were on ice at the morgue. Compared to that, it's been a New Year's Eve party."

He was a monolith in the night, as ever an enigmatic presence.

"Please don't worry. Nothing needs saying," he said.

"Of course it does."

"What would you say? That in some other life, some other time, it would be the two of us?"

"I wouldn't say something that trite to a Vigilante."

"If . . ."

"There is no if. There's only the way it is."

He jammed his hands deeper in his pockets and turned to face me. "Fine. No if. No other life, no other world. This life. This time. There's you, and me, and there's now." He smiled. "And there's someday."

Heat was pouring off him, an invisible pulse. His eyes were luminous.

"Be happy. He loves you," he said.

Inside my house, the phone rang. The cops had plugged it back in. Lieutenant Rome leaned out the door and called to me.

"It's Keith Blackburn," he said.

That was odd, and possibly worrying. I jogged to get it.

Keith said, "Why is a police officer answering your phone?"

He had no clue what had happened. This was about something else. "What's wrong, Keith?"

"Could you come over? Please. Patsy's asking for you."

Never, in three and a half years, had Patsy Blackburn asked for me. "Keith?"

"I don't know what's wrong. She won't explain; she just says you have to come. Please, she's close to hysterical."

Great. I ran my hand through my hair, looking outside. Marc was gone. I heard his truck pulling away.

Jesse pulled the Mustang into the driveway at his parents' house. The moon was rising in a black sky, clouds streaking past in the wind. We could see Keith inside the living room, pacing back and forth. Spotting us, he rushed outside.

He opened Jesse's door. "I don't know what's going on. I can't get a straight answer out of her. Maybe you can."

This was not going to be good. For *straight answer*, read *slurred speech*. Jesse pulled his gear from the backseat, snapped the wheels onto the frame, and got out of the car. When he slammed the door, I got a look at his face. Nightmare, it said.

Keith backed out of his way. "You didn't bring your crutches?"

"Don't start, Dad."

"But she'll want to see you. And she's upstairs."

"Get her to come down."

We headed for the porch. Jesse spun around backward and I lugged him up the steps. Keith averted his eyes, staring into the night.

He followed us through the door. "She won't come down."

"She's too drunk?"

"She's too upset." He ran a hand across his face. "She asked for Evan, but you should talk to her too." His tone was pleading. "It's only sixteen steps."

Jesse looked at me. He didn't have to say anything. I ran up the stairs.

On the landing it smelled stuffy, as though the upstairs windows had been shut for years. The closeness was overlaid with the cloying scent of potpourri. The lights were dim.

Downstairs, Keith said, "Can't you just try?"

Jesse laughed, a bleak sound. "Now why didn't I think of that? Hell, I'm going to just try and speak Mandarin while I'm at it."

I called Patsy's name and pushed open a bedroom door. Inside was an unmade bed, and P.J.'s clothes on the floor. I crossed the hall to what I recalled had been Jesse's old room. The lights were off.

From inside, Patsy said, "Keith?"

"It's Evan."

The bedroom curtains were open. A streetlight illuminated Patsy sitting on the floor beneath the window, knees curled to her chest, rocking back and forth. Her hair was messy and she reeked of alcohol. I flipped on a desk lamp.

It cast an amber light that seemed to set the walls

sizzling. I stepped back, startled. Shine and glitter confronted me. Floor to ceiling, wall to wall, on every surface, were trophies, photos, medals, certificates. Everywhere.

And it was all Jesse.

One wall was solid trophies, arrayed like the Manhattan skyline. Above the bed hung clusters of medals, from age-group swimming, from Junior Olympics, and from the California State Championships, Big West, NCAAs, U.S. Nationals, Pan Pacifics. A bookcase bulged with scrapbooks and videos, neatly labeled: WORLD UNIVERSITY GAMES, OLYMPIC TRIALS, WORLD SWIMMING CHAMPIONSHIPS. But gleaming brightest was the wall of framed photos. Travel shots—Jesse with the U.S. team in Red Square, at the Forbidden City, and on top of Sydney Harbor Bridge. And all the competition photos: at age six, an impish kid bounding with enthusiasm. At sixteen, cute and cocky. At twenty-two, predatory, unstoppable, magnificent. Swimming the butterfly, attacking the water. Leaping from the starting blocks, the camera catching his fire and shocking physical power.

There were even a few triathlon photos, taken the summer I met him. The display ran virtually right up to the day he went cycling with Isaac Sandoval and came back down the hill strapped to a backboard. Then it stopped. Patsy had archived his Before.

She had taken every remembrance of him from downstairs where he could see it, and where it would fan the family's grief about After, and she had hidden it here. In her secret shrine.

She and Keith weren't embarrassed by Jesse. They were crazed with pain.

"I didn't know." Her voice rasped of Marlboros and vodka. Her mascara was smeared. "How was I supposed to know?"

I sat down on the desk chair. "Tell me what's happened."

"Is Jesse here?"

"Downstairs with Keith. Patsy, what didn't you know?"

"That I shouldn't let her in. Nobody told me not to."

I got a bad feeling. "Sinsa Jimson?"

"She came by looking for Patrick. She's been over before. Pint-sized thing, a real cutup." She squeezed her knees. "She brought cranberry vodka. Where's the harm in having a drink with one of his friends?"

Downstairs, Jesse and Keith raised their voices.

"She was chatty. She seemed so understanding. Telling me she can see they really care about each other. In spite of it all."

"Jesse and P.J.?" I said.

"And she's right, they do, they just can't get past whatever it is that sets brothers off."

"Where are you going with this, Patsy?"

Her cheeks were crimson. She tried to look at me but her eyes kept clicking off to one side.

"I couldn't see the harm." She blinked and made a severe effort to focus on me. "She was so concerned. Patrick asked me not to tell anyone where he was going, but Sinsa asked. And I just couldn't see the harm in telling her."

My mouth felt dry. "But?"

Her eyes shimmered. "But then she left so suddenly. And I got worried, thinking maybe I should have kept my mouth shut."

From the entryway Jesse called, "Are you coming down?"

She cringed. "No. He can't see me like this."

"We're staying here," I called back.

I heard him say, "Fuck it." A minute later footsteps stammered up the stairs. Turning, I saw Keith helping him. Jesse had one arm slung over Keith's shoulder and the other gripping the banister, fighting upward as though working a crazy set of parallel bars. He was biting his lower lip with the effort, and looking fully pissed off. He caught my eye, and then his gaze stretched past me to the spangled bedroom walls. Astonishment spread across his face.

They reached the top of the stairs and Keith stopped, exhausted. He looked weirdly buoyed that his son had made the climb on foot, until Jesse said, "Get the chair."

Keith's face fell. But though Jesse could stand up, without his braces and crutches walking simply didn't work. He grabbed hold of a hallway table for balance.

"Please," he said.

Looking crushed, Keith lumbered back down the stairs. Jesse gaped at the display in the bedroom, mystified. And pained by the sight of Patsy on the floor.

"Mom."

Her head lolled back, and she blinked. "Jess?" Hand to her chest.

"Why did you do all this?" he said.

Smoothing her hair, she lurched to her feet. "I . . ."

She tottered. Putting out an arm, she aimed for the bed and sat back down. Keith brought the wheelchair up to the landing. Jesse took it and wheeled into the bedroom.

I drew his eye. "Sinsa stopped by, looking for P.J."

Patsy turned her head, hiding her face from him. Her voice was thin. "After she left, I called him to say that I had . . . that she knew where he was. He got upset." Her hands curled into fists. "And while we were talking, people came in where he was. I heard noise, and a fight."

Jesse put a hand on her arm.

She resisted his touch, looking at the floor. "They were hitting him. I heard them hitting him." She looked up at me. "And then they talked about you. They said Evan should stay tuned."

For a moment her face was accusatory. I felt sick to my stomach. But she crumbled.

"How was I supposed to know?" Her shoulders jerked. She began crying.

Jesse looked at me, and straight on through. I could sense his mind working behind his eyes. He had paled.

Patsy gripped his arms. "You have to help him."

He didn't react.

"Jess." She shook him. "Patrick can't help himself. He's not strong like you."

My cell phone rang. I felt no surprise. I knew what was coming, and from the dead chill in his eyes so did Jesse. I answered the call and heard a voice I had hoped was gone for good.

"Some unfinished business."

I closed my eyes. "Hello, Toby."

36

"The money. You never delivered, so now there's a late fee," Toby said.

"How much?"

"Principal, plus interest. Also my loss of income over the past week, plus a penalty for the fucking inconvenience. Round it up to fifty thousand."

"Let me speak to P.J.," I said.

"Don't interrupt me. You bring it in cash, tonight, if you want to see Junior here alive again."

I didn't plan to give him a dime. I had no money to give. But I thought I'd better make it realistic.

"I'll go forty," I said. "Now put him on the phone."

He breathed into the receiver. "I know you have fifty."

As I suspected: Sinsa had told him I had that much. The better to screw you with, my dear. She was setting me up in every way possible. Telling him I had an unobtainable amount.

"Put P.J. on the phone," I said.

The sound went muffled, as if he'd put his hand over the receiver. "Bring him here." A second later I heard P.J.'s frightened voice.

"Hello?"

"It's Evan. Just answer yes or no. Do you know where you are?"

"Not really."

"Are you on Toby's boat?"

"Guess it's his."

"Are you in the harbor?"

"No idea."

I heard a clattering sound on his end, as though he had dropped the phone. His voice rose, and he sounded like he was struggling. "Ow, shit, stop, what are you doing?"

The sounds increased. He screamed out a string of invective. I clenched my hands. He shouted, "Jesus, man, why'd you do that?"

More clatter, and he came back on, breathing hard. "They shot me up."

Shot . . . "With what, P.J.?"

"A needle. A fucking needle. Shit, man, it's bleeding."

Toby came back on the line. "That will just calm him down. Yeah, he's already looking happy."

"What did you give him?"

"His first hit. The second will put him under. A third will turn his lights out for good."

I put a hand against my belly.

"But you won't let it get to that stage. Because you'll bring the money. And you'll do it fucking fast, if you want to know what I just gave him."

Heroin, probably—but Toby may have thrown something else into the mix.

"You get it together," he said. "All fifty thousand. I have to replace Avalon's guitar player, find a dude willing to wear a fucking leisure suit, which isn't easy. I'll call back and tell you where."

"I—"

"And no cops. I even sniff a badge, Junior gets a straight shot to nirvana."

I looked at Jesse. He was tight as a drum.

"Oh, and one last thing," Toby said. "In case you'd be just as happy to have him float off to his cloud. I don't think you want his friend to."

"What friend?"

"Hang on. What's your name, baby?" More muffled noise. "Devi Goldman."

Jesse and I stared at each other. Patsy pulled herself to her feet, using him for balance.

"You heard?" she said. "They're holding Patrick. You have to get him back."

His face was icy. He nodded to me. "Call Lily Rodriguez. I'll call Lieutenant Rome."

Patsy dug her nails into his shoulder. "You can't. They told me no police."

He grabbed her wrists. "We need the police. We can't help P.J. by ourselves."

"Don't tell me that. I can't hear that."

She fought him. He held her hard in his grip. But then it seemed that her internal mechanisms slipped a cog and all the springs blew. She stopped fighting and flopped down on the edge of the bed, motionless, vacant to the point of incoherence. Keith hung in the doorway. I looked at Jesse.

"Sinsa gave them P.J., in order to get me. She knows there's no money. She wants them to take me instead," I said.

"Them," he said.

The nausea swelled again, a sickening wave. "Toby isn't alone. Somebody else brought P.J. to the phone."

Neither of us said it. Murphy.

Simultaneously we took our phones and dialed the cops.

The living room was a hive of activity, with deputies, Lily, and Gary Zelinski all buzzing around, on phones and radios, coordinating a search with the Santa Barbara police, the Highway Patrol, Harbor Patrol, and the coast guard.

We heard their theories. P.J. and Devi must be in the Santa Barbara area, considering they'd been taken only a couple of hours earlier and the fact that Toby had contacted me via a cell phone. He hadn't used a ship-to-shore radio.

Lily stood in her boxer's stance, feet spread. "He'll be close to shore too. Doubt he's out very far in the channel, unless whoever grabbed them had a speed-boat."

Jesse hung up his phone. He had just finished telling Lavonne about Devi.

"How is she?" I said.

"Tough. Scared to death."

Patsy sat on the sofa holding a tiger-print throw pillow. "Why don't we pay them? Can't you all arrange the money? If it would get Patrick back. Jesse?"

She looked at him, her eyes pleading.

"Mom, I don't have fifty thousand dollars in cash," he said.

Patsy curled over the pillow. Keith sat down beside her and set an arm on her back.

Jesse said, "Dad, maybe you could take Mom in the other room to lie down."

Keith seemed to sense that Jesse wanted to discuss worse things with the detectives. It looked as though the earth had eroded from beneath him. He took Patsy's elbow and stood her up, leading her to the family room.

Jesse turned to Lily. "They're going to kill my brother."

She shook her head. "Toby Price isn't a killer. That's simply off the chart for him."

"But not for Murphy Ming."

She didn't disagree.

I said, "This is not a kidnapping for ransom. This is a setup to get rid of me and P.J."

Jesse nodded.

"And I doubt that this is Sinsa's final gambit," I said.

"What do you mean?"

"If I show up at a rendezvous, Murphy, or Shaun,

will kill me along with P.J. If I don't show up, or show up without the fifty thousand, they kill P.J. right then and come after me later. Any money drop will be an ambush."

Lily blew air through pursed lips. "You're not going to make any money drop. Don't worry about that."

Jesse put his hands up. "Of course she isn't. Jesus Christ. The point is, we have to find P.J. *before* the drop time. That's our only chance."

"We have good information. Water location. Time window. Gary's already contacted the Harbor Patrol and the coast guard."

"I can't sit still. I have to go look for him."

"No," Lily said.

"You can't keep me here. What are you going to do, arrest me?"

My phone rang.

Toby sounded smooth. "Put the money in a backpack. Catch the twenty-two bus at the downtown station. Leave the pack under the next-to-last seat, and get off at the Santa Barbara Museum of Natural History, ten o'clock. Can you handle that?"

"I don't drop the money until I know P.J. is free."

"He'll be waiting outside the museum."

"Unhurt."

"He has a tendency to injure himself. No promises."

Toby's voice wandered away from the receiver. I was unprepared to hear Murphy come on the line.

"Just thought you should know, your little friend here is more of a man than you realized. He's made a manly choice. Here, let him tell you."

Snuffling sounds, and P.J. came on. "For fucksake, help me. He's got Devi tied up. He says he's going to shove a whiskey bottle into her until it breaks off, unless I let him do it to me instead—"

The phone was torn out of his hand. Then there were sounds of a struggle, and P.J.'s voice shearing into incoherence. Toby came on the line.

"Not yet, Murphy." He was laughing. "He's just jerking your chain right now, but boys will be boys. However, you get the money to me, and Junior here might come away intact. Hope you're getting it in order. We'll see you in two hours."

I stared blankly at the walls. "Don't hurt them."

Toby's voice shifted down a gear. "Murphy can't wait. He has a crush on you."

My skin wanted to slough off. "Murphy can eat shit and die."

Toby laughed. "See you at ten."

He broke the connection.

Lily clicked off the tape recorder, pulled out the earpiece, and nodded at Zelinski. I heard them talking about cell phone coverage, triangulation, and service areas, estimating where the call had come from.

She put a hand against my back. "Good job."

My limbs felt like the strings had been loosened. I sat down on the couch. Their voices became a buzz. After a few seconds I felt Jesse's hand on mine. His face was indecipherable.

"Murphy," I said.

I felt weak and frightened. Jesse pivoted onto the couch and pulled me into his arms. He held my head against his shoulder. I unwound against him.

He held me, comforting me as though I were the one suffering, but it was his brother whose life was on the line. And I knew he didn't plan to let P.J. come home in a body bag. If he sat here while P.J. died, he would end up turning his gun on himself. Pledge or no pledge. But he wouldn't let me put myself in danger. He was going to do it himself. If that meant he sacrificed himself for P.J., that was what he'd do.

And I couldn't let that happen.

Lily and Zelinski continued conferring, bringing in the deputy, calling their watch commander. Jesse kissed my forehead. He let go of me, saying, "Keep Mom and Dad calmed down if you can. I'll be back."

I stood up and followed him. "No."

At the step up to the entryway he wheeled and held his hand out. I didn't think twice; I gave him a lift.

Lily turned around. "Where do you think you're going?"

"Murphy isn't going to let Toby overdose P.J.," Jesse said. "He'll want him coherent enough to suffer. He's going to rape him, possibly to death."

Lily said nothing.

"We don't have much time. Murphy's going to sodomize him. Then Toby's going to shoot him up. He'll die. You can't negotiate with them, or plead for more time. Our only chance is to find him before that happens."

She glared at him.

"You know I'm right," he said.

He looked at me. "Get P.J. a jacket and a warm shirt from upstairs, would you? It's a cold night and he may need them."

I was upstairs rooting through P.J.'s clothes when Keith stuck his head around the corner. His face was drawn.

"I overheard you talking with the detectives about a drug overdose," he said. "It's probably heroin. If they injected him, it's likely to be an opiate of some kind."

"Yes."

He held out a packet of pills. "Naltrexone. It's an alcohol antagonist. It'll also reverse an opiate overdose."

I took them, frowning.

"They were prescribed to P.J." He looked at the floor. "He had inpatient treatment a couple of years ago. These were for aftercare, to help him maintain. They're left over."

"He never took them?" I said.

"Give them to the detectives, or whatever. Just get

them to P.J." He pressed them into my hand. "But don't tell Jesse. He doesn't know any were left. He'd probably think all the money was wasted."

Clang, like an anvil hitting the floor between us, I knew that Jesse must have paid for P.J.'s alcohol detox. And P.J. had gone straight back to drinking and getting high. No wonder Jesse was so disappointed in him, and searching for a way to get P.J. to own up.

"I'm not keeping anything from Jesse. He's going to try to get P.J. out of this." I put the packet in my pocket. "How much would he need?"

"Stuff them down his throat."

I turned, and he said, "I know you think she's a crackpot."

Across the hall I could see the glint of the shrine. His gaze followed mine.

"That room, the trophies . . . The boys mean more to Patsy than anything in the world. She would never hurt them. She didn't mean for this to happen to P.J. If they . . . if he . . . It'll kill her."

I had no reply. His eyes broke from mine.

I rushed down the stairs. Jesse was waiting. I handed him P.J.'s things and he opened the door.

There stood Marc.

His hand was out, ready to ring the bell. He and Jesse stared at each other for a moment before Jesse let him in.

"I forgot to give Evan her house key. When I came back Lieutenant Rome told me what was going on," he said. "I couldn't leave. Murphy wanting payback, that's on me. Tell me what you need me to do."

Jesse hesitated only a second. "Let's get the hell out of this house."

Jesse unrolled a U.S. Geological Survey map of the coastline on his kitchen table. He put his finger on the Goleta neighborhood where Devi Goldman lived.

"Two hours ago they grabbed P.J. and Devi here,"

he said. "Half an hour ago P.J. told Evan he was on Toby Price's sailboat. Which gives us a range . . ."

He spread his hands, tracing the coastline. "Could be anywhere in a ninety-mile radius. Could be all the way up in Arroyo Grande, or in the harbor down in Port Hueneme. Shit."

Marc rubbed a thumb across his lips. "So where do we concentrate?"

"To collect the money, they have to come ashore. That means Toby either has a skiff that can run in to the beach, or he's going to moor the sailboat."

I leaned on the table. "The day I was on the sailboat, I didn't see a skiff tied to it."

Jesse stabbed his finger at the map. "Oil company piers. Here, here . . . maybe five or six possibilities."

I rubbed the back of my neck. "They're spread out, from Ventura County all the way up to Point Arguello."

Marc looked at his watch. It was a diver's watch with a luminous blue dial. "It's eight thirty. Can we cover all of them in an hour and a half?"

"No," Jesse said.

"We have to narrow this down," I said.

I walked to the plate-glass windows. The surf was pummeling the beach. South of the horizon a storm was brewing, shedding wind in our direction. Spray flew white under the moonlight.

"I bet anything Sinsa and Shaun know where the boat is," I said. "They had no trouble contacting Toby to send him after P.J. and Devi."

"So we get them to tell us, or show us, or lead us there," Jesse said.

"How?" Marc said.

I watched the ocean churning black. Thinking of depths and crosscurrents.

"We trick them. Turn them against each other." I turned from the window. "I have an idea."

*　　*　　*

I got hold of Shaun's cell phone number from Ted Gaines, Brittany's father. I didn't tell him why I wanted it. While I was on the phone with Gaines, Jesse got the Glock. It was our lone weapon; Lieutenant Rome had insisted on keeping hold of Brian's gun because I'd discharged it into my bathroom—and maybe even into Shaun. Jesse checked the Glock's magazine, cleared the chamber, and set the gun on the table next to an extra ammunition clip. Then he took off his sweater and reached for P.J.'s shirt. I hung up, giving him a look.

He pulled on P.J.'s shirt and jacket. They were tight across his shoulders.

"You know Lily Rodriguez wants to disguise herself as you and fake the money drop, don't you?"

"That's my sense," I said.

"But that won't get P.J. back. If we're going to pull a fast one with a disguise, there's only one that'll work. Me."

He held out a pair of kitchen scissors. "Cut my hair."

I took them. "Hold still."

Five minutes later, I said, "Done." He ran a hand over his head.

"Don't look in the mirror," I said. "It'll work. In the dark, from far away. The clothes will do most of the trick."

Marc rolled up the map. "Don't take offense. It's a decent imitation, but face it. They're going to notice the wheelchair."

Jesse spun around. "I know. Believe me, it's the only thing a lot of people notice. So if I'm not in it, it'll never dawn on them who I am. All I have to do is stand up and we're home free."

As long as you don't lose your balance, I thought.

Jesse nodded to me. "Okay. You're on."

I phoned Shaun's number. My stomach was the size

of a walnut. The phone rang, and he answered. I took a breath.

"Pick the glass out of your scalp and listen to me," I said.

There was a pause. "Delaney."

"When you tape people's mouths shut, you keep them from giving you vital information."

"What in hell are you talking about?"

"I have a proposition for you."

Another pause. "Is this some kind of joke?"

"On you and me. Sinsa's playing us. And it's time to turn the tables."

He breathed into the receiver. "What do you mean?"

"Tell me if I have this right. Sinsa wants you to ambush me tonight when I get off the bus at the natural history museum."

Quiet on the line. I listened to background noise, hearing traffic.

"But I won't be there. I don't need to put any money under the seat on a bus. The money has already been delivered."

Jesse and Marc watched me. Their faces were tense and focused.

"I paid the fifty thousand dollars to Toby Price an hour ago," I said.

"You gave Toby the money?"

"All of it."

He was quiet again. I forced a sick laugh from my throat.

"Let me guess. Sinsa told you there wasn't any money."

"I know there wasn't any money."

"You idiot. Of course there was money."

"Then where was it?"

"In the safe at the law firm, Sanchez Marks. I got it out tonight."

"You're lying."

"They grabbed Devi Goldman along with P.J. Don't you know who she is? She's the daughter of the firm's chairman. Of course there was money to ransom her. They're *lawyers*."

Hesitation. "I don't get it."

"I'm trying to tell you. Sinsa set us both up. P.J. and Devi are already home having a beer, and Toby's getting ready to sail."

Hard breathing. "You're full of shit."

"Shaun, you're into film. Doesn't the phrase *femme fatale* ring any bells?"

Did I hear him wiping his hand across his forehead?

"She's the femme, and you're going to be the fatale. Think about it. She hasn't done a bit of the dirty work. She's set you up to take every fall. Brittany, Ricky, and now P.J. and me."

"No."

"So who's on the surveillance tape closing down the fake checking account at Allied Pacific Bank—her, or you?"

"Stop—just stop. What the fuck are you saying?"

"That she's going to split that fifty thousand with Toby. Meanwhile, you're walking into a SWAT ambush at the natural history museum."

Outside a train whistle rose on the night, bellowing past up on the tracks, followed by the clack of the wheels. All right, time to light the second-stage booster.

"But I don't want them to have that fifty K. And if we get it back from Toby, nobody's the wiser. It doesn't have to go back into the safe at the law firm. You and I can split it."

Long, long quiet. "Why should I help you?"

"You get us on board, I bring the gun. The rest is ballistics."

He breathed noisily. "I don't know."

Come on, Shaun, buy it. I was running out of bluffs.

And then I heard, on Shaun's end of the line, the same train whistle I had just heard. He was close. Real close.

He was coming here. Shit. The bastard, jumping the gun, trying to get me.

"Forget it," I said. "I'll do it myself, and keep all fifty thousand bucks."

"No, I never said that—"

"Call me back if you change your mind."

I hung up. "He's coming. We're getting out of here."

They looked at me. Jesse put his hand on the Glock.

"Not yet," I said. "He's on the scent. We're going to let him lead the hunt, like a hound dog." I ran for the front door. "Marc, throw me your keys. Move it, men."

37

I floored Marc's truck up the driveway and out into the road. In the rearview mirror I saw Jesse and Marc pull out in the Mustang. Jesse didn't follow me but turned off the road and backed the Mustang into the bushes past his drive. He switched off the headlights. I turned the corner and saw a freight train racketing past the railroad crossing. The lights and bells were going and the gate was down. I pulled up and waited. If Shaun was on the other side, I was going to have to do this fast. I hoped to hell he didn't have a gun.

The caboose clacked past. For a few seconds the bells and lights kept going. Across the tracks, beyond the other gate, I saw a single bright headlight.

Shaun was riding P.J.'s Suzuki.

The gate swung up. I put down the window. Jamming it in first gear, I popped the clutch and bounced across the tracks. I stuck my arm out the window and flipped Shaun the bird.

I shouted, "Forget it, asshole. The money's mine."

He wasn't wearing a helmet. Even in the darkness I could see the shock on his pretty face. I hit the gas.

This truck had plenty of power but not what I wanted right then, acceleration. I upshifted, shot a glance at the mirror, and saw Shaun turning the bike around to follow me.

Fumbling with the headset mike for my phone, I called Jesse. "He's on my tail. Driving P.J.'s bike."

"We're coming."

The pickup's headlights swallowed the road. Trees streaked past. "I'll be at the freeway on-ramp in about a minute."

"We just crossed the tracks."

The trees thinned, and I passed the Miramar Hotel. The road curved. The freeway overpass was ahead, past a stop sign. Checking the mirror, I saw that I was out of sight of the bike. I turned off the headlights, braked, and swerved into a driveway. I shut off the engine. I could hear the bike coming up the road. I held my breath.

In the mirror I saw the bike race past behind me. Shaun stopped at the stop sign, turned onto the overpass, and cruised slowly across, as though looking over the railing to see which way I had gone. I lost sight of him. I stuck my head out the window, trying to hear the Suzuki.

Into the phone mike I said, "He didn't follow me. But I can't tell whether he got on the freeway north-bound, or stayed on San Ysidro heading toward the mountains."

I put the pickup in reverse and spun the wheels backing out of the driveway.

In my ear Jesse said, "Whoa."

I saw him streak past behind me. He cut the corner at the stop sign and gunned the car onto the freeway heading north.

"Ninety percent sure he's heading up the coast," Jesse said. "But you take San Ysidro, just in case." In the background Marc said something. "And Dupree says the truck goes faster if you drive forward."

I headed up San Ysidro Road in the night, past a grove of oaks, cruising toward the mountains, slowing to look up and down side streets. I saw no sign of Shaun.

In my ear Jesse said, "Got him."

I braked.

"He's heading north on One-oh-one, and there's plenty of traffic to screen us. Now let's see if he takes us to Toby."

I pulled a three-point turn and headed back to catch up with him. "Is it time to call Lily?"

"No."

We were ripping along. I was doing eighty, and it still took me ten miles to catch up with Jesse. By then we were heading through Goleta. Shaun streaked up the freeway. We shadowed him, hiding in traffic, taking turns getting behind him so he wouldn't become suspicious. We rolled through the commercial flare of the town, and on past long miles of suburbia that gradually thinned into countryside. The highway began to snake over hills and gullies, past canyons thick with eucalyptus, through the big ranches where prize cattle grazed the hills and the scent of lemon flowed from the orchards. Wind buffeted the truck. Traffic dribbled to a minimum.

I was a hundred yards behind the Suzuki. Jesse was another hundred behind me. I pinged him on the phone. "It's starting to feel naked out here."

"Only a few places he can turn off between here and the point. Drop back if you're nervous."

"We can't lose him."

We headed into open countryside. To my right the mountains blocked the sky. To my left the ocean spread in a satin void across the horizon. Only the occasional wink of light from an offshore oil platform broke the blackness. We passed El Capitán Beach, and Refugio. Passed dirt roads that turned off toward coves and cliffs. Passed a half-hidden road leading through trees to an oil refinery. We crossed the Tajiguas Canyon bridge.

Jesse said, "I think I know where he's headed."

"Where?"

"The Cojo Oil pier, out past Gaviota Beach. Moor a sailboat there in the dark, and it would be impossible to spot from the road. And a coast guard search boat would have to come way around the point to spot it."

"Then I'll call Lily Rodriguez."

Over the phone, I heard him talking to Marc. "No, we have a decision to make. There are two roads to the pier. The first is the one everybody knows about, but it's slower, with cattle guards, a creek, and gates. The second one's farther up the freeway, but if we push it we can beat Shaun by miles."

"So take the second road."

"Here's the problem. The first road also leads to Aubrey's Cove. You could anchor a boat there and row a rubber raft to the beach. If that's where Shaun's going, we'd lose him. And we wouldn't get back for half an hour. Way too late."

"Your call," I said.

The engine droned. "Okay, stick with me."

"What are you going to do?"

"Improvise."

The truck swallowed the road. The white line blurred past. "I'm giving Lily the heads up. We're way the hell out here. It's going to take deputies God knows how long to catch up. But they can send a car to the cove as well as the pier."

"Do it."

But Lily's phone was switched off. I got Gary Zelinski, who sounded irked in the extreme. "Following Shaun Kutner? Do you know there's a warrant out for his arrest? He's a wanted murderer. You should have phoned in this information when you first found it."

"You can scold me, or you can send the deputies to this pier."

"I'll send them. You just sit tight. All of you."

Hanging up, I strained to see Shaun ahead. We

crested a rise, and his brake lights came on. He pulled off the highway, turning toward the beach. I backed off the gas.

The Mustang came screaming past me, blowing right by the turnoff. I punched Jesse's phone number.

"Blackburn. You're improvising at a hundred miles an hour."

"We're taking the chance. Come on."

His taillights were diminishing. I passed the first turnoff, seeing a sign that read COJO OIL. Sitting tight wasn't an option. I followed him.

38

Dust thickening in the moonlight. With the headlights off, that was the only sign I had that the Mustang was still on the road ahead. We were curving downhill along a gully toward the beach, and the asphalt had run out half a mile back.

Jesse's brake lights came on. I stopped behind him, and through the swarm of dust saw Marc jump from the Mustang and run ahead. He pushed open the gate to a cyclone fence. We drove through. Posted on the gate was PRIVATE PROPERTY, NO TRESPASSING. COJO OIL.

Trickling water lit up the ground to our left. The road paralleled a stream. Ahead, moonlight tickled the ocean's surface. We drove across the stream and Jesse stopped. I got out and my breath frosted the air. The salt bite was sharp on the night. Jesse put down his window.

"I don't want to drive any closer. But if you go up to that rise, you'll be able to see the beach and the pier."

Marc got out of the Mustang. We jogged up the rise. In the brush uphill from us, oil pumps rocked up and down. They looked like giant grasshoppers see-sawing in the night. As soon as we topped the hill, the wind caught us. It was bitter. The surf was angry, spraying white mist in the moonlight. The pier stretched ahead of us, running half a mile into the water. On it were more oil pumps, a couple of derricks, and stacks of drilling equipment. The cyclone gate onto the pier was chained shut in the middle. The surf roared through the pilings.

Marc crouched down and pointed at the far end of the pier. "Boat landing."

I squinted at the darkness. I could barely make out a wooden staircase leading down from the top of the pier to the water.

His voice rumbled. "And Toby's boat's moored alongside."

"You can see that?" All I could make out was a bobbing blob. "Are those the lights in the cabin?"

"Can't distinguish any movement. The curtains must be closed." He continued staring. "How much time do we have?"

"Sheriffs might take twenty minutes. Shaun, ten minutes max."

He glanced at his luminous blue watch. "It's five till ten. Whoever's downtown hoping to collect the fifty thou off the bus, in five minutes they're going to know it's blown."

"We can't wait. We have to go." I turned.

He took my arm, stopping me. "Jesse won't be able to get down the stairs to that boat. What's he going to do?"

"Whatever it takes, Marc. He'll go all the way, and beyond."

Marc's eyes were black under the moonlight. The wind kicked up, raking my face. The surf slammed through the workings of the pier. Marc turned and ran back to the Mustang.

He clasped the windowsill. "We only have a few minutes. I say we screw stealth."

Jesse nodded. "Absolutely. You have the tonnage. I'll run interference."

Marc pounded his hand on the roof of the car and sprinted for the pickup.

"Wait." Jesse held out the Glock. "Take it."

Marc jammed it in the small of his back. "When I get your brother and the girl, I'm going to rip straight out of here and keep going until I reach safe ground. Make sure I have a clear path out."

He ran to the truck. Jesse called to me, pointing at the hillside and telling me to get down behind the rise, out of sight. Marc slammed the pickup door and started the engine. His headlights flipped on, high beam. Jesse started the Mustang.

Marc was going to get P.J., and Jesse was going to throw himself in front of anybody who tried to stop that. He wanted me out of harm's way. And I knew what counted, and what he needed.

I ran to the pickup and climbed in. Marc gave me a critical eye, but didn't stop me.

"Buckle up and cinch it down."

He jammed it in gear. The engine groaned, the truck gaining speed over the rise. I buckled my seat belt, feeling the truck gather itself and power down the hill toward the pier.

Marc upshifted. "Hang on."

I braced myself. This wasn't a movie, and that was no breakaway prop straight ahead, and hell, here it came, a big metal gate chained shut in the middle, shining silver in the headlights. We crashed straight into it.

Sparks jumped. The truck shuddered. I swung against the seat belt and felt a stabbing pain in my ribs. The gate ripped from its hinges and flipped onto the hood, shrieking. Marc kept his foot down. The gate screeched across the windshield, flew aside, and we careered out onto the pier, climbing the incline, hearing the wooden rattle of the planks beneath us.

Marc's voice was calm. "I'll go down the stairs to the boat. You take the wheel. Turn the truck around so that when I come back we're ready to roll."

We raced out onto the pier, passing oil pumps and

equipment sheds, a derrick spiking into the sky, a
flatbed truck stacked with drill casings. There was no
guardrail, just railroad ties spiked along the edges of
the pier like curbs. The ocean spread on either side
of us far below, a maw. Straight ahead, where the pier
ended, were a crane and hoists and then darkness.
Marc steered, eyes straight ahead.

I looked back through the rear window of the cab.
The beach was a thin strip, immensely distant. The
Mustang was parked at the foot of the pier, blocking
it.

"Get ready," Marc said.

I braced. My ribs were aching. He braked sharply
and we screeched to a stop next to the staircase, ten
feet from the end of the pier.

"Take it."

He leaped from the cab. I clambered over the gearshift into the driver's seat. He had the gun in his hand.
He racked the slide and charged down the stairs out
of sight.

I put the truck in gear. My legs felt like water. Spinning the wheel, I began turning around. The pier was
narrow, and when I got the truck angled sideways all
I could see, fore and aft, was night. I turned by feel,
knowing that the truck's big tires could easily run
over the eight-inch curbs and swan-dive straight
down to the water. Inching, forward and reverse,
teasing the clutch, I got the pickup aimed back
toward shore. I put down the windows, hoping to
hear something. Anything. The wind howled. I pulled
forward of the staircase so that when Marc returned
he could jump straight in. P.J. and Devi could climb
in the cargo bed.

I heard the screech of the wind, and the slur of the
ocean rushing through the pilings. The clang of metal
from the crane at the end of the pier.

Low sounds. Hard, popping sounds swallowed by
the wind. My airway constricted. God, tell me those

weren't gunshots. In the rearview mirror I peered at the top of the staircase.

Footsteps pounded up the stairs. I saw someone. Wild curls, skirt swirling around her legs. It was Devi Goldman, running toward me.

She jumped in. "Drive!"

"Where's Marc?"

"They're shooting. Fuck, fuck, drive!"

I looked at the stairway. "Does Marc have P.J.?"

She stared at me, wild-eyed. "P.J.'s dead."

It felt as if an archer had loosed an arrow deep into my forehead. Shock, pain, electricity running down my chest and through my limbs. A high-frequency ringing in my ears.

"Go, crap, go." She looked back at the staircase. And screamed.

A new figure was climbing the stairs. The moon shone off a white T-shirt and a gleaming skull. It was Murphy.

He had a gun in his hand. He raised it and fired. The back window of the cab shattered. Devi and I jumped, and she screamed again. I slammed the truck into gear.

And reversed straight into him.

I hit him, heard a thud, and braked, because the crane was right behind me, and the crane was at the end of the pier. Devi kept screaming. I put it in first and drove forward. I couldn't see Murphy behind me anymore.

"You ran him over. You ran him fucking over." Devi's mouth was wide.

I certainly fucking did. I put it in reverse and backed up again. And forward. And back again. I felt like I was in a trance. Up and down the pier, swerving, stomping on the gas and the brake, hearing the tires spin, smelling rubber, trying to cover every inch of wood. Flatten you like a tick, Murphy. But I heard no more thuds. Felt no bumps.

"Where'd he go?" I said. "Where the hell is he?"

"Who cares? Get out of here."

Murphy had to be down. Dead or unconscious, or gone over the edge. Otherwise he'd be shooting at us.

Devi slapped my arm. "Why are you sitting here? Go. Go, go, go."

I grabbed her by the hair. "Stop it. Who's still down on the boat?"

Her mouth yawned into an oval. "What is wrong with you?"

"Toby Price?"

"No, he left."

"When?" I pulled harder on her hair.

She tried to claw my hands loose. "Forty-five minutes ago, to get the money."

"So tell me. Who. Is. On. The. Boat."

"The black man who came charging down."

"Where's P.J.?"

"Murphy took him off. Toby told him he didn't want any mess on the boat."

"Mess? You mean killing?"

"Yeah. Right before he left," she said.

"So when Marc came down—"

"It was just me and Murphy on the boat. Let go of my hair."

So where had Murphy taken P.J.? The arrow of pain dug into my skull. He had dumped him. My stomach was churning. I looked at the staircase. No sign of Marc.

I looked toward shore. Jesse was waiting there for his brother. No, don't think about it. Think and I would lose it, uncontrollably. I'd be useless. And I had to hold on.

I opened the door. "I'll be right back."

"What?"

I stepped carefully out onto the pier. The wind keened around me. My foot touched the wood. Nothing grabbed my ankle. Murphy wasn't under the truck, pulling a *Cape Fear*. I reached into the bed for Marc's golf bag and pulled out the driver.

"Marc's down there on the boat. Is he hurt?" I said.

Her face was disbelieving. "You're leaving me here?"

"I'll be right back. Was he hurt?"

"I don't know."

"Right back. You're okay. Sit tight."

And holding the golf club like a mace, I charged down the stairs toward the boat landing. The wind needled my hands and face. The water roared below me. After five steps, my courage started flaking off like old paint. I wanted help, but I'd never get Devi back down here. I kept going. Halfway down, the stairs hinged—from fixed to floating, so that along with the landing platform they could rise and fall with the tide. I stepped onto them and felt as if I'd mounted a bareback horse at a gallop.

I took my eyes off my descent and saw a bad sight: The sailboat had come unmoored from the landing. It was wallowing loose, starting a slow spin. The ocean shrugged and slammed the boat against the landing. Fiberglass shrieked.

I cupped a hand to my mouth. "Marc."

The hinged stairs bucked with the rise and fall of the water. The boat slammed against the landing. It jolted me. I grabbed for the railing, slipped, and fell back on the stairs. The golf club twirled loose and fell. I heard my cell phone crack.

Shit.

I held fast to the railing, feeling as though I were trapped in a funhouse. And then I heard the carnival music. I heard the truck being put in gear.

And driving away.

I ran up the stairs two at a time, out onto the pier, and saw the pickup racing toward shore. For possibly five seconds I stood there, mouth hanging open, watching Devi make tracks.

Then I got a grip. No, I told myself, this is actually all right. Jesse's there. When she tells him, he'll come get me.

I looked around. All I saw was night. All I felt was wind. All I heard was the dwindling rumble of the pickup, and the chink of the hoists and crane swaying in the wind. Murphy was nowhere to be seen. I had knocked him off the end of the pier. I looked back over the edge, down at the boat landing. The sailboat was wallowing, its bow scraping the pontoons of the platform and rasping on past. The tide was coming in, strong. The boat wouldn't stay here for more than a minute. If Marc was down there, I had to find him now.

I looked again at the shore. The pickup's taillights had shrunk to red bug bites. She was nearing the beach. I held my breath, squinting, watching for her to stop. Come on, Jesse, come on. I'm right here.

The pickup hit the road and kept going, without even slowing down. And the Mustang lit out after it.

I was hosed.

Gripping the railing of the funhouse stairs, I edged down to the landing platform. I felt nauseated. From the rocking motion, from the roar and chill of the ocean. From knowing that Marc, if he was alive, was hurt. And that getting to him would be a bitch.

Holding the railing, I stepped onto the landing platform. It pitched on the surf. The surface was wet and slick.

"Marc," I called.

The sailboat was still there. Rolling, lurking just off the platform.

"Marc."

The boat rose on a wave, like a beast, and rammed the platform. Metal and fiberglass screamed. The platform juddered. I lost my footing and fell backward on my butt. The platform reared. I slid back-

ward, swearing. Heading for the edge. I flung my
arms out and grabbed the bottom stair. I clung to it.
Oh, crap.

The platform dropped. The ocean stormed through
the pilings. Holding on to the step as though it were
my own mother, I tried to see where the sailboat
was.

One more time I yelled, "Marc."

The boat rolled and snapped upright again. The rigging was coming down. The mooring lines were dragging along the edge of the dock. If I could grab one,
I thought . . .

If I could grab one, the next swell would pull me
straight off the platform. Unless I could catch it on
the trough of a wave, and maybe wrap it around the
railing for the staircase.

No, it was too much. If Marc was even on the boat.
If Marc was even still alive.

He had gone down here for P.J. Run into the teeth
of danger for Jesse's brother. For me, and for the man
I had chosen. And he had children. Two girls, Hope
and Lauren.

I couldn't leave.

The boat subsided and lazed toward me. The mooring line hung free from the bow, dragging on the dock.
Hunkering down on all fours, I lunged across the platform, sliding across marine paint, arm extended,
stretching for it. It swung toward me.

I grabbed it. Crawled back as fast as I could for the
railing. But not fast enough. An incoming swell lifted
the boat and heaved it away from the platform.
Caught sideways to the wave, it heeled over, near to
capsizing. The rope yanked in my arms, pulling me
belly-down across the dock. My injured shoulder and
arm went loose, uncontrollably helpless. The rope
slithered from my grasp into the water. The boat
heaved. And was sucked away from the platform for
good.

I lay spread-eagled, facedown on the platform, watching the boat rasp into the pier. Even if I'd been a lifeguard, not in a million years could I get aboard it now. The tide was going to run it aground.

I got to my feet and staggered for the stairs. The ocean boomed. The wind slapped the crane and hoists around above me.

I climbed, fighting tears. My ribs and shoulder ached. Everything was screwed.

And I had to hurry. Shaun was still coming. So were the sheriffs, but I couldn't count on their getting here first. Eventually Jesse would realize that Devi had run off with the truck and he'd return, but I didn't know when.

Just that I'd have to tell him about P.J.

He had wondered aloud how people dealt with finding a loved one's body. What was he going to do when they found P.J.'s? A fat sob jumped up my throat. I climbed, hearing clattering and moans on the wind. Ghost hecklers.

Or not. I looked around. Below the end of the pier where the hoist cables swung in the wind, I saw a big metal hook. Standing on it, clinging to the cable, was Murphy Ming. Staring at me. His varnished skull gleamed in the moonlight.

He started climbing.

I ran up the stairs and out onto the pier. Looking back at the hoist cable, I saw Murphy's head and shoulders appear. The studs on his dog collar shone like nails.

I'd never beat him to the beach. My ribs hurt like hell. I had to hide.

Ahead were an oil pump and an equipment shack. Parked beside the pump was a flatbed truck stacked with drill casings. I ducked behind it.

I stepped gingerly, barely able to see my footing,

and set my foot down on a hose. It gave under my weight and I stumbled, hitting a valve assembly.

I clambered onto the flatbed and crouched next to the drill casings. They were heavy steel, cold under my touch. In front of me was a set of chain tongs. They were a heavy tool, a long metal handle with a length of what looked like bicycle chain attached at the end. Rig crews used them as wrenches, but I could use them as a whip.

By the edge of the pier, the oil pump thrummed and whined. Its rocker beam swung up twenty feet into the air and back down, as if the pump were a praying mantis dipping its head repeatedly for a drink.

I heard Murphy running toward the flatbed. His footsteps slowed to a walk. I reached for the chain tongs and looked at the deck for a spot to jump down. I saw the hose I had tripped over.

It wasn't a hose. It was P.J.

He was lying facedown near the flatbed. His Converse tennis shoes were untied. It made him look like a little kid.

It took my breath away. I crouched there, unable to tear my eyes from his body. Gritting my broken teeth so I wouldn't cry out loud. From the way his cargo pants sagged on his rear end, it was obvious that they were unzipped.

Bastard. Son of a bitch. Suck-ass, pissing shithead Murphy.

Heat soured in my gut. On the far side of the flatbed, Murphy's footsteps stopped. He knew I was nearby. I picked up the chain tongs and the chain dragged across the flatbed, clinking.

"Come out, come out, wherever you are," he said.

His voice was moving. I held my breath.

"This can go easy or hard. Your choice."

He stepped around the flatbed. He had a revolver

in his right hand. He bent down and grabbed P.J.'s ankle.

"Why don't I show you what's gonna happen if I have to hunt for you any longer?"

He began dragging P.J.'s body, looking around. He saw me. The heat, the arrow of grief, my fear and rage erupted. I stood up, raised the tongs over my shoulder, and swung the chain.

39

Twelve minutes.

Now, counting it, I know that's how long it took from the time Marc and I crashed through the gate till the end with Murphy. I don't drink a beer in twelve minutes.

But that night, adrenaline frenzy drove me out of my skin. I couldn't reconstruct the choreography if my life depended on it. But it had.

Murphy stepped around the flatbed. The chain whipped down, hitting him across the shoulders. He staggered in pain. I swung again, hysterically, aiming for the gun in his hand.

I missed.

He should have killed me. He had a prizewinning shot. But the chain had wrapped around his neck, and instinct made him claw at it. I pulled up as hard as I could, choking him.

He swung the gun around, aiming in my general direction. His empty gaze centered on me. I leaped off the flatbed, holding on to the chain tongs. He gurgled. His hands clawed at his throat. The chain had tangled in the studs of his leather dog collar.

He was fighting for breath, but I knew I couldn't hold him. His strength was immense. I might as well have grabbed the tail of an F/A-18 as it took the catapult shot off a carrier deck. Damned if I held on, damned if I let go.

I had to secure him to something, now. And it was right there.

The oil pump, rocking up and down, humming and squeaking, pulling the pump cables that ran down into the well. I yanked him back, off balance. The head of the pump rocked down. I jammed the handle of the tongs through the rigging of the pump cables and twisted, lodging it there.

The pump rose. Murphy went up with it, hanging from the chain.

His legs jerked. His body spun. I watched, thinking, *So help me, I just hanged a man.* Feeling deep, crazed numbness, and disbelief that his greasy body wasn't wrapping itself around me. I stumbled back, watching with horrified fascination.

The pump rocked down. Murphy's feet landed square on the deck, releasing the pressure on his neck. He reached overhead and scrambled to dislodge the chain from the rigging. The pump rocked up. He gagged and jerked into the air again. But though he writhed he held on to the chain, keeping himself from strangling.

He raised the gun over his head and fired, trying to shoot the chain.

That was when fight-or-flight made me crazy. Firearms and oil wells: Don't try this at home. I scrambled away from him, around the flatbed. He fired another shot. It pinged off the pump.

And the pier began to rattle, like a faint drumroll. I looked toward the beach. A single headlight was driving toward us. It was Shaun.

I was so hellaciously tired. And God the lousy comedian had an infinite supply of jokes.

The motorcycle was still almost half a mile away. He couldn't see me yet. There was only one place left to hide—behind the equipment shed, on the edge of the pier. I ran and hunkered down against the wall, a foot from the drop. My teeth were chattering from the cold. My hands were numb. The wind ran through my hair.

Murphy had stopped shooting. I hesitated to look, but the oil pump was just beyond the corner of the shed. I stretched, and peeked.

He was still swinging from the chain tongs. Alive. He had shoved the revolver in his jeans and was holding frantically to the pump cables with both hands, doing a pull-up. When the pump swung down, he planted his feet on the deck and fought to disentangle himself. When it rose he rode it up, keeping the pressure off his neck.

The motorcycle cruised closer. The headlight couldn't reach me behind the shed, but I heard the bike rumble along the pier, driving carefully over the planks. The sound dimmed for a moment as it passed the far side of the shed. Shaun was heading for the boat landing.

Murphy grunted. I turned my head, saw his feet on the deck, his hands jerking at the tongs. He was watching me.

Up he went.

The motorcycle stopped. It idled a second, and the engine shut down. I heard Shaun's voice.

"Murphy. Holy shit."

Though I pressed myself against the wall of the shed, I couldn't help but turn my head and peek around the corner of the building. I saw Shaun hop over the valve assembly and trot to the oil pump. Murphy came down.

"Power," he groaned. Back up.

Shaun watched Murphy's feet swing into the air. "You want me to shut down the power?"

Murphy reached the apex, feet twirling above Shaun's head, and came back down. "There."

He pointed. At the edge of the shed, where I was hiding.

Shaun spread his hands. "Hang on. I'll cut the power."

Murphy was jerked off his feet. His finger lingered, aimed at me, for just a second. His eyes were holes. He grabbed the cables. The pump hit its apex.

Shaun climbed over the pipes. "Here it is."

He hit the emergency shutoff switch. The pump stopped—just past the apex, on the downswing. Murphy's inertia ripped his hands loose from the cables. He swung, feet pinwheeling, spinning, letting out a strangled roar. His hands tried to reach the cables again, but missed.

I pushed myself back against the wall of the shed. The sounds twisted the air for long seconds, and stopped. I turned my head. Shaun was watching Murphy dangle from the chain.

"Lights out, shithead," he said.

A female voice said, "Jesus, shut up with the punch lines. You're not funny."

It was Sinsa. She had to be riding pillion on the bike. Shaun must have picked her up before he reached the beach—no wonder it took him so long to get here.

"Stop smiling, Shaun, that's sick." Footsteps. "Fine, stand there preening. I'm going to find out the deal with Delaney and this supposed money."

He spread his hands. "Don't be such a bitch. Sin—"

"You blew the chance to get her downtown on the bus. You'd better be right that she's out here."

"Of course she's out here." He waved at Murphy. "What do you think happened to him?"

"Shit." Her boots clunked across the planks, faster. "Then she's either somewhere in this junk or she's down on the boat. Find her. And don't let her get away." Her voice receded.

Shaun stood for a moment, looking around. The wind feathered his tangles. He crouched and peered under the flatbed truck. He stood and looked up at the top of the oil pump. He watched Murphy dangle.

He took a deep breath. He seemed to be relishing the sight of it.

Distantly on the night came the sound of tires humming over the road. I laid my head back against the weathered wood of the shed. Cops. Or Jesse. But someone was coming. Just stay here, I thought. Just stay quiet. Don't move. Make yourself a mouse, an ant, a speck of dust, invisible. Help will come.

Shaun flipped the power switch. Murphy swung down like a sock puppet. When the body came down, eye to sightless eye, Shaun lifted the revolver from the waistband of Murphy's pants.

I crept to the corner of the shed facing the beach. A single car was coming. Fast. No flashing lights or siren. It bucked over the rise in the road and sheared down toward the pier. Sliding sideways, not backing off the power.

Damn, Jesse knew how to make an entrance. Did they teach that at stupid-ass driving school?

I couldn't see Shaun, but I knew he had to hear the engine too. I was going to have to time this right—when Jesse came close enough, run to the Mustang and hop in. He'd have to back it off the pier, fast, to keep out of Shaun's firing range. I gauged the distance.

Behind me I heard a choking sound. I turned my head. Murphy was going up and down on the pump like a yo-yo, hanging limp. He was dead.

The choking sound again. It was coming from the deck, near the flatbed. And then I saw movement, no more than a twitch.

It was P.J. He was alive.

40

P.J. twitched again. He made a choking sound, and his arms flailed. I felt astonished, joyful, and instantly horrified. Shaun's footsteps headed for the noise. P.J. was struggling to sit up.

Endgame. Brawn wouldn't work; running away wouldn't work. The only way out was straight ahead, finishing what I'd started with Shaun.

I stood up, counted to three, and strode out from behind the shed.

"We're too late. The money's gone."

He turned and aimed the revolver at me. "And you're full of shit. P.J.'s not home having a beer. He's right here."

"You still can't tell them apart, can you? That's Jesse."

My mouth was so dry, my lips so numb, I was surprised I could speak. "You should have come with me earlier. And you should not have brought Sinsa with you now."

P.J. was fumbling around, uncoordinated. He tried to get to his hands and knees, but his pants were coming down. The Mustang's headlights swelled. I walked out to the center of the pier, where Jesse would be able to see me.

"What in fuck happened here?" Shaun said.

"It went bad."

He looked doubtful. He aimed the gun at P.J. "What's Jesse doing here?"

"He tried to get the money back for the law firm. Leave him. He's not worth worrying over."

The gun remained aimed at P.J.

"Shaun, don't waste a bullet on a frickin' lawyer."

He pointed at the headlights, now racing toward us. "Who's that?"

"It's your proof."

"Of what?"

"That Sinsa double-crossed you."

I balled my hands inside the pockets of my coat so that he couldn't see me shaking like a popcorn popper. I glanced at the end of the pier. Sinsa had gone down to the dock. But she wouldn't stay down for long.

"She's setting you up to take the fall for killing Ricky. And then she's looking to get the big bonus."

The headlights approached, illuminating Shaun's face. "Bonus? What bonus?"

"Selling the story to Hollywood."

"You're wack," he said.

Okay, leap of intuition. "She filmed it, Shaun. Ricky's murder."

"No. No, she didn't. She refused."

Grab the thread. "Wrong. She just didn't want you to be the one to get possession of the tape. She wanted an exclusive."

His eyes narrowed. "You're fucking with me."

"There're CCTV cameras all over Green Dragons. You didn't know? Karen installed fiber-optics everywhere, to keep tabs on Sinsa. You know how tight she keeps Sinsa's leash, right?"

He grabbed a glance at the stairs. "She got it on video?"

"Of course she did. And she's got big plans for that video."

"The cops? Fuck, that would implicate her too."

"No. Think, Shaun, who's on the video? What will it show?"

His face seemed to go blank. "Oh, fuck. Fuck her

bitch ass. It'll show her punching me, make it look
like . . ."

"Like what?"

"Like she was trying to stop me. Fuck her. I don't
believe it."

"Believe it. She plans to sell the tape, big-time. A
major studio. Or cable, if the story's fading. And you
won't get a voice in it. They'll get some B-lister to
play you. Some soap actor. Or a boy-band singer."

"No, no, no."

"And she gets all the money. And all the credit."

His shoulders swelled. He shook his head and swung
the revolver up at my face.

"You're lying. Prove it. Show me proof," he said.

P.J. crawled out from under the flatbed truck.

The headlights of the Mustang hit us full force. The
engine growled and the car braked to a stop. I couldn't
see beyond the lights, but I knew Jesse could see everything that was going on.

"Put the gun down. If you use it on me, you'll waste
the last bullet and never get the money."

Ping, his eyes went wide. He stared at the gun, and
at me, and at the car. He lowered the gun and flipped
open the cylinder to check the bullets. I couldn't see
how many were in fact loaded, and the fuzzy expression on Shaun's face didn't tell me much either way.

I looked at the car. I jittered my knee the way P.J.
always did and lifted my chin in greeting, his way.

For a moment we held there, a frieze. Under the
blinding high beams, we couldn't see more than a silhouette. Shaun put his hand up, shading his eyes.

Jesse opened the door and got out. Hauling himself
up, he stood next to the car, leaning heavily against
the roof. With the sun-white glare, it looked as though
he was casually hanging a hand on the door. We could
barely see his face.

"I'm just here to pick them up, dude. Okay?" he
said.

Shaun's face shaded into rage. "Fuck the bitch."

He turned around just as Sinsa came up the stairs. I pointed Jesse back into the car and ran for P.J.

Shaun walked toward her. "Lying traitor."

I grabbed P.J. and pulled him, crawling, toward the car. His breathing was slow and labored. His pupils were pencil dots. He made it to the edge of the pier, put a hand on the railroad tie, and tried to stand. He collapsed on the deck like gelatin.

"Something's weird." He looked at his cargo pants and the undone zipper. "Oh, man." A moment of pain erupted on his face. He bent double.

Sinsa and Shaun were striding toward each other.

"Shaun, what's wrong with you? It's Delaney. Do her," Sinsa said.

"She was telling the truth. P.J. wasn't being held out here. You lying bitch."

"What do you mean? That's him right there." She waved. "Peej."

P.J. pulled himself up onto the railroad tie. "Sin?"

Checkmate.

Shaun stopped, swung the gun around, and aimed it at P.J.'s head. Out of time, out of luck, out of everything. There was only one thing to do.

I yelled to Jesse. "Go."

I pushed P.J. over the edge.

He dropped like a stone. Shaun gaped. Shouting, "*Shit*," he fired down at him. I leaped from the pier into the night.

Air surrounded me. I flung my arms wide, feeling the cold, sensing my feet swing out. How high, thirty feet? Falling through the wind at the black ocean roaring below me.

I hit. Hard, like getting whacked with a door right in the ribs, and I went down into harsh cold, solid dark. The air bubbled out of my mouth.

I kicked for the surface. My clothes dragged on my

limbs. My boots filled with water. I broke the surface gasping, mouth wide, and inhaled seawater. I coughed, choking, and my head slipped under. I kicked maniacally back up. Hacked and spit. The wind sheared water across my face. My ribs were stabbing with pain. I couldn't breathe in.

"P.J."

Nothing. The water heaved, lifting me. I could hear it rushing through the pier. But that was all—I didn't hear the Mustang. Shit. Jesse had to get out of there.

Above on the pier, Sinsa's voice cut through the wind. "Hey, stupid."

"I'm not stupid." I heard Shaun's footsteps. "Calling me names when I'm holding the gun, *that's* stupid."

What had happened to Jesse? And where was P.J.? The water lifted me. The pier was far above, the water deep below. So deep, the thirsty mouth of the earth. I floundered around and looked toward the beach. Jesus God, it was three time zones away. Panic cinched around me.

Beyond me in the dark I heard thrashing. A swell passed, dropping me into the trough. There was P.J., wallowing.

I splashed toward him. He was ten feet away, toward shore. The tide was going in. I went with it, my legs kicking like stones, and grabbed his hand. He sank. I scissored my legs, holding on to his arm, and brought him back up.

He looked at me, terrified. "Evan?"

"I gotcha."

Above us Shaun cried, "You were going to go public and take the credit."

A gunshot cut through the wind and the roar of the ocean. On the far side of a pier came a splash. Body-sized. God, why didn't I hear the Mustang?

I had to get P.J. to shore. Get behind him, I knew that much. Turn him on his back. Cup a hand under his chin to keep his head above water, and so he couldn't grab me in a panic and take us both down.

I slung my arm around him. Water washed over our faces. I choked. He didn't. Shit, the heroin was suppressing his respiratory system. Could he drown without even submerging? Frantically I felt for the naltrexone. It was still jammed in the pocket of my T-shirt, but I couldn't possibly give it to him now.

Half a mile to the beach. Five minutes earlier I'd assessed that I couldn't run that far. Swimming that far would be immensely harder. But I didn't have to make the beach—I could swim back to the boat landing platform. Waiting for a swell, I looked. It was about eighty yards behind us, farther than I'd thought. The tide was giving us a real run. Terror, like a smooth, cold sheet of metal, planed through me.

My arms were stiff with the cold. My legs were burning with the effort of merely treading water. I had to get my clothes and boots off.

"P.J., keep your head back and spread your arms. Float faceup."

He must have heard me, because he did it. Kicking hard, I slipped off my coat. Then I fought my feet out of the cowboy boots. The water slid us into a trough. I unzipped my jeans and wrestled them down. For a jarring second I went below the surface with my Levi's around my knees, binding me so I couldn't kick. My chest went tight. I shoved them off and scissored back up.

The wind bit into me. P.J. was ten feet away again. In the time it had taken me to strip down, the tide had carried him farther away from the platform. I dog-paddled to him. I was seriously, crazily scared. I floundered with him, paddling into the wind, swallowing water.

Above on the pier, the motorcycle buzzed to life. The headlight came on.

Swim, I told myself. Ninety yards to the dock. Jesus,

I hated the ocean. If I got out of the water tonight, I was moving to the desert. The Gobi. The Sahara. China frickin' Lake. I kicked, I paddled. I looked. The dock was farther away.

The motorcycle cruised the edge of the pier. The headlight swung back and forth. Somebody was searching for us.

P.J. looked up. "That's my bike."

"Shaun and Sinsa brought it."

"Shaun wants to kill me."

"We're not going to let him do that." I kicked. My quads were burning.

"Because of Britt," he said.

"He killed Britt, P.J."

He blinked. "I know." His voice was distant. "He shut the door."

The wind sheared water across my face. I kicked for the platform. And abruptly I realized what he had just said.

"That night at the party—you saw Shaun shut the bedroom door?"

"Never thought he'd . . ." He breathed. "Never do it."

His voice trailed off. I tightened my arm around him.

"P.J." Oh, God. "You saw Shaun take Brittany in the bedroom to kill her?"

"Not my fault."

The water lifted us. "What's not?"

"Sin said."

We sank into the trough of the wave. I felt twice as cold as I had a moment earlier.

"Tell me what Sin said."

He gazed nowhere, but seemed to be remembering. "Shaun'll take it from there."

"What, P.J.?"

He opened his mouth, seemingly waiting for the

words to wind their way to his tongue. "I just got Britt to the party."

Water washed over our faces. He gagged and went under. He came up gurgling, but still not coughing.

I gritted my teeth. "Sin said that if you got Britt to the party, Shaun would take it from there?"

He didn't respond. I pinched him.

"You knew that Shaun was going to kill her?" I said.

"No. Gonna scare her." His voice faded. "His friend . . ."

I felt ill with shock and disgust. But I couldn't think about it. Pain seemed to catch him. His head went back and his chin slipped out from under my elbow. I clasped him, kicking, and slung my arm back around him. He was barely breathing. His face was pale, his eyes remote.

"P.J. You can't go to sleep." If he dropped from consciousness, that was it. "Patrick John Blackburn. Wake up, jackass."

I bit him on the ear.

His mouth opened wide. "Ow."

I took a big breath and kicked into the teeth of the wind. I had to make it to the dock. The water lifted us. I held P.J., feeling the ocean pull us up, up, waiting to pass the crest of the swell.

And then I felt it tipping us backward. It was going to break and surf us toward the shore. I turned and looked.

And slammed into a pier piling.

Face-first, full frontal. Stars burst behind my eyes. P.J. was torn away from me. The water swept over my head and I felt what it had become. The black wing, shearing the night. Snapping our lives in two.

A hand buried itself in my shirt and pulled me to the surface.

"Evan."

I hung, unmoored. The stars trailed across my vision like sparks ignited by the black wing. The hand gripped me against the drag of the waves.

"Kick."

I kicked. Jesse hauled me in.

He was clinging to a pier piling with one arm, and to me with the other. He pulled me against his side.

"Grab hold."

I gripped the piling. I tried to speak, to say his name, and nothing came out.

Tears scalded my eyes. "P.J."

"I see him."

He sliced away into the ink under the pier. A wave rushed past, echoing off the wood around us. In its wake I heard another sound: the Suzuki, rolling slowly across the planks above our heads. I held the piling. Thirty seconds later Jesse swam back, hanging onto P.J. His stroke was strong but labored. His face was strained. P.J. looked incoherent.

"That splash off the pier was you," I said.

"Sorry it took so long."

"I can't believe you spotted us."

"Ev, your *Star Trek* panties are visible from outer space."

The motorcycle grumbled overhead. He kept P.J.'s head tilted back.

"I was swimming for the dock," I said.

"We can't do that."

"Why not?"

"Don't you smell it?"

And I did: oil. Shaun or Murphy must have shot a hole in a pipe.

"But it didn't ignite," I said.

"Yet." A wave slapped water into his mouth. He spit. "But if it's leaking there may be vapors. Heat or a spark could set it off."

Such as from the exhaust pipe of the motorcycle.

"We have to swim to shore," he said.

For a second I sensed the black wing circling. There had to be another way.

"We can do it. But you're going to have to help me," Jesse said.

"How?"

"My kick is crap. Take my shoes off."

His jacket and shirt were already off. By the time I got his high tops untied, I worried that P.J. had taken on more water. But Jesse kept up a stream of chatter with both of us, keeping our attention on him, and not the likelihood of drowning. The stink of crude oil was getting stronger.

His shoes came off. He said, "Let's go."

We pushed away from the piling. The sound of the breakers hitting the beach was a distant sigh. Beside me Jesse protected P.J., stroking with one arm, glancing up at the pier. The Suzuki trolled up and down, looking for us.

Jesse's mouth was near P.J.'s ear. I heard him talking to his brother.

"We're getting there. Stay strong."

The wind battered us. The water rode around my face.

"I love you, P.J. Fight this. Keep breathing."

I swam harder. Behind me, on the pier, the Suzuki revved.

There wasn't an explosion, or even a sound. But slowly a red glow emerged from the area near the oil pump. It bloomed, flickering to life. The bike roared away. The pier lit up the night, the water, and our struggling band. Jesse looked at me.

"Six hundred meters, Delaney. Race you to the shore."

41

The breakers were roaring onto the beach. Two sheriff's cruisers barreled past us on the pier above, racing out toward the fire. They didn't see us in the surf. I fought the white water, arms thrashing. And felt sand beneath my feet.

"I can touch bottom." Four unbelievable words. I looked at Jesse.

Yards away, he was barely holding P.J. by the arm, and they were being pulled back with the receding wave.

"He's vomiting." He struggled to turn P.J. onto his side. "Ev, help, take him."

I pulled P.J. through the shallows and dragged him onto the sand. He was unconscious. Under the orange light of the fire I saw that his eyes were rolled back in his head. His lips were blue.

"Turn his head to the side," Jesse called.

I did. Water and vomit drained from his mouth. Jesse shouted over the crash of the waves.

"You have to give him the Heimlich. Kneel down with your legs on either side of his hips."

I straddled P.J. He didn't look to be breathing.

"Put your hands one on top of the other. Heel of your bottom hand between his navel and rib cage." He cleared the surf and pulled himself toward us. "Lean on him. Use your body weight; give him quick upward thrusts."

I pushed. Vomit and water poured from P.J.'s

mouth. I kept pushing, hard and sharp, until nothing more came out.

Jesse was right beside me. "I got him."

I collapsed on the sand. Jesse began CPR. He cleared out P.J.'s mouth, tilted his brother's chin back, and when he heard nothing, began breathing into his mouth.

Jesse was shivering convulsively. His hair hung in strings across his eyes. The wind whipped sand over his skin. He ignored it all. Two breaths, slowly, and he turned his head to watch P.J.'s chest subside. He checked for a pulse. Breathed for him again.

Out on the pier the fire writhed in the wind, but it wasn't getting any purchase. Fire suppression equipment had turned on immediately. The yellow flames were dying down.

I heard a gasp of breath.

"Yeah, P.J., that's it," Jesse said. "Come on, bro."

His voice was broken with cold. His teeth were chattering. His hand, when he put it on P.J.'s forehead, was shuddering.

P.J. moved his legs. He hacked out a breath and opened his eyes.

"Jess?"

Jesse pushed his feet out straight and stretched out alongside P.J., trying to warm him with his own body heat. He pulled P.J. against his chest and rubbed his back.

P.J. heaved in a breath. "You came to get me."

Jesse laid his cheek against P.J.'s forehead, holding on to him as if he were three, not twenty-three.

P.J. put his arm around him. "You rescued me."

Jesse looked at me. "We have to get those deputies' attention."

Nodding, I fumbled the naltrexone packet out of my pocket and gave it to him. I staggered to my feet. I knew what I had seen in Jesse's eyes: belief. That P.J. could, in fact, be rescued.

I walked. The light bar on the sheriff's cars flashed red and blue. I wondered if the Mustang had gone up in the fire.

Jesse couldn't abandon P.J. Not in a million years.

My shoulders jumped with the cold. P.J.'s words rattled in my head: *Sin said.* If he got Britt to the party, Shaun would take it from there.

He knew. He enabled.

I stumbled toward the pier.

He was an accomplice.

When Brittany found the fraudulent credit cards, P.J. must have told Sinsa. Who decided to stop Brittany from exposing their scheme. She knew Brittany was obsessed with P.J. She knew Brittany would follow him anywhere.

On the pier, one sheriff's car was slowly backing up and turning around.

So at Sinsa's urging P.J. lured Brittany Gaines to the party on Del Playa, where Shaun Kutner was waiting for her. A big surprise. Not supposed to be back from Barbados yet. Nobody else saw him sneaking in the back of the house, waiting for Britt.

And when Shaun closed the door, P.J. knew what was going to happen and did nothing to stop it. And he could have. He had literally tons of backup: He was in a house full of fired-up college students. Instead he cowered in the bathroom, horrified by the knowledge that he'd set the trap.

I kept walking toward the pier. The flashing lights edged their way back from the fire. The strobe lit up the surf in hallucinogenic colors. The pier looked eerie. The water shone red.

I stopped. On the far side of the pier, where the light faded again, I saw the sailboat wrecked on the sand. My stomach grabbed.

I ran, stiffly, under the pier and out the other side. The breakers thundered onto the beach. The boat lay tilted to one side, mast broken, rigging a tangle.

"Marc," I called.

I ran around the boat. The cabin windows were broken. Spilled on the sand were soggy junk food, the television, and the first-aid box. It was open, and bandages, the flare gun, and Toby's silver cigarette case lay strewn in the sand. A bunch of gauze packs were ripped open, as though someone had needed them recently and urgently. I staggered around the wreck, trying to find a way to climb inside.

Motion caught my eye. My head popped around. Past the sand was Bermuda grass, the road, the hillside, all deep in shadow. But I'd seen a jet of light.

At the foot of the pier, someone hopped down onto the sand and walked toward me. Almost a hole in the night, darker than dark, hair streaming like a black corona in the wind. Sinsa.

The moon gleamed off her silver earrings and bracelets. And off the pistol gripped in her right hand. She was thirty feet away. Escape was my best option. But the last thing I could shout to Jesse was, *Run*.

I could see her face now. Those eyes, which swallowed light, watching me. As if eating the night, drawing upon it. I stepped back.

Behind her, in the dimness of the grass and road, shadows twisted. Darkness flicking forward. Soundless, air itself striking out. Marc lunged from the shadows, running at her. She saw him and brought the gun up.

I shouted at her. "Sin."

She looked. I held the flare gun in both hands. She pointed her pistol at me.

I fired. And made her a star.

42

The coast guard helicopter medevaced P.J. off the beach. The engines spooled up to a howl and we turned our backs, hunkering away from the sandstorm blown by the rotors. They rose and swooped away over the water. The engines faded. The helo's running lights skirted the coastline and disappeared.

The roar of the surf remained. And the pinwheel flash of the fire engine's lights out at the far end of the pier. We had drawn a crowd. Three sheriff's cars, the engine, an ambulance, and a fire department EMT truck. To the carnival, a free concert of death.

The paramedics were giving Marc the once-over. Bandaging a bloody gash on his head. Murphy had attacked him with a broken Bushmills bottle, and his scalp would need stitches. So would the stab wound in his arm. He had managed to open the gauze packs from the first-aid box and tear his shirt to make a tourniquet, but glass was embedded in his forearm and he'd lost some blood.

I approached the EMT truck. Marc's face, considering it was the color of coffee, looked distinctly gray. A paramedic was checking him for concussion, flicking a miniflashlight in front of his eyes.

"It's a headache, nothing more," he said.

"You upchucked," the paramedic said.

"I was seasick."

The paramedic put down the flashlight. "Aye-aye, skipper."

He climbed into the truck to find some supplies. Marc sat on the tailgate, pressing a gauze pack against his forehead.

"Damned small boats make me seasick. Give me something displacing a hundred thousand tons. With nuclear reactors and an air wing."

I tightened the blanket around my shoulders. "Devi Goldman said there was shooting onboard the boat."

"Afterward." He explained. "Murphy had her, and I didn't have a clear shot." He looked away. "He had a whiskey bottle and was getting ready to use it on her."

The wind caused him to squint. Neither of us said what we feared: that Murphy had been taking a break from raping P.J. with the bottle.

"When Murphy hit me with the bottle, Devi made a break and got out. He chased her. He was up the stairs and on deck before I pulled it together and clocked off four rounds. He locked me in the cabin when he left."

His face was smooth, but I shook my head.

"Uh-uh. That doesn't sound right."

I pulled the gauze pack off. His head was creased with a long trough of a wound.

"Christ, Marc. Murphy shot you."

"Grazed me."

My legs felt weak all over again. "I should have tried harder to get the mooring lines."

His eyes remained cool, but his mouth softened. "You did all right."

"So did you. You got Devi out."

"Bet she's halfway to Arizona. I filled the tank with gas this afternoon."

The deputy walked up, his utility belt creaking. "Miss? Think you're ready to give us an explanation now?"

"Five minutes. Please."

Shaun was dead. Point-blank through the forehead, the deputies said. Some of his last words were a boast—telling Sinsa she was dumb for calling him names when he had the only gun. He was wrong on all counts. Sinsa had a gun wedged in her boot. And Shaun had a gun that had run out of ammunition.

Sinsa was gone, taken away in another ambulance. The flare hadn't been close enough to kill her, but the magnesium fuel had exploded on her chest. She was down, would be for a long time, and wouldn't ever look the same. And I couldn't find any compassion to care.

I exhaled. Toby was in custody. Lily Rodriguez had been onboard the number twenty-two bus when he boarded it downtown—and so had three plainclothes SBPD officers. Shaun may have been supposed to ambush me, but Toby had wanted to grab the money himself. The cops took him without a fight. We were safe now.

Marc reached out and brushed my hair from my eyes. He tucked a lock behind my ear. His eyes were calm. He nodded toward the beach.

"Go on," he said.

I hiked to the verge between the Bermuda grass and the sand, where Jesse sat trying to get warm beneath a fire department blanket. He was gazing at the sky in the direction the helo had flown.

"I need to get to the hospital. I don't want him to be alone," he said.

"Then let's go."

He looked at the pier. "Mustang's gotta be toast." He raked his fingers through his hair. "And my wheels were in the backseat."

I tried to see the end of the pier. I turned to the EMT truck. "Marc. Can you see Jesse's car?"

He took a look, eagle-eyed, and gave us the thumbs up. Jesse blew out a breath.

I stood up. "Give me the keys and I'll get it."

He kept looking at the sky. "Maybe this time. I think this may finally scare him straight."

I saw the wish in his eyes. My heart sank.

I could keep quiet about what P.J. had confessed. I could protect Jesse's fragile reconciliation with him, and hope that this disaster did indeed scare P.J. straight.

P.J. had let Brittany die out of fear and misplaced love for Sinsa Jimson. If I told the sheriffs, P.J. would go to jail. If I told Jesse, it would drive a stake into his heart. After everything that he had been through, how could I do that to him?

He looked up at me. His lips were nearly as blue as P.J.'s had been.

P.J. had lured a trusting friend to her death. If I didn't speak for Brittany, nobody would.

And I knew that Jesse was strong enough to take it, and would hate me for doing anything else. I had to tell the truth. And it might end everything with him, right now.

He sensed my distress. He took my hand. "What's wrong?"

I sat down and told him.

43

Strange light shot the sky. Sunlight raking green oaks and black clouds. Dragon-red bougainvillea shimmering along the fence in front of my house. Hot yellows in front of a charcoal wall of cumulus. I dug my hands into my jeans pockets, watching Marc toss his duffel bag in the back of his pickup.

Devi had taken the truck only as far as Lavonne's house. Which was where she was now reduced to living, at her parents' insistence. She didn't argue the point.

Marc sauntered up to me, putting on his aviator shades.

"Tough day for flying," I said.

"Would be." He panned the horizon. "But not if you got above it."

"Then here's to high flight. Clear skies and a tailwind," I said. "Take care of yourself."

He nodded.

"I'll see you," I said.

"That you will."

Smooth and fast, he had me in his arms, tilting my head back, kissing me. Cool as anything, and taking his time. Pressed to his chest, I felt my heart pound.

"Just so you know," he said.

And so I did. Marc Dupree never sneaked in under the radar. He smiled a dazzling smile and drove away.

He headed into the sun. I was giving him a wave,

shading my eyes with one hand, when the Mustang turned onto the street. They both stopped. I heard them exchange a good-bye.

When Jesse pulled up to the curb, the stereo was pounding. Springsteen, "Born to Run." The Big Man's sax practically shattering the windshield. Jesse put down the window.

"Ready to go?" he said.

"Not quite. Get out."

He scrunched his mouth, nonplussed. I held his door open, leaning on the frame, and he pulled his hardware from the backseat.

"Did you see P.J.?" I said.

He nodded, avoiding my eyes. "He's going to plead. They're offering accessory after the fact to murder." He got out of the car. "He'll do a year in county."

Considering everything, it was a light sentence. Jesse backed up. We faced each other, silent. He couldn't say he was glad, and I couldn't say I was sorry. This was how it was. And how it was between us. No ifs, no going back, no somedays. Only forward.

I took the envelope from my pocket. "Trade."

"For what?"

"Keys."

"Delaney?" He took the envelope, perplexed, and opened it. "It's a check."

"My best offer. Take it or leave it."

"What's this for?"

"I'm buying the Mustang. It's for sale, right?"

"You're serious."

"Had to get rid of that pain-in-the-ass Explorer sooner or later. And this pony needs a good home."

"You're sure you want to spend the money on this?" He looked at the check. "I know you turned Lavonne down on the job offer."

I'd spoken to her an hour earlier. I was honored by her offer, I said, but preferred to work on my own. She took my decision graciously. And I felt free—

as if the wind were at my back and the skies open above me.

"I'm sure." I held out my hand. "Deal?"

That look was skewing Jesse's face. He leaned back, ran his gaze over the low black lines of the car, and handed me the keys.

"Pink slip's at home. And I get to borrow it until I buy another ride," he said.

"And I get to take a test drive."

"Fair enough."

"Get in." I opened the door and dropped into the driver's seat. "I can use the gas pedal, right?"

"Yeah. Just remember, it's a lot more responsive than the Explorer. Where are we going?"

I fired up the engine. Waited while he got in the passenger seat.

"Lunch?" I said.

He closed the door. "And dinner."

"We'd better throw in breakfast, too."

"You need a long stretch of empty highway to really open it up."

I put my hand on the gearshift. "How about Vegas?"

I believe that he was trying not to smile. He put on his wraparound sunglasses, changed the track on the stereo, and turned it all the way up. Springsteen's guitar chimed, hanging in the air, the chord refusing to resolve, until the band came crashing in, piano and drums hitting the offbeats, propelling the song hard, and higher, and soaring. It was "She's the One."

"Drive," he said.

I put the pedal down.

Read on for an exciting preview
of Meg Gardiner's brand-new thriller,

THE DIRTY SECRETS CLUB

Available wherever books are sold
or at penguin.com

Fire alarms sang through the skyscraper, piercing and relentless. Under the din people poured across the marble lobby toward the doors, dodging fallen ceiling plaster and broken glass. Outside, Montgomery Street crackled with the lights of emergency vehicles. A police officer fought upstream to get inside. The blonde was ten feet behind, struggling through the crowd.

The man in the corner paced, head down, needing her to hurry.

People rushed by him, jumpy. "Everything crashed off the bookshelves. I thought for sure it was the Big One."

The man turned, shoulders shifting. The Big One? Hardly. This earthquake had just been San Francisco's regular kick in the butt. But it was bad enough. On the street, steam geysered from manholes. And he could smell gas. Pipes had ruptured under the building. The quake was Hell saying, *Don't forget I'm down here—you fall, I'm waiting for you.*

He checked his watch. Come on, girl, faster. They had ten minutes before this building shut down.

A fire captain glanced at him. He was tall and young and moved like the athlete he was, but nothing clicked in the fire captain's eyes, no suspicion, no *Is that who I think it is?* Out of uniform he looked ordinary, a plain vanilla all-American.

The blonde neared the doors. She stood out from

the crowd, platinum sleek, hair cinched into a tight French twist, body cinched into a tighter black suit. A cop stuck out an arm like he was going to clothesline her. She flashed an ID and slid around him.

He smiled. Right under their noses.

She pushed through the doors and walked up, giving him a hard blue stare. "Here? Now?"

"It's the ultimate test. Secrets are hardest to keep in broad daylight."

"I smell gas, and that steam pipe sounds like a volcano erupting. If a valve blows and causes a spark—"

"You dared me. Do it in public, and get proof." He wiped his palms on his jeans. "This is as public as it gets. You'll supply my proof."

Her hands clenched, but her eyes shone. "Where?"

His heart beat faster. "Top floor. My lawyer's office."

Upstairs, they strode out of the express elevator to find the law firm abandoned. The fire alarm was shrieking. At the receptionist's desk, a computer was streaming a television news feed.

". . . minor damage, but we're getting reports of a ruptured gas line in the financial district . . ."

The blonde looked around. "Security cameras?"

"Only in the stairwells. It's bad business for a law firm to videotape its clients."

She nodded at a wall of windows. The October sunset was fading to dusk, but downtown was ablaze with light. "You plan to do this stunt against the glass?"

He crossed the lobby. "This way. The building's going to shut down in"—he looked at a red digital clock on the wall—"six minutes."

"What?"

"Emergency procedure. If there's a gas leak the building evacuates; they shut down the elevators and seal the fire doors. We have to be out by then."

"You're joking."

The wall clock counted down to 5:59. He started a timer on his watch.

"Yeah. I was meeting with my lawyers when the quake hit. It limits damage from any gas explosion." He pulled her toward a hallway. "I can't believe you're scared of getting caught with me. Not Hard-girl."

"What part of 'secret' do you not you get?"

"If we're caught, they'll ask what we're doing here, not what we're hiding in our pasts."

"Fair point." She hurried alongside him, eyes bright. "Were you waiting for an earthquake before you did this?"

Good guess—this was the third minor quake in the last month. "I got lucky. I've been looking for the perfect opportunity for weeks. Chaos, downtown—it was karma. I figured seize the day."

He rounded a corner. A glass-fronted display case along the wall had cracked, spilling sports memorabilia onto the floor.

She rushed past. "Is that a Joe Montana jersey?"

His stopwatch beeped. "Five minutes."

He opened a mahogany door. Across a conference room the red embers of sunset caught them in the eyes. The hills of San Francisco rose in front of them, electric with light and packed to the rafters like a stadium.

He shrugged off his coat, took a camera from the pocket and handed it to her. "When I tell you, point and click."

He crossed the room and opened the doors to a rooftop terrace. Kicking off his shoes, he strode outside.

"You complained I was using the club as a confessional. You told me I was seeking expiation for my sins, but said you couldn't give me absolution," he said.

Deep below them, the building groaned. She walked outside, breathing hard.

"Damn, Scott, this is dangerous—"

"Your dare was—and I quote—for me 'to offer a public display of penitence, and for Christ's sake, get proof.'"

He pulled his polo shirt over his head. Her gaze seared its way down his chest.

Now, he thought. Before his courage and exhilaration evaporated. He unzipped and dropped his jeans.

She gaped.

He backed toward the waist-high brick railing at the edge of the terrace. "Turn on the camera."

"You came commando-style to a meeting with your lawyers?"

Naked, he climbed onto the brick ledge and stood up, facing her. Her lips parted. Thrilled to his fingertips, he turned to face Montgomery Street.

A salt breeze licked his bare skin. Two hundred feet below, fire and police lights flickered through steam boiling from the ruptured pipe, turning the scene an eerie red.

He spread his arms. "Shoot."

'You have got to be kidding me."

'Take the photo. Hurry."

"That's not penitent."

He glanced over his shoulder. She was shaking her head.

"*Bad?* You tattooed *Bad* on your tailbone?"

His watch beeped. "Four minutes. Do it."

"You're a badass?" She put her fists on her hips. "You get all torn up about a nasty thing you did in college, and want to unload it on us—fine. But you can't tattoo some preening jock statement on your butt and call it repentance. That's not remorse. Hell, it's not even close to being dirty."

Frowning, she stormed inside.

He turned around. "Hey!"

Was she leaving? No, everything depended on her getting the photo. . . .

She ran back out, holding a piece of sports memorabilia from the display case. It was a jockey's riding crop. He swallowed.

She whipped it against a potted plant with a wicked crack. "Somebody needs to take you down a notch."

He nearly whimpered. She wanted points, too. This was even better.

Snapping the crop against her thigh, she crossed the terrace. Evaluating the ledge, she unzipped her ass-hugging skirt, wriggled it down, and stepped out of it.

"It's time to make your act of contrition," she said.

In the tight-fitting black jacket, she looked martial. The stilettos could have put out his eyes. The black stockings ran all the way to the tops of her thighs. All the way to—

"What's that garter belt made from?"

"Iguana hide."

'Jesus, help me."

"I have a drawerful. I got them in the divorce." She held out her hand. "Don't let me fall."

"I won't. I have perfect balance." He felt crazed and desperate and *God*, he needed to get her up here, now. "I get paid four million dollars a year to catch things and never let them drop."

A wisp of her blond hair had escaped the perfect 'do. It softened her. He wanted her to put it back in place. He wanted her to put on leather gloves and maybe an eye patch. He pulled her up on the ledge beside him.

She gripped his hand. Her smooth stocking brushed his leg.

He could barely speak. "This is penance?"

"Pain is just one step from paradise."

She looked down. Her voice dropped. "Christ. This is asking for a heart attack."

"Don't joke."

She looked up. "No—I didn't mean it as a crack about David."

But if David hadn't dropped facedown with a coronary, they wouldn't be here. The doctor's death had created an opening, and Scott wanted to fill it. This was his chance to prove himself and gain admission to the top level of the club.

The breeze kicked up. In the lighted windows of the skyscraper across the street, people gazed down at the fire trucks. Nobody was looking at them.

"Right under their noses," he said. "Bonus points for both of us."

"Not yet." She handed him the camera. "Set it so we're both in the frame."

He set the autotimer to take a five-shot series and set the camera on the ledge. His stopwatch beeped. Three minutes.

She planted her feet wide for balance. "What happens to guilty people?"

Blinking, he turned around and carefully knelt down on all fours. "I've been bad. Spank me."

She slapped the crop against her palm. "What's the magic word?"

Relief and desire rushed through him. "Hard."

The camera flashed. She brought the crop down.

The pain was a stripe of fire along his backside. He gasped and grabbed the ledge.

"Harder," he said.

She whipped the crop down. The camera flashed.

He clawed the bricks. "*Mea culpa.* I've been very, very bad. *More.*"

She didn't hit him. He looked up. Her chest was heaving, her hair spilling from the French twist.

"My God, you actually want to be punished, don't you?" she said.

"Do it."

She swung the crop. It slashed him so hard, he shouted in pain. She wanted to dish out punishment, all right, but not to him. She would use this to send a message to somebody else. The watch beeped.

"Christ, two minutes," she said. "Let's get the hell out of here."

His eyes were watering. "Not yet. Nobody's looking."

"*Looking?* You're nuts. If there's an aftershock I'll lose my balance. We—"

A thumping sound echoed off skyscraper walls. A helicopter swooped over the top of the building above them.

It turned and hovered above Montgomery Street, rotors blaring. Everything on the terrace blew about in the air. Dust, leaves, their clothes. The camera tipped over. Scott grabbed for it but it fell off the ledge.

She yelled, "No, the evidence—"

The camera dropped, hit the building and sprang apart. He let out a cry. His penance, his memories—

The terrace lit with a blinding white searchlight.

"Oh, no—it's a news chopper," she said.

She leapt from the ledge to the terrace. Landed like a gazelle on her stilettos. He scrambled after her, buttocks stinging. They grabbed their clothes and ran for the door. The chopper rotated in the air, searchlight sweeping after them.

She looked back, her eyes brimming with joy and fury. The searchlight lit her hair like a halo.

"Turn around," he shouted. "You want them to get a close-up?"

"The city knows your face, not mine."

"But it's about to know your glorious ass."

He ran into the conference room, stopped and wriggled his left leg into his jeans. The spotlight caught them. He bumbled for the door.

Fumbling her way into her skirt, she sprinted into the hallway. "It's chasing us like those things from the damned *War of the Worlds.*"

He urged her forward. "Take the service elevator. The lobby downstairs is full of cops."

She ran beside him, agile in the heels. His watch beeped.

"Oh, crap. No time."

In the lobby, the fire alarm wailed a high-pitched tone. The digital clock flashed red: :58, :57. The TV news was showing pictures from the chopper's camera.

"Two people are trapped on the roof," shouted the reporter. "A woman was signaling for help. If we swing around . . ."

The alarm rose in pitch.

"How long to get down?" she said.

They ran to the service elevator and she pounded on the button. The searchlight panned along the windows. Like a white flare, it caught them in the eyes.

"I see them. They're attempting to escape from this deadly tower. . . . "

She whacked the elevator button with the riding crop. *"Open."*

With a *ping*, the elevator arrived. They lunged inside.

On the ground floor they burst out a back exit into an alley. The asphalt was wet and steaming. Scott clicked his stopwatch.

"Seven seconds. Time to spare."

"Maniac," she said.

They dashed through puddles toward the end of the alley. On the street a police car blew past, lights flashing. The helicopter thumped overhead, searchlight pinned on the roof.

Scott nodded at it. "They got it on tape. You have evidence."

"You're reckless. I think you actually want to get caught."

"I carried out the dare. Did I make the cut?"

She fought with her zipper. "We'll put it to a vote. No promises."

They rushed out of the alley. The street, lined with banks and swanky stores, was being cleared by the police. They slowed to a walk, trying to look normal. He buttoned his jacket. She smoothed down her hair.

Elation flooded him.

"Admit it—that was awesome."

"It was outrageous." She pointed at him. "And do not tell me it ended with a flourish."

"Really?" He reached into his coat pocket and withdrew a baseball.

"What's that?"

He tossed it to her. She caught it.

"A Willie Mays autographed ball?" She looked up, surprised. "From the law firm's memorabilia collection? You stole it?"

"On our way out. And it's not just any baseball. It's *the* ball—from the 1954 World Series. The greatest catch of all time."

She gawked. "It's got to be worth—"

"Hundred thousand." He smiled, broadly. "Right under *your* nose."

Anger flashed across her face. She shoved the ball back into his hands. "Okay, bonus points for chutzpah."

He laughed and tossed the baseball into his other hand. "Fear not—it'll be returned. That's the next challenge."

"How? The building's locked down. And your fingerprints are all over it."

"So? I'm a star client. My lawyer let me hold it. It doesn't matter that my fingerprints are on it." He glanced at the police car down the block, then back at her. "How will you explain that yours are?"

She stopped dead on the sidewalk.

He held up the ball. "Return it without getting prosecuted. I dare you."

He turned, faced the jewelry store they were passing and hurled the ball straight through its front window. Glass crashed. An alarm shrieked. He spun back around.

"Have fun, Hardgirl."

He took off running down the street.